THE QUEEN'S

Christopher Mitchell is the author of the epic fantasy series The Magelands. He studied in Edinburgh before living for several years in the Middle East and Greece, where he taught English. He returned to study classics and Greek tragedy and lives in Fife, Scotland with his wife and their four children.

By Christopher Mitchell

The Magelands Origins

Retreat of the Kell
The Trials of Daphne Holdfast
From the Ashes

The Magelands Epic

The Queen's Executioner
The Severed City
Needs of the Empire
Sacrifice
Fragile Empire
Storm Mage
Soulwitch Rises
Renegade Gods

The Magelands Eternal Siege

The Mortal Blade
The Dragon's Blade
The Prince's Blade
Falls of Iron
Paths of Fire
Gates of Ruin
City of Salve
Red City

City Ascendant
Dragon Eyre Badblood
Dragon Eyre Ashfall
Dragon Eyre Blackrose
Dreams of Kell
God Restrainer
Holdfast Imperium
World's End

———

Copyright © Christopher Mitchell 2019
Cover by Miblart
Cover Copyright © Brigdomin Books Ltd 2019

Christopher Mitchell asserts the moral right to be identified as the author of this work.

All the characters in this book are fictitious, and any resemblance to actual persons living or dead is purely coincidental.

All rights reserved. No part of this book may be reproduced in any form or by any electronic or mechanical means, including information storage and retrieval systems (except for the use of brief quotations in a book review), if you would like permission to use material from the book please contact support@brigdominbooks.com

Brigdomin Books Ltd
First Edition, May 2019
ISBN 978-1-912879-03-8

For my wife

ACKNOWLEDGEMENTS

I would like to thank the following for all their support during the writing of the Magelands - my wife, Lisa Mitchell, who read every chapter as soon as it was drafted and kept me going in the right direction; Graeme Innes for reading the manuscripts and sharing many discussions over whisky; my parents for their unstinting support; Amy Tavendale, Sandra and Donna Wheat and Vicky Williams for reading the books in their early stages; James Aitken for his encouragement; and the Film Club and Stef Karpa for their support.

Thanks also to my Magelanders ARC team, for all your help during the last few weeks before publication.

DRAMATIS PERSONAE

Rakanese

The Kanawara Siblings

Shella, Flow Mage

Obli, Sister

Sami, Brother

Pavu, Brother

Tehna, Sister

Clodi, Sister

Klebo, Brother

Dannu, Sister

Noli, Sister

Chapu, Sister

Lenni, Brother

Zonnie, Sister

Asta, Sister

Marru, Brother

Others

Janno, Obli's husband

Thymo, Noli's husband

Thelo, Flow worker

Pannu, Flow worker

Barro, Flow worker

Joanie, Flow worker

Lorri, Commuter

Jayki, Shella's guard

Braga, Shella's guard

Cano, Flow Mage

Polli, Shella's assistant

Bowda, Shella's advisor
Tanni, Officer of the Wardens
Darra, Army Commander
Barri, Army Commander

Rahain

Politicians
Laodoc, Capital City Councillor
Niuma, Centrist Councillor
Riomac, Centrist Councillor
Juarad, Centrist Councillor
Ziane, Conservative Party Councillor
Myella, Conservative Party Councillor
Yaelli, Merchant Party Councillor
Pleonim, Liberal Councillor
Nueillin, Liberal Councillor
Wyenna, Liberal Councillor
Ruellap, Patriot Party Cllr, son of Laodoc
Heoran, Patriot Party Councillor
Kaeotip, Patriot Party Councillor
Flanouac, Patriot Party Councillor

Others
Stoelica, Laodoc's ex-wife
Simiona, Slave in Laodoc's household
Niniat, Professor at Laodoc's Academy
Likiat, Army Officer, son of Laodoc
Douanna, Entrepreneur from Jade Falls
Jaioun, Douanna's butler
Teolan, Douanna's husband
Meiolan, Friend of Douanna
Paeotan, Young Student at Laodoc's Academy
Geolaid, Professor at Laodoc's Academy
Baoryn, Renegade Peasant

Kellach Brigdomin

Killop, Captive from the Clan Wars
Kallie, Captive from the Clan Wars
Bridget, Captive from the Clan Wars
Kylon, Terrorist/freedom fighter
Bedig, Terrorist/freedom fighter
Leah, Terrorist/freedom fighter
Klai, Terrorist/freedom fighter
Kilynn, Terrorist/freedom fighter
Keira, Fire Mage
Lacey, Keira's Aide
Kalayne, Crazy old man

Holdings

Daphne Hold Fast, Exile, Vision Mage
Quentin Hold Terras, Ambassador to Rahain
Joley Hold Vale, Embassy Official
Shayba Hold Elance, Embassy Official
Getherin Hold Liant, Embassy Guard
Brookes, Embassy Official
Dale Hold Anster, Embassy Official
Rijon, Mage-Priest
Ghorley, Mage-Priest

THE PEOPLES OF THE STAR CONTINENT

There are five distinct peoples inhabiting the Star Continent. Three are descended from apes, one from reptiles, and one from amphibians. Their evolutionary trajectories have converged, and all five are clearly 'humanoid', though physical differences remain.

1. **The Holdings** – the closest to our own world's *Homo sapiens*. Excepting the one in ten of the population with mage powers, they are completely human. The Holdings sub-continent drifted south from the equator, and the people that inhabit the Realm are dark-skinned as a consequence. They are shorter than the Kellach Brigdomin, but taller than the Rakanese.

2. **The Rakanese** – descended from amphibians, but appear human, except for the fact that they have slightly larger eyes, and are generally shorter than Holdings people. They are descendants of a far larger population that once covered a vast area, and consequently their skin-colour ranges from pale to dark. Mothers gestate their young for only four months, before giving birth in warm spawn-pools, where the infants swim and feed for a further five months. A dozen are born in an average spawning.

3. **The Rahain** – descended from reptiles. Appear human, except for two differences. Firstly, their eyes have vertical pupils, and are often coloured yellow or green, and, secondly, their tongues have a vestigial fork or cleft at their tip. Their heights are comparable to the Holdings and the Sanang. Skin-colour tends to be pale, as the majority are cavern-dwellers. Their skin retains a slight appearance of scales, and they have no fingerprints. They are the furthest from our world's humans.

4. The Kellach Brigdomin – descended from apes, and very similar to the Holdings, they are the second closest to our world's humans. Their distinguishing traits are height (they are the tallest of the five peoples), pale skin (their sub-continent drifted north from a much colder region), and immunity to most diseases, toxins and illnesses. They are also marked by the fact that mothers give birth to twins in the majority of cases.

5. The Sanang – descended from apes, but evolved in the forest, rather than on the open plains that produced the Holdings. As a consequence, their upper arms and shoulders are wider and stronger than those of people from the Holdings or Rahain. They are pale-skinned, their sub-continent having arrived from colder climates in the south, and they occupy the same range of heights as the Holdings and Rahain. The males bear some traits of earlier *Homo sapiens*, such as a sloping forehead and a strong jaw-line, but the brains of the Sanang are as advanced as those of the other four peoples of the continent.

NOTE ON THE HOLDINGS CALENDAR

In this world there is no moon, so there are no months.

Instead, the four seasons are divided into '**thirds**', each lasting thirty days. To make the year up to 365 days, five extra days are added, two between Winter and Spring, and one between the other seasons, roughly corresponding to each solstice and equinox.

New Year starts on the vernal equinox (our 21st March).

--- New Year's Day – 21st March

- First Third

- Second Third

- Last Third

--- Summers Day – 20th June

- First Third

- Second Third

- Last Third

--- Autumns Day – 19th September

- First Third

- Second Third

- Last Third

--- Winters Day – 19th December

- First Third

- Second Third

- Last Third

--- Year's End – 20th March

Examples:

Daphne's fort was built in the last third of spring (i.e. our 21st May to 19th June)

The goat gave birth on the fourth day of the second third of autumn (i.e. our 23rd October)

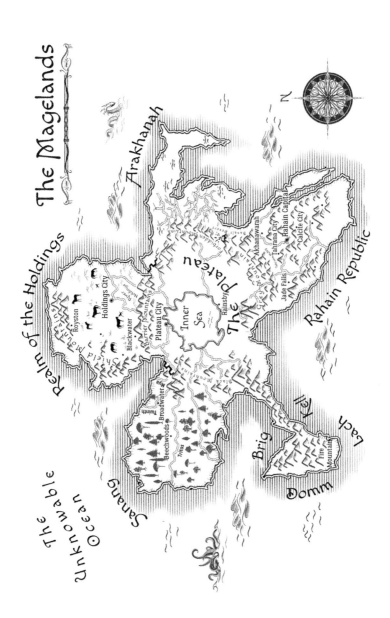

CHAPTER 1
THE BLOCKAGE

Arakhanah City – 5th Day, First Third Summer 504

'Stop fidgeting, Shella. Keep your hands still, and quit making that noise.'

The teenage girl tutted. Her arms were folded, and she wore a sullen expression on her face. Her mother sat next to her, frowning as they waited in the draughty hallway.

An office door opened, and a young man walked out.

'Missus Kanawara?' he said to the girl's mother. 'Please come in.'

'Thank you doctor,' the woman said as she stood, her back straight. She gestured to her daughter, and the girl got to her feet, slouching. The young man smiled, and went into the office.

'Behave yourself in here,' the woman said, as she and the girl entered the room. The young man closed the door and took a seat behind a desk.

'Please,' he said, gesturing at two chairs.

The mother and girl sat.

'Feet off the chair,' the mother said, glaring at the girl until she complied.

The young man smiled again. 'I have some good news for your

family,' he said. 'Your daughter here has tested positive for flow mage abilities, all the way up to grade four.'

The mother arched her eyebrows. 'Well, well. I always knew there was something funny about her. Still, my great uncle had flow powers, so I suppose it's not completely unexpected.'

'I've been in contact with the district council to register her as a new flow mage,' the young man went on. 'It means that you'll be able to claim vouchers for her healthcare and education.'

'She'll be schooled with the rest of her brothers and sisters,' the mother said. 'She doesn't need to go to some fancy academy. She already wastes her days dreaming. Still, at least I know that she'll be an earner for the family. Grade four, eh? What does a grade four make working for the council these days?'

The young man frowned. 'Considerably more than me.'

The mother laughed. 'Did you hear that, Shella? In a few years you'll be supporting the family. Your old dad will be able to retire at last. That should put a smile on his miserable face.'

The girl shuffled in her chair. 'But I don't want to.'

'It doesn't matter what you want,' her mother said. 'You're a registered flow mage; you have to get a job – it's written in the law. You've a life of hard work ahead of you, my girl, putting rice on the table for all your brothers and sisters, until one of them gets a licence to spawn. It'll be Noli, I reckon. That girl...'

Shella scowled, dread filling her as her mother mapped out her future.

It sounded like a nightmare.

Shella lay on her back, floating in the warm water. Above her, the vast open sky was endless, its colour a deep, hot, summer blue. Her ears were submerged, and she felt the silence permeate her, the raw, rare and beautiful silence. She welcomed it.

Peace.

At last.

The sun had climbed halfway up the eastern side of the sky, and she could feel its warmth on her skin. Another gorgeous day in the Rakanese wetlands. If only she could lie there and enjoy it for a bit longer.

Hands grabbed hold of her shoulders, and she was hauled out of the water and up onto a brick-built pier, where she lay, drenched.

'Shella!' a man shouted in her face. 'Are you okay?'

A crowd was forming around her on the wide retaining wall.

'What happened?' said someone.

'The mage fell in,' came one reply.

'Is she alive?'

The overseer pushed his way through the surging bodies, and approached Shella. He stared down at her, his tapping foot on the ground.

'Get up, Mage Kanawara,' he said. 'It's not break-time.'

Shella sat up, pushing her wet black hair from her face. Her overalls were soaked through.

'Maybe I should go and get changed, boss,' she said.

'No time for that,' he scowled; 'the sun'll dry you off soon enough.' He stuck out his hand to help her up, but she ignored him and got to her feet unaided.

'Right, everyone,' the overseer shouted; 'the mage is fine. Back to work!'

The disappointed crowd of workers dispersed, leaving Shella and her team of twenty alone on top of the wide brick wall.

'You really okay?' said the man who had pulled her from the water.

'Yeah, Barro,' she said. 'Just slipped. Tired.'

'I'm not surprised, mage,' Barro said; 'this is your eighth double-shift in a row.'

She stared at him, her eyes narrow.

'I checked the rota,' he said, shrugging.

'Need the pay,' she muttered.

She didn't need the pay. She just wanted to get out of the house,

3

and its crushing, suffocating atmosphere; and she couldn't think of anything else to do but work. She looked over at Barro. He was kind enough, though a little neurotic at times, but he wasn't someone she was about to confide her troubles in.

Barro nodded, his attention having drifted back to the water-lock, and the job they were supposed to be getting on with. Eight workers in overalls were clambering on top of the giant structure, which separated two large pools. Shella walked along the top of the retaining wall that ran between the artificial basins, her clothes dripping and her shoes squelching on the rough brick surface. The pool on her left, the one she had fallen into, was filled to the top with clean, treated water, almost ready to be fed back into the city's waterways. The basin on the right held all of the contaminants that had been extracted from the cleaned and treated pool.

The valve in the water-lock was blocked, stopping the last of the toxins from being flushed out of the clean pool. As she approached the lock, she found herself standing where she had been when she had fallen. She had been leaning over the pool, concentrating on identifying and pulling the waste from the water, and flowing it through the valve. She remembered something large being pulled in, and jamming, and it was this abrupt break in her concentration that had made her topple over.

'It's big,' she said to her crew. 'Whatever's blocking the valve. Someone's going to have to go down there.'

The workers looked at the water, the wall, anything but meet her eyes.

'Uh, mage,' Thelo said, 'seeing as how you're already wet and all...'

A few others sniggered.

'What's the point of being a bloody mage,' she muttered, picking up one end of a rubber breathing pipe, 'if you have to do all the work?'

She put the end of the pipe into her mouth, and climbed down the brick steps set into the retaining wall next to the lock. As her crew gathered to watch, she descended back into the pool until she was fully submerged, breathing through the pipe.

4

Silence again.

She let her eyes adjust to the shimmering and wavering sunlight under the water, and turned to the valve. It was shaped like a funnel, with the open end facing her. The sides were made of rubber, and its tip would open under pressure, allowing fluids out, but not back in again. She moved closer, until she was sitting on the funnel's lip. It was dark in there, but she could make out the shadow of an object ahead, blocking the valve as it narrowed. She reached out a hand.

Her fingers touched something, grasped it. She pulled. It didn't budge.

She put her foot up onto the side of the retaining wall, and reached in with both hands, pulling.

Something gave, and she was propelled back off the wall. She looked at what she was holding. It was an arm. A man's arm.

She opened her mouth and the breathing pipe fell away, sending a stream of bubbles rising. She kicked out of instinct, and the powerful muscles in the backs of her legs carried her up to the surface.

She took hold of an offered hand, and was pulled up onto the bricks. She fell to her knees, dropping the rotten and mangled arm she had been holding. The workers gasped, and started talking all at once, crowding round her.

Amid the noisy chatter, the overseer barged his way in.

'You again?' he said. 'What is it this time?'

She pointed at the arm lying on the bricks next to her.

'Oh,' he said.

'Yeah. Found our blockage.'

Work came to a halt as someone was sent to fetch the local constabulary.

When the officers arrived, they sent divers down to retrieve the corpse. It was brought back to the surface in pieces, which were laid out on a sheet, while the workers sat about in the sunshine, watching and commenting.

'Vagrant?'

'Nah, a drunk.'

'A drunk vagrant?'

The crew laughed.

Shella looked away.

'What's eating you, mage?' Pannu asked.

'Halfwits who ask stupid questions.'

The crew raised their eyebrows and nodded to each other knowingly.

The overseer glanced over from where he stood by a couple of constables.

'Can we go?' Shella called over to him.

'You're staying here,' he shouted back. 'I want that valve clean and working again, even if it takes all night!'

The work crew groaned.

'Thanks, mage,' Thelo muttered.

'She's been nothing but bad luck today,' Pannu said.

Several made gestures to ward off evil fortune, and a few edged away from where Shella was sitting.

She ignored them.

She was going to be late for her sister's big announcement, she realised, almost smiling in relief. Obli had told everyone in the family to be there for what she hoped would be a successful decision in her application for a spawning licence. Shella shook her head. Her sister was delusional. The Spawn Control Board never handed out licences to women who had a sibling who had already spawned, and Noli, one of their other sisters, was the proud mother of sixteen spoiled and noisy toddlers.

Obli was not someone to listen to reason however, and had painstakingly gone through every step of the tedious and expensive application process, from painful medical examinations, to intrusive inspections of their home. The inspectors, of course, had been there four years earlier, when processing Noli's application. There was no doubt in Shella's mind which way the decision would go, and it bordered on cruelty for the Board to have kept her sister's hopes going for so long. Poor Obli. Shella imagined that evening's dinner at the

Kanawara family home, with everyone present, and Obli delivering the bad news. She imagined the smug told-you-so expression on Noli's face. Shit, she thought, she needed to be there, to stick up for Obli if nothing else. Or to stop Obli from killing Noli...

'Hey, mage!' the overseer yelled. 'Wake up! Valve's clear.'

Shella glanced up. The sun had passed the point of noon, but was still high in the sky.

There was time enough to make it if they got a move on.

Hours later, Shella stood waiting in the queue for the water-bus. It was almost dusk, and the lines by the long dockside were packed with hundreds of workers all trying to get home. Her clothes were damp and the skin underneath had been rubbed raw, but the valve was spotless and working again, and they had drained the purified contents of the clean pool back into the city's water system.

A bus arrived, a forty-oared vessel. It slid in towards the dock, its rowers lifting their oars along one side as it touched the quay. The queue surged forward, as three hundred commuters crammed themselves on board. Dock workers shoved the vessel away with poles just as the doors were closing, and the water-bus pushed off. Behind it, another was lining up.

'It shouldn't be too long, Shella,' said Barro, standing in line next to her, 'the rate these buses are coming in.'

'Yeah,' she said. 'Should be getting home just in time to go to bed, so I can get up before dawn to do it all over again.'

'You still upset about finding that body?'

'Yeah, maybe,' she lied. She had hardly thought of it.

'Do you want to go up town for a drink?' he asked. 'Talk about it?'

She thought for a moment. She had gone with Barro a few times in the past, mostly when one or the other had been bored or lonely. She looked upon him as a bad habit, one she regretted indulging in, but somehow kept finding herself going back to. He wasn't interested in settling down, neither was she for that matter, but he would always act in a certain way at work the next day that infuriated Shella, as if he possessed some claim on her.

'Not tonight, Barro,' she said. 'Obli's got a thing.'

'Oh, okay,' he said. 'Wait; you mean today's the day Obli gets the decision from the Board?'

'Yeah.'

'No offence, Shella,' Barro said, 'but she hasn't got a chance.'

'Yeah, I know.'

'They never give out licences if you've already got a sister with kids.'

'Yeah, Barro, I know.'

'You should have told her,' Barro went on, oblivious to the irritation in Shella's eyes; 'and saved her the trouble.'

Shella resisted the urge to punch him.

'She should forget all about it,' Barro said. 'We're way too over-crowded as it is. It's selfish to want children when there's no space for the people who are already here. My cousins over in Evergreen District say that the families above them are living twenty to a room. The housing department need to sort that out. Did you go to the assembly this morning?'

'Sure.'

He paused for a moment, uncertain if she was telling the truth.

They moved forward a few paces amid the throng of bustling bodies as another full bus pushed off from the dock.

'Did you hear?' he went on. 'They're going to bring forward the vote on whether to turn Waterheart Park into a thousand new homes. It's disgusting, Shella; building over our district's only park? I'm voting against.'

'Were you not just complaining about over-crowding?'

'Yeah, so?'

'Well,' she said, 'how are we supposed to fix over-crowding if we can't build any new homes?'

He squinted at her. 'But, Shella, over the park?'

She shrugged. 'Can you think of anywhere else to build?'

'There's plenty of land up north,' said a woman to their left. 'We just need to start sending people up there.'

'Nah,' a man said. 'There's not enough freshwater; it's like a desert.'

'And what would you know?' the woman replied. 'You've never been there.'

'I can read the newspapers,' he said. He turned to Shella. 'You're a mage; is it true what they're saying? That the northern reclamation is a complete fiasco?'

'I don't know any more than you,' she lied. 'Progress has been slow.'

As the political debate rolled among the workers by the dockside, Shella stayed quiet. It was better to remain tight-lipped about the truth. The massive reclamation project going on over a hundred miles to the north, at the extreme edge of the vast sprawl of the Rakanese city, had seen an enormous amount of money invested over the previous three years. Shella's district, like the hundreds of other districts, had been heavily taxed to pay for the work going into creating a new area of freshwater marshland suitable for habitation. Almost all of the money, Shella knew, had been wasted. The land was arid, and sloped, and the rock beneath porous, altogether most unlikely terrain to be converted into wetlands. Frustratingly however, it was the most suitable land left on the peninsula. All of the level temperate land was already developed. To the west, the ground slowly rose beyond the city boundary, to become the foothills of the vast Forbidden Mountains. To the south, the land was rocky and barren, and then blocked by the basalt flows from the still-active volcano which lay there.

The north was their only hope for expansion; their only hope to ease the suffocating, mass over-crowding. And for Shella, it represented the chance for a new start, an escape from her dull routine, for she had recently been offered a position on the project as a third-level flow mage. It was a pay-grade higher than what she was on at her current job at the Sewage and Waterworks plant, but it would mean uprooting herself from her family and living alone, far from everything and everyone that she knew.

Right at that moment, caught among the heaving press of bodies on the quayside, Shella could imagine nothing more idyllic than living alone.

Another water-bus arrived, its oars chopping through the air, spraying water onto the crowd. Shella boarded, along with the three hundred closest to the vessel. She descended the steep wooden steps to the lower deck and grabbed hold of a hanging knotted rope as workers piled in around her. She glanced up, and realised she had lost Barro. Scanning the dense crowd, she noticed him standing over by the stairs, laughing with the woman from the dockside. Shella scowled and lowered her eyes.

The packed vessel lurched and they set off. The crammed-in crowd braced their feet, and hung on as the boat dipped and swayed. Shella could feel an elbow in her ribs, a shoulder jutting into her back, and a knee prodding her thigh. Well, she hoped it was a knee.

She held her breath.

All these people.

Too many people.

The vessel was steered through Dewy District, the brick ware-houses and docks visible through the boat's circular windows. The great banks of oars pulled in rhythm, guiding the vessel down the centre of the wide canals towards the residential areas. Smaller boats of all dimensions and types used the lanes to either side, keeping well clear of the giant water-bus, and bobbing in its swell once it had passed.

Shella groaned in relief as half of the workers disembarked at Dewy District's main docks, while only a few got on. Shella recognised a woman she used to work with out east on the salt pans. She lowered her head, but too late, and the woman came over to join her.

'Hi Shella,' she said. 'This is not your usual bus.'

'Hi Lorri,' Shella replied, a forced smile on her face. 'Been working late today.'

'Oh.' Lorri wrinkled her nose. 'What happened to your clothes?'

Shella flushed. 'Fell into a pool.'

'At the sewage works?' Lorri said. 'How revolting. You should probably burn those overalls.'

If she did, Shella thought, she would have nothing to wear the next day. All of her other pairs were lying in an unwashed heap on the floor of her room at the family house. She would have to wash some as soon as she got home, and hope they had dried by the morning.

'You look tired, Shella,' Lorri said.

'Mmm. Too much work.'

'Are you looking after yourself?'

'Sure, Lorri,' said Shella. 'It's just been a rough day, that's all.'

'How's the family?'

Shella smothered a deep sigh. 'Fine, thanks.'

'How old are Noli's kids now? They must be coming on.'

Shella thought for a moment. 'They'll be three in a couple of thirds.'

'Wow,' Lorri said. 'Three.'

Shella nodded, wishing Lorri would go away.

'Must be a busy house!' Lorri said, laughing. 'Was it ten boys, six girls she had?'

'Yeah, that's right.'

'My brother's kids are thirteen now,' Lorri said, her gaze drifting into the middle distance. 'Quite a handful at that age.'

Shella shuddered at the thought of sharing the family home with sixteen teenagers.

'And my sister-in-law,' Lorri went on; 'she's hopeless at keeping them under control. Lets them walk all over her, so she can have a quiet life. Don't know what my brother ever saw in her.'

Shella squinted through a side window, and saw that they were approaching Crossmarket District.

'Looks like my stop, Lorri,' she said.

'Yeah,' said Lorri. 'We really should get together; have a night out.'

'Sure,' Shella said, as the boat docked, and she started for the exit. 'I'll check when I'm free and get back to you on that.'

Who was she kidding, she thought as she stepped up onto the dockside. She would never be free.

The quayside at Crossmarket was packed with people, some rushing home, others standing talking, while numerous hot-food stalls were doing busy trade. The great market hall, from where the district got its name, bulked ahead of her, an enormous three-storey brick edifice. Everything that could be bought and sold in Arakhanah could be found somewhere inside the hall. Its doors were open, as business continued each evening right up to midnight, and the light from inside spilled out onto the quayside. Shella elbowed her way through the noisy crowd, heading for a road at the southern end of the quay.

Her route home was criss-crossed with canals lined by towering blocks of brick tenements. That part of Crossmarket was one of the most densely populated areas in that quarter of the city, and the majority of its inhabitants were poor. The large apartment blocks were packed with families, with many having upwards of a dozen sleeping to every room.

Every utterable sound was heard: babies crying, children laughing and shouting, young couples arguing, drunks singing, old folk gossiping. Every emotion was exposed; every secret laid bare. Privacy was a dream beyond all but the wealthiest and, Shella reflected, it was also on offer to those who chose to abandon their families and go north to work on the reclamation project.

After a brisk ten minute walk, Shella crossed over into Brackenwell, her home district. A line of willow trees marked the boundary, their long thin branches trailing into the water of a canal. She entered a long street of large townhouses, detached five-storey blocks, each home to a large extended family. It was a richer area than the one she had just passed through, though the quality of the street was well past its prime. The brickwork was crumbling in places, and the pavements were cracked and untidy. Most of the truly wealthy had long since departed for more spacious and private accommodation; those who remained represented the families struggling to maintain their positions, their wealth old and faded.

It was dark by the time she reached her family's townhouse. She opened the front door and let herself in. The hall was dark, and silent. Shella paused, hearing nothing from the children or adults who lived within.

She passed the dining-room, where the family sat each evening for their shared meal. The room was in darkness, and looked like it hadn't been in use that day. Shella frowned, and went downstairs to the kitchen.

The lamps were burning, but no one was around. Shella prepared herself some food.

She filled a bowl with rice and some cold fish curry from a pot on the stove. Just as she was getting a spoon from a drawer, she heard a noise behind her.

'You're home.'

Shella's heart sank, and for a moment she couldn't bring herself to face her sister, or reply.

'Sorry,' she said. 'Had to work late.'

'Today?' Obli said. 'You just had to work late today?'

Shella turned. 'Sorry.'

'The one day I really needed you?' Obli went on, her face matching her voice's lack of emotion.

'They turned you down, then?'

A flicker of rage mixed with grief swept over her sister's face for a second. Obli cast her eyes downwards.

'I know what I did wrong this time,' she said. 'I won't make that mistake again, when I re-apply.'

Shella said nothing, her heart aching for the pain she felt coming from her sister.

'I'll need you to help me, Shella,' Obli said. 'You know, with the new application.'

'Of course I will.'

Obli looked up, a fierce glare in her eyes. 'You think I'm stupid, don't you?'

'No, Obli,' Shella said. 'I'll help you.'

Obli nodded, then turned and walked in silence from the kitchen, like a ghost.

Shella stood for a moment, watching the space where her sister had been, then she took her bowl of curry and went upstairs to her room. She lit her lamp and pushed the pile of clothes and books from her table onto the floor. She sat, and started to eat her cold dinner.

There was a knock at the door.

'Yeah?' said Shella.

The door opened and Sami, one of her five brothers, poked his head round.

'Hi, Shella,' he said, coming in.

'Sami,' she replied.

He took a seat next to her at the table. Without asking, he picked up a glass, wiped a smudge from its lip, then poured himself a long drink of rice spirits.

'Some evening,' he said.

'Pour me one, too,' she said, 'and tell me what happened.'

'We were all down in the sitting room,' he said, handing her a fresh drink. 'Except you, of course. We were sitting waiting for Obli and Janno to come and give us their news. We waited and waited, and they never showed up, so we started talking about what might have happened. Noli had just finished saying that Obli was crazy to even think that the Board would give her a licence, when who should suddenly appear, having overheard everything?'

Shella groaned. 'Oh no.'

'Exactly,' Sami went on. 'Well, you can fucking imagine what happened next...'

'Language, Sami,' Shella said, out of habit.

'Sorry, sis. Anyway, Obli and Noli started shouting at each other, and their husbands went at it, too; and soon the whole family was arguing. Obli stormed out, and the whole dinner was called off. Noli and some of the others took the kids out for the evening. Poor Chapu, after cooking all that food as well.'

'Obli told me she was going to re-apply,' Shella said.

Sami snorted, shook his head, and poured himself another drink. 'Noli will never allow it.'

'I'm not sure she'll be able to stop her.'

Sami shrugged. 'Anyway, what happened to you?'

'Had to work late,' she said. 'Found a body in the sewage works, blocking a valve.'

'Fuck!' Sami said. 'Sorry.'

'About the corpse, or about your foul language?' Shella said, smiling for the first time that day.

Sami laughed. 'Both.' He refilled Shella's glass. 'Want to get seriously drunk?' he said.

'Working another double shift tomorrow.'

'And when has that ever stopped you, sis?'

Shella sighed, and took another drink.

CHAPTER 2
REQUISITION FORM

R ahain Capital, Rahain Republic – 6th Day, First Third
Summer 504

'You're a stubborn old fool, Laodoc,' Stoelica said. 'He's our son.'

'I cannot be seen to be making an exception,' said Laodoc from behind his desk. 'My enemies would say I was being hypocritical. And they would be right. To have been opposed to the war from the start, only to be a guest of honour at a victory celebration? It would look as though I were trying to claim the credit for someone else's success.'

'But Likiat has been away for over a year...'

'Then,' Laodoc said, 'I will catch up with him on some other, less public, occasion, and pass on my congratulations more discreetly.'

'Once again, Laodoc, you put your political ambition ahead of your family. I am reminded of why I divorced you in the first place.'

Laodoc glanced up from the piles of paperwork in front of him. 'It has been a pleasure as always, Stoelica, but as you can see, I'm a little busy this morning.'

'Busy,' she repeated, her tongue flickering out, the cleft at the tip visible for a second. 'Of course. Well, I won't disturb you any longer.' She picked up her hat, and strode to the door of the study.

Laodoc flinched as she slammed it shut behind her.

He took a sip of his cold bitter lemon drink, and rubbed his temples. He had a headache coming on.

Outside, in the underground caverns, he could hear the low rumbling echo of the continual parties and festivities. Twenty days of public holidays had been ordained by the High Senate, following the successful conclusion of the conflict in Kellach Brigdomin. The capital city of the Rahain Republic reverberated with victory, and was swaggering with success. For twelve days, Laodoc had barred his front door and closed his windows to the boisterous and cheering crowds. Only another eight to go before he could leave the house again.

The governing war coalition had organised daily parades through the capital's wide, arterial thoroughfares, displaying captured booty and slaves from the campaigns, along with marching companies of heroic soldiers. Laodoc laughed to himself. Heroic? To steal some land from a band of impoverished and backward savages? A few well-armed reservists should have been able to accomplish it, and yet it had taken the army nearly a hundred thousand requisitioned soldiers from the servile classes a whole year to achieve victory.

And the cost? Seven hundred dead officers from the ruling elite, a bloody harvest of the republic's youngest and brightest. Along with thirty thousand chattel from the lower classes who would be expensive to replace, though no one was talking about that.

He shook his head, picked up his spectacles, and got back to work.

As a gentleman of Rahain, he had no formal occupation, but was burdened with several responsibilities. While the most important was his position on the City Council, he decided to look over some neglected correspondence from one of his other roles, as the patron of a small science academy.

He sorted the requests for money into a separate pile, which soon became the largest, and skimmed through the rest, until one caught his eye.

It was a letter from the academy's Head of Biological Sciences, informing him that she had successfully petitioned the government for a requisition of three Kellach Brigdomin captives, for the purposes of examination and study. Due to the demand for slaves however, there had been a delay in processing the request, and the Head was asking in the most polite terms if Laodoc could use his influence to intervene. Attached to the letter was a copy of the requisition form.

Laodoc checked the date of the letter. It had arrived ten days previously.

'Oh, bugger,' he muttered. 'Simiona!'

The door to his study opened, and a young woman entered.

'Yes, master?'

'Clear the rest of my day,' he scowled. 'We need to take a trip out into the city.'

If the requisition had been for three native Rahain slaves, Laodoc reflected, as his carriage jerked through the subterranean streets, he would have simply ordered them to wherever he had needed them to be. For three Kellach captives, he wasn't so sure. Would they require an armed escort? Defeated they may be, but were they broken?

'Here it is, master,' Simiona said, an open scroll in her hands. 'The recommendation is four guards for every adult Kellach Brigdomin slave.'

Laodoc raised an eyebrow. It was uncanny how she always seemed to anticipate what he was thinking. She may be new to his household, but she was fast becoming the most useful slave he owned.

'Now, that's interesting,' she went on, her eyes scanning the page.

Laodoc smiled. He should reprimand her more often for her over-familiar manner, but as there was no one else in the carriage he decided to indulge her.

'What's that, then?' he said.

'It says here,' she said, looking up with earnest enthusiasm on her face, 'that we must keep them away from naked flames, at least for their initial period of captivity.'

'Ahh, yes, of course,' he said, nodding.

'Why is that, master?'

'Their mages, Simiona,' he said. 'They are few in number, but some among them can control fire, build it, concentrate it, and throw it. I hear they were responsible for a high proportion of our casualties in the war.'

'And could some of the captives be mages?' she said, her voice rising.

'It seems unlikely. I imagine they were all killed in the fighting.'

'It would be amazing to be able to study one of them.'

'No doubt,' he chuckled, 'though also a little dangerous. No, I'm afraid our humble science academy will have to make do with a few common specimens of savage barbarism.'

'Something confuses me, master,' she said, though she looked far from confused. 'You are a speaker for the peace coalition, and yet you show the same contempt towards the Kellach Brigdomin captives as those who were in favour of the war.'

'It is not your place to question my motives, slave.'

'Apologies, master,' she said, her head downcast. 'I meant no offence.'

Laodoc fidgeted in the awkward silence that followed. He was too soft on his slaves. It had been one of Stoelica's constant refrains over the many years of their marriage.

The carriage rolled and juddered to a halt.

Laodoc lifted the window-blind a crack and peered out. They were in a well-lit street outside the gates of a slave clearing-house; one that he had heard was filled to capacity with new arrivals from the savage tribal lands.

'We're here,' he said.

They sat and waited as the driver opened the side door for them, before stepping down to the smooth stone pavement.

Simiona gazed up at the vast cavern roof overhead. 'Master,' she said, 'are we in the wine merchants' district?'

'We are indeed,' he said. 'How did you know?'

She pointed upwards. 'This cavern has seams of dark red quartz running through the southern roof buttresses. The wine merchants' district is the only large cavern with that type of quartz, master.'

'Well done!' he said. 'At least someone pays attention to my mineralogy lectures.'

She blushed.

'Beoloth,' Laodoc called up to the driver. 'Be sure to stable the carriage as closely as possible to the main entrance. We shouldn't be too long.'

'Master,' he nodded. He lashed the four-limbed gaien into movement, and they lurched down the street, their scales gleaming in the lamp light of the underground city.

Laodoc brushed the dust from his tunic, and smoothed his grey hair.

Simiona was gazing up at the walls of the clearing-house.

'Have you ever been inside one of these places?' he said to her.

'Of course I have, master.'

'How silly of me,' he said. 'Of course you have.'

Laodoc smothered a curse. Talking to the girl as if she were a student, rather than a possession. He strode towards the gate, and she followed, keeping two paces behind, as properly befit her station.

The walls surrounding the compound were high and smooth, merging seamlessly into the sides of the cavern, and the barred gate was guarded by a whole company of servile troops. Laodoc looked through the bars at them, searching for whoever was in charge.

An officer glanced over.

'Good morning, Councillor,' the captain said. He called out to his soldiers. 'Open up.'

The great gates swung open, and Laodoc and Simiona entered.

Inside, the entrances to the holding blocks rose before them, each capable of confining thousands of slaves at a time. Each block was dug back into the side of the cavern, extending for hundreds of yards through the heart of the mountain. There were twenty such circular entrances on the dark face of the high cavern wall in front of them, four rows of five; and stairs had been carved into the wall to allow access to the three upper rows. At the base of the stairs were the administrative offices, barracks and buildings for storage.

'Good morning, Captain,' Laodoc said, as they walked to the offices. 'And how may we assist you today, sir?'

Laodoc handed him the requisition form.

The captain studied it, frowning.

'I want this expedited immediately, if you don't mind; there's a good chap,' Laodoc said.

The officer swallowed.

'Is there a problem, Captain?'

'Of course not, Councillor,' he said. 'Official channels...'

'Have been found wanting in this case, I'm afraid,' Laodoc said. 'Hence the reason I am forced to come in person. Tedious, I know, but what's to be done?'

They reached the office.

'The difficulty is, sir,' the captain said, 'all of this lot here,' he waved his arm up at the entrances to the holding blocks, 'have already been requisitioned.'

'What?' Laodoc cried. 'By whom?'

'Well, let me see now,' the officer said, counting on his fingers. 'Four thousand for the silver mines south of Granite Heights, eight thousand for the preliminary works on the Grey Mountains Tunnel Project, three thousand for the new iron foundries being constructed in Calcite City...'

'Yes, yes, I see,' Laodoc said, his tongue flicking in irritation. 'Are there none left whatsoever? After all, I'm only looking for three.'

The officer shifted nervously. 'What would you be wanting with them, sir?' he said. 'If you don't mind me asking.'

'Of what possible relevance is that?' Laodoc snapped.

'Well,' he muttered, looking at the ground. 'I heard there were a couple of other science institutes apparently interested in picking up a few slaves, for, for experimental purposes, if you catch my meaning, sir.'

Laodoc paused, saying nothing.

'And,' the captain went on, 'if that were the case with your academy, sir, then there might be something we can do.'

'I see,' said Laodoc, masking his confusion.

'It's just that we have a pen filled with those deemed unsuitable for any requisitioning work, where three slaves might not be missed.'

Laodoc frowned, and lowered his voice to a whisper. 'And what is due to happen to these creatures?'

'Once the pen's full,' the officer said, 'they're all destined to be turned into gaien-feed. Sir.'

Laodoc thought for a moment. 'Tell me,' he said, 'exactly how does a slave come to be deemed unsuitable?'

'Mostly because they're crippled, or diseased, or proven trouble-makers, sir.'

'And their slave licences?'

'Oh, they're still perfectly valid, sir. I would just need to remove a stamp or two.'

Laodoc glanced around, checking that no one was listening. 'Take me to this pen.'

The captain led Laodoc and Simiona to the furthest corner of the compound, where there was another entrance, one he had not previously noticed. At a nod from the officer, guards unbarred the iron rimmed circular door, and they entered.

The foulest stench Laodoc had ever experienced assaulted his senses, and he gagged, putting a hand to his mouth as the bile surged.

'Master?' said Simiona. 'Are you quite all right?'

He looked at her face, her eyes cold and expressionless.

'Quite,' he coughed.

The captain had halted a few paces ahead, waiting for them. The corridor behind him extended for fifty yards in a straight line. Every ten feet, there were grilled hatches set low into doors on either side.

Laodoc started walking again, though he was feeling decidedly unwell.

They stopped at the first grille on the left. The captain knelt down and peered through. He nodded to himself, and straightened up. He took a scroll down from a peg on the wall and gestured for guards. A dozen formed up by the door, their crossbows levelled and ready.

'Is this really necessary?' said Laodoc, his gaze on the drawn weapons. 'For the crippled and ill?'

The officer bent down to the grille.

'Back! Back!' he shouted through it, then he unbarred the door and shoved it open.

Laodoc glanced inside, and retched again. 'Oh my.'

Inside the large cell was a scene of squalor and filth such as Laodoc could not have imagined. Bodies lay prostrate on the floor, several of whom were clearly dead. Some had even started to show signs of decomposition. Those alive lay huddled in excrement-plastered rags up against the walls of the cell, on the low stone benches that ringed the room. Some looked up at him in hatred, but most gazed listlessly into the distance.

The captain turned to him. 'Do any of these suit your needs, sir?'

Laodoc considered calling the whole thing off. After all, surely the academy could wait a little longer for their specimens? Damn, if only he hadn't delayed opening the letter.

'I'll need to take a closer look,' he said, adding 'unfortunately' under his breath.

The captain nodded, and gestured to his soldiers. Six of them entered the cell and took up positions by the door, their crossbows remaining pointed towards the captives at all times.

Laodoc went through the entrance, being careful not to tread in anything too unpleasant, his eyes stinging from the ammonia filling the air. He noticed Simiona by his side. Her face continued to display no emotion, but she had paled considerably.

He turned back to the captives, distancing himself emotionally from what he was looking at, much as he did when he was dissecting a specimen for an anatomy demonstration. These are just specimens, too, he said to himself. Nothing more.

'What about these three?' he said, pointing to a small group crouching together in a corner. 'They look alive, at least.'

The officer squinted at the numbered tags attached to the captives' ankles, and consulted his scroll.

'Trouble-makers, those ones.'

'And what did they do?'

'Not recorded, sir,' the officer said. 'It could have been one of a hundred things. Fighting, stirring up dissension; you name it.'

Laodoc studied the small group. Two females and a male. This was the closest he had ever been to any of the Kellach Brigdomin, having stayed indoors and missed the great parades.

They were pale-skinned, and very large, but those differences notwithstanding, they appeared to him to be remarkably similar to people he had seen from the Realm of the Holdings, far to the north.

'Ape,' he muttered.

'I'm sorry, sir?'

'What? No, nothing,' Laodoc said, breaking out of his thoughts. 'I'll take them.'

'Excellent, sir,' the officer grinned. 'Now we can go and do the paperwork, while the guards prepare your specimens for travel.'

Back at the office, Laodoc sat enjoying a cool drink, while the captain carefully erased the 'unsuitable' stamp from the three slave licences.

'There you go, sir,' the captain said, winking as handing the licences over. 'Good as new, they are.'

Laodoc put them into the inside pocket of his overcoat.

'Now,' the captain went on, 'about our administrative fee. Sir.'

———

'The gall of the man!' Laodoc spluttered, as the carriage bumped and lurched its way to the academy. 'One thousand ahanes apiece? Robbery, Simiona, that's what you've just witnessed.'

'Yes, master.'

She had been uncharacteristically quiet the whole way back, he noticed. And for the entire time since they had seen the Kellach slaves.

'What's bothering you, girl?'

'Master, may I ask a question?'

'Proceed.'

'I don't want to anger you.'

He frowned. 'Get on with it.'

'Master,' she said, 'are you going to experiment on the slaves, like that soldier said?'

'You mean, dissect them?'

She nodded, her face paling.

Laodoc laughed. 'Of course not. Is that it? You're worried the academy will cut up our new Kellach captives for science? Ha! You're feeling sentimental about them, eh?'

Simiona looked away, her face reddening.

'No, Simiona,' he said. 'The academy wants live specimens. There will be experiments from what I understand, but they will be more like, "Is it possible to teach them to understand our language?" for example, or, "Are they capable of rational thought?" You know, that sort of thing.'

'And what if they are?' she asked in a whisper.

'Excuse me?'

'What if your academy proves that the Kellach Brigdomin are capable of thinking rationally, and that they can learn our language?'

'Well,' he said, 'then they'll be more useful to us as slaves. Frankly though, after our visit today, I doubt we'll find much intelligence in them. Nature seems to have endowed them with physical gifts, but possibly to the detriment of their brain development. Of course, that in itself would be interesting to study.'

'Of course, master.'

'What about you?' he said. 'What would you like to learn from our specimens?'

She looked away for a moment, thinking. 'Songs,' she said. 'And stories. Of their people. I could compare them to ours.'

Laodoc looked over his spectacles at her.

'My,' he said, 'you are optimistic. Though I would suggest that this sort of thing belongs more in an art college than our dear old science academy. However, this promise I make to you. If, by some miracle, we are able to glean stories from the captives, then you will be afforded the opportunity to record them for your studies.'

'Thank you, master,' she said, beaming.

He smiled to himself. It was all fantasy, of course. Slaves didn't study. They didn't have the mental capacity for it.

The carriage jerked to a stop.

'Ahh, here we are,' he said.

The door opened and Laodoc and Simiona stepped down. They were in the academy's rear courtyard, enclosed on three sides by a high wall. The fourth was taken up with the solid back of the faculty buildings: three storeys high, in pink granite.

Lining the steps up to the rear entrance were a dozen or so staff and students, awaiting their arrival, word having been sent ahead.

Laodoc waved at them as he ascended the steps. 'Chancellor, professors, good day to you all,' he said.

'Patron Councillor Laodoc,' said the academy chancellor, bowing.

There was a gasp from the students, and Laodoc turned back to the courtyard to watch, as two dozen soldiers marched in, escorting an enormous covered wagon.

'Councillor?' said the chancellor, his tongue flickering.

Laodoc smiled. 'Don't worry, old chap; it's not an armed takeover of the academy. No, these fine soldiers here are kindly escorting a new and, I hope, valuable addition to the Biology Department.'

'You mean...?' said Professor Niniat, her eyes widening.

'Indeed,' he replied. 'Your requisition. It took a little arm-twisting if I'm honest, but what's the point of having a councillor as your patron if there aren't a few perquisites now and again, eh?'

'Professor, kindly explain,' said the chancellor.

'Oh, Chancellor,' she said; 'don't you remember? I requested three Kellach Brigdomin captives for study.'

'You mean all these soldiers are for three slaves?' he said, waving his arms at the growing crowd. The covered wagon had halted next to the steps, and guards were forming a circle round it, their crossbows bristling inwards. 'Just how dangerous are they?' he whispered.

It seemed as though the entire student body was watching, crowding into the small courtyard and leaning out of the tall windows overlooking it.

Two soldiers approached the wagon and pulled back the tarpaulin covering it, revealing a large steel cage fixed to the chassis of the cart. The crowd let out a gasp, while Laodoc looked on, struggling to suppress a grin.

'There they are,' he said. 'Your new specimens.'

The three Kellach were sitting in the middle of the cage, warily eyeing the hundred or so soldiers, students and academy staff surrounding them. Each had been burdened with heavy chains, linking their ankles and wrists.

'Now,' Laodoc said, thinking aloud; 'I assume the best place to keep them would be the gaien facility in the basement. It is empty at the moment, isn't it?'

'Yes,' Niniat said. 'It's been unoccupied since the last one died. I don't think it's been properly cleaned though, councillor.'

Laodoc shrugged. 'I don't think these three will mind. It'll still be a step up from their previous conditions.'

She nodded and patted her belt. 'I have the keys.'

The soldiers removed the heavy crossbars from the back of the cage, and a hatch fell open with a loud clang onto the flagstones of the courtyard. Silence descended over the onlookers as the Kellach male rose to his feet, and dragged his chains to the hatch. He was truly enormous, Laodoc thought, seeing him upright for the first time. His long dark brown hair and beard were filthy and matted, but his eyes held a fire. He jumped down from the back of the wagon, and the crowd seemed to flinch as one. Soldiers waved their crossbows at him, but he ignored them. He turned back to the carriage and picked up one of the women, the red-haired specimen, carrying her and her weight of chains in his big arms. The woman's head hung limp, her long red hair tangled through the metal links of her shackles. Her eyes were closed.

She had better not be dead, Laodoc thought in dismay. Waste of money.

The other woman jumped down. She was dark-haired, and shorter than the other two, though still a head taller than any Rahain. She put her hands on her hips and glared at the crowd.

'They are giants!' the chancellor gasped.

'Beasts!' cried someone from the crowd.

'Murderers!'

The dark-haired Kellach woman laughed, and shouted something back, her guttural and barbarous voice filling the air.

Laodoc glanced over at Niniat. 'We'd best have that gaien cage opened up soon, I think.'

'Get them inside!' the chancellor cried, his high voice wavering. The guards responded, and started herding the captives towards the door, crossbows aimed at their backs.

Professor Niniat led them through the corridors of the academy, and down to the basement level. They passed the archives and records halls, and the mineralogy test laboratories, stopping when they reached the door to the animal room. Niniat unlocked it and went ahead, lighting the interior lamps.

'Master,' Simiona whispered. 'The lamps.'

'Don't worry,' Laodoc said, as they waited for Niniat to finish lighting up the room. 'It is believed that a Kellach mage requires a direct line between them and any fire for their powers to work. The lamps here are enclosed in glass, except for the small opening at the top. We're perfectly safe.'

Niniat lit the final lamp, and nodded for them all to enter.

A stale odour of gaien filled Laodoc's nostrils. Unpleasant enough, but nowhere near as bad as the slave pen had been. The large chamber was filled with birds, mammals, and small reptiles in cages, which were stacked up against each side wall, and on tables running down the centre of the room. At the far end was an enormous single cage, where the academy had been keeping a small group of gaien.

The cage sat on a raised platform a foot and a half above the floor of the room, with the back resting against the rear wall. The bars of the other three sides were twelve feet high, and made of steel.

Niniat unlocked a gate at the rear of the cage.

'We'll need fresh straw, and lots of water,' she said.

The soldiers escorted the three captives to the entrance. The man went in first, still carrying the red-haired female. The dark-haired woman stopped at the gate however, and turned to look at Laodoc, who was standing next to the chancellor.

Contempt shone in her eyes, and unbroken pride. She smirked at them.

Just as the guards were motioning for her to move, she stepped up into the cage and shut the gate behind her.

'She's got spirit, eh?' Laodoc chuckled, as Niniat re-locked the cage.

The chancellor puffed his cheeks in relief. 'Now I know why none of the better families are taking on any of the Kellach as house slaves.'

'Yes,' Laodoc said. 'They are a little intimidating. Still, they're back behind bars, ready for research and investigation by the academy's finest young minds.'

'Indeed,' Niniat said, her set of keys swinging from her belt. 'I'll send you a copy of the programme I've been planning. We're going to start with basic cognitive functions, and responses to external stimuli. Jahaieni has been working on a most interesting...'

'Yes, quite,' Laodoc said. 'Well, it's been a long and tiring day for an old man. Come on, Simiona, let's be getting home.'

'Thank you again, Councillor,' Niniat called out as Laodoc made his way back to the door.

'No, really; it was nothing,' he said.

Merely three thousand ahanes. They had better be worth it.

CHAPTER 3
JADE FALLS

Tahrana Valley, Rahain Republic – 7th Day, First Third Summer 504

'Are you ready?'

Daphne said nothing, her gaze fixed on the mountain range stretching out into the distance.

This was not how her powers were to be used.

She turned, eyed the opposition, and drew on her battle-vision.

A dozen heavily armed Rahain soldiers stood in the field before her. Daphne took in every detail of their positions: their stances, the way they held their weapons, and then set off like a hunting dog after a hare. She dived and rolled under the first clumsy sword swing, sprang to her feet and leapt over the second, her foot touching the soldier's arm on the way up. She dug her heel into his shoulder and jumped clear, landing in the space between two others. As they lunged with their weapons, she dodged to the left, then right, moving faster than the soldiers could follow, their sword edges flashing through the air where she had been. She faced the final soldier, and sidestepped his frontal attack, the tip of the sword missing her neck by an inch. She turned out of his reach and crossed the finish line, to a cheer and round of applause from the Rahain merchants and traders, sitting on their wooden foldaway chairs on the grass.

'Bravo!' cried Douanna, getting to her feet and striding towards the Holdings mage. The man next to her also got up, a look of disbelief on his face.

'It was just as you said, my girl; well done,' said Douanna, shaking Daphne's good right hand.

Daphne nodded, and eased off her battle-vision. Her intensive practice over the previous three thirds since their escape from the Holdings meant that she barely noticed any after-effects from such a short burst of her mage skills. What would have left her doubled over and nauseous a year ago was now over in a minute or two. She wondered whether the cramps in her stomach were due to her powers, or her unease at having let Douanna persuade her into putting on a display.

'My dear Meiolan,' Douanna said to the man next to her, 'I do believe you owe me one hundred ahanes.'

The man frowned, and took out a purse from within the folds of his voluminous robes. He counted out some coins, and passed them over to the beaming merchant.

'Something tells me that I have just been played.' He nodded to Daphne. 'Most exquisitely; but played nonetheless.'

'Come now,' Douanna said, laughing, 'it's been such a long and tedious journey, and I've been waiting so long to show off my new companion. Surely, you wouldn't want to deny me a little fun? I mean her skills are, as you only just said, exquisite.'

'Quite. I just wish I wasn't the first old friend you happened to come across on your return to Rahain.'

'Oh,' Douanna said, putting her hand on the man's arm. 'You won't tell, will you? Promise you won't tell. I intend to repeat the trick on quite a few others!'

Daphne coughed.

Douanna turned to her. 'If that's all right with you, dear? I mean, you told me you wouldn't be in any real danger.'

'One tiny slip,' the man laughed, 'and your trick might take on a more tragic flavour and, well, that could prove a little embarrassing.'

'And painful,' Daphne said. 'No, I think one demonstration will suffice.'

'You two ruin all my fun,' Douanna said in mock sadness. 'Though I can see advantages to keeping these skills a secret.'

'Are you homeward bound, then?' the man said.

'Yes,' Douanna replied. 'After two long years of sweat and toil, I am returned.'

The man gestured at the lines of wagons and carts by the roadside. 'And it looks as though it were a most profitable endeavour.'

'I did do rather well, didn't I?'

'I'll say. Did you leave anything behind, or have you stripped the Sanang forest bare?'

'Come now,' she said; 'I've brought plenty from the Holdings as well.' She began pointing down the lines of wagons. 'Tea, tobacco, coffee, sugar, and yes, glory of glories, crates of chocolate. All high end; all top quality, and enough to send even the most hard-headed traders in the capital into delirium.'

Daphne watched as Douanna showed off some of the stock to her friend. When she had met the Rahain trader during the previous autumn, she had been living in a rundown apartment block in seeming poverty, and Daphne had assumed that business had been bad. Douanna had not thought to disabuse her of this notion until after they had fled the Holdings on horseback at the tail-end of winter. When they had reached the new city being built on the northern shore of the Inner Sea, Douanna had taken her to a heavily guarded warehouse near the docks. The guards had recognised her as the owner, and Douanna had shown Daphne the true fruits of her trading business – crates piled high, packed with produce from both the Sanang forest and the rich fields of the Holdings savannah.

Douanna had chartered a Rahain boat at the docks to transport her, Daphne, and all of her stock across the Inner Sea to the Rahain port on the southern shore, a bustling, lively, but ramshackle township called

Rainsby. The settlement was nominally under Rahain law, but behaved as if it was an independent city-state. It was cut off from the rest of Rahain by a long trip round the Grey Mountains, the road that Daphne and Douanna had just travelled, after transferring their cargo onto wagons and carts, and employing an entire company of Rahain guards as an armed escort.

Daphne had kept the horse Douanna had bought for her in the Holdings Capital when they had made their escape, a young hazel-brown stallion. Jamie, as Daphne had named him, was most likely the only horse in the Rahain Republic. The locals used large lumbering reptilian beasts known as gaien to pull carts and perform other heavy work, and many Rahain had stared as she had ridden her horse along the coastal road down from the Plateau. Douanna had told her that she could earn a good price from the stallion if she chose to sell him, whether for food or sport, but Daphne's stomach had turned at the thought.

She looked up as Meiolan was making his farewells to Douanna. He was clutching onto a small box of treats that Douanna had made up for him as a gift.

'It's been delightful seeing you again, my dear,' Douanna was saying.

'The pleasure was mine, my lady,' he said, bowing. 'And might I say what a privilege it was to meet you, Lady Daphne of Hold Fast,' he said, bowing to her as well.

Daphne started to frown, but remembered her upbringing.

'It was an honour, my lord,' she said, bowing in return.

He smiled. 'Most charming.'

Daphne put a foot into the reins of her horse, and pulled herself up with her good hand. Her useless left arm she kept close to her body, but once she was up on the saddle, she wound the reins round the withered fingers of her damaged hand. It was only on a horse that she felt her left arm was of any use to her, allowing her to ride while keeping her right arm free. A year had passed since her crippling injury, and although most of the pain had been healed by a Sanang hedgewitch, its constant discomfort nagged away at her. She could still be sent to her knees in agony if she bumped her left elbow against something, and she was always aware of the wrongness of how it felt.

Though they would never hold a sword again, the fingers on her left hand had, after much painful exercise, regained enough grip to enable her to hold the reins, and she smiled as she watched Douanna climb up onto the bench of the lead wagon, alongside her butler Jaioun.

Douanna raised her arm, and the long caravan lurched into motion, the guards marching on either side. Daphne kicked her heels, and Jamie responded with a slow trot. She fell into position to the left of the lead wagon, as they moved off south along the highway, leaving Meiolan's country estate behind.

After they had travelled for a few hours, Douanna called out to her. 'My dearest Daphne, soon we shall see my home; my beautiful city of Jade Falls, the most perfect jewel of the seven cities of Rahain. Wait until you gaze upon the most magnificent sight of the falls at dusk, when the last glimmerings of sunset flood the caverns! Ahh. How I long to see it again.'

Daphne squinted up at the barren mountain range ahead of her, as uninviting and desolate as the Grey Mountains had been. There was no sign of any city, just a few estates dotted about the arid valley floor. The road ran straight along towards the side of the mountains in front of them, before disappearing into the haze.

'How far away is it?' she said. The sun had passed its zenith, and the early summer afternoon was warm, even in the lengthening shadows of the mountains to their right.

'We're almost there,' Douanna said. 'Look; the eastern gate is ahead.'

Daphne gazed into the distance, scanning the side of the mountain. The road was aiming towards a dark area, and as they came closer, she saw that it was a large entrance, burrowed into the side of the mountain. The opening was shaped like a horseshoe, and was bordered by a dark green band, set bold against the dull brown rock of the steep hillside.

'The city is underground?'

'Of course,' said Douanna. 'Naturally, there are farms up in the high valleys, but the city itself is built into the mountain, delved out through countless ages. All Rahain cities are such; did I not mention this to you?'

'You talked about caverns and caves,' said Daphne, 'but I hadn't really imagined that the whole city had been built inside a mountain, like a coalmine.'

'It is nothing like a coalmine, my dear. And I should know, as I happen to own a few. The cities of Rahain are thousands of years old, and over time enormous airy caverns have been dug out, and houses and buildings constructed within. There are hundreds of light and ventilation shafts; and remember what the Rahain mages can do with stone, my dear. They can carve it, twist it, strengthen it; and build with it structures that would be impossible in the Holdings, for all your skill with stone and metal. Slender bridges of onyx, marble as thin as paper, granite compressed into beams to reinforce the ceilings of domes a hundred yards wide. Ahh, Daphne. A coalmine, indeed.' She shook her head and flickered her tongue in mock outrage.

Daphne laughed.

They joined other traffic at a crossroads about a mile from the entrance, and followed the smooth flagstoned road as it rose up into the foothills of the mountain range. The gate was massive, able to fit six wagons side by side, and was three times as high as it was wide. The solid jade archway was carved in delicate relief, depicting dozens of different images of Rahain at work: builders, miners, farmers; then higher up the arch there were mages and merchants. At the apex, a carved figure sat upon a throne, gazing imperiously down on the travellers below.

'That,' Douanna said, 'is the work of the great Toeimus, a renowned master arch-builder from nearly four thousand years ago, during the Second Goanian Tyranny. A terrible time, if the histories are correct, but it was also a period when many of the republic's greatest architectural masterpieces were created, such as the High Senate in the capital.'

'I shall have to read some Rahain histories,' Daphne said. 'My mind can hardly begin to imagine records from thousands of years ago. I think I'll start with recent events, and work my way backwards.'

Douanna laughed. 'A sensible choice. If you started at the very beginnings of our recorded history, it would take a lifetime's study to work your way up to the present! But don't you worry about books, my dear; my husband has a most excellent library.'

'Your what?' cried Daphne, a little more loudly than she would have liked.

Jaioun smiled, but remained silent, flicking the reins over the sturdy backs of the lumbering gaien.

Next to him on the wagon's bench, Douanna fidgeted. 'Oh dear. Did I forget to mention him?'

'I think I would have remembered something like that.'

'I confess that maybe I have been keeping it from you, Daphne dear, though please don't take offence. It's just that I thought you might disapprove. I know how Holdings morality on such matters differs from Rahain.'

'On what matters?' Daphne said. 'Marriage?'

'Yes,' Douanna replied. 'My marriage is one purely of convenience, you see. I married Teolan for his extensive business contacts, and because he was a perfect gentleman, and he married me to earn a little respectability, and to hide the fact that he prefers boys to girls.'

'Why would he need to hide that?'

'I'm afraid the republic is not quite as liberal on this point as the Holdings. Of course, nobody cares what the lower classes get up to, but among the better born, the social imperative is to produce children, especially if you are of mage blood. Traditions run deep in Rahain.

'However, Daphne,' Douanna went on, 'please don't forget that, even though the queen of the Holdings survived the attempted coup last winter, she remains profoundly ill. Consider what will occur when she dies. All those freedoms that your generation have taken so utterly for granted: what you can wear, who you can sleep with, drinking alcohol, ignoring the proclamations of your prophets and priests – it will all come to an end once her brother Prince Guilliam ascends the throne, and the church takes control. On that day, Daphne, we can reflect again on which society is the most free.'

Daphne fell silent, thinking of her homeland, and the precarious balance of power that existed there between crown and church. The war in Sanang that was so strongly opposed by the church was entering its fourth year, despite the calamitous end to the previous year's campaign. With Summer's Day having passed several days before, the Holdings advance forces would be deep within the Sanang forest. And somewhere, waiting for them, was the warlord Agang Garo, and his army.

Daphne looked up as they passed through the jade archway and entered a wide tunnel, smooth on all sides, and as wide and high as the entrance. Elegant lamps were suspended from the curved ceiling of the tunnel, while traders lined the walls, with stalls set out for the early evening traffic.

'Welcome to my city,' said Douanna. 'Look up there.' She pointed to the ceiling.

Daphne craned her neck and followed the line of Douanna's finger.

'That's the seam of jade from where the city takes its name,' the Rahain woman said. 'This is where it begins. It stretches throughout the city; in fact, the original settlement was planned around this seam, and the oldest streets and caverns follow where it leads.'

Daphne saw it, a dark, jagged smear of polished green stone, running the length of the tunnel.

The wagon climbed the road's gentle incline, and they came into an enormous cavern, the largest interior space that Daphne had ever seen.

Her mouth opened in astonishment. Inside the cavern were towering spirals of slender stone, light beams of bridges spanning the air, and a clustered mass of houses and buildings that climbed the walls and rose from the cavern floor like sculpted stalagmites. All of it sparkled and glistened in the evening sunlight which streamed through apertures cut into the cavern roof.

She gasped.

'Daphne, my dear,' Douanna said, chuckling to herself, 'this is merely the entrance hall.'

They travelled along the main road, stopping at a fortified building by the cavern's exit. There, Douanna had the wagons and carts unloaded, and the cargo stowed into one of the vaults inside the building. She left her own wagon full, stacked high with her most expensive goods. She paid off the guards and the custodians of the warehouse, from the seemingly inexhaustible supply of golden coins she kept in a strongbox under the wagon's bench.

She retained two guards, and once they had clambered up into the back of the wagon, Jaioun flicked the reins, and they set off again, with Daphne and Jamie alongside.

After a short journey, they passed through a gated and guarded tunnel and emerged into a cavern containing some of the most exclusive addresses in the city. Douanna's house was piled up the side of the cavern wall, with terraces and balconies, and a light shaft positioned over a walled garden, high up on the fifth storey. The wagon pulled up in front of the main entrance, and Daphne eased herself to the ground.

'Home again,' Douanna said, smiling as she stepped down from the wagon and looked up at the great mansion, its red sandstone blocks towering above them. 'Go on,' she said, 'give your horse to Jaioun. I want to go straight in.'

Daphne handed the reins to the butler, and followed Douanna through an archway into a marble-floored hall. Douanna led Daphne up a wide flight of stairs, and gestured for silence when they came to a doorway. She held up her hand, and counted down on her fingers.

When she got to zero, she flung the door open, and strode into a large bedroom.

'Greetings, my husband!' she cried.

A handsome middle-aged man looked up from the bed, a pair of spectacles balanced on his nose. A younger man lay under the blankets next to him, sleeping.

'Still not mastered the art of knocking, I see,' the older man said, as he put down a book; 'beloved wife.'

'It must have slipped my mind, darling. After all, it's been two years.'

Douanna walked over to the massive, luxurious bed and sat down on its edge. She ran her eyes over the form of the sleeping man.

'I'm glad to see that your standards haven't slipped.'

The older man smiled.

'Daphne,' Douanna went on, 'this is my husband Teolan. Teolan, my dear, this is Miss Daphne Holdfast, a companion and a trusted friend.'

Teolan looked over at her, interest piquing in his eyes. 'Really?' he said. 'Then you've told her…'

'Nothing, beloved husband,' Douanna cut in. 'As of yet. Perhaps if you would care to get dressed and meet us downstairs in the dining room? We are most famished; maybe we could talk while we eat?'

Teolan nodded. 'You two go down. I'll follow shortly.'

Douanna gestured to Daphne and they went down a flight of stairs to a severe room containing a long dining table, where Jaioun was waiting for them.

'A feast, if you please,' Douanna said, 'and set a place for my dear husband.'

Jaioun nodded and got to work.

Within minutes, servants were setting down plates and cutlery, and soon Daphne and Douanna were served roasted poultry, racks of pork in brandy sauce, piles of warm ryebread, and deep jugs of red wine.

By the time Teolan joined them, Daphne was sitting back, her stomach full. She sipped from her wine glass, enjoying the new taste, but wary of getting drunk. Her mind was turning over on itself after hearing what Douanna and her husband had said. Tell her what?

Teolan poured himself a glass of wine, and picked up a few grapes from a plate.

'So,' he said to his wife, 'business first, I suppose; though I don't doubt for a second that you have made us even more fabulously wealthy than we already are.'

'I'm afraid so, dear husband,' said Douanna; 'such is the burden of being married to me. I estimate somewhere in the region of eight million ahanes in profit, taking both taxes and insurance into account.'

Teolan raised his glass, and blew out his cheeks. 'I'd guessed from your letters that you had been busy, but eight million? For two years' work? My gorgeous, most beloved wife, I always knew my mother was wrong about you.'

Douanna smiled, and clinked her glass with his.

Teolan took a drink, then he turned to study the Holdings woman. 'Miss Daphne Holdfast,' he said, looking over the table at her. 'Tell me about yourself.'

Daphne put down her glass. She was unsure if she should trust this man, but he was married to the only friend she had.

'I'm a fugitive,' she said, 'on the run from the church and crown of the Realm of the Holdings, and sentenced to death for disobeying orders while in command of a fort in the middle of the Sanang forest.' She paused. Teolan said nothing, but continued to stare at her. 'I did no such thing, of course,' she went on. 'I was set up by the church.'

'Why?' he said.

'Because of her father,' said Douanna. 'Lord Holdfast is a powerful noble close to the queen. Who is dying, by the way. Daphne has the powers of a Holding mage, and can fight like a jackal. She is perfectly suited to our requirements.'

'She's the daughter of a lord?' Teolan said. 'Won't the Holdings come after her? Their embassy in the capital is bound to hear of her presence sooner or later.'

'And what if they do?' she said. 'Their laws do not apply here. We plan on going to the capital next, and I'll be more than happy to march Miss Daphne right up to the Holdings ambassador, to show them that they cannot touch her, not while she is a guest of this household.'

Teolan turned his gaze back to Daphne, eyeing her up and down. 'What happened to your arm?'

'It was crippled while I was fighting the Sanang,' Daphne said. 'When I was captured by a warlord.'

'I shudder to think what a fighter she would be if she had the use of both arms,' Douanna said. 'Believe me, husband, she is deadly enough with one.'

'I'm not sure I can trust someone from the Holdings,' he said. 'After all, their culture is so young, they know nothing of the world.'

'That isn't true!' Daphne said.

'Oh? And how far back does your history go?'

'Five hundred years,' she said, 'from the founding of the realm.'

Teolan smirked. 'Five hundred years? Did you know that there is a journal some eleven thousand years old, that still exists in the Hall of Records in the capital? I know; I have seen it. Eleven thousand years, Daphne Holdfast. During the time of the actual Collision.'

'The what?'

Teolan raised an eyebrow. 'The Collision; the formation of this continent from the five original subcontinents? Your history tells you nothing of this?'

She shook her head.

Teolan stood up and walked to the wall of the room, where books and scrolls lay on dark wooden shelves. He picked up a large scroll and brought it to the table. He laid it out flat, weighing it down at each corner with an assortment of utensils.

'This,' he said, 'is a map of our world. Our continent, the only one on this world that we know of.'

She gazed at the large, square parchment. Upon it was the outline of a five-pointed star. The points were all differently shaped, from large and bulbous to long and spindly. Each point met the centre in a wall of mountains, shaded darker on the map. They created a thick ring encircling a central plateau, with the great Inner Sea at its heart. Daphne leaned closer, to be able to see the tiny script. Rainsby, she read, under a dot on the southern shore of the Inner Sea.

'The Holdings,' Teolan said, pointing to the large, almost round mass at the far north of the star. 'Probably the continent least damaged by the Collision. The Rakanese, on the other hand,' he said, pointing at the twisted fingers of the ragged area making up the north-eastern point of the star. 'We think they lost most of their land to the tidal waves and earthquakes that occurred during that period. Their lifestyle restricts them to freshwater wetlands, swamps basically, and the entire population is now crowded into this area of marshland here. A most miserable existence, for a most miserable people. Fortunately, our way to them is blocked by this volcano here, for they would be a nuisance as a neighbour, and their culture has absolutely nothing to recommend it.'

'That's a little harsh, husband,' Douanna said. 'I met some delightful Rakanese when I visited.'

'You've been?' Daphne said. 'I confess I've only heard rumours about the frog-people living there.'

Teolan laughed.

'Please, Daphne,' Douanna said, 'promise me you'll never use that phrase again, especially if you ever meet one. It is true that they are descended from amphibians, as we are from reptiles, just as you Holdings come from apes.'

'We what?'

'Don't confuse her, dear,' Teolan said. 'We have thousands of years of science and the study of biology and geology behind us.'

'Another time, maybe,' Douanna said, waving away Daphne's questioning look.

Teolan looked back at the map. 'Then, we have Rahain.' He pointed to the south-eastern point of the star. 'We suffered greatly in the Collision, with only seven of our once twenty-one cities surviving the catastrophe. However, those that did survive remained relatively intact, sheltered within the mountains, allowing our culture to continue uninterrupted.'

'And here,' he said, moving over to the long, thin, spindly peninsula on the south-western corner of the star. 'The site of our recent conquest,' he said. 'Kellach Brigdomin, the southern tribes.'

Daphne looked up, his words triggering a deep memory of lying in the dark Sanang forest, grievously injured, dying. In her agony she had heard, or thought she had heard, the voice of the Creator in her ear, talking to her of his grief at the wars ravaging the land, and of his wrath at the Rahain aggression against the southern tribes.

She frowned. 'Is the war over?'

'War?' He snorted. 'It was a slaughter. We estimate that about half a million people of the southern tribes were inhabiting those lands before our soldiers invaded. Now, we think that fewer than one hundred thousand remain.'

Daphne gasped.

'About one hundred thousand were killed, and about twice that number were put into cages and transported back here as slaves.'

'I noticed that we don't seem to have any here,' said Douanna. 'A pity. I was curious to take a look at one.'

'They are too fierce to be of any use as house slaves,' Teolan said. 'I heard that most of them are being sent to the mines or to the big construction projects.'

He caught Daphne's expression across the table, despite her efforts at smothering it.

'Is something the matter, miss?' he said.

'She doesn't approve of slavery,' Douanna said, before Daphne could respond. 'Thinks it barbaric. Well, that's what their holy book says.'

'It's not just that,' Daphne said. 'We believe it's wrong to enslave another person.'

Douanna and Teolan shared a glance.

'What about the rest of the Kellach Brigdomin?' Daphne went on. 'You're still one hundred thousand short.'

'Indeed,' he said. 'They are currently swarming over the Plateau as refugees. Many of them I believe are being fed and watered in a camp at Rainsby, while I hear that others are making their way up to the new Holdings town on the northern shore.'

'But we were in Rainsby,' Daphne said. 'I didn't see any.'

'As my husband mentioned,' Douanna said, 'they are in a camp to the east of the town. I saw no reason to divert our route to visit them. I believe it is a scene of quite dreadful squalor.'

'They do seem irredeemably savage,' Teolan said. 'I watched them in a victory parade, massive they were, muscles like granite.'

'Also descended from apes,' Douanna said, smiling.

'Quite,' Teolan said. 'And finally,' he pointed to the last point of the star, the large subcontinent in the north-west. It was coloured green to depict a vast forest, but was otherwise featureless. 'Sanang. The one people that the Rahain have not yet successfully made contact with, excepting tales from the Holdings frontier. I hope, Daphne, that you will oblige me by telling me everything you remember about it.'

Daphne put down her glass and glanced at the two Rahain. 'This has all been very enlightening, but why am I here? What is it that you think I'm suitable for, exactly?'

'My dearest Daphne,' Douanna said, taking a sip from her wine-glass, 'nothing that is beyond your more than ample skills.'

'What?'

'It's simple, really,' Douanna said. 'We would like you to kill a few people.'

CHAPTER 4
ICE BATH

R ahain Capital, Rahain Republic – 12th Day, First Third Summer 504

Killop awoke shivering, a deep cold penetrating his skin, right down to his bones. He felt a rough hide blanket cover him, and gentle hands placed a folded bundle under his head as a pillow.

'Kallie,' he groaned.

'No,' a voice said. 'The other one.'

He opened his eyes, a headache pounding behind his temples.

'Bridget?'

'Aye, Killop,' she said, sitting in her ragged clothes on the dirty floor of the cage next to him. 'Kallie's sleeping.' She nodded over to a figure lying wrapped in furs by the back wall of the cage.

Killop looked around. The large room was dark, with just a solitary lamp burning in a wall sconce high up on the left. The strange noises of the birds and animals, and their accompanying smells, filled the air.

'Where did the lizards take you this time?' Bridget said.

He lay back down and closed his eyes.

'The same room as before,' he said, his teeth chattering as he spoke. 'Except this time they had a bathtub filled with ice. They kept the chains on and threw me in.'

Bridget tutted. 'Fucking animals. At least yer clean, but.'

'The Rahain just stood around and watched,' he went on, 'just like the times before. Watching, and writing things down on scrolls. In the end, I guess I must have passed out from the cold.'

She touched his arm. 'You're freezing! Your skin's almost blue.' She started to rub his hands and fingers vigorously, then worked up to his wrists and forearms.

Killop gazed out through the bars of the cage at the other trapped animals, stacked high against the walls of the room. We are just like them, he thought. Dumb animals in cages.

'I thought we were going to die in that pit,' Bridget said, 'before we got moved here. I mean, this is a shithole, but it's paradise compared to that other place. But I'm not so sure that we're better off after all. Are they going to keep torturing you until they kill you? What do they want?'

'Knowledge, I think,' Killop said, his voice barely a whisper. 'They know we're tougher than them; they just want to discover by how much.'

'Then they're going about it the wrong way,' Bridget said. 'Take our chains off and we'll show them exactly how much tougher we are.'

Killop raised a faint smile. 'Did Kallie wake up while I was away?'

'Aye, for a bit,' she said. 'Didn't say anything, but.'

'We need to keep her strength up.'

'Oh, Killop,' Bridget said, 'when are you going to realise that Kallie might never be coming back? She hasn't spoken in a third; some days she completely forgets to eat or drink and, if I'm honest, I'm getting a little tired of cleaning up after her.'

Killop turned his face away.

He hadn't been able to protect her. He knew it was his fault, even though Bridget had told him a hundred times that there was nothing he could have done. The lizard soldiers had been looking for revenge, and there had been too many for him to stop on his own. But he also knew that they had chosen Kallie for the beating because of him, because they had believed that he had been responsible for stirring up the trouble at the transit camp.

Killop closed his eyes, trying to keep the memories from flooding his mind.

He heard Bridget get up. He opened his eyes a crack and watched the young Brig woman gather up more blankets in her arms. She came back to his side, and piled them on top of him. He pulled the filthy covers around his body, feeling the deep cold slowly start to fade.

He felt Bridget lift the blankets up, and snuggle in behind him.

'Bridget,' he whispered, 'I'm not sure this is a good idea.'

'Don't be a numpty,' she said, pulling him close, her front to his back. 'You're the only person in this world that I need and trust, and I'm not letting you die from the cold.'

He closed his eyes, feeling the press of her warm body against his back, her arm round his chest, her breath on his neck. He tried to imagine it was Kallie, but that threatened to bring back too many painful memories, so he emptied his mind instead, took the offered comfort, and sank into an exhausted sleep.

When he awoke, the room was bright and busy, with young Rahain going from cage to cage, feeding the birds and animals. Killop yawned and stretched. Bridget was already up, and was standing by the bars, watching the Rahain. At the back of the cage, in the shade, Kallie sat against the wall, hugging her knees, with blankets wrapped around her. She was staring into the middle distance.

'Morning,' he said to her.

Her eyes flickered over to him for a second, then resumed staring.

He stood up, letting the grimy covers and blankets fall to the stone floor. A few of the young Rahain stopped what they were doing and gazed at him as he walked to the front of the cage. He jumped up and grabbed hold of a horizontal beam above his head, and pulled himself up, stretching his muscles as he exercised.

'Stop showing off,' Bridget muttered.

After twenty pulls he dropped to the floor. 'We need to keep in shape,' he said, 'for when the time comes to rip off their heads.'

Bridget laughed. He was always surprised at how, despite everything they had been through, she had managed to keep her spirit. It rubbed off on him, he knew. Without Bridget, he would have long ago lost his daily battle with despair.

Attracted by the laughter, a few of the Rahain ventured closer to the cage. They looked young, Killop thought. Students, he guessed, which would make the middle-aged woman in black robes their teacher. For the six days since they had arrived, they had been observed, discussed, and made to undergo all manner of strange, and sometimes painful, tests. The previous day's ice-bath had been the worst yet, although being tied upside down by his ankles until he had passed out the day before hadn't been much fun, either.

'Come on,' Bridget called out to the students in a cheerful tone. 'Come closer, ya wee bastards, and I'll wring yer fucking necks for you.'

Killop smiled.

One of the Rahain approached until he was almost within touching distance. He was a young man, practically a child, and held his hands out to show they were empty. He edged forward, while his companions stayed where they were.

He pointed at his chest. 'Pay-oh-tan.'

Bridget looked at Killop, an eyebrow raised. 'Is this one actually trying to talk to us?'

Killop leaned his arm out through the bars and pointed at the Rahain boy.

'Pay-oh-tan,' he said. He then pointed to himself. 'Killop.'

The Rahain laughed out loud, and looked back at his companions, speaking excitedly. The others looked nervous and uncomfortable, and went back to feeding the animals, but the young man remained.

He pointed at Killop. 'Klee-hop.'

Bridget laughed. 'No, you dumb twat; it's Kill-op, Kill-op, Killop.'

'Killop?' the Rahain tried again.

She grinned. 'Aye, that's it.'

The young Rahain pointed at her.

'Bridget,' she said.

The Rahain looked confused. 'Bree-got?'

'Close enough,' she laughed.

The doors to the room swung open, and the rest of the class entered, led by the woman in black robes. She saw the young Rahain standing close to the Kellach cage.

'Paeotan!' she shouted in alarm.

The young man blushed and ran to the others, and Killop watched him receive a dressing down from the teacher.

As the class settled, Rahain guards brought the captives their daily supply of food and water. Killop knew the routine well. He and Bridget moved to the back of the cage, next to the wall where Kallie sat motionless, while long pikes were thrust through the bars to keep them from moving. A small hatch was opened, and the previous day's empty food-crate and water barrel were removed, and full ones put in their place. At the other side of the cage, the reverse operation was carried out on their toilet trough.

Both hatches were relocked, and the pikes withdrawn. Bridget made straight for the crate of food. As she rooted through the contents, Killop noticed the class position their chairs in a semi-circle facing the cage. The teacher was lecturing the students, while frequently pointing at the captives.

'Look what they've brought for us today, Killop,' Bridget said, as she pulled items from the crate. 'Roasted meat, dark bread, fruit... I think, if that's what this orange thing is.'

He crouched down by her, gathered a selection of food, and took it over to Kallie.

'Sweetness,' he said. 'You should eat. It'll help you heal.'

Her eyes flickered over him, but she remained silent.

'I'll get you some water,' he said. He went over to the fresh barrel, and took a metal cup, filling it and placing it by Kallie's side.

'You'll get better,' he whispered, stroking a loose strand of red hair from her eyes.

'This tastes good,' he heard Bridget call over. 'Things are looking up!'

He went back over to the bars where Bridget was sitting, and pulled a chunk of meat from the crate.

He sniffed. 'What is it?'

'Fuck knows,' Bridget said, her cheeks stuffed with food. 'Meat.'

He chewed a piece and recognised the taste from the rare occasions he had eaten it before.

'That fat, pink animal they have here,' he said. 'I think it's called a pig.'

'Pig, eh?' Bridget said, nodding. 'I like pig. Not sure about this bread, but,' she went on, picking up a piece of the dark, hard loaf.

'Don't think they have wheat in Rahain,' he said.

Bridget stopped eating. She dropped the bread, and clutched her stomach.

'Oh, Killop,' she gasped, her face turning green.

Killop heard the background chatter from the students fade into silence.

'What's wrong?' he cried.

Bridget fell to the floor, writhing in pain, sweat pouring from her forehead. She retched and choked, and held onto her stomach, as Killop watched helplessly.

Then he started to feel it himself, a searing pain shooting through his stomach and bowels, and an intense tightening of his throat. He fell forwards, crashing into the food-crate, and sending its contents spilling across the floor. He bit his tongue as his jaws clamped shut, and his insides felt like they were burning up.

He saw Bridget on the floor in front of him, shuddering in a fit, foam spraying from her blue lips, her face swollen up like a ripe plum.

His eyes shut involuntarily, and he felt himself drift.

Fingers grasped his head, prising his mouth open. He felt a stream of water flood over his face, much of it forced into his mouth. He bit the fingers holding his jaw, and received a slap across the face, as more water was poured down his throat.

Killop pushed the hand away, and rolled onto his knees, his gag reflex causing him to vomit over the floor. He collapsed in relief, as the pain subsided into a throbbing ache. He lifted his head from the pool of vomit, and saw Kallie on her knees, forcing water down Bridget's throat. Kallie held her by the shoulders as she too vomited, mostly down the front of her ragged clothes. Bridget's head lolled backwards, and Kallie dragged her over to the wall, and covered her with a blanket.

'Kallie,' he gasped.

She turned, and looked at him.

'Killop.'

'Thank you.'

'I wasn't going to let them win,' Kallie said, pointing out of the bars towards the Rahain students, who sat transfixed.

She approached the bars, rage across her face.

'Do you hear me, ya bastards!' she cried. 'You'll never beat us! Never!'

She sank to her knees, weeping, holding onto the bar in front of her. Killop staggered over, and took her in his arms. He felt tears come to his own eyes, but they were tears of relief.

By the time he looked around again, the room was still and empty, the students gone.

He helped Kallie to her feet, and she went and lay down next to Bridget. Killop gathered up the poisoned food and pushed it out of the cage, down onto the marble floor of the animal room. He cleaned up the vomit with spare straw, and pushed that out as well.

His stomach still ached from cramps, and his throat felt raw, but the water was cool and clean. He wondered what the Rahain had been trying to learn. Maybe they had decided to kill them, and were intending to make a lesson through watching them die.

They were left alone for the rest of the day, and when the lamps were dimmed, Killop guessed that it must be evening outside. Bridget had awoken, and Killop had told her everything that had happened.

Kallie was still sleeping, and hadn't spoken since saving them both, but Killop felt more hope than he had in a long time.

Some hours later, the door to the room opened and Paeotan entered, a sack over his shoulder.

He closed the door behind him, and shuffled down the room between the rows of cages, while Killop and Bridget watched.

When he got to just out of arm's reach, he stopped. He opened the sack, to show them a fresh supply of food. He pointed at it, and spoke to them in Rahain.

'We should get him to eat some first,' Bridget said.

Killop nodded, and leaned through the bars. He gestured to Paeotan, then the food. The Rahain looked puzzled, then snapped his fingers in realisation. He picked up some bread, tore off a piece and took a bite. Next he did the same with some of the pig-meat and a handful of grapes.

He smiled at them, and patted his stomach.

Bridget beckoned him to come closer.

He hesitated, looking from Bridget to Killop, his forked tongue flickering.

'Come on,' Bridget said. 'It's not you we want to eat.'

Paeotan gulped. He approached the cage and pushed the sack through the bars into Bridget's arms.

As Killop and Bridget ate, Paeotan got a chair and positioned it next to the cage. He opened his grey robes, and pulled out a book. Killop looked up.

Paeotan opened the book. It was filled with pictures of objects, with words written underneath.

Killop had never learned to read in Kell. One scribe for each village had been deemed adequate for anything that required to be written down. He knew what writing was, having often watched scribes at work, but the marks on the Rahain book looked like nothing he had seen before.

Paeotan pointed to the first picture, which was of a giant lizard, and said the word in Rahain.

Bridget and Killop looked at each other.

'This is going to be a long night,' she groaned.

Paeotan visited with food and books every night after that, while during the day the captives were subjected to further tests, none of which were as painful or life-threatening as the poisoning had been.

Although Kallie was improving, she continued to sleep for most of the day. When awake, she could fall into a trance-like state, unresponsively staring into space for hours at a time. Sometimes she would be talking, then stop mid-sentence, her eyes glazing over. Killop and Bridget would sit and wait, then eventually get up, only for Kallie to continue from where she had been speaking, sometimes after hours had passed.

That evening, as they awaited Paeotan, Kallie was in good form.

'So you just stood there while they drew you?' she said to Killop.

'Aye,' he said. 'Easiest day I've had yet. I had to take my clothes off, and then they all sat around in a circle, and sketched on these big sheets of parchment. There was a different teacher, not the woman in the black robes. She's called Niniat, by the way. I heard the students call her that.'

The door opened, and Paeotan entered the animal room. Behind him walked a young woman, her expression troubled.

'Shit,' said Bridget. 'I hope this doesn't mean he's been caught.'

'I thought you didn't like him?' Killop said.

'I don't,' she said, 'but he breaks up the boredom of being stuck in here.'

Paeotan approached the cage. He halted well out of reach, and lowered his sack of food. He looked at the captives, and shrugged.

The woman stepped to his side, and they talked together, their voices low. Paeotan seemed to be trying to explain something to her. He reached into his robes and pulled out one of the picture books he had been using to teach the captives. He looked worried, but came closer to the bars of the cage, until he was standing next to where the prisoners sat.

The woman put her hand to her mouth in apprehension, but remained out of reach.

Paeotan opened the book, and pointed to the first picture.

'Gaien,' Bridget said.

Paeotan pointed to the next page.

'Book,' said Kallie in Rahain.

'Ball.'

'Orange.'

'Shoe.'

The woman said something to Paeotan, and the boy put the book down.

She approached.

Paeotan pointed at her. 'Simiona,' he said.

'Simiona,' Bridget repeated.

Killop stared at the woman. She had been there, he thought, the day they had been moved to the school. She had been with the old man who had saved them from the pit.

'Hello, Simiona,' he said to her in Rahain.

Her mouth opened in astonishment.

'Hello,' she replied.

Paeotan smiled, and pulled over the sack of food, and a couple of chairs. He pushed the food through the bars, and sat. Simiona settled down next to him, and watched as Paeotan began the lesson.

The three captives learned the Rahain words for numbers that night, reciting them over and over, and watching as Paeotan drew the symbols that represented them onto blank sheets of paper. They were also tested on the words he had taught them over the previous evenings. Simiona sat back and observed, her face a bewildering mixture of emotions. Finally, as the night wore on, she interrupted Paeotan, asking him something. Killop listened to her voice, trying to discern any words he recognised, and trying to get a feel for the rhythm of the language. Bridget seemed to be picking it up faster than he was, her mind never forgetting a word once it had been taught to her.

When Simiona stopped talking, Paeotan turned to the captives. He spoke to them in Rahain, enunciating each word with care.

'Simiona,' he said, 'wants you to sing.'

'Sing?' Killop repeated. It wasn't a word he knew. He looked at Bridget, who shook her head.

'Yes,' Paeotan nodded. 'Sing. La la la…'

'Ahh, he means sing,' Bridget said in the Kellach tongue.

'Well, I'm not singing,' Killop muttered.

'I'll do it,' Kallie said.

'Yes, we sing,' Bridget said in Rahain to Paeotan and Simiona.

Kallie edged closer to the bars, shut her eyes, and started singing – a low, mournful song, a lamentation for the death of a twin. It was a song Killop had heard many times during the war, at the graveside, a song of loss for the heartbroken. Painful and beautiful, it rose shivering into the still air, chilling his heart. Killop lowered his head, to hide the tears falling down his cheeks.

He wiped his face as the song finished, and saw that Simiona was also in tears. He noticed for the first time that she was wearing a thin silver chain around her neck, a sign that she too was a slave, though one in a rare and privileged position.

'Very good,' Paeotan said, his eyes moist. 'Thank you.'

Killop took Kallie's hand, and they sat in silence.

Simiona and Paeotan stood up, and pushed the chairs back away from the cage.

'Good night,' Paeotan said.

Simiona's eyes lingered on the captives for a few more moments. She shook her head, and followed Paeotan to the door.

When they had gone, Bridget turned to Killop. 'Did you recognise her?'

'Aye,' he said. 'Her master is the old man who brought us here.'

'Aye.'

'I don't remember her,' Kallie said. 'Do you think she might help us?'

'I don't know,' he said. 'They seem amazed that we can learn their language, as if they think us no better than beasts. If we can prove we're not, then... I don't know.'

'What the fuck can she do, but?' Bridget said. 'She's a slave.'

'Aye,' Killop said, 'but she's a slave that gets to walk about on her own at night. She must be close to the old man; he must trust her.'

'Aye,' Bridget said, 'but can we?'

CHAPTER 5
PARTY OF ONE

R ahain Capital, Rahain Republic – 18th Day, First Third
Summer 504

'As far as I can see, my good man,' Laodoc said, resting his glass of
brandy on the dark pine table, 'there remains no reason for us to stay
together.'

'Are you saying that you want to disband our alliance?' asked
Pleonim, his eyes widening.

'The war is over,' said Laodoc. 'We lost. Well, Rahain won, but we,
the peace coalition, were defeated.'

'But someone in the council needs to stand up to the war coalition,'
Pleonim said. 'Their arrogance grows by the day. They'll be casting
their greedy eyes on the Plateau next; you know it! Do you think war
with the Holdings will be as easy as it was against those southern
savages?'

'Now, now, Councillor,' Laodoc said. In the shadows around the
table sat the rest of the Hedgers, the small bloc of eleven city councillors led by Laodoc. 'I'm sure you Liberals will do a fine job of opposing
the war coalition. For us Hedgers, however; well, some of us feel that it
might be time to rebuild a few bridges...'

'Cross over to the other side, you mean.'

'See here,' Laodoc said, getting irritated, 'you Liberals knew perfectly well why we were opposed to the war, and even though those reasons were different from yours, you still welcomed our votes in the City Council. But we lost, Pleonim. Rahain went to war. And with our defeat today on that damnable Kellach Slave Bill, the Hedgers no longer see any purpose in maintaining our coalition with you. As of the next session of the City Council, we shall consider ourselves free to vote as we wish.'

'You're right,' Pleonim said, sliding back into his comfortable armchair, a brandy glass balanced between his slender fingers. 'We did know your reasons for opposing the war. The market being flooded with cheap imports of coal and iron from the conquered Kellach territories would destroy your little mining cartel, and cost you all dearly.' He looked around the table at the men and women of the Hedgers, who were glowering at him. 'I see I am right,' he said, 'but this does not gladden me. I had harboured foolish hopes that once you saw the brutality and senseless waste of the war with the Kellach Brigdomin, and witnessed the imperialistic hubris of the high-handed bullies in the war coalition, you would come round to our view.'

He rose to his feet. 'I now realise I was mistaken. I will convey your intentions to the Liberal Party leadership.' He put down his glass. 'Thank you for the drink, and good night.'

He turned and strode across the floor of the members' bar, picking up his jacket and hat from a servant by the door.

'He took it well enough, I thought,' Laodoc said, gesturing to a waiter for more brandy.

'And now, Laodoc,' Niuma said, frowning as she pointing at him, 'we need to talk about how to undo some of the damage our ill-fated alliance with the Liberals has caused us.'

'We should have dissolved the coalition as soon as war was declared!' said someone else.

'We no longer have confidence in your leadership of the Hedgers,' Riomac said.

Laodoc spluttered. 'Hold on, old chap.'

'Before the war,' Riomac said, 'we Hedgers could lend our votes to whichever bloc best suited our interests; play off all parties against each other and, I'll admit, it was good fun while it lasted. But you went too far, Laodoc, and the war coalition will never trust the Hedgers again, at least not under its current leadership.'

Laodoc chuckled. 'So you're after my job, then, Riomac? You clearly haven't understood the party's constitution, my fine fellow, since it explicitly states that, once elected, leaders serve a term of five years, with no recourse to being replaced, unless through death or criminal conviction. I have two years to go, I'm afraid.'

'And I'm certain,' Riomac said, 'that you'll make a wonderful leader of a party of one.'

'What?'

'We can't replace you,' Niuma said, 'but we can leave.'

She stood, and the others followed her to their feet.

'With immediate effect,' Riomac said, 'we all hereby resign from the Hedgers.'

Laodoc sat, his mouth hanging open, as they shuffled past, averting their eyes. The last to leave, Juarad, stopped next to him.

'Best of luck, Laodoc,' he said. 'No hard feelings, eh?'

'What will you do now?' said Laodoc.

'Most of us,' Juarad said, 'are joining the Merchant Party.'

'But they're in the war coalition!'

Juarad shrugged. 'Sometimes it's just easier to be on the winning side, for a while at least. What about you?'

'I don't know,' Laodoc said, his hands trembling. 'I'll admit to being a little bewildered by what has happened.'

'If you would take my advice,' Juarad said, 'join the Liberals. They're the only party that would have you now, I imagine.'

He stuck out his hand. Laodoc grasped it limply.

'Farewell, old chap,' Juarad nodded, then he walked away.

Laodoc sat back in his leather armchair, staring at the empty table in front of him.

'Sir?'

He glanced up. It was the waiter he had summoned.

'Your brandy, sir,' the servant said, placing a full bottle onto the table.

Laodoc stared at it. Some occasions, he reflected, positively cried out for drunken oblivion.

———

Several brandies later, a small group approached Laodoc, as he sat brooding in the deep shadows of the alcove.

'Father,' his eldest son Ruellap, said. 'May we join you?'

'If you must,' said Laodoc. 'Though if you're here to gloat I would suggest another time.'

'No gloating, father. I promise.'

Ruellap sat, along with two other politicians from the war coalition. One of them, Ziane, a famous old member of the Conservative Party, gestured to a servant for drinks and glasses. Next to him sat Yaelli, a prominent Merchant.

'I assume you've heard?' Laodoc said.

Yaelli nodded. 'We have. I've just returned from a meeting with the Merchant Party, where we voted to accept your old Hedgers.'

'All ten of them?' Laodoc cried.

'Indeed,' Yaelli said, grinning, 'which, at a stroke, doubles the Merchant Party's representation in the City Council, making us the third largest party...'

'Yes, yes,' Ruellap said, raising his eyebrows, 'and over-taking my Patriot Party, as you have already informed us, Yaelli. Several times, in fact!'

'So the damned war coalition is now utterly dominant,' Laodoc muttered, the brandy loosening him. 'You outnumber the Liberals two to one. I suppose you'll be planning the next invasion soon, eh?'

'You cannot fight destiny, father,' Ruellap said, as servants set down drinks for them.

'Ahh, destiny is it now?' said Laodoc.

Ruellap shook his head. 'Why is it so painful for you to admit that we are the superior species in this world, father? Technology, wealth, culture, science; no one can match us. Only the Holdings come even close.'

'So, son,' Laodoc said, 'what will the Patriot Party's advice be? What will they propose in the High Senate as our next adventure?'

'If I had my way, father, I would have us take the Plateau.'

'And how would you accomplish this feat?' Laodoc said, his voice rising. 'Where would you find another hundred thousand soldiers, eh?'

'The answer is staring us in the face, father,' Ruellap said, while Ziane and Yaelli listened in. 'We should organise the Kellach Brigdomin into a new slave army. Imagine it; they would smash their way across the entire continent!'

Ziane spluttered, spraying wine across the table.

'My young friend!' the old conservative cried, wiping his face with a napkin. 'The very last thing we want to do is arm the savages in our midst! And you should forget these bold notions of conquest, at least for now. We have a peace treaty with the Realm of the Holdings, and a clearly defined border across the Plateau. We would hardly be leading by example if we were to break our word, and invade without good cause. No, we should be negotiating with the Holdings, each defining our spheres of interest on this continent.' He looked around the table. 'I hear they're having a spot of trouble with their war in Sanang. We should be pushing them hard for talks, while they are distracted.'

'I heard some gossip today you may find interesting,' Yaelli said. 'Apparently, their queen is dying; poisoned in a conspiracy involving their religious leaders, who are stridently opposed to the war.'

'Really?' Ziane said. 'That is interesting, indeed.'

'There's more,' she went on. 'I also heard that their king-in-waiting, the queen's brother, is in the pocket of the Holdings church; and he'll end the war in Sanang the moment he is crowned.'

'Their church is pacifist?' Ruellap said. 'That would be excellent news, neutering the only armed force on the continent that could possibly stand up to us.'

'It's terrible news!' Yaelli cried. 'Just as our trade with the Holdings is picking up, and our access to Sanang goods is improving, the Holdings turn isolationist? Have you any idea how popular and lucrative this trade is?'

Ruellap shrugged. 'I prefer Rahain products, myself.'

'I confess a certain fondness for chocolate,' Ziane said, patting his ample stomach, 'and sugar, and, yes, a few other things. You are correct Yaelli, that is a valid concern.'

'There's a trader from Jade Falls newly arrived in the capital.' Yaelli went on. 'She has just returned from two years at the frontier between the Holdings-occupied Plateau and the Sanang forest. I met her, and she provided us with some samples of her goods. Their quality is astounding, and by my calculations, she's going to be one of the richest merchants in Rahain once it's all sold. It would be tragic indeed if we allowed trade to suffer due to the backwardness of the Holdings religion. We need to focus on pushing ahead with the tunnel through the Grey Mountains, so we can move our traders, and if necessary our army, up onto the Plateau as quickly as possible. *That* is how we should be using the Kellach slaves.'

'What say you, father?' said Ruellap.

He shifted in his seat, looking at his political opponents: conservative, merchant and patriot. He suspected they were only being friendly to him because they no longer saw him as a serious threat.

'You lot squabble as much as the peace coalition did,' he said, taking a drink.

They smiled politely.

'No, really, father,' Ruellap said. 'What do you think?'

Laodoc straightened, slurring his words. 'Son,' he said, 'you utterly humiliate me in the City Council, ensure my every suggestion and amendment is soundly defeated, and now you are asking for my advice?'

'Come, Laodoc, old fellow,' Ziane said. 'Don't be like that. We're here to show you that we can still be friends, once we're off the floor of the council chamber. Politics is a filthy business, but we needn't carry the dirt with us wherever we go.'

Laodoc stood up, swaying. He steadied himself, putting a hand on the top of the armchair. He picked up the half empty bottle of brandy, and slipped it into the folds of his dark robes.

'You are not my friends,' he said, earning disappointed and aggrieved scowls.

He turned and staggered towards the door of the bar, hearing someone's voice call 'pompous old fool' at him. He hoped it wasn't his son.

Beoloth was waiting for him in the courtyard of the council chambers, along with the other politicians' slaves and servants.

'Master,' he said, bowing. 'Let me collect your carriage.'

Laodoc waited in the warm, dry air of the enormous cavern that held the majority of the capital's government buildings. The lamps had been dimmed for evening-time, and they would be darkened further nearer midnight, to mimic the natural world outside. To his right, the towering domes and spires of the High Senate loomed, making the council chambers, for all its architectural glory, seem small and insignificant by comparison.

Laodoc sighed.

The High Senate. While each of the seven cities had its own council to run its local affairs, the High Senate ruled all of Rahain; its fifty senators elected for life. Seven were appointed from each city, with the capital alone contributing eight. Whenever a member of the High Senate died, the others would select a new candidate from the City Council where the dead senator had originated. This was Laodoc's dream, to be selected to join the High Senate. At sixty-three, he was still two years away from meeting the minimum age for a senator, but the campaign to be selected took long and careful planning. After having managed to offend every other party in the City Council during the course of a single evening, he knew that his hopes had been set back by a few years at least.

He got into his carriage as soon as Beoloth swung it round to the steps of the council building, and pulled the window blinds down. He sat in silent self-pity as the carriage lurched its way home.

When they arrived, Laodoc staggered through his cold and empty mansion, until he came to his small study, which held an old desk, two snug armchairs, and shelves overloaded with books. He took a glass from a desk drawer. As he was standing pouring himself a large brandy, there was a knock at the door.

'Go away.'

The knock came again, a little louder.

'Damnation!' Laodoc cried. 'Enter, then!'

Simiona shuffled in, her head down. 'Sorry, master...'

'Well?' he shouted at her. 'Out with it!'

'I've been waiting to speak with you all day, master,' she said, keeping her eyes lowered. 'Maybe now is the wrong time.'

'No,' he said, calming a little. He should really watch his temper with the girl. 'Go on, tell me.'

'It's the Kellach slaves, master,' she said. 'I visited them last night. They have been learning to speak Rahain, and have been making great progress! And, master, the woman with the red hair, she sang me a song!'

'Wait a minute,' he said, his anger rising again. 'They're learning Rahain? On whose authority? I hope this has nothing to do with you. It must cease at once, of course.'

'I thought that learning the language was one of the aims of the research programme, master?'

'Was it?' Laodoc slurred. 'I don't recall that. It seems a foolish idea to me. They're savages, Simiona; nothing but wild apes. It's surely for the best that we don't allow beasts to understand what we're saying.'

'But, master...'

'Are you questioning my authority, slave?' he shouted, rage filling him. After the day he'd had, this was the last thing he needed, to be pestered about some ignorant barbarians by a nagging slave.

'No, master!' she cried, putting a hand in front of her face as he raised his fist to strike her.

Laodoc looked down into the eyes of his terrified slave, his right fist poised to punish her impertinence. He knew others who regularly beat their slaves, taking out their petty frustrations and troubles on them. He hated people like that.

He lowered his fist.

He walked round the desk to his armchair and settled down, relieved that Stoelica was not present. She had despised his moments of weakness, especially those concerning his inability to administer appropriate discipline to his slaves.

'I apologise for my temper, Simiona,' he said. 'I have had the most dreadful day, although that is no excuse. Come; sit.'

Simiona sat down in the armchair on the other side of the desk from him. Her face was pale, and she was shivering. He got another glass from the drawer, and poured her a small brandy.

He passed her the glass. 'So, tell me all about the Kellach's song.'

CHAPTER 6
LEAVING HOME

Arakhanah City – 20th Day, First Third Summer 504
'Wake up, Shella,' Barro said, nudging her with his elbow. 'It's time to vote.'

'What?' she croaked.

Shella opened her bleary eyes, a string of drool hanging from her lip, while a monstrous hangover held her in its grasp. The dawn air was crisp and cool, but the blue sky overhead heralded another hot and sunny day to come. All around her were hundreds of other Rakanese, sitting on the tiered stone benches of Brackenwell District's local assembly. 'What are we voting for?'

Barro scowled at her. He took his democratic rights very seriously, and rarely missed the morning debates. 'The proposal to implement the two-shift school day, Shella. You know, the one we were talking about last night?'

'Oh yeah,' she said, her head pounding. 'Which way are we voting? For or against?'

Barro sighed. 'Do you ever listen to anything I say?'

She shrugged. 'Sometimes.'

From a raised podium, the speaker of the assembly held up her hand for silence, waiting until a relative quiet had descended over the half-filled benches.

'Those in favour of proposal seventeen!' she thundered.

There was a flurry of hands in the air. Shella noticed that Barro's hand was not raised, so she put hers up. Counters to either side of the speaker noted down the citizens' response.

'Those opposed!' the speaker called out.

A far smaller number of arms, including Barro's, were raised.

The speaker didn't bother to wait for the counters to finish.

'Proposal seventeen carries!' she shouted. 'Next item. Proposal eighteen regarding the re-allocation of funds from the budget to refurbish the riverside harbour. Here to speak in favour of the proposal...'

As the speaker continued, Barro turned to Shella in fury.

'You voted in favour!'

'Well, yes,' she said. 'The average classroom size in the district is over sixty, Barro. The teachers can't cope, and most lessons are useless. We split the classes in half, and run two shifts back-to-back; at least we get the class sizes down.'

'But, Shella,' said Barro, 'they didn't include adequate provision for childcare. What are parents whose kids are allocated the early shift going to do when their children are let out of school at lunchtime?'

She shrugged, squinting into the sunlight. 'Make do, I guess.'

He snorted and shook his head.

She smothered a smile. As much as she enjoyed winding him up, she found his inability to realise whether she was joking or not a little disconcerting. She yawned, and stretched out her arms. It was going to be a rough day. She had turned up drunk at Barro's apartment the previous evening, and spent the night. They'd had sex, though her mind was hazy on the details, and she had a horrible feeling that she may have fallen asleep while he had been grunting away on top of her.

'Can we go to work, now?' she said. 'I'm bored.'

'Actually,' he said, 'I want to stick around for the vote on the new rent control restrictions.'

She raised an eyebrow. 'And when will that be?'

'Another forty minutes, maybe?'

'Sod that,' she said. She staggered to her feet. 'I'll see you at work, yeah?'

'Sure.'

Shella pushed her way through the crowds of people towards the western exit. The majority of the attendees were elderly, being those with the most time to spare, as well as the strongest opinions on how Arakhanah was in terminal decline. A few old folk tutted as Shella passed them, or commented on how her early departure proved how fickle and apathetic the younger generations really were.

She ignored them. Her hangover was all she cared about.

Once out of the building, she made her way along the canal front towards Crossmarket to catch the water-bus. It took her a few minutes to realise that the streets and waterways were much quieter than usual. Odd, she thought. It was still early, but the dawn wave of workers heading to their jobs tended to make this a busy time.

She reached the large quayside in front of the great market hall, and her mouth opened. The queues for the water-buses were tiny compared to usual. A few hundred people stood around, where normally there would be thousands at this time of the morning.

Her stomach rumbled. Barro lived like a man who had never cooked a meal in his life, and she had yet to have any breakfast. She walked over to a hot-food stall, her hand reaching inside her overalls for her purse.

'Morning,' the woman behind the counter said, her apron greasy and stained.

'Yeah,' Shella replied. 'I'll take one, please. Large.'

The woman leaned over a deep fat fryer to her left, and extracted a long thick locust on a stick from the bubbling oil. 'How spicy do you want it?'

'Very.'

The woman nodded, and rolled the fried insect in a tray of dark red powder, before wrapping it neatly in paper.

'Three and a half bits,' she said, handing it over.

'Ta,' Shella said, giving her the money. 'Quiet today.'

'Yeah.'

'Any idea what's going on?'

'Nope,' she replied. 'It was busy at dawn, then, about an hour ago it started to thin out. Is there a strike on that I didn't hear about?'

Shella shrugged as she turned away. 'Don't think so.'

She walked to the queue for her water-bus.

'Hi, Joanie,' she said, recognising a woman from the sewage works.

'Hi, Shella,' she replied. 'Do you know...?'

'No idea,' Shella said. 'Just come from the Brackenwell assembly, nobody said anything about a strike while I was there.'

'We heard it was religious,' said a man from the neighbouring queue. 'Everyone's gone to listen to a new visionary or prophet or something.'

'Not another one,' Shella said. 'That guy last winter was a complete fraud.'

'Yeah,' the man said. 'My sister totally bought into it as well, she...'

'Shella! Shella!'

Her head turned as she heard her name shouted across the quayside.

'Is that your brother?' Joanie asked, pointing.

Shella saw him in the distance, as he scanned the crowd looking for her.

'Lenni!' she yelled. 'Over here!'

He ran over, out of breath.

'You been running?' she said. 'Why are you not at work?'

'Where were you this morning?' he asked. 'You weren't at breakfast.'

'I was out.'

'Noli sent me to look for you,' he went on. 'Obli and her husband had a huge row and, well, Noli needs you to come home. Now.'

Shella sighed. 'Can it not wait until after work?'

Lenni shook his head.

Shella raised her eyebrows at Joanie. 'Tell the overseer,' she said; 'I don't know, tell him I've found religion.'

She unwrapped the fried locust as she left the quayside with Lenni, her stomach aching.

'Can I have a bite?' asked Lenni, spying it.

'I'll leave you some,' she said, biting the head off, 'if you tell me what's going on.'

'Can't,' he muttered. 'Noli asked me not to.'

She shrugged, and finished off the insect in another couple of bites, chewing on its warm, crunchy flesh, her mouth burning from the rich spices. Lenni looked away, scowling.

'Mmm,' she mumbled.

'I'm definitely not telling you anything now.'

'You weren't going to anyway,' she said, belching. 'You always do whatever Noli tells you to. Isn't that right, loyal little Lenni?'

He lifted his palms up. 'She is the head of the family, Shella.'

'Yeah,' Shella nodded, 'because giving birth magically imbues wisdom, doesn't it?'

'Giving authority to mothers is only fair,' he said, 'as they're the ones with the biggest stake in the future.'

'So,' Shella said, 'not only are they lucky enough to have children, but they get to lord it over those of their brothers and sisters who are denied the same right, and who are left to wither like dead branches on a tree?'

'I didn't think you wanted any kids.'

'I don't,' Shella replied. 'But that's not the point. There are plenty who do.'

'Like Obli.'

'Yeah,' she said, her voice low. 'Like Obli.'

They walked in silence along the quiet canal-lined streets.

'Where is everyone?' Shella muttered, mostly to herself.

'I assumed the unions had called another strike,' Lenni said.

'If they have,' she said, 'nobody told us. Guy in the bus queue said he heard it was a new religious craze.'

'People are so gullible.'

'I know,' she said, nodding. 'By the way, did you remember to perform the ritual sacrifices to the household spirits this morning?'

He scowled at her. 'That's different, and you know it.'

'Of course it is,' she winked at him. 'Completely different.'

They walked into their street, keeping to the shade under the trees, as the summer morning warmed up.

The family house was in uproar as they entered. Children were crying and shouting, and adults sat about looking depressed, or stood and argued. Brothers, sisters, nephews and nieces crowded the main hall, and the sitting rooms beyond. Lenni led her to the dining room, where Noli sat at the head of the table, frowning. Next to her sat Sami, another sister Zonnie, and Obli's husband, Janno. Zonnie had two of Noli's children sitting on her knee.

'I found her,' Lenni said as he came in, taking a seat next to Janno.

Noli looked up at Shella.

'I'm not going to ask you where you were last night,' Noli said. 'Right now, there are more important things to worry about than your lack of respect for yourself.'

'And a good morning to you too,' Shella said, sitting next to Sami.

Zonnie scowled at her from across the table.

'You got something to say?' Shella asked her.

'You're an embarrassment to the family,' she blurted out.

'Thanks!' Shella replied. 'One tries one's best.'

'Enough!' Noli cried. 'While you two bicker, Obli is out there somewhere, alone.'

'What?' Shella said.

'I need you to go and find her, Shella,' Noli said. 'You're her closest sister. If she'll listen to anyone, it'll be you.'

'Wait a minute,' Shella said. 'Where has she gone? What happened?'

'I'll let Janno tell you,' Noli said, waving her hand at the man, who Shella noticed was sitting with his eyes downcast, shame beating from him.

He said nothing.

'Come now, Janno,' Noli said. 'Best if you tell her.'

He mumbled something too quiet to hear.

'What?' Shella said.

'I've been having an affair,' he whispered.

Shella gasped, looking around the table. From the sullen looks on everyone's faces, she guessed they already knew.

'You've been cheating on Obli?' she said, her anger growing. Her hands clenched into fists.

Janno nodded.

'Bastard!' Shella shouted, and launched herself out of her seat. She swung her arm, and her right fist connected with the side of Janno's head. He yelled out, and Shella felt Sami's arms pull her back across the table.

Shella sat down, with Sami's arm over her shoulder. Janno stared at Noli in protest, holding a hand to his face.

Noli shrugged, a half smile on her lips.

'How long?' cried Shella. 'Who with?'

'Nearly a year. You don't know her,' Janno said. 'You don't understand what it's like, living with Obli; it's been so difficult...'

'I don't care,' Shella said. 'I don't want to hear you speak again. In fact,' she turned to Noli, 'why is he even here? Why is his backside not out on the street?'

'I'm tempted to throw him out,' Noli said, 'but I wanted to wait and see if that's what Obli wanted, too. We need to find her, and bring her back here, and then we can talk about what to do.'

'Okay, sis,' Shella said, 'I'll go. When did she leave?'

'About two hours ago.'

Shella stood, wracking her brain for places that Obli could have gone.

'This could take a while,' she said. 'I'll need Sami to help me.'

Noli nodded to their brother, who pushed himself to his feet.

'If you can,' Noli said, 'try to get a message to us by lunchtime, even if you haven't found her, just so we know.'

'Okay, will do,' Shella said.

Noli reached over, and hugged Shella. 'Good luck, sister.'

Shella nodded, and she and Sami left the dining room.

Back out on the street, she headed right, towards the centre of Brackenwell.

'So,' Sami said, 'where were you last night?'

She tutted. 'Not you as well, Sami?'

'Come on, sis. I'm not judging you; I'm just curious.'

'Barro's,' she muttered.

Sami snorted. 'Him? Oh, sis, you can do better than that.'

'You don't even know him.'

'No,' he said, 'but I've heard you complain about him often enough.'

Shella slowed as they reached a small market square bordering the riverside docks.

'Where are we going to look first?' Sami asked.

She had no idea. Not the first clue where Obli could have gone.

Sami gazed around the square. 'Why's it so quiet?'

Shella glanced up. The usually bustling fruit and vegetable stalls were almost deserted. There were a few elderly people, and a handful of older children running messages for their families, but no one else.

They went up to the first stall.

'Where is everyone?' she asked the stall-keeper.

The old woman leaned forward. 'They've all gone west, dear.'

'West?' Shella said. 'Why west?'

'They're following a new holy man,' the stall-keeper said. 'One minute, the market was busy, the next, a rumour spread through the square, that someone was going to speak, someone in the west of the city, someone blessed and holy, and then all the young folk left. It was the oddest thing I ever saw.'

'It's not just here,' Shella said. 'The quayside up at Crossmarket was deserted as well.'

'It's rattled me, dear,' the old woman said, her eyes worried.

Shella turned to Sami. 'What do you think?' she said. 'Would Obli have gone to listen?'

Her brother shrugged. 'Maybe, I don't know. She was doing a lot of superstitious stuff before the Board made their decision, so she might have.'

'West it is, then,' she said. 'Come on.'

They walked to the main road by the western entrance to the market. It ran alongside a major canal that cut across one of the loops in the river. Shops lined the street on one side, while on the other the tables and chairs of the local cafes sat out by the canal. Waiters stood around the empty seats, looking slightly embarrassed by the lack of customers.

'Definitely not a strike, then,' Shella said. She shook her head. 'I can't believe another crank holy-man has duped half the city, so soon after the last one.'

'People are desperate,' Sami said. 'They want to believe in something, anything.'

'That's pretty deep,' she said. 'For you.'

'Do you think you're the only person in this city who feels like they're drowning?'

'Generally I try to avoid other people's feelings.'

'Except when you're stepping all over them.'

'What's gotten into you?'

'Our family's breaking apart, Shella,' he said. 'Noli didn't say anything, but did you not wonder why so few of us were at the dinner table?'

She thought. Of her siblings, Noli, Lenni and Zonnie had been there with her and Sami. She had also seen Chapu, Marru and Asta in the hallway looking after the children.

That left her sisters Dannu, Clodi and Tehna, and her brothers Klebo and Pavu.

'I assumed they were all at work.'

'Nobody went to work,' Sami said. 'Not after what happened at breakfast, with Obli screaming at Janno, and everyone fighting.'

'So where are they?'

'Not sure,' he said. 'I think they slipped out after Obli. Followed her.'

'Followed her? What do you mean?'

'Something Obli said, before she stormed out.'

'What did she say?' Shella said. 'Something that made the others walk out, too?'

'When Noli asked her what she was going to do,' Sami went on. 'Obli replied *I'm leaving*, that's what she said. *I'm leaving*.'

Shella stopped, and her heart lurched. An intense feeling rose from the tips of her toes, rippling upwards through her body. I have got to get out of here, she thought, closing her eyes, dizziness overcoming her.

Leaving.

She was shaking with the *rightness* of how the word felt.

'You feel it too?' Sami asked, snapping her out of her trance in an instant.

'What?' she said. 'No. I felt nothing.'

Sami half-smiled. 'Fair enough, sis. Anyway, that feeling that you didn't feel just now, well, when Obli said those words, everyone in the room felt it. No, almost everyone. I don't think Noli batted an eyelid. I think the others slipped out because of that feeling, to follow Obli.'

They started walking again. Shella's mind was racing, trying to process the emotions that had surged through her like a current.

How could a mere word cause such feelings? How could it make her brothers and sisters get up and follow Obli?

She stopped again, a fearful panic rising in her, threatening to choke her as she grappled with its implications.

'You okay?' Sami asked.

'What if it's not a holy man, Sami?' she said, her voice quavering. 'What if... holy fuck, oh no, please no.'

She collapsed to her knees, trying to breathe.

'Shella!' Sami cried, putting his arm around her.

She stared at him. 'What if they're all following Obli?'

They ran together through the streets, over long bridges, alongside canals, into the steadily thickening crowds.

Masses of people were all heading in the same direction: west. Everywhere Shella looked, more were joining the flow, having come from every corner of Arakhanah within reach. If the rumour spread to the entire city, then tomorrow would be even busier, and the days to come. No child or older person could be seen in the crowd, whose ages ranged from late teens to forties. Many were smiling, or laughing, and looked relaxed, as if they were on a day out.

'What are you doing?' she had asked the first group they had come across.

'Leaving,' they had replied, laughing as if a load had been lifted from their shoulders.

'Why are you going west?' Shella had persisted.

'To hear the one who called us to leave.'

When he had heard that, even Sami was convinced that Obli was somehow involved.

They pushed their way through the masses of people, edging closer to the front of the crowds, then halted as they reached a bridge over an arm of the river. Hundreds were lined up in queues waiting to cross.

'We need to move faster,' Shella said. 'Where is there on the western side of the city that could hold thousands of people?'

'There are the big fields over in Newmarsh District,' Sami replied. 'Used to grow rice, but they all dried up when they diverted the canals a few years back.'

'Big, dry, empty fields?'

He nodded.

'Okay,' she said, 'how do we get there quicker than everyone else?'

'Boat,' he whispered.

She nodded, and they slipped out of the crowd to the left, away from the bridge, and toward the riverside quay a mile upstream.

She swore as they reached the dockside's long pier.

'Seems like others have had the same idea,' Sami said, looking down at the empty wharves.

'Wait,' she said. 'There's one.'

They sprinted down the pier, towards a single-sailed barge, the captain punting from the rear of the craft.

'Hoy!' Shella shouted.

The captain looked up.

'You for hire?' Shella asked, as they came alongside the craft.

'Sure,' he said. 'Jump aboard.'

Shella and Sami stepped down into the flat-bottomed barge, and the captain moved across to the other end, which then became the rear.

'Let me guess,' he said, smiling. 'Newmarsh District, by any chance?'

'Yeah,' Shella replied. 'How did you know?'

'This will be my fourth trip in the last couple of hours,' he chuckled, patting the stuffed money-belt at his waist. 'Thirty bits each, please.'

'What?' Sami shouted. 'You're joking!'

'You can go back to walking if you like,' the captain said. 'I can turn around now?'

'No,' Shella said, sitting on the wooden bench running down the centre of the barge. 'We'll pay.'

The captain pushed the pole down into the shallow mud-bed, and the barge moved off. The wind picked up as they left the shelter of the harbour, and the sail snapped and filled. The captain pulled the pole back up into the barge, and squatted by the rudder, guiding the craft as it skipped through the rougher waters of the river.

Brick-built houses, workshops, warehouses, depots, harbours and quays flew past on either side, as their craft raced through the city.

'There's so much of it,' Shella said.

'And this is just one tiny corner,' Sami said. 'Imagine going on a tour of the whole thing.'

'Imagine leaving it.'

He looked at her.

'Do you want to?' he asked.

'Do you?'

'Yes,' he said. 'And no. I want to, but I'm scared. Where would we go?'

'There's nowhere to go,' she said, spitting over the side of the barge. 'That's the problem.'

'And how would you know?'

'There's something I haven't told you,' she said. 'A while back, I went up north for a job interview at the big reclamation project.'

'When?' he asked. 'Wait, that time you told me you were working a short contract out on the salt pans?'

'Yeah.'

'It worries me Shella, that you can lie so easily, even to me.'

'I didn't tell anyone about the job,' she said. 'I didn't want it getting out, when I hadn't decided if I even wanted it or not. Anyway, I went up there for a couple of days, saw the project, and got to read through their survey reports. Did you know that we've been sending out scouts for years, decades even? Searching all around, looking for anywhere to settle.'

She turned to face him.

'There's nowhere, Sami.'

'So that's it, then?' he said. 'Is that what you're going to tell Obli when we find her?'

Shella shook her head, saying nothing. Her mind was a blur of emotions, raging against each other. Desire against fear, hope against despair. What would she say to Obli?

'Here we are,' the captain said, as they pulled alongside a section of dilapidated harbour. 'Can't take you any closer, I'm afraid. As you can see, the waterway ahead is blocked.'

Shella paid the captain, and they climbed up the wooden pier. From the top they could see hundreds of vessels, from tiny skiffs to large galleys, filling the river upstream of where they stood. To their left, behind the harbour buildings, were the big fields that Sami had mentioned.

They were filled with thousands of Rakanese, who packed every corner of the vast open space, and the streets and roads round about. There were tents dotted across the fields, and everywhere the noise of people echoed through the air. The atmosphere was festive, as if everyone was enjoying one of the more relaxed holy days.

'There must be sixty thousand people here,' Sami said, looking around.

'And this is just the beginning.'

Shella and Sami barged and elbowed their way through the pressing crowds, heading towards a cluster of tents in the middle of the first field, guessing that this might be where Obli could be found.

It was slow going, and the sun had passed its peak by the time they approached a cordoned-off area. Surrounding the cluster of tents was a ring of men and women, each with a scarlet sash tied round their left arm. Every one of them held a long spear, and they were keeping the crowds from getting too close to the tents.

Several of them aimed their weapons at Shella and Sami as they pushed their way to the front. The noise was almost overwhelming, with thousands of raised voices.

'We need to see Oblikanawara!' Shella shouted at the guards.

'Yeah,' one replied, 'you and everyone else.'

'She's our sister!' Shella yelled.

The guard smirked. 'We're all brothers and sisters now.'

'Wait,' Sami cut in, before Shella could say something stupid. 'What about our brother, Commander Pavukanawara? Can we see him, please?'

The guards looked at each other. 'Names?' one said.

'Shella and Samikanawara,' Sami replied.

'Okay, stay here,' the guard said. 'I'll be back in a minute.'

As he raced off towards the tents, Shella looked at Sami.

'How did you know?' she said.

'I had a hunch,' he said, 'that if anyone in the family was going to start up a group of vigilantes, it'd be him.'

Shella nodded. 'Fair enough.'

Their brother Pavu soon approached, and Shella and Sami were waved through the cordon, and into the relative calm of the cluster of tents.

'Glad to see you made it, Shella,' Pavu said. 'I'm surprised at you though, Sami. I had you down as a stay-at-home.'

'Noli asked us to come,' Shella said, earning a snort of derision from Pavu. 'We haven't decided if we're part of... whatever this is, yet.'

'This is the beginning of the new world, Shella!' Pavu said, stretching out his long muscular arms. 'Obli will lead us to a future where we can live freely, and...'

'Cut the crap, Pavu,' Shella said. 'None of you know the first damn thing about what you're doing.'

Before Pavu could respond, she swept past a couple of guards into the largest tent.

There, in the centre, she saw Obli standing, a crowd assembled in a half circle before her.

She looked radiant and composed. Sunlight was entering the tent through an opening, and a shaft fell across her, illuminating her long, white gown. She was wearing a wreath of flowers on her head; water-lilies and orchids.

'She looks like a vision!' Sami gasped.

Obli saw them both, and smiled.

'Come,' she said. 'Friends, this is Shella, who I have spoken of before. She is to be treated with the utmost respect.'

The crowd moved to let her through.

'Sister,' Shella said. 'May we speak in private?'

Obli nodded. She took Shella and Sami through to a small enclosed sitting room at the rear of the tent, while a guard took up position outside.

As soon as they were alone, Shella reached out and grabbed Obli's arm.

'What the hell are you doing, Obli?' Shella whisper-shouted. 'Where are you leading these people?'

Obli's mouth opened in shock.

'We're leaving!' she said, her smile returning.

'Yeah, so I hear,' Shella said. 'Only, where? Where are you going?'

'Oh, I don't know yet, exactly,' Obli replied. 'In some ways, it doesn't matter. We will choose a direction, and begin. And somewhere along the way, we will find our new home.'

'Are you fucking insane?'

'Calm down, Shella!' Sami said, pulling Obli free.

Shella closed her eyes and breathed, trying to regain her composure.

'So, Obli,' she said, 'there's no plan?'

'Plan?' said Obli. 'How could there be a plan? This migration is fated, it's destiny, and I am merely the spark that lit the fire.'

Shella shook her head.

'But what about water supplies, food, maps, tents, wagons, or where people are going to take a dump? You'll need to list all the flow and clay mages you have, and get them organised. And how are you going to gather the money to pay for everything? You'll have to fleece the migrants for cash and donations. Also, you'll need...'

'This is good, Shella,' Obli said. 'This is exactly why I need you here. I don't know anything about these details, but you do.' She opened the tent flap and called for someone.

Moments later a young man came in, with a pencil and paper.

'Write down everything she says,' Obli instructed him.

'Shella,' she said. 'From the very beginning, please.'

Shella sighed, a long sigh of resignation.

'Okay,' she said. 'Water; let's start there.'

A few hours later, Shella and Sami stumbled back out into the daylight.

'My head hurts,' Sami said. 'How do you know all that stuff?'

'What I advised back there,' she said, 'is probably out-weighed ten to one by what I don't know, and can't foresee.'

'Seemed pretty thorough to me.'

One of her recommendations had already been put into action. All members of the leadership now carried a token, moulded on the spot by a clay mage, which would allow them passage through Pavu's guards.

Others were entering the cordoned-off area just as they were departing. To their right stood representatives of the Rakanese parliaments, councils, unions and assemblies. Beyond them, Shella could also see a party of delegates from the embassy of the Realm of the Holdings, their height and dark skin standing out among the shorter, paler Rakanese.

Sami raised an eyebrow. 'What do they want?'

'If I had to guess,' Shella said, 'it would be to make sure that Obli doesn't set off in the direction of their lands.'

'Which way do they live?'

'Far to the north-west,' Shella said. 'The Forbidden Mountains run north almost to the ocean, but there's a narrow pass at the coast that leads to a plateau, which the Holdings farm. The pass is blocked with a wall.'

'Who built it?' Sami asked, as they moved back through the thick crowds.

'They did.'

The sun was low in the western sky by the time Shella and Sami reached their family home in Brackenwell. Exhausted and hungry, they trudged up the steps to the front door and let themselves in. The sound of children was coming from the dining room, so they headed in that direction.

Noli was at the head of the table, exactly where they had last seen her. Shella wondered if she had moved from the seat the whole time. She looked more tired than they did. Around the table sat all of the brothers and sisters who had remained, and the children sat two to each adult.

'Shella!' Noli cried as she saw them approach. 'Where is Obli?'

Shella sat at the table, and pulled a dish of food towards her.

'She's not coming back,' she said, as she started to eat.

'Is it true?' said Lenni.

'Is what true?' Shella replied, mouth full of food.

'That Obli is leading them?' he said, his voice rising in exasperation.

'Yeah.'

The adults at the table let out a collective gasp. Noli put her head in her hands.

'We didn't believe it,' Zonnie said, 'when people started coming round to tell us that Obli was in charge of this madness. I mean, half the city following Obli?'

'Did you speak to her?' Chapu asked.

'Yeah.'

'I take it she didn't listen to what you had to say?' Lenni said.

Sami glanced at her.

'Look,' Shella said. 'This whole thing is way bigger than us now. Half the family are sat here, while the other half are out in a field on the edge of the city, but remember that the same thing is happening in every house in this entire quarter. And tomorrow it will spread to the rest of the city.'

'At least you've come back to us,' Noli said. 'Thank you for that.'

'Well,' she said, shifting in her seat, 'not exactly.'

'What do you mean?' Noli asked, her face hardening.

'Sami and I,' she said, 'are only here to tell you what happened. And to get our things.'

The table fell into silence.

'You're not leaving,' Noli said. 'I absolutely forbid it.'

Shella sat back in her chair. 'Ahh, Noli,' she said. 'I've been meaning to have this conversation with you for a while. I'm a grown adult, and you cannot tell me what to do.'

'While you live under my roof...'

'Precisely,' Shella said, 'and as of today, that is no longer the case. I'm leaving.'

'This madness will lead to nothing but ruin!' Noli cried, angry tears spilling from her eyes.

'Maybe,' Shella said. 'Maybe not. It'll be hard, but we may find a new home.'

'Not for the ones that leave!' Noli screamed. 'For those left behind! Who will work in the fields and factories? Who will keep the salt and sewage from the water? Who will grow the food for the spawn pools? We will be a land of children and old folk, with almost everyone of working age gone!' She wept, rage twisting her face. 'You selfish bastards. You've got an hour. Get your things, then get out.'

Shella and Sami were packed and ready in half the time, and stole out of the house, avoiding the anger and resentment emanating from those siblings choosing to stay behind.

In the dimness of the street lamps, they made their torturous way back west to Newmarsh District. The crowds were still growing, heaving, and flowing like a river towards Obli.

At the inner cordon their new clay tokens got them through the lines of guards, and they walked into the command tent as Obli was speaking.

They waited in a corner, as Obli delegated out several responsibilities, for wagons, a treasury, stores, logistics, water stocks, sometimes repeating word for word what Shella had told her earlier.

Please don't rely on me, Shella silently begged her sister.

When Obli had finished, she looked up and beckoned Shella and Sami over.

'Listen friends,' she said to the crowd in front of her, as Shella positioned herself by Obli's side. 'This is my sister Shella. She is my most trusted mage and counsellor, and stands to my right at the very heart of this holy migration. And bear witness to me now, as I hereby appoint Shella as my deputy and second in command. You will listen to her words, and obey them as if they were my own.'

She turned, smiling at Shella, who felt a weight the size of a mountain range form in the pit of her stomach.

'I present to you Shellakanawara,' Obli said to the crowd, who fell to their knees, their heads bowed. 'The Most Holy Migration's High Mage!'

With that, Obli stood aside, to allow Shella to bask in the adulation of the kneeling crowd.

Oh shit, she thought.

CHAPTER 7
BARS BETWEEN

Rahain Capital, Rahain Republic – 26th Day, First Third Summer 504

Rahain Capital, Rahain Republic – 26th Day, First Third Summer 504

Daphne tried to imagine herself as a killer. True, she had taken the lives of many in the Sanang forest, and during her escape from the Holdings, but that was as a soldier, or in self defence. What she was being asked to do now was different. Murder.

Douanna and Teolan had filled her head to bursting that first night in Jade Falls, trying to persuade her of the righteousness of their cause. They had targeted several key members of the war coalition for their greed, arrogance and aggressive natures. They had no interest in creating the conditions for a coup, they had told her. They merely wanted to nudge Rahain back onto its proper course, as they saw it.

She looked around the brightly-lit restaurant, filled with lunchtime customers in their rich robes, jewels and finery, while servants in brown tunics rushed to fulfil their every whim. If Douanna and her husband had wanted real change, Daphne thought, she would have had no qualms about joining them. However, they were not interested in abolishing the institution of slavery in the republic, and had smiled patronisingly at her every time she had brought it up. It was much too embedded, they had told her, with four out of every ten in Rahain a slave, and a further four in ten an indentured peasant farmer or labourer. The small elite at the top were privileged because they belonged to the families that held the mage bloodlines, and carried them forward into the next generation of rulers. It was a wise system, perfected over millennia, and it was futile to argue that such traditions could ever be over-turned.

Douanna had insisted that Rahain society was fair, pointing out that anyone from the servile or peasant classes who exhibited even the slightest signs of magery would be whisked out of their environment, along with their entire extended family, and brought into the comfortable embrace of the elite, where they would be re-housed, educated, and given every right and privilege that their abilities had earned them.

The most convincing argument that they had used on her was to raise the possibility of a new war between Rahain and the Holdings, which, they had suggested, might occur if the war coalition got its way. Intoxicated by their success in the Kellach Brigdomin tribal lands, their ambition seemed boundless, and unless they could be restrained, a future conflict was likely, if not inevitable.

To prevent the Rahain Republic from going to war with the Realm of the Holdings – this was to be her motivation to kill, but she wasn't convinced it was enough. It was too abstract, and her feelings for the Holdings were mixed. She hadn't shared her reservations with Douanna, preferring to keep her thoughts to herself while deciding what to do. At the same time, her trust in the Rahain trader had taken a blow. When she had helped Daphne escape from the Holdings, it had seemed out of honest friendship, but now she worried if perhaps Douanna had held an ulterior motive the entire time.

'I'm sure you would agree, Miss Daphne?' Douanna said, snapping her out of her thoughts.

Daphne glanced around the table, smiling at the assorted merchants, politicians and socialites present.

'As you say, my lady,' Daphne said, hoping this would be an appropriate response, her attention having drifted away from the conversation some time before. It was the same sales pitch she had heard

Douanna deliver several times, during the ten days since their arrival in the capital. Although Jade Falls was more than two hundred miles away, they had made the journey in hours, transported in a giant carriage through the air by enormous flying reptiles. Like an excited child, Daphne had stared through the small windows, gazing down at the view of the Rahain mountains and valleys from hundreds of feet up, judging it one of the most wonderful experiences of her life.

Seeing the capital of the Rahain Republic for the first time was somewhere near the top of that list as well. As much as Jade Falls had a soft and delicate beauty to it, the capital dwarfed it in scale and grandeur. The enormity of its central caverns defied belief, and the structures within seemed to have been built by an act of divine creation, rather than by the labour of thousands of Rahain over millennia.

Compared to Jade Falls, the disparity between the elite and the lower classes was more apparent in the capital. The ubiquitous brown tunics were everywhere, performing the laborious and menial tasks essential to the running of the great metropolis. Daphne saw them wherever she looked, and marvelled that Douanna didn't seem to notice them at all, as if they had become invisible to her.

On her fifth day in the capital, their private salon had been visited by an official from the Holdings embassy, who had come to greet Daphne, and to remind her that the warrant for her arrest remained valid. Douanna had been very polite with the young Holdings man, and very firm. Under Rahain law, foreigners had no legal rights, unless they were being sponsored by a respectable citizen. Douanna had shown the official the paperwork proving that she was Daphne's sponsor, laying it on the table for everyone to see. He had smiled, seeming almost relieved, and he and Daphne had chatted amicably for an hour about news and gossip from the Realm. She had liked his smile.

'Daphne,' Douanna said, 'you're day-dreaming again.'

She looked up. The seats around the table were empty, and Douanna was packing her samples away.

'What were you thinking about?' the Rahain woman said. 'No, let me guess. It was that young Holdings man from the embassy again, wasn't it?'

Daphne laughed. 'Am I that obvious?'

'Well, my dear,' Douanna replied, raising an eyebrow, 'it has been a while, hasn't it?'

'Maybe you could use your contacts to find out if he's seeing anyone?'

'Do you think that's wise, Daphne dear?' Douanna asked. 'Dating a man who wants to arrest you?'

'Would make it interesting.'

'Sometimes, Daphne,' Douanna said, 'I think that everything you've been through has affected your mind; made it a little peculiar.'

'Well, I'm not going out with a Rahain,' Daphne said. 'No offence.'

'None taken.'

'And, as he's probably the only Holdings man my age in the city, it's not as if I'm left with much of a choice.'

'But you can't settle for just anyone, Daphne.'

'I'm not looking to marry him,' she said. 'Just, you know...'

'Daphne Holdfast!' Douanna cried. 'And to think I was worried about my morals offending you.' She stood, gathering her coat, and her shoulder bag. 'I shall make some discreet enquiries.'

Daphne smiled, and they walked to the door of the restaurant.

'Now, my dear,' Douanna said as they reached the street, 'I know I've said it before, but I really wish you'd let me buy some new dresses for you, something more befitting a lady.'

'But I like my Holdings clothes,' she said, looking down at her dark green tunic, leggings and riding boots. 'I like to feel as if I could jump onto a horse any time I needed to.'

'But dear, your animal is being cared for back in Jade Falls.'

'Unfortunately,' Daphne replied. 'I miss him.'

They walked through one of the more moderately-sized caverns, its curving walls lined with cafes and bars, laid out around an elegant square with a marble fountain. The underground street lamps were lit to indicate mid-afternoon, and Rahain ladies and gentlemen strolled, or bought cake and iced drinks.

'What do we have planned for the rest of the day?' Daphne asked.

'We're going to visit someone I have heard some interesting things about,' Douanna said. 'His name is Laodoc. He is a politician in the City Council, a rather successful one until recently. It appears that his party of misfits and schemers have deserted him, seemingly because he was too close to the Liberals, and kept up strenuous opposition to the war coalition, long after the war itself was over.'

'Are you hoping to enlist him?'

'Oh, much too early for that,' Douanna said. 'No, I just want to sound him out, see where he stands on things. His hatred of the war coalition has made him quite unpopular in certain quarters, yet several days ago he disbanded the peace coalition, earning him the contempt of the Liberal Party as well.'

'Sounds like he's good at annoying people,' Daphne said, as they left the cavern, and entered a wide tunnel.

'I fear you may be right. My little spies tell me that he's working in his science academy today, which is close by, so I thought we'd chance a visit. While we're there Daphne, you should take a look around the place. It's one of the most expensive schools in the city for the youngsters of the better families, specialising in geology, biology, that sort of thing.'

'Maybe I should enrol in a few classes.'

'That's not such a bad idea,' Douanna said, laughing. 'I had been pondering how best you could improve your knowledge. Although I daresay the biology professors would be more interested in you as a specimen, rather than as a student. I don't imagine they've had the chance to examine many people from the Holdings recently.'

Daphne snorted. 'Well, they're not starting today.'

They followed a branch of the tunnel into a smaller cavern, which was occupied by a single three-storey structure, surrounded by a high wall. The building's pink granite shone in the afternoon lamplight.

'Laodoc's academy,' said Douanna, sweeping out her arm.

They went through the outer wall's main entranceway into a court-yard, with long, wide steps leading up to a massive set of double doors. Many of the tall windows on the upper storeys were open, and the sound of students and teachers at their lessons filtered down to them as they climbed the steps.

The doors opened with a gentle push, and they walked into the reception hall. At the front desk, they were informed that the school's patron was working in the animal section down in the basement, and were given visitor badges and directions.

At the bottom of a staircase, they found a long carpeted corridor, its walls adorned with diplomas, certificates and prizes won by the students. They passed by doors marked 'Archives', and rooms filled with boxes of rocks, labelled and stacked against the walls. At the end of the corridor, they heard the cries of birds and animals, squawking and calling. Douanna pushed the door open.

Ahead were rows and rows of cages, filled with a wide variety of birds, small mammals, snakes, and other reptiles. Students were gathered at the back of the room, clearing away chairs.

Daphne gazed at the animals, most of which were unfamiliar to her. She caught the sound of people talking, and smiled at a group of young students in front of her, as they looked up in surprise at the sight of the Holdings woman walking towards them.

Movement beyond the group drew her attention, and she saw a large cage taking up most of the rear wall. Behind its bars stood three people.

Daphne frowned as she approached. Three people. In a cage.

Her mind jolted as she recalled her own time in prison, in a cage with no privacy, exposed in front of mocking guards, starved, tortured, and beaten. She halted, her right hand moving unconsciously to her crippled left elbow, the old pain remembered.

She closed her eyes and controlled her breathing. She was free now, she reminded herself. Free.

She looked up. The three people behind the bars were tall, and well-built, and their skin was pale, as pale as the Sanang had been. They didn't look like Sanang though, they looked more like her.

There were two women, and a man. The man was coming closer to the bars, just as she was approaching from the other side. He was large, the tallest man she had ever seen, with long dark hair, bearded, and dressed in rags.

She looked at him, he looked back, and their gazes caught.

His gaze turned into a stare, and they mirrored each other for a long, slow moment, as they stood two yards apart, staring at each other, thick steel bars between them.

He was beautiful, she thought, though also frightening. A savage, the Rahain claimed. An untameable beast, who knew nothing but violence. Passion gripped her, exhilarated her, made her feel more alive than she had felt in a long time. She maintained her gaze, drinking him in, unwilling to break away first, wanting to remain in the moment.

She felt a hand touch her shoulder, and she blinked.

'My dear Daphne,' Douanna said, laughing. 'Quite shameless, the way you were staring at that barbarian. Please don't tell me your desires now include the Kellach Brigdomin. I shall have to make enquiries into that embassy boy right away.'

Daphne looked away from her, saying nothing, and turned her attention back to the cage.

The man had shifted, and was looking over at the two captive women. The shorter, dark-haired Kellach woman was standing with her hands on her hips, smirking in bemusement. The taller woman with red hair was staring wide-eyed at Daphne, a look of shock on her face. They were all dressed in tatters, and the cage stank, filthy straw littering the floor.

Tears came to Daphne's eyes, surprising her, and she looked away, sobbing.

The dark-haired woman approached. She reached her arm out through the bars, and took Daphne's right hand.

'Who are you?' she said in Rahain, her accent thick.

Daphne gasped.

She noticed that the students had gathered round her, watching and listening, and she heard their young voices murmur in excitement.

'I am Daphne Holdfast,' she said, looking the Kellach woman in the eye.

She was young, Daphne thought, younger than she, and her eyes shone with a deep, sad longing that Daphne recognised. She felt guilty that she was free, while they were caged, and almost turned away in shame, but the yearning in the Kellach woman's eyes kept her drawn in.

'Where are you from?' she asked Daphne.

'The Holdings.'

'I am from Brig,' the woman said, smiling. She released Daphne's hand, and pointed her thumb at her chest. 'I am Bridget.'

Daphne smiled back, hot tears spilling down her cheeks.

'My dear,' Douanna cut in, 'it appears that Councillor Laodoc has not been down to the animal room today. The students here tell me he is working in his personal study upstairs.'

A rage started to build in Daphne, and she kept her eyes on Bridget.

'Shall we go and meet him there?' she said, keeping her voice calm.

'Yes, let's,' Douanna replied, taking Daphne's hand, as if reclaiming it from the Kellach.

'I will see you again,' Daphne said to the caged prisoners, as Douanna turned her towards the door.

As they climbed the stairs to the upper levels, Douanna looked Daphne in the eye.

'Are you quite all right, my dear?' she asked. 'Those slaves seemed to have affected you deeply.'

Daphne stayed silent, not trusting that she would remain calm if she started to talk about how she felt.

They reached a landing at the top of the stairs, where the governors of the academy had their personal offices.

Douanna knocked on the door marked Patron.

A pretty young Rahain woman in a simple brown tunic opened the door, and Douanna gave Daphne a quick sideways glance.

'Can I help you?' the young woman asked.

'Yes, my child,' Douanna said. 'We are looking for your master, Councillor Laodoc. We were hoping to have a few words, if he could spare the time.'

The woman looked embarrassed for a moment. She cleared her throat. 'If you are here to request a financial contribution for your charity, then master Laodoc would prefer you to send your submission by post.'

Douanna sniffed. 'We're not here to beg, child.'

The woman relaxed.

'Who is it, Simiona?' said a voice from behind the door. 'If they're after money, then...'

'No, master,' the woman replied. 'They're not.'

'Then show them in, girl,' the voice said.

She opened the door and Daphne and Douanna entered a luxurious office, with ornate armchairs, a massive darkwood desk, and thick carpets. Paintings and bookshelves covered the walls. Behind the desk, with a mountain of paperwork in front of him, sat an old Rahain man. He had an impatient expression, as if he loathed meeting visitors, which he tried to hide with a forced smile.

'Good afternoon,' he said. 'And what can I do for you?'

'A glass of wine would be most wonderful,' Douanna replied. 'May I?' She pointed at an armchair by the desk, and sat in it before the man had a chance to respond.

'Of course,' he stuttered. 'Sit, please. Wine, yes, let me see. Simiona?'

'Yes, master?'

'Wine for our guests,' he said, recovering his composure, 'and for me as well, I think. Paperwork is such a chore. I judge I've done quite enough for today.'

Simiona placed a tray of slender-stemmed glasses onto the desk, and started to open a bottle of wine.

'I am, as I assume you know, otherwise why would you be here, but anyway, I am Laodoc, patron of this little school for the scientifically gifted young folk of Rahain. And who might you be?'

'I am Lady Douanna of Jade Falls, merchant and trader of goods from the Holdings and Sanang.'

'Ah, yes,' he nodded. 'I think I may have heard mention of you. Did you meet with a city councillor by the name of Yaelli, by any chance?'

'I did,' Douanna said. 'A few days ago, in fact. She asked me to join the Merchant Party.'

'Did she, indeed?' Laodoc said. 'And what did you... Wait, sorry. Your friend, here?' he looked up at Daphne, who was standing by the chair. 'Won't she sit?'

Douanna looked embarrassed. 'Miss Daphne, please.'

Daphne put on a polite smile, and sat.

'Miss Daphne, you say?' Laodoc said, looking her up and down. 'Is she from the Holdings? Does she not speak any Rahain?'

Daphne saw Douanna consider for a brief second whether or not she should lie.

'Yes,' she said. 'She is from the Holdings. She can speak Rahain fluently, I taught her myself, but I'm afraid she's been feeling rather unwell today.'

'Oh dear,' Laodoc said. 'How unpleasant. Perhaps I could have one of the biology professors take a look at her?'

'You're not putting me in a cage to be examined!' Daphne exploded, rising to her feet, her right fist clenched. 'You Rahain!' she cried. 'Your culture of slavery disgusts me, but what I saw just now in the basement was the worst wickedness I have ever witnessed! How can you cage people like animals? Have you no shame?'

Laodoc shrank back in his chair, gripping its arms, a look of terror on his face, his tongue flickering in bewilderment.

'Miss Daphne!' Douanna said. 'Please leave the room immediately.'

Daphne stood up straight, and held her head high. She caught the eye of the slave Simiona, who was staring at her in utter astonishment. Daphne flashed her a quick smile, then turned and walked from the study, closing the door behind her.

On the opposite wall of the landing was a glass door, through which she could see an exterior balcony. She opened it, stepped outside, and took a long, deep breath. She shook her head. Had her outburst just ruined any chance of Douanna winning Laodoc over?

She stood at the railings, and realised that she didn't care. Her thoughts raced back to the three Kellach in their basement cage. She remembered the way that she and the man had stared at each other through the bars that separated them. Her heart filled with painful longing. Why hadn't she asked his name?

She heard someone, turned, and saw Simiona standing to her right.

'I came to see if you were all right.'

'Thank you,' Daphne said. 'I'm fine.'

'May I ask you something?'

Daphne nodded.

'About what you said in there. Are there no slaves in the Holdings?'

'None,' Daphne said. 'It's illegal, and even if it weren't, everyone is taught from a young age that slavery is a great evil. And,' she went on, 'like the Kellach Brigdomin, I was once a prisoner. No, twice,' she corrected herself. 'Once in a foreign land, and once in my own country.'

'How did you get free?'

'I escaped,' Daphne said. 'Both times.'

Simiona grinned at her.

'Now,' Daphne said, 'it's my turn to ask you something.'

'Please, ask me.'

'Have you spoken to the Kellach captives in the basement?'

'I have,' the slave replied, her eyes lighting up.

'Do you know their names?'

'Yes,' Simiona nodded. 'The most talkative one, the woman with dark hair, she's called Bridget. The other woman, the gorgeous one with red hair, she's called Kallie. She doesn't speak as much, often just sits quietly, but she takes everything in. The man is called Killop.'

'Killop,' Daphne repeated, her face flushing as soon as she realised she had said it out loud.

'Yes,' Simiona said, studying Daphne. 'He can speak Rahain well, though not as fluently as Bridget. It is amazing how quickly they have picked up the language!'

'My heart aches,' Daphne said, 'to see them caged like animals.'

'I feel the same way.'

There was a noise from the corridor, and they turned to see Douanna leaving Laodoc's office. Daphne went back through the balcony door.

'Ah, there you are,' Douanna frowned. 'My incorrigible companion. Come, let us be away, before you threaten any more respectable citizens.'

Daphne nodded a silent goodbye to Simiona, and followed Douanna.

'I think I may have just about repaired the damage you caused in there,' she said as they descended the stairs. 'I explained to him that you were still suffering from the after-effects of your own imprisonment. I had to exaggerate your torture somewhat to suggest that you were a troubled individual, prone to nervous episodes. I also had to promise him a whole box of free samples. His slave is being sent over later to collect it. Did you see her, Daphne? Of course you did, you were just talking to her on the balcony. An old man like Laodoc, getting himself a pretty young thing like that as his personal slave? I didn't think he had it in him!'

Daphne shuddered at the thought.

'Now,' Douanna went on, 'I think it's about time that you started to pay your way, and earned some wages.'

Daphne looked up. 'You have something for me to do?'

'I might have just the thing.'

CHAPTER 8
BRIDGET IN CHAINS

Rahain Capital, Rahain Republic – 26th Day, First Third Summer 504

Killop watched Bridget from the dark shadows of the cage as she crept over to where he sat on the dirty floor.

'That's her asleep,' she said in the dim lamplight, scooping a mug of water from the little barrel.

Killop looked over her shoulder at Kallie, rolled up in blankets by the rear wall.

'Now,' Bridget whispered, 'will you tell me what in Pyre's name was going on today? What were you thinking, staring at that woman?'

'It was shock, Bridget,' he said, almost certain he wasn't lying. 'I was just surprised.'

'Come on, Killop, I'm not stupid,' she said. 'I was surprised. You and Kallie on the other hand...?'

He brooded in silence.

'Fine,' she said. 'So neither of you will tell me.'

Bridget sipped her water, then gathered some blankets round her, getting ready to sleep.

'She's not supposed to exist,' Killop whispered, just as Bridget was lying down.

'Who?' Bridget said. 'That woman? Daphne?'

'Aye, her.'

'I don't understand.'

'Neither do I, Bridget. Last year, me, Kallie and the rest of the squad were travelling with the old Kell chief, and we stopped in at this place in the mountains where a holy man lived. A crazy old holy man. He used his strange mage skills to see where the Rahain armies were, and then afterwards he told some of us our future.'

'Whose?'

'Mine, Kallie's and Keira's,' he said. 'He told me that he saw me with another woman. A dark-skinned woman. Of course, I told Kallie not to worry, that there was no such thing.'

Bridget swore. 'That explains what Kallie was saying to me before, that it was destiny, and that she couldn't stop it.'

'Maybe she's right.'

'Oh Killop, don't you start!' Bridget said, rolling onto her side to see him better. 'Telling the future? What a load of crap. No one can see into the future.'

'That's what I thought,' Killop said. 'Until this afternoon.'

'What else did this holy man claim to see?'

'For me, it about being with a dark-skinned woman, and something about fighting death, or the dead. For Kallie, he said that the Rahain would kill her soul, but that she would be reborn when the Fire Goddess came to her.'

'The Fire Goddess? You mean Keira? That's what the captives were calling her, back in the transit camp.'

'My sister is many things, but a goddess isn't one of them.'

'What did the old man say about her?'

'That she would destroy half the world with fire.'

Bridget smiled. 'So what's new?'

'And,' Killop continued, 'that she would topple an empire.'

'He was probably just saying this stuff to wind you up.'

'Aye, but he was right about a lot of other things,' Killop replied.

'About where all the armies were positioned. And about what would happen to the clans.'

'Sounds like you want it to be true.'

'No,' he shot back. 'I love Kallie.'

'Aye,' she nodded. 'I believe you. But the way you and that woman were looking at each other? Well, if I were Kallie, I'd be angry too.'

The door to the animal room opened, and Simiona walked in.

'Hello,' Bridget called out as she approached them.

'Hi,' Simiona said, smiling. 'I heard you met with someone from the Holdings today.'

'The Holdings?' Killop said.

'The place where Daphne is from,' Bridget said.

'Yes,' Simiona said, her eyes shining. 'Daphne. I spoke with her. There are no slaves in the Holdings, did you know that? She was very angry...'

'Angry?' Bridget queried.

Simiona acted out anger for them, until they nodded.

'Why was she angry?' Bridget asked.

'Because she believes it's wrong to put people in cages,' Simiona said. 'As do I.'

'Can she help us?'

'I don't know,' Simiona said. 'She was asking me about you, asking for your names.' She glanced at Killop. 'She shouted at my master,' she went on. 'Terrified him.'

Bridget shrugged. Simiona mimed being scared witless, and Bridget laughed and nodded.

'I like this Holdings woman,' she said. 'Do you think what she did will make any difference?'

'To what?' Simiona asked.

'To what Laodoc thinks about us being in here.'

'I don't know,' the slave pursed her lips. 'He sat up alone all evening. I don't know.'

Bridget nodded.

Simiona pulled up a chair. 'Listen,' she said, 'I have decided that you should continue with your tuition, but the academy is no place for a young boy like Paeotan to be alone at night.'

Bridget and Killop looked at each other.

'So,' Bridget asked, 'who will be giving us lessons instead?'

'Me,' Simiona said. 'What would you like me to teach you tonight?'

'Angry, terrified,' Bridget answered without hesitation. 'Words like that.'

'Feelings? Emotions?'

'I already know happy, and sad,' Bridget said. 'Teach me more.' She looked at Killop. 'Teach us more.'

'Should we wake Kallie?' said Simiona. 'Maybe she'd like to join in?'

'No,' Killop said. 'She is sad.'

Bridget glanced at him. 'I think you mean angry.'

———

Several days later, Killop sat at the bars of the cage, listening as Paeotan chatted to him about his schoolwork. The boy was setting out chairs for that morning's lesson and Killop wondered what it would be. The previous day, guards had escorted Bridget out of the cage, the first time she had been selected, and Killop and Kallie had sat worried sick for hours until she had been returned to them.

The students had been drawing her, just as they had done with Killop before, and Bridget laughed to see the relieved expressions on Killop and Kallie's faces. Until that moment, it hadn't occurred to Killop what it must have been like for Bridget and Kallie, each time he had been led out of the cage for another lesson. Waiting for Bridget's return had felt worse than being taken. He wasn't sure how he would react if they came for Kallie.

She was still being cold to him, not that he could blame her. Why had he stared at that Holdings woman? The truth was, he didn't understand why. There had been something about her that had held him frozen, a spark deep within her green eyes. He had stared at her, and she had stared back as if she had wanted to devour him whole. No one had ever looked at him that way before, not even Kallie. If the bars hadn't been there to separate them, he wasn't sure what he would have done, so lost had he been.

He saw Bridget sit to his left, eating an orange.

'Hi, Paeotan,' she said. 'What are you doing to us today?'

The boy flushed. 'I don't know.'

'Will the lesson be in here?' she asked, pointing at the chairs in front of the cage.

'Yes,' he replied. 'The other rooms are busy.'

The door opened, and Paeotan straightened up as the teacher entered, followed by six guards, armed with crossbows and long pikes.

Kallie joined Killop, sitting by his right. 'They're coming for one of us.'

'Aye, no doubt,' he said, then nodded towards the chairs. 'Though this time the others will get to see what happens.'

'I'm not sure if that's better or worse.'

'I hope they don't want to draw you again, Killop,' Bridget said. 'I've seen quite enough of your hairy arse.'

'Then I'll be sure to point it the other way.'

'Fuck off,' she said. 'That's even worse.'

The teacher approached. It was Niniat, the biology professor. She pointed at Bridget, and gestured to the guards.

Four of them pushed their pikes towards Killop and Kallie, forcing them to the rear of the cage, while the other two levelled their crossbows at Bridget, who walked casually to the side door.

Niniat unlocked the gate, and Bridget went down the steps, two crossbows trained on her. The professor relocked the cage, and the guards fitted Bridget with heavy shackles. They led her round to where the seats were laid out.

The students were sitting in rows, in front of a selection of metal equipment. Bridget was placed against a tall board, etched with numbers and lines, and measured. The students wrote in their jotters as Niniat lectured them. Killop concentrated, and tried to pick out words he knew, but Niniat was speaking too quickly.

'She is saying,' Kallie whispered in their own tongue, as they crouched together by the front of the cage, 'that Bridget is shorter than you and me, but she is still taller than any Rahain.'

Bridget was then made to stand on a squat metal platform, attached to an arm, which was balanced by weights. Niniat placed several metal blocks onto the balancing tray, counting aloud, until Bridget's platform was raised just above the ground.

'It seems,' Kallie said, 'that Bridget is also heavier than any Rahain. Though please don't tell her I said that.'

As Bridget was being led down from the platform, Niniat reached up to touch her face, and the Brig woman brushed the Rahain's hand away. Four crossbows closed in on Bridget, one of them jutting into the skin of her neck, under her left ear, a loaded bolt two finger-widths from her skull.

Killop tightened his grip on the bars as he watched.

The two other guards approached Bridget, carrying a tall metal frame, to which they attached her chains. Her wrists were clamped by each side, and her ankles were fixed to the bottom of the frame. A thick leather strap was fastened around her throat, and the guards retreated, keeping their weapons trained on her.

Completely secured in an upright position, Bridget could only glare at her captors in defiance. Several of the young students shifted in their seats, their faces pale.

Niniat approached the captive. She reached up, and with her thumb and forefinger pulled Bridget's right eyelid wide open, all the time talking to her students.

'Our eyes are different,' Kallie translated, her voice low.

Niniat spoke to a guard, who approached Bridget. With one hand on her forehead, he prised open her mouth. Killop could see the hatred burning in Bridget's eyes, and the fear.

'Niniat is telling the students to draw her tongue,' Kallie said, spitting each word out.

'I can't stand this,' Killop said, his knuckles white.

Kallie looked at him, her face fierce with anger.

Killop got to his feet. 'Stop! We are not animals.'

There was a collective intake of breath as everyone in the room turned to look at him.

Niniat stared, a look of surprise and confusion passing over her face. It hardened, and she gestured to a pair of guards.

Two Rahain strode towards the cage, their pikes levelled. Killop backed away from the bars, watching as one approached him. The other came at Kallie, who also stepped back. The guards were relaxed, having carried out this procedure dozens of times before. The one in front of Killop glanced at his colleague, a complacent smile on his face, and the Kell man struck.

His left arm flew out, and he gripped the shaft of the pike, just behind its serrated steel blade. He heaved it as hard as he could, and the guard was pulled forwards, cracking his forehead off the bars of the cage. He groaned, and slumped to the marble floor. Transferring the weapon to his right hand, Killop hurled it, blunt end first, and it struck the other guard on the temple. As he fell, Kallie relieved him of his pike, pulling it into the cage, and spinning it round so the blade pointed outwards.

Children screamed, while the four guards who were still standing looked at each other in alarm. Niniat called to them, and they pointed their crossbows at Kallie and Killop.

'Don't shoot!' Paeotan cried, jumping up from his seat, and running towards the cage, as the guards took aim.

The boy stopped halfway between the guards and the cage.

'Paeotan!' Niniat cried. 'Come away! They will hurt you!'

'We will not!' Kallie shouted back. 'Unlike the Rahain, the Kell do not harm children.'

Niniat's tongue flickered, and she stared at Kallie in amazement.

The guards glanced at the professor, waiting for their orders, as they kept their weapons trained on the captives. Bridget squirmed against the shackles keeping her to the upright metal frame, while children sobbed, or sat frozen in terror.

Killop stood by Kallie, looking from guard to guard.

Niniat appeared to have made a decision, and she started to raise her arm.

The door swung open, and Laodoc strode in with Simiona at his heels.

The old man's mouth opened as he surveyed the scene.

'Nobody move!' he commanded, his voice filling the room.

'Patron!' Niniat cried. 'The Kellach slaves have injured two of the guards!'

'They were only trying to protect their friend!' Paeotan yelled.

Laodoc approached, saying nothing. He glanced at the two unconscious guards on the floor, then over to where Bridget was shackled, and finally up at the Kell in the cage.

'Put the pike down,' Killop whispered.

Kallie paused for a moment, then threw the weapon to the ground.

Laodoc reached the cage.

'We are not animals,' Killop said to him, holding his palms aloft.

Laodoc stared at him a good while, before looking down at the dropped pike on the cage floor, lying amid the dirty straw.

'They are dangerous, patron,' Niniat said.

'Yes, professor, they are.'

Simiona stepped forward.

'Master,' she said. 'This is Killop and Kallie. Bridget is the one in chains.'

Laodoc nodded at his slave, his face emotionless.

He turned to Niniat.

'Have that one escorted back into the cage, if you would, professor.'

She nodded, and the guards obeyed. One started to unshackle Bridget's restraints, the others covering her with their crossbows. Laodoc turned to Kallie.

'Give me that,' he said, pointing at the pike.

Kallie stared at him, doubt and defiance on her face.

Laodoc kept his hand out, silent and patient.

Kallie reached down, and slid the pike across to Laodoc, who took it, and placed it on the floor of the room.

'Thank you,' he said.

Laodoc waited as Bridget was taken to the cage. Killop and Kallie rushed over and embraced her as she was led in, and the gate was locked.

'Children!' Laodoc called out. 'This lesson is over. Consider carefully all that you have learned, and ponder it. Professor Niniat, please escort the students to their next class.' He pointed down at the unconscious guards on the floor. 'Don't forget those two when you leave.'

As the students began to file out of the room, Laodoc put a hand on Paeotan's shoulder.

'Please remain here,' he said to the boy.

Paeotan nodded, his face flushing. Guards picked up the fallen soldiers by their arms and legs, and carried them out of the room.

Laodoc sat down the moment they had shut the door behind them.

'Such excitement certainly takes it out of an old man,' he sighed. 'Simiona, would you be so kind as to fetch me some water?'

'Yes, master.'

'Come, child,' he said to Paeotan, patting the chair next to him. 'Sit, and tell me everything that happened.'

The captives listened as Paeotan related what had occurred during the lesson. The old man said nothing, letting him talk. Soon, the boy was also telling him about the extra lessons he had been giving them.

'This boy, then,' he asked Simiona, as she handed him a glass of water, 'is the one whose identity you were protecting, when I questioned you regarding who was responsible for teaching the Kellach Brigdomin to speak our language?'

Simiona's face went red, and she looked away.

'You say Kellach Brigdomin,' Bridget said, 'but there are no Lach in this cage, nor are there any Domm.'

Laodoc stared up at her, his tongue flickering. 'I beg your pardon?'

'I don't know those words,' Bridget replied.

'I, I mean...'

'She is making the point,' Simiona said, 'that we use the term Kellach Brigdomin, but that is not what they call themselves.'

'I am Brig,' Bridget said, then pointed at Killop and Kallie. 'They are Kell.'

'Ahh, so the army must have amalgamated their tribal appellations into a new compound word,' said Laodoc. 'Most interesting.'

'What?' Bridget said.

'Master,' Simiona said, 'although their tuition has been progressing rapidly, they have not yet acquired an extensive vocabulary.'

'What?' Bridget repeated.

'You don't know all the words yet,' Simiona said to her.

Laodoc's eyes roved over them, taking in their tattered and filthy rags, and his nose wrinkled at the smell they were giving off. He frowned, and Killop could sense the conflicting thoughts struggle in the old man's mind.

'Do you have a family?' Killop asked.

The old Rahain scowled.

'I had two sisters,' Bridget said. 'They didn't like me, and I didn't like them, but I miss them.'

'I don't like my sister either,' Paeotan said.

Laodoc frowned. 'I have two sons.'

'The master's sons are very important men,' Simiona said.

'They are fools, Simiona, but I love them anyway. And please, call me Laodoc.'

Killop noticed the way Simiona looked nervous as well as pleased at her master's informality.

'No slaves in Kell,' he said. 'Why are there slaves here?'

Laodoc stared at Killop, his yellow-green vertically-slit eyes boring into him.

'You have caused a lot of trouble today,' he said.

'They were hurting my friend,' Killop replied. 'What should I have done?'

Laodoc ignored him.

He stood, and walked to the front of the cage.

'Simiona,' he said, 'unfortunately, it seems that you will not be getting the chance to carry out any more research on the captives, thanks to their behaviour this morning.'

'But why, master?'

'Come now, girl,' he said, 'you must realise what will happen once the children from today's class get home and tell their parents what occurred. You can't seriously believe that they will continue to allow such dangerous savages to be close to their little ones.'

Simiona stood. 'What will happen to them?'

Laodoc snorted. 'That is what I am trying to decide, girl.'

He paced up and down in front of the cage, shaking his head.

'There is still so much to learn from them,' he said. 'I can't keep them here, but if I withdraw them from the academy, they will become available for someone else to requisition and, well, I don't like the thought of that. The new Slave Act makes it illegal for Kellach to become house-slaves, therefore that avenue is also closed to us.'

Simiona clasped her hands, trying to remain patient. Laodoc glanced over at her, and Killop thought he saw the old man's eyes soften.

'I could,' he said; 'I know, I could establish a new faculty of... of Cultural Studies.' He began pacing again. 'I would need to find a suitable arts professor, and commission them with researching and recording the Kellach Brigdomin language and history, for comparative purposes, of course.' He paused, then snapped his fingers. 'As for the location, I hardly ever go near the northern wing of my home any more; I could have it converted into secure living quarters for the captives, with teaching areas, guardrooms, and a suite of rooms for the new professor.

'I will need your assistance with this Simiona, and your utmost discretion. No one must think for a moment that I have been swayed by sentiment.'

'Yes, master,' she said, 'of course I will help.'

'It will take a few days to arrange,' he said to her. 'Until the quarters are ready, I will instruct the departments here that no more lessons are to take place involving the captives. There. Does that satisfy you?'

'Yes, master,' Simiona said. 'Thank you.' She turned to the captives. 'What do you think?'

'I don't know,' Killop shrugged. 'There were too many big words.'

'In a few days,' she said, 'you will be moving to the master's house. You will still be prisoners, but you will have your own rooms.'

'No cage?'

'No cage.'

'A bath?' said Bridget.

'Oh yes,' Simiona laughed, looking at their filthy rags. 'I will insist.'

CHAPTER 9
CINDERS

Rahain Capital, Rahain Republic – 30th Day, Last Third Summer 504

Laodoc stood.

'Lord Speaker,' he said, 'I am quite sure that, for once, I speak for the majority here when I say that I hope this delay doesn't inconvenience us much longer. Like many others present, I have plans for tomorrow's Autumn's Day holiday, or should I say today's holiday, as this session has now passed midnight.'

There was a low rumble of agreement from across the chamber.

As Laodoc resumed his seat, the lord speaker of the council raised his arm.

'I understand the esteemed councillor's concerns,' he said. 'Rest assured, I have been informed that the matter is of the utmost importance, and I would beg the indulgence of this chamber while we wait. I too have vacation plans I would be loath to miss.'

The semi-circular tiers of benches facing the lord speaker were filled with tired councillors, impatient to be going home or to the bar after a long day's debating and voting. It was the final session of a five-day stretch, and they had been due to finish when word had come down from the High Senate that a matter of vital concern had been brought to their attention.

'Nice try, Laodoc,' muttered Pleonim from the bench next to him, 'but I think we're going to be stuck here a while yet.'

Laodoc nodded. Following the dissolution of the peace coalition, and the desertion of his own party's membership, Laodoc had spent a lonely and isolated third in the City Council. Without any colleagues to support him, he had never been picked to speak, his opinions were ignored, and his votes an irrelevance. Finally, he had pushed back his pride, and approached the Liberals. After much painful negotiation, he had been allowed to join, and had moved to sit by them, making them the largest single party in the council. This status was meaningless, however, when set against the solid alliance of the Patriot, Conservative and Merchant parties, dominant and all-powerful since the war with the Kellach.

There was movement by the doors of the large chamber, and Laodoc saw a group enter, dressed in the fine uniforms of clerks of the High Senate. They strode across the floor of the City Council, and presented a paper to the lord speaker, who put on his glasses to read.

'I have a proclamation from our honourable colleagues in the High Senate,' he said. Everyone leaned forwards in their seats to listen.

'The High Senate regrets to announce that mining operations at all State Company-held locations in the occupied territories of Kellach Brigdomin have been suspended with immediate effect, following the destruction of the coal mining and storage facility in the north-eastern annexation.'

There was a collective gasp in the chamber. The facility, as was well known, had just been finished. It had cost a fortune to construct, being the single largest mining depot the Rahain had ever built. Its purpose was to store and process all coal taken from the Kellach mines, ready for shipment back to Rahain. It was also the site of an enormous colliery, one of the biggest that had been dug into the Kellach mountains.

Laodoc suppressed a wry smile. The war coalition's promise of cheap coal from Kellach remained only that, a promise.

The lord speaker raised his hand to still the anxious chatter.

One of the High Senate officials stepped forwards, holding out an open scroll.

'The facility,' he said, 'was assaulted on the eighteenth day of the Last Third of Summer, twelve days ago, by a band of barbarian renegades, led by a Kellach Brigdomin fire mage. They slaughtered the soldiers guarding the perimeter of the compound, and burned the entire stock of coal that had been collected there, estimated at approximately three and a half million tonnes.'

Several councillors cried out in shock, and Laodoc could see the horrified and desperate expressions on the faces of those who had invested in the new mining operations. He could have laughed out loud at that moment, thinking of how his shares in the decrepit Grey Mountain coal mines, which had been virtually worthless since the war had been won, would be of great value again.

'Furthermore,' the official continued, 'all equipment was destroyed, including the entire minehead, which was systematically blocked, and razed to the ground. In consequence, some six hundred and forty-three miners underground at the time were asphyxiated. The barbarian rebels then fled the scene, and escaped into the nearby mountains.'

'Shame!' someone shouted from the benches of the Patriots.

'Total personnel losses,' the official went on, 'amount to some nineteen members of the Merchant Guild, thirty-six army officers, and nine hundred and eighty-eight soldiers and miners requisitioned from the servile classes. The High Senate has this night passed a resolution, ordering a fresh requisition of ten thousand of the servile classes into the army, to be dispatched forthwith to the Kellach Brigdomin territories, to hunt down and arrest or kill the renegade fire mage, and to destroy the rebels. Major Likiat has been appointed commander of this expeditionary force, on account of his honourable record in the previous campaigns on the Kellach peninsula.'

Laodoc lowered his head, all smugness fled. His younger son, a celebrated hero of the war, had volunteered for action in the tribal lands again, this time as commander.

'The High Senate therefore requests,' the official concluded, 'that the City Council release reserve funds without delay, to ensure that Commander Likiat's forces are adequately provisioned for the season's campaign.'

'We get to the heart of the matter,' the lord speaker said. 'Do I have a sponsor...?'

Laodoc's elder son, Ruellap, rose to his feet at once.

'Lord Speaker, I would be honoured to make such a proposal,' he said, 'to release the necessary funds without delay, and also to send this chamber's highest commendations to the esteemed commander, my honourable brother, and to wish him all the best in this endeavour!'

The benches around Ruellap roared their approval, stamping their feet and cheering.

'Do I have a seconder?' the lord speaker shouted over the noise.

Several Conservatives stood.

The lord speaker pointed at Ziane, their leader in the council, and the clerks noted his name for the records.

'And a dissenter?' the lord speaker said, looking over at the Liberal benches.

Pleonim nudged Laodoc's arm. 'I'll let you off this one, old man,' he whispered. 'I'm not so cruel as to ask you to speak out against both of your sons.'

'No,' Laodoc said, as he pushed himself to his feet. 'A deal's a deal. I gave my word.'

There was a chorus of exaggerated tutting and head-shaking from the war coalition benches, as Laodoc glanced at the speaker, who nodded his permission.

'I must set aside my feelings as a father, Lord Speaker,' he said to the watching councillors, 'and ignore the pain in my heart as one son happily sends the other off to slaughter more ragged savages.' There were boos and shouts of derision, but no more than he was used to. 'We have stolen from these tribes, we have taken their land, and their lives, and their freedom, and then we wonder with amazement and anger why they would retaliate against us, as if we were the injured party. More lives thrown to the winds for the insatiable greed of men and women already rich beyond belief. More death, more waste, more futility.' The boos and insults were growing louder now, drowning him out. He fell silent, waiting. The lord speaker thumped his fist down, shouting for order.

'I counter-propose that we recommend to the High Senate that they think again,' Laodoc said, when the chamber quietened, 'and vote to deny them the resources they request, to stop them from continuing down the foolish path they have chosen.'

The lord speaker nodded. 'Do I have a seconder for the counter-proposal?'

For a moment it looked as if no one was prepared to support Laodoc, then Pleonim grimaced, and rose to his feet.

'A vote is therefore called,' the lord speaker said. 'Those in favour of the proposal from Councillor Ruellap raise your hands.'

The ranks of benches opposite the Liberals lifted their arms as one.

'And those in favour of Councillor Laodoc's counter-proposal?'

The thirty-four on the Liberal benches raised their arms.

'Councillor Ruellap's proposal is hereby carried, by sixty-two votes to thirty-four,' the lord speaker said. 'Officials will be sent to the High Senate to inform our honourable colleagues of our decision. Commander Likiat is hereby authorised to use the city's reserve funds as he sees fit in pursuance of his assigned tasks. This session is now ended. Good night, and have a most joyous Autumn's Day.'

Everyone rose as the lord speaker got to his feet and stood down from the podium. Councillors chatted in groups as they made their way to the front doors, which were being swung open by servants.

'Laodoc!' he heard a woman call.

He turned. 'Good evening, Niuma,' he said, watching his old Hedger ally walk over from the opposite benches.

'May we speak in private?' she said.

'The members' bar?'

She nodded. They left the debating chamber, and strolled down the finely decorated corridors to the cavernous bar, where countless shadowy nooks and alcoves offered as much privacy as desired.

A servant approached as they sat in a dark, secluded corner.

'Brandy for me, my man,' Laodoc said.

'And white wine for myself,' Niuma added.

'Now,' Laodoc said to her as the servant departed, 'what can I do for you?'

She looked him up and down. 'You seem to be in a better mood recently.'

'It was a difficult time,' he said, 'being isolated and spurned for so long. I suppose I'm happier now I'm with the Liberals.'

That was a lie, he thought. That was not the reason.

Their drinks arrived.

'So,' Laodoc said, 'how is the Merchant Party treating you?'

Niuma shrugged. 'They're a lot stricter than you were.'

'I imagined that might be the case,' Laodoc said. 'How else is one to explain all of the old Hedgers voting the way they did tonight? Hastening the flow of coal from Kellach only hastens their own impoverishment.'

'Believe me,' she said, 'not all of them are happy about it. That's why I'm here. The Grey Mountain Mining Cartel might not be as dead as we all assumed.'

'I thought you'd sold your stake.'

'I tried,' she said. 'No one would take it. At least not at a sensible price. I know of only one ex-Hedger who sold out. He accepted a ridiculous sum, just to be rid of it. I'll be willing to wager that he might be regretting his folly now.'

'And what of it?'

'What of it?' she repeated, staring at him. 'Well, it means that we have interests in common once again, and we may find it is to our mutual benefit if we work together.'

'What? Reform the Hedgers? After I've spent the last third abasing myself with the Liberals?' He laughed. 'A little late for that.'

'But, Laodoc…'

'No, Niuma.'

She looked at him with scorn. 'Then,' she said, 'you meant everything you said in the chamber, about how we stole from the barbarians, and that we were in the wrong? We all assumed you had been forced to repeat that Liberal rhetoric. We were sitting there thinking, "poor old Laodoc, being made to look a fool", but no, you are a fool. You actually believe that nonsense. Well?' She looked at him. 'Deny it, then.'

He sipped his brandy. 'Good night, Niuma.'

She laughed, and stood. 'Always knew you were soft at heart. Your sons must have their mother to thank for their courage, for it certainly didn't come from you.'

She walked from the alcove, leaving Laodoc to his brandy, the dim shadows reflecting his mood.

Did he believe what he had said in his speech? It was true that he had stood several times in the council chamber over the last third, delivering the lines the Liberals had fed him, as part of the deal when he had joined, and accepted their protection. They had been just words, words he hadn't thought too deeply about.

Nevertheless, his convictions were starting to change, but from a different source altogether. For the last two thirds he had been spending more time working on the academy's new faculty, than worrying about politics. It had taken much longer than he had assumed to convert the upper storey of the northern wing of his mansion into a secure holding area for the three Kellach Brigdomin slaves. And it had cost him a small fortune for the building work, and to endow the faculty with books and materials, hire guards, and appoint a new professor. It had been twenty days before the captives had been able to move in.

Since that time however, the reports of their progress had astonished him, and he had the budding idea that his new faculty might develop into the foremost academic department specialising in the language, culture and history of the Kellach Brigdomin. For now, he assumed, no one else was interested, and he detected no other academies, schools or research institutes looking into this field of study. If he could somehow publish their initial research within a year, and thereby set the standard textbook on the subject, the fame of the academy would only increase his own prestige, as part of his long-planned bid for the High Senate.

He had read a portion of the translated and transcribed poems and stories from the collection that Simiona was compiling. Some he found interesting, such as their rudimentary origin stories, which appeared to contain echoes of the catastrophes that had assailed the world at the time of the Collision. Others had touched his heart, such as the ballads from the mountain-dwelling hunters and trappers, romantic tales of lost love and the mysterious bond that seemed to exist between brothers and sisters.

One thing was certain, he realised. He was no longer looking upon the Kellach Brigdomin as dumb brutes, as animals to be controlled. They had had their own civilisation, though backward and primitive, and the Rahain had destroyed it. His people. For what? More coal, iron, gold, timber, copper, and all of the other resources they were going to systematically strip from the Kellach lands? The war coalition had portrayed the native inhabitants as no better than animals, who happened to be in the way of progress. And when animals bit back, you struck them down.

The Slave Bill that had banned the use of the Kellach as house slaves had been cleverer than Laodoc had suspected at the time. For it was not solely, as it had been advertised, to protect Rahain civilians from the dangerous, murderous savages, but it was also to ensure that there were no opportunities for the foreign slaves to be seen as anything but animals, removed as they were from the cities, and placed to work in remote areas, in appalling conditions, labouring like beasts of burden.

He recalled the words that the frightening, dark-skinned woman from the Holdings had shouted at him, when she had visited with the trader. Although he had no desire to ever meet her again, a tiny part of him wished that she could see how the three Kellach slaves were faring, now that they were living in Laodoc's mansion. She would probably still disapprove, he reflected.

'No slaves in the Holdings.'

Foolish utopian dreamers. Nature pointed the way to the best solution, it was right before their eyes. Mages and their kin ruled Rahain, their powers and abilities making it obvious that nature had favoured them. The rest of society, they were there to be ruled, and guided, and protected, for there was also a responsibility to the lower orders, one that seemed to be ignored in the confusion of the Holdings constitution. An egalitarian-religious-monarchy, he laughed. What a foolish and irrational nation.

'Here you are,' a voice said. 'Hiding away in a corner, grinning to yourself.'

Laodoc looked up. It was Pleonim, with a couple of other Liberals, Wyenna and Nueillin.

'Mind if we join you?'

'Please do,' he said, signalling a waiter.

'You've got guts,' Wyenna said as she sat. 'Must have been hard to say what you did about your sons in the chamber tonight.'

'They are grown men, my good woman,' he replied, directing the waiter to set glasses and pour wine. 'I'm sure they know it's just politics.'

'Never mind that,' said Nueillin. 'Laodoc, did you notice who was missing from the chamber tonight?'

He considered. The votes had tallied up to ninety-six, whereas a full council contained one hundred members. Two of the missing were long-term vacancies to replace deaths from old age earlier in the year, for which applications were being narrowed down before a final vote. One of the other two spaces on the benches was more recent, caused by the death of a Patriot by the name of Heoran, who had drunkenly drowned in his bath almost a third before. That left one. Laodoc pondered, remembering how the council benches had been filled that evening.

'Myella, the Conservative,' he said, to nods from the others. 'I don't recall seeing her this evening.'

'We just heard,' Nueillin whispered, leaning in close across the table, 'that she was found dead in her rooms.'

'What?' said Laodoc, his eyes wide. 'When?'

'Just now,' Pleonim replied. 'After the session ended, some of her fellows went up to see why she hadn't attended, and found her collapsed on the floor.'

'A heart attack?'

'No,' Wyenna said. 'Murdered.'

'Oh my,' Laodoc said. 'I'm shocked, but not, I must confess, completely surprised. I know she had her enemies.'

'I can think of at least half a dozen people who wanted her dead,' Nueillin said. 'She was a known blackmailer and extortionist, who held several of the City Council in her pocket, not to mention at least two of the High Senate.'

'And a couple of Liberals,' said Laodoc.

'You knew about her?' Pleonim asked him.

'Oh come on,' Laodoc said. 'I'm not completely addled.'

'Well,' Wyenna said, 'I'll bet you didn't know that she controlled at least two of your old Hedgers, including Riomac, your erstwhile deputy.'

Laodoc's face fell. 'He was working for her?'

Pleonim nodded, a smug smile on his lips.

Laodoc shook his head in disappointment. 'How exactly did Councillor Myella die?'

'I believe she was struck with a knife,' Pleonim said. 'In the head.'

'Oh dear,' he said, suppressing a slight smile. 'Have there been any arrests?'

'None so far,' said Wyenna. 'There will be a thorough investigation, I'm sure.'

'It must have been someone on the inside,' Nueillin said. 'No one else has access to the members' private rooms.'

'So there could be a murderer in our very midst?' Laodoc said. 'How barbaric.'

'That reminds me,' Wyenna said. 'I've been meaning to ask what happened to your academy's resident barbarians. My cousin's daughter attends, as you know, and she told me that the savages have been removed, after they caused a ruckus a while back.'

'Really? I didn't know that,' Nueillin said. 'Did they harm anyone?'

'A couple of guards got knocked about a little,' Laodoc said. 'Nothing serious, but I felt it best if the academy's specimens were placed in a more secure environment.'

'So your school is still experimenting on them?' Pleonim said. 'Whatever do you think you might learn from such savage beasts?'

'The purpose of the research is to learn more about ourselves,' Laodoc said, 'by holding the Kellach Brigdomin up as a comparison.'

'It sounds like a waste of time,' Pleonim smiled. 'And money.'

'I'm sure you're right,' he said. 'It is rather an expensive hobby.'

'Some spend their wealth on wine,' Pleonim said, laughing. 'I suppose spending it on a school is no more foolish.'

'He can afford it,' Wyenna chuckled. 'All those coal mines...'

'It does put you in a tricky position, however,' Nueillin said, 'as regards your sons. It would appear that the worse they do, the richer you get. And if they were to succeed...'

Her voice tailed off.

Laodoc sighed. 'Then we all lose.'

CHAPTER 10
ASH

Basalt Desert, between Arakhanah and Rahain Republic – 30th Day, Last Third Summer 504

'I wish we'd never left, Shella,' Clodi sobbed, as they crouched in the darkness of her cramped tent. 'This is a nightmare.'

Shella hugged her weeping sister, biting down her impatience.

'I want to go home!' Clodi cried.

'We're going to our new home,' Shella whispered. 'You'll see.'

'No, we're all going to die in this horrible wasteland.'

'We shall pass through it,' Shella said, worried that she was starting to sound like Obli. 'We will find a green land with broad rivers beyond.'

'Do you really believe that, Shella?'

'Of course I do,' she lied.

Clodi's sobs quietened to a sniff. 'Sorry, Shella,' she said. 'Sometimes I feel so low, like this is never going to end.'

'I know,' she replied. 'Look, will you be okay? I have to get back to work.'

'Sorry,' Clodi repeated. 'You've probably got a hundred important things you need to be doing, and here I am, being stupid as usual.'

'No, you're not,' Shella said. 'Look, I'll come and check on you later, see if you're okay.' She kissed Clodi on the forehead and crawled to the tent's entrance. 'Bye, Clodi,' she said as she left.

Outside, she stood up, her boots crunching on the black basalt beneath her feet. She gazed up into the morning skies, looking for clouds, but seeing none.

'Shit,' she muttered.

The pair of militia guards that escorted her everywhere got to their feet from where they had been sitting by the tent.

'Miss,' one nodded to her.

'Jayki,' she replied. 'Braga. Let's go.'

They followed her between the lines of shabby tents, across the hard, dry, black volcanic rock, that stretched for miles in every direction. To her left was the rising sun, shining low over the vast reaches of the endless ocean to the east. On her other side loomed the smoking bulk of the great volcano in the distance. Lava flows of centuries past had spilled their way down the eastern slopes of the peak, creating a vast desolate landscape of black, inhospitable rock; barren, dust-blown and lifeless. Between the volcano and the ocean nothing lived, nothing apart from the hundreds of thousands of Rakanese migrants, choking with thirst as they snaked their way southwards.

As they approached the inner circle of command tents, she saw her brother Pavu jog towards her.

'We have a situation, Shella,' he said, panting as he reached her.

'What is it now?'

'Possible riot brewing in Willowbrook camp,' he said. 'Didn't take kindly to having their water ration cut.'

'So?' she muttered. 'The gangs there are always fighting.'

'Sami and Klebo are cut off right in the middle of it,' he said, as they walked to the largest tent in the inner circle.

'What were those idiots doing in Willowbrook?' she snapped. Her brothers should have known better than to go into one of the most gang-infested camps, named, as they all were, after the migrants' home district. Willowbrook was an enormous, densely populated slum in the east of the city centre back in Arakhanah, notorious for its violence and squalor.

'They were supposedly negotiating with the camp's leaders,' Pavu said, keeping up with her. 'Over what, I don't know. It certainly wasn't me who authorised the trip.'

She halted, as she realised what needed to be done.

'Will you go?' he asked her.

'Are there no other flow mages available?'

'None at your level, sorry,' he said. 'They're all still exhausted from yesterday's attempted cloud-gathering.'

A knot of stress grew in the pit of her stomach.

'I don't think I can do this any more, Pavu.'

He took her hand.

'You must,' he said. 'If you don't, we'll have to send in the militia, and many more will die, innocents, guards, possibly Sami and Klebo.'

She felt disgusted.

'I'm not made for this.'

'What kind of person would you be if you enjoyed it?' he asked. 'I'm glad you hate it, for it shows you are still the same Shella, that you haven't changed.'

He's wrong, she thought. She wasn't the same.

'Let's go, then,' she said.

Pavu had assembled a whole company of armed militia, numbering about two hundred. They all wore dark red shirts and black kilts, and carried batons and shields. They were a nasty bunch, mostly made up of thugs and bullies who had got lucky. They were fierce in their loyalty to Obli, cherishing her with a devotion bordering on worship. Most of the officers behaved obsequiously to Shella and Pavu, the kind of toadying little sycophants that she felt ashamed to be associated with.

The company marched out, with Pavu and Shella walking near the head of the column. They passed by the ragged and dirty camps of several districts on the way, while their occupants watched them warily from the shadows of their tents.

Willowbrook camp was a chaotic, sprawling mess of wagons,

luggage, crates, tents and people. A large crowd had formed on what passed for the main road through the camp, bordered on either side by rows of hastily assembled wooden buildings, constructed from dismantled water-wagons from when they had stopped a few days before. The mob were attacking the structures, ripping them apart with their hands, shouting with rage.

'They're wrecking their own camp,' Shella sighed.

'They must think there's water inside,' Pavu said. 'Instead, it's our foolish brothers.'

He turned to the column behind him.

'Form up!' he bellowed, and the guards of Obli's militia shuffled into position, making a wedge shape, pointed at the crowd.

'Targets are in the main building to the left ahead,' he shouted. 'Once the mage has cleared the way, go straight in, secure the hostages, and get out again.'

He turned to Shella. 'Ready?'

She nodded. 'Come on, boys,' she said to Jayki and Braga, who trailed along after her as she walked out from among the guards towards the mob, a hundred yards away.

'I enjoy this bit,' she heard Jayki say in a low voice behind her.

'Which bit?' Braga replied in a whisper. 'Watching rioters' heads go pop, or checking out the mage's ass?'

'Both,' Jayki laughed.

'Do you think I'm fucking deaf?' she snapped back, without turning her head.

'Sorry, miss,' they mumbled.

When they got within twenty paces of the mob, she halted. Many had turned to look at them, and some were already starting to run, seeing Shella, and recognising her.

'Do the honours, please Jayki,' she said.

The guard stepped forward.

'Clear the streets!' he yelled. 'We have a mage!'

The effect was instant. Screams rose, and people broke from the mob, fleeing down the road in the opposite direction from where

Shella stood. She readied herself, her right hand raised. Usually there were a few brave idiots: the young, the ignorant, or those who had never witnessed what a high mage could do.

She sighed as she saw them approach, a knot of youths, who stared at her, then charged, jumping over the debris littering the street, while others around them continued to scatter.

Shella concentrated, focussing on the six rioters in the lead row of the mob rushing towards her. She reached out, sensing the fluids pumping through their bodies, and, with a sudden sweep of her hand, she pushed the liquid powerfully up into their brains, felling the six, blood bursting from their nostrils, eyes and ears, their corpses convulsing on the basalt rock.

The other charging rioters stopped, staring with horror at the shaking, bloody bodies of those fallen at their feet. Shella raised her arm again, while Jayki bared his teeth and growled, 'Want some more?'

The rioters fled, leaving the road deserted within seconds.

Shella lowered her arm, as the company of guards moved up past her, jogging towards the largest wooden structure alongside the road.

'Good job,' Pavu said, as he drew up next to her. 'How are you feeling?'

'Knackered,' she replied. 'And sick. As usual.'

They watched as the militia raided the building, emerging a few minutes later with Sami, Klebo, and half a dozen others.

'Sorry, sis,' Sami said, as they reached her.

'What were you idiots thinking?'

'That'll have to wait, Shella,' Pavu said, as the militia assembled around them. 'Let's get out of here first.'

Pavu gave the order, and the column started jogging back towards the command tents at the head of the great camp.

Shella looked back as they moved off, seeing the lifeless and bloody bodies of the six young Rakanese that she had killed, sprawled out across the dark rock.

Another small piece of her lay dead with them.

'I've already said I'm sorry, Shella,' Sami muttered. 'I didn't know what was going to happen, that you'd have to... you know.'

'Kill people?'

Sami looked at the ground.

'Shit; I wish I could get drunk,' Shella said. She noticed Sami's expression. 'What are you smiling at?'

'You,' he laughed. 'After so many years of telling me off for swearing.'

'Don't change the subject,' she scowled. 'What were you doing in that camp? If you're looking to get your stupid head kicked in, I'll happily volunteer, no need to go all the way over to Willowbrook.'

Sami looked away, his face dark in the shadow of the tent's interior.

'Well?' she asked again.

'I can't say, Shella,' Sami replied, holding up his hands.

'Ohh, I see,' she said, narrowing her eyes. 'So you're covering for that oaf Klebo? I should've known. Let me guess.... Okay, he's in trouble, gambling, maybe? He owes someone nasty a lot of cash, and had gone to Willowbrook to pay up. No, that doesn't sound right. He went there to offer them a deal, some off-the-books water to forgive his debt?'

She looked at Sami. 'Am I close?'

He shrugged.

'Great,' said Shella. 'So now I have six more deaths on my conscience to add to the others. Obli said it was all for the greater good, that I wasn't to worry, that by killing people I actually save lives.'

'It's true, Shella,' Sami said, looking up at her. 'It's horrible, but it's true. You and the other flow mages have stopped many riots before they could get started, just by being there.'

'The migration is turning us into monsters.'

'You're not a monster, Shella.'

'Not yet, maybe,' she said, 'but I don't know how much more I can take. Everyone stares at me with fear in their eyes. Fear and hatred.

With a flick of my hand I can burst their brains with their own blood, or stop their hearts from pumping, or send fluid into their lungs and drown them, quickly or slowly. That sounds like a monster to me, Sami.'

'But you're second in command. Only Obli ranks above you,' Sami said. 'Couldn't you get the other mages to do it instead?'

'I already make them do it! But how could I ask them to do what I refused to? It's taking its toll, though, some of them are close to cracking up. And they're the decent ones. The mean ones are more of a worry, a few of them seem to enjoy it a little too much.' She sighed. 'If we make it across this wasteland, then they'll be the ones we'll have to watch out for.'

'Have you mentioned any of this to Obli?'

'Yeah,' she said. 'She told me she'd take care of it, whatever that means. Anyway, that reminds me, Obli wants me in her tent. Meeting.'

'We moving out soon?'

She got to her feet. 'Yeah, probably.'

'See you later,' Sami said.

'Bye,' she replied, leaving the tent, and stepping back outside into the harsh sunlight.

She looked down the row of grimy tents, where most of her brothers and sisters slept. This part of the camp was guarded, to protect those closest to the leader, and she saw Jayki and Braga chatting to a couple of female militia, near Dannu's tent.

She whistled on them, and they trudged back towards her.

'Miss?' said Braga.

'Command tent,' she said. 'Come on.'

She led them through another ring of guards, into the inner circle. When she entered the crowded main tent, she saw that the meeting had started.

Pavu was standing arguing with one of the supply bosses, while Obli sat impassively on a raised chair at the head of the room, dressed in a long white gown. Her flowers had long since died, and upon her brow sat a slender silver band, with a large diamond inset.

The jewel had been created by the migration's foremost clay mage, who had worked on it for many days. He had presented it to Obli, while on his knees, as if she were a queen, and he her humble subject.

Obli saw her as she approached.

'Mage Shella,' she said, causing the room to fall silent, as all eyes turned to her.

'Sister,' Shella replied.

'We were just discussing a date for our departure,' Obli said. 'What would you recommend, mage?'

'We should leave tomorrow,' Shella said without hesitation.

'But, Shella,' Tehna said, 'the people are exhausted, they cannot walk without water. Should we not wait for rain?'

'And while we wait,' Shella said to her priestess sister, 'the camps riot, and hundreds die each day from thirst. We have to keep moving.'

'It will soon be autumn,' Obli said. 'The rains will come.'

'And they will come sooner, the further south we get,' Shella said.

Obli nodded. 'It is decreed, then. We leave tomorrow. Mage Shella, ensure the camps are informed.'

'Will do.'

'Now,' Obli went on, 'our friend from the Holdings has performed a sighting for us.' She looked over at a tall, dark-skinned man, standing close by. He had accompanied the migration as a representative of the Holdings, sent by their embassy in Arakhanah. Shella didn't trust him, but the mage-priest had a useful skill, which allowed him to see things at great distances, though it made him quite poorly for hours afterwards.

He stepped forward, looking ill and grey.

'I scanned the way south,' he said, in faultless Rakanese. 'The basalt plain stretches out for at least another two hundred miles. I would estimate that we are not yet half way through.'

The tent fell into silence.

'Our water supplies will never last that long!' said one of the supply bosses.

'How can this be?' Obli said. 'I was told that we had adequate supplies for the entire journey across the desert.'

'The people are squandering the supplies,' he said.

'What?' Obli cried, her face darkening in anger.

'He's right, sister,' Shella said. 'No matter how many rules we make, most camps break them, trying to take as much water as they can. We've put more guards on the wagons, but they've been overwhelmed by rioters on a few occasions. It's been impossible to get the camps to stick to the rationing, and we haven't got enough militia to enforce the orders.'

'The mages must make more rain!' Tehna said.

'Then, sister dear, why don't you pray for some clouds?' Shella said. 'Then the mages will be only too happy to oblige.'

'Did you see anything else, Priest Rijon?' Pavu asked the Holdings mage. 'Rivers, trees?'

'Nothing,' the man replied. 'The way south is desolate.'

'Wasn't it you who advised us to go this way?' Shella asked.

'That's not how I remember it, madam mage,' said Rijon. 'I recall trying to dissuade you from the entire enterprise, but, seeing that you had determined to leave, I merely pointed out the fact that the way south, although long and dangerous, was the only possible direction you could take.'

'Just a coincidence, then,' Shella said, 'that south also happened to be in the opposite direction from the Holdings?'

'But madam,' he said, 'our lands are already settled. Whereas the Rahain valleys and lowlands, where plentiful rivers run, are not. The Rahain prefer to build their cities within the hearts of their mountain ranges, and are not interested in the wet, empty lowlands.'

'But...' Shella began.

'The way has long been decided, Mage Shella,' Obli said. 'There is no need to go over old arguments.'

'Sister,' Shella nodded, scowling at the Holdings priest.

'Water must be conserved at all costs,' Obli said. 'Thieves, cheats, and anyone wasting water must be severely punished.'

Shella shared a side glance with Pavu.

'The migration will continue,' Obli went on. 'It must continue. When we began, we knew the way would be hard, and that there would be losses. If only half of us remain, once we have found our new home, I shall still count it a success.'

The tent hushed as they listened. Shella noticed most people in the room looked up at Obli with awe, as if her every pronouncement was sacred, immutable and true. To Shella, Obli still seemed to be the same sister she had always known, a self-righteous attention-seeker, who had finally found the role of her life.

There was a low rumble beneath Shella's feet.

She looked up, and saw from the apprehension on everyone's faces that she hadn't imagined it.

Before anyone could speak, the ground lurched, throwing everyone to the ground amid cries of terror. The tent collapsed, its poles snapping, and the canvas fell down on top of them. Shella curled her body up, clutching her face, as she waited out the earthquake, her heart pounding with fear.

The earth stopped shaking, and Shella began to crawl, trying to remember where the exit was. With the tent smothering them, she could see almost nothing as she struggled under the weight of the canvas. She saw a glow ahead of her, and made for it. A few guards were holding up the edge of the great tent, letting in the blinding sunlight, as they tried to look for those within.

'Miss!'

She saw Braga. He was gripping onto the canvas, holding it high.

'This way!' he cried.

Shella scrambled to her feet, and ran the last few yards.

'Get in there!' she called to the guards. 'Start propping up the tent. Find Obli!'

Others were now crawling out, dazed and bleeding.

The earth shook again. Braga grabbed Shella's arm to stop her toppling over, and she braced her feet until it stopped.

As soon as the earth steadied, Shella pushed through the crowd of guards, and climbed one of the large rocks that littered the basalt landscape.

Crouching on its rough summit, she gazed up at the volcano, almost due west of where the camp stood.

A thick pillar of dirty black and grey smoke was belching from the top of the mountain, towering up into the blue sky.

Shella watched in fascinated horror as the tower of smoke billowed ever higher, to a background roar from the heart of the volcano. The sky darkened, as the ash blotted out the sun, casting the land below into shadow.

The earth shook again, and Shella clung on to the top of the rock with all her strength. The screams and shouts from the camp around her grew louder. She stared up at the volcano as the smoke increased. Ash and small, red-hot stones started to land all around. The earth stilled, and Shella scrambled down from the high rock.

At the front of the collapsed tent, she saw Obli and the others emerging from the darkness.

'We must go!' Shella yelled, as they looked up at the volcano in confusion. 'Sound the alarm! Get everyone moving!'

Obli staggered forward, blood trickling down her face from a wound on her forehead. Dannu and Tehna were supporting an arm on either side.

Larger stones started to rain down, the size of river pebbles, but hot like burning coals. Shella saw a guard struck in the face with one, and other stones were setting tents alight throughout the camp.

Shella took Obli's hand.

'Sister?' she said, but Obli looked dazed.

'She took a blow to the head,' said Dannu.

'You're in charge,' Tehna said. 'For the moment.'

Shella nodded, and turned to Pavu and his militia.

'Order the departure!' she shouted at the top of her lungs.

Pavu looked stunned, but obeyed, taking a whistle out from beneath his tunic. He blew on it three times, harsh notes that cut through the air. Within seconds, other whistles were heard, three short blasts on each, as the message rippled outwards through the camp.

'Get Obli onto a stretcher,' Shella shouted to Tehna, then turned back to Pavu. 'Brother, take a company, and escort her. Lead the way south. I will make sure everyone follows.'

'Okay, Shella,' Pavu said, sounding relieved that someone had taken command.

She gave out a series of rapid orders to the other militia officers to secure the remaining water-wagons, and ensure they were rigged up and on their way south as soon as possible. She sent some to pack up the tents, some to guard the supply caravans, and others to gather the rest of the mages and get them moving.

Whistles were echoing from every part of the vast camp, and amid the ash-fall, Shella could see tents being pulled down, and people crowding around their district assembly points. She watched them, from the higher ground of the inner circle.

Her people.

Scattered, weary, and thirsty beyond imagining, they assembled, as fiery stones rained down upon them from the heavy, leaden skies. The air was thick with ash flakes, and growing hotter, and the low rumble beneath her feet was continuous.

We might just manage this, she thought, as the camp migrants started moving south like a slow wave.

There was a tumultuous roar as the volcano erupted, and Shella stared wide-eyed as lava belched from the broken summit, first a narrow bright stream then, with a pulsing heave, a burning flood of molten rock was vomited down the mountainside in their direction.

The ash was falling faster, and the fiery rocks smashing into them were now the size of watermelons.

'Miss,' Jayki said. 'We should go.'

She ignored him, trying to estimate the path the lava was taking. It was rolling smoothly and slowly down the long slopes of the volcano, and she knew it would be a few hours before it reached their current position. The camp stretched for miles northwards however, and it would take all day for the rearmost camps to catch up. She coughed, her throat parched and burning. A man ran out in front of her, screaming, his hair on fire.

'Miss!' Jayki yelled.

She took her eyes off the mountain for a moment and looked around. A full company of militia were assembled in the swirling ash, ready to leave, awaiting her command. Several wagons, piled up with the tents of the inner circle, stood by, their oxen lowing in fear. Shella wrapped a cloth over her face as it became difficult to breathe, the hot air filled with burning dust. She shook her head, sending ash flying.

She glanced back at the camp. There was nothing more she could do. There was no point in waiting, or going back to warn them. The migrants at the northernmost end of the camp could see the danger as clearly as she, and would run all the way if it came to it. How many more would die that day?

She turned away, and raised her hand. 'Move out!' she cried, and the guards in her company got underway, trudging southwards as ash buried the ground. Periodically, a rock would crash nearby, sometimes missing, sometimes smashing into the ranks of the militia in an explosion of fire and glowing shards.

She nearly stumbled, the grey carpet covering the cracks and jagged stones on the ground. She shrank into herself, her head empty of all thoughts except keeping her feet moving.

CHAPTER 11
DOUBLE DOWN

Rahain Capital, Rahain Republic – 30th Day, Last Third Summer 504

'Whoever you're working for,' the old woman said, aiming her hand-sized crossbow at Daphne's heart, 'should have warned you that people have tried to kill me before.'

Daphne, her eyes flowing with battle-vision, stared at the city councillor. She saw the Rahain's finger about to tighten, and flung her left arm up over her chest as the old woman pulled the trigger. The bolt glanced off the armour that protected her crippled limb, and Daphne pounced. She pulled a knife from her boot as she sprang, directing it towards the old woman's heart. The Rahain ducked at the last moment, and Daphne slammed the blade into the side of her head.

She let go of the knife, and the old woman fell to the ground, three inches of steel in her brain.

Daphne gazed at the dead Rahain at her feet. Myella, the second name on Douanna's list. Lying on the floor, she didn't look like someone who was capable of doing the kinds of things that Douanna had listed. Like a spider at the centre of a web, she had said. With her death, the network of those she had controlled, both in the City Council and High Senate, would weaken, and the alliance between the parties that made up the war coalition might start to fracture. And that would make war with the Holdings less likely, Daphne guessed, running through Douanna's logic in her mind, trying to justify what she had done.

Murder.

Her mind turned to Killop, as she remembered seeing him two thirds before. While the threat of war against her homeland seemed remote and hard to imagine, her motivation for carrying out Douanna's commissions felt viscerally real when she thought of the condition of the Kellach slaves. Eliminating some of those responsible felt like a better justification to her, and so revenge for what the Rahain had done to the Kellach Brigdomin had got her through her first assignment, a third before, and it would get her through this.

She hoped.

Daphne left the knife where it was, and crept to the door of the old woman's office, four floors up in the City Council building. She knew the layout well, having sneaked around before, on her nocturnal wanderings through the city. Breaking into the mansions of the rich, and the more heavily guarded public buildings had become a habit for Daphne as she practised her skills. Prowling alone at night, and then sleeping and studying during the day, had become her routine since Douanna had left over a third before. The Rahain merchant had travelled back to Jade Falls, to put some distance between herself and the execution of her commissions.

Crouching low, Daphne looked out through the keyhole.

Bending her sight with line-vision, she scanned the corridor in both directions, finding it empty.

She left the room and ran down the corridor, her feet making no noise on the thick carpet. She searched the wall at the end of the passageway, finding the concealed door leading to the servants' stairwell. She heard voices approach from the left, crowing over some victory in the council, and she went through. She put her ear to the door as she shut it, listening as the voices came closer.

'When you see your brother,' a low voice said, 'give him my hearty congratulations. I'm sure he'll do a fine job bringing those recalcitrant savages to heel.'

'I will, thank you,' a younger voice replied, as they passed the door.

'Now, let's see what excuse Myella has for not turning up this evening.'

'I'm sure it'll be a good one, she never likes to miss giving the Liberals a bloody nose!'

Oh, it's quite good, Daphne thought, smiling in the darkness.

Thirty minutes later, she was well on her way through the dark streets of the city. It was past midnight, the streets were quiet, and she slipped through the shadows, keeping close to the walls and back alleys.

Her night wasn't over, and she turned towards the High Senate, towering above her in the central cavern of the city.

She had questioned the value of assassinating members of the City Council, first the drunken brute that she had poisoned, and then drowned in his bath, and now the old woman, when those who sat in the High Senate seemed to hold all the power. Douanna had explained about the virtual veto the City Council wielded over matters of war, as they held the keys to the capital's treasury, the largest reserve of coin in the republic.

She recalled the words of the Rahain she had overheard by the stairs. If the city councillors were talking about crushing savages and beating Liberals, it could only mean that they had passed a resolution to supply funds for some sort of expedition that the High Senate had needed approval for. More pertinent to her assignment that night, it also meant that the senators would have to wait for word of the City Council's vote before they could disband for the Autumn's Day holiday, and that her next target would therefore still be inside.

From a nearby roof, she noticed that the security surrounding the High Senate appeared to be normal, meaning that news of Councillor Myella's death had not yet arrived. She settled in to wait, watching the guards patrol the streets around the huge complex. Her view also encompassed the large courtyard at the rear, where the senators' carriages were stationed. Slaves and gaien stood in the night air, waiting for the orders to take their masters home, or to a party, or wherever else the elite in Rahain society went while the rest of the city slept.

As she leaned back against the stone roof, Daphne inspected the damage to the armour covering her left arm. It had been fashioned by a Rahain stone mage, who had crafted thin, compressed plates of a black, green-veined rock, held within a hinged steel frame. The entire piece fitted her from shoulder to wrist, and was so light and thin that it was unnoticeable when worn under a cloak.

She saw a tiny chip in the smooth, dark stonework halfway down her forearm, from where Myella's bolt had struck. Douanna had assured her that the work was of the highest quality, and that the mage was not only the best at what he did, but was also discreet regarding his paid commissions.

At her wrist, the forearm guard extended past her knuckles, ending in a studded steel bar, capable of delivering a punch. She had been practising fighting using her left arm, to parry, and to strike. Her elbow remained fused at an angle, but the freedom the arm-guard gave her had improved her overall movement, as she no longer had to worry about protecting her crippled limb at every turn.

Movement in the courtyard below caught her eye. She watched from the shadows as the rear doors of the senate building opened, and small pockets of senators started to emerge, hailing their carriages.

Daphne slipped into battle-vision, drawing on just enough to allow her to pick out individual faces among the crowd forming below. Her eyes focussed as she recognised her second target of the night.

Flanouac, a senator from the Patriot Party. One of the main proponents of the war strategy against the Kellach Brigdomin, sponsor of the laws authorising the invasion, and one of those most responsible for the death and enslavement of hundreds of thousands. Douanna had told her that he was now agitating for the transfer of troops into the demilitarised Plateau, as soon as their tunnel through the mountains was complete. Ostensibly about protecting trade routes from the Kellach and Sanang bandits who roamed the mountains, Douanna had insisted that Flanouac's true motive was to provoke a fight with the Holdings. She had explained that the Conservatives were loath to begin hostilities in light of their signed peace with the northern realm, and so the Patriots were attempting to provide a pretext that would allow them to go to war without formally breaking the terms of the treaty.

Daphne's mind had already glossed over these details. He was one of the politicians who had caused untold suffering among the Kellach tribes, and that, for the moment, was enough for her.

She watched as Flanouac said his farewells to a group of senators, and boarded his carriage. The gaien lurched ahead, and exited through the large, double-arched entrance, and onto one of the main streets surrounding the walled senate complex. Daphne scrambled up and over the top of the roof where she had been hiding, to observe the direction the carriage chose. Over the last half-third that she had been tailing the senator, he had once or twice gone out to a restaurant or party, but tonight she saw that he was taking his normal route homeward, to his mansion in Silverlight Caverns, one of the most exclusive addresses in the city.

Daphne sprinted across the roof of the tall building where she had been crouching, until she reached an access shaft, high up the cavern side. A network of service tunnels ran between the main caverns, and she had learned the layout by stealing a map from a city library. There was no direct route to Flanouac's mansion, so she emerged from the tunnels into a large vertical ventilation shaft directly above Silverlight Caverns.

They were beautiful. Natural pillars, formed of stalagmites merged with stalactites, seemed to hold up the brooding, heavy ceiling. The grey rock was streaked with polished seams of silver, which ran along the ground, and across the cavern walls. A score of large mansions appeared to rise out of the stone, their silver seams shimmering in the lamplight.

A network of high roads linked the main entrances of the mansions, while, below them, a narrower web of trenches and tunnels criss-crossed the cavern, to allow the servile classes to move around without being seen by the nobles who lived there. At this hour, the servants' passageways were silent and deserted. Daphne lowered herself into the closest one, and began to make her way to the home of Flanouac.

As she passed the high walls of a private garden, she heard the sound of a carriage approaching along one of the high roads. She withdrew into the shadows, and used a short burst of line-vision to confirm that the passenger was indeed her target. Waiting until it had passed, she put her hands on her knees. A wave of nausea washed through her, and she gagged.

Even with all of her practice, switching back and forth between her skills could still cause her difficulties.

The feeling passed, and she reached into a pocket sewn into the inside of her vest. She took out a small stick of keenweed, brought all the way from the Sanang frontier by Douanna, and lit it after striking a spark with a Rahain match.

She closed her eyes as she inhaled, knowing that her senses would be flooded with the combination of the narcotic with her battle-vision. She felt her energy increase, and the last traces of her nausea vanished. Preparing herself, she opened her eyes, taking in every detail around her in an instant.

An alert calmness filled her as a surge of energy rippled through her body, and she ran down the passageways towards Flanouac's mansion.

She had never been in his home before, but it was as unprotected as the other mansions in Silverlight that she had broken into. There were a few complacent guards posted on the main gate, but none watching the low back walls, and she was over and into the marble flagstoned yard without being seen. The avenue running towards the large house was lined with statues of ancient Rahain notables. According to Douanna, this cavern had been continuously inhabited for thousands of years, and had gained its present form under the rule of a tyrant some three and a half millennia before.

Daphne felt a little surge of pride that an upstart Holdings renegade was able to infiltrate the inner sanctuaries of a society as ancient as the Rahain. Bringing their arrogance down a peg or two was its own motivation.

She studied the mansion from the shadow of a statue, noting where lamps were lit. She shot her line-vision up to the index finger of a massive figure of a Rahain warrior, her marble hand pointing to the sky, and gazed into each room in turn.

She paused when she scanned the third room. Inside, a woman was helping two young children pack some bags and travel cases with clothes and toys. They were laughing, as the boy was trying on a selection of his sister's hats.

So he has a family, she thought. Doesn't matter. Changes nothing.

She continued examining the rooms. In the fifth one along, she saw a study, where Flanouac was facing the window, sorting out some documents on a desk. The room to the left of where he was standing seemed empty, its windows dark.

Daphne ran to the side of the mansion, under the dark window to the left of Flanouac's study. The wall was faced in the grey, silver-shot stone that was present everywhere in the cavern, and had been moulded with deep rusticated blocks.

She looked down at the armour covering her crippled limb. The stone mage who had constructed it had set a retractable iron claw into the framework under her left wrist. She released a catch to extend it, and approached the wall. She hooked the claw onto a ledge above a stone block, put some of her weight onto her left arm, and began to climb. It was hard work, and she was sweating as she scaled the wall, guessing that it was the keenweed that was allowing her to push past her normal limits.

She clambered up onto a balcony, and sat for a moment to recover her breath.

The tall windows leading off the balcony were dark. She got up, listened at the doors, then entered the mansion. She crossed the floor, and put her ear to the inner door. She heard nothing, and crept out of the dark room and into a corridor. She padded to the next door along, and opened it a crack.

Flanouac was still within, his back to her as he stood at his desk.

Daphne entered. She drew a knife from her belt, and aimed at the space between his shoulder blades.

He must have heard something, as he started to turn just as she threw the knife. His eyes opened wide as the blade struck him in the chest under his left shoulder, missing his heart.

Daphne ran towards the desk as he fell. She caught him, and lowered him to the ground.

There was a choking, gasping sound coming from his mouth, along with flecks of blood. Must have punctured a lung, she thought.

He stared at her in shock, pain, and a raw fear of death.

'Who are you?' he gasped, as she lay him onto the carpet.

'The spirit of vengeance,' she whispered, putting her foot against his shoulder, pinning him to the floor.

'Why?' he groaned, his tongue flickering. 'Why?'

'For what you did to the Kellach Brigdomin.' She extracted the knife from his chest, stepping aside to avoid the spray of blood that followed. Flanouac's face paled, as his life pulsed out through the wound.

'You don't have to kill me,' he whispered, trying to raise his head, but failing, his neck flopping uselessly.

'I know that,' she said, 'but I'm going to do it anyway.'

'For the Kellach?' he asked, his breath ragged and laboured. 'But you are Holdings.'

'I am,' she replied, kneeling in close, her knife at his neck.

'You hypocrite!' he gasped. 'If you want to kill warmongers, you should have started at home.'

She paused.

'Look at what you are doing in Sanang,' he went on, blood trickling down his chin. 'You think the Holdings are innocent?'

He pointed up at her. 'You are the same as us...'

She slit his throat, silencing him. Blood pumped out through the slash she had made, and his vertical pupils dilated.

She stood, the bloody knife dripping onto the cream-coloured carpet.

'I am nothing like you.'

She stooped, wiping the knife on the dead Rahain's tunic, then approached the balcony doors, and slipped outside. The air was warm, and she remembered that she was not really outside, but deep underground. She resolved to visit the surface as soon as she could, so she could feel fresh air blowing on her face. The air down in the caverns was stale and close, and she started to feel claustrophobic.

Don't falter now, she told herself, as she leaned against the balcony railing. She had to get far away from there, before the keenweed could wear off. She slung her legs over the edge, and climbed back down to the ground.

With no sound of any alarm, she sprinted to the rear wall of the garden, and hoisted herself up. Sitting perched upon a ledge just below the top of the wall, she looked back at the mansion, sending a surge of line-vision back up to the stone warrior's raised finger. She gazed into the room where she had killed Flanouac.

The study was crowded with terrified servants and tearful guards. Next to the body, a woman stood, her face crumpled and distraught, as she looked down at her dead husband. Two small children were hugging the corpse, crying hysterically. Each clung onto one of their father's arms, while servants tried to pull them clear.

Daphne looked away, shielding her heart from the waves of pain that she could feel coming from the people within the room. She jumped down from the wall, lowered herself into the servants' trenches, and started to run.

It took half the night to reach Douanna's home, in the fashionable area of the Topaz Caverns. She had been forced to hide for hours until the Silverlight entrance tunnel was clear enough for her to escape back through the ventilation shaft. Her nerves were shot, the keenweed all but worn off, and her use of battle-vision, as well as the numerous bursts of line-vision, had left her body exhausted, but her mind buzzing.

She let herself in through a small side door, and nearly collapsed with relief. Holding onto the wall, she straightened herself, and stumbled down to the basement. The lamps were dimmed, and the kitchens were empty. She staggered over to the deep sinks and began washing the blood from her hands, pouring freezing cold water from a large jug.

'Good evening, my lady,' she heard behind her.

'Good evening,' she replied to the old servant, one of Douanna's longest serving, and the only other person living in the house.

'Busy night, my lady?'

'So-so,' she said, never sure how much Douanna had told him about what she was doing. It made for a strange and uncomfortable relationship, with Daphne dancing around her true role in the household, while the old servant often hinted that he knew more, without ever confirming it. Daphne had no doubt that he reported her every word back to his mistress.

'Is my lady hungry?' he asked.

Daphne turned to face him, drying her hands on a towel.

'Not much appetite this evening.'

'As you say, my lady,' he said, his eyes scanning her.

'I would be grateful,' she went on, 'if you could bring some wine up to my room in half an hour.'

'As you wish, my lady,' he replied. 'Red or white?'

'Actually, make it brandy,' she said, walking towards the stairs.

'Very good, my lady.'

She trudged up the stone steps to the top floor, where she had a bed chamber and washroom. She changed out of her night-stalker clothes, unfastening and removing her arm-guard with care, and placing it on the small table at the end of her bed. She put her knives away, and pulled on a light cotton robe, just as the old servant entered with a tray.

She lit a cigarette as he set down the bottle of brandy and a single glass on the bedside table, next to her armour.

'Would my lady be requiring anything else?'

'Not tonight, thank you.'

'Very good, my lady,' he nodded, leaving her room and closing the door behind him.

She sat on the edge of her bed, and poured herself a glass.

The keenweed had worn off, and the brandy hit her quickly, sending her mood downwards into a morose cycle of guilt and shame. As self-pity engulfed her, she tried to reason with herself, knowing the alcohol was fuelling the after-effects of the narcotics, but it was too late.

Tears started to fall down her cheeks, and the image of the slain politician's grieving wife and children shone in her mind as if seared there. They had been getting ready to go off on their autumn holiday, packing their little bags with toys. But she had intervened in their lives, to destroy them, in one night of blood they would never be able to forget.

Daphne refilled her glass.

She had a sudden desire to see Killop, and a longing grew within her. Feelings flooded through her, feelings she could normally suppress when not coming down off narcotics and her vision power. She wanted to see Killop. No, more than just see him. She wanted to be held within his arms, she wanted to feel his skin next to hers, she wanted him. She wanted...

But it was pointless. She had no idea where he was, or even if he was still alive. She had gone back to Laodoc's academy, not long after Douanna had returned to Jade Falls, only to discover that the three Kellach had been moved to a more secure location, as the clerk at the reception desk had informed her.

If Killop had been mixed in with the great mass of other Kellach

Brigdomin slaves, then Daphne knew that her chances of ever seeing him again were as good as zero.

She poured herself another brandy.

She felt wretched. And drunk.

She unlocked a small drawer built into the table, and took out a polished wooden box. She opened it, and looked inside at the little rows of Sanang drug-sticks. There were the ones for keeping alert and unemotional, like the keenweed she had smoked earlier. There were also ones for pain, that numbed the mind as well as the body, and she selected one of those, putting the box back into the drawer.

Dullweed, she thought, as she gazed at the little cigarette.

Bringer of oblivion.

She lit it, and inhaled.

CHAPTER 12
DREAMS OF DAPHNE

R ahain Capital, Rahain Republic – 3rd Day, First Third
Autumn 504

Killop lay asleep, dreaming that he was in bed, a woman held close
in his arms. He heard her soft breathing, felt her skin against his, and
opened his eyes to look upon her.

He awoke, alone in bed, an empty space on the mattress next to
him where Kallie had lain.

He turned over onto his back, sighing. The glowstone lamp in his
bedroom had been turned up, signifying that it was morning in the
sunless caverns. He had lost count of the number of days that had
elapsed since he had last seen the sky, but reckoned it couldn't be far
off a hundred now.

The bedroom was furnished simply, with whitewashed walls, a
plain wooden bed, two chairs and a table. Clean clothes, regular food
and a bathroom added to the list of relative comforts.

He got up, pulled on a pair of knee-length cotton shorts and a vest,
and went out of the room into the main hall, from where every room in
their new living quarters could be accessed. His bedroom, which he
usually shared with Kallie, was next door to her own room, where she

sometimes slept if they'd had a fight. Bridget's room came next, then the bathroom, and then their large common room, where they ate the meals that were brought to them each day. The final room was fitted with blackboards and desks, and it was there they continued to learn Rahain, their lessons having expanded to include reading and writing.

On the west side of the rectangular hall was a large gate, with steel bars running across it. Beyond was a corridor, where a squad of armed guards were stationed. Killop knew, from when they had been brought in, that there was another gate with more guards, just out of sight round a corner in the passageway. Between the two gates, where the captives were never allowed, Simiona had her office, and there were guardrooms, and a kitchen where their food was prepared.

Killop knocked on the bathroom door, and tried the handle. Locked.

He knocked again.

'I'm busy!' yelled Bridget from inside.

'But I'm bursting on a piss!'

'Well, cross yer fucking legs!'

Killop swore under his breath, and made for the common room. Food and water had been laid out on the large wooden table by the slaves assigned to look after them.

Killop sat, ignoring the cool water in the covered jug, and picked at the fruit. The room had several tall bay windows, letting in the bright lamplight from the cavern outside. Each window had been fitted with a sturdy set of bars, so that even if they smashed through the glass, there would be no way out. Simiona had blamed the delay in moving out from the cage in the academy basement on the extra time it had taken to fit the bars to all of the windows. In the end, it had been twenty days following their encounter with Laodoc before they had been transferred to this suite of rooms in his mansion. Throughout that time, he had been as good as his word. The tests and experiments had ceased, but it was still a squalid animal cage, and they had been happy to leave it.

He looked up at the bars, criss-crossing the window panes of their common room. It was still a cage, just a more comfortable one.

There was a noise behind him of a door opening, and he got to his feet.

'About time; I was away to...' he tailed off as he saw the cold expressions on the faces of Kallie and Bridget, as they walked into the common room.

He turned to Bridget as Kallie passed by, stony-faced. He shrugged, mouthing 'what?', and Bridget mouthed back 'tell you later', as she scowled at him.

Saying nothing, he rushed into the bathroom to relieve himself.

The room remained a marvel to Killop, with water that ran from metal taps, one for hot and one for cold. There was a ceramic bath, and a sink, and a flushing toilet, the greatest invention he had ever seen. As he washed his hands, he looked up into the mirror above the sink.

Back in Kell, thirds could pass between seeing a clear reflection of yourself, but here he saw his own face every day, looking back at him. The novelty had worn off, but this bathroom mirror had obsessed the captives when they had first moved in, each spending time staring at themselves. They had then watched as their appearances were transformed. The new professor, who was now in charge of the captives, had decided that something needed to be done about how the Kellach looked.

Their rags were removed and burned, and they were measured for full sets of new clothes. These looked similar to those worn by the servant classes, but were in larger sizes, and were comfortable and clean. They were all given haircuts. Kallie and Bridget had their long hair trimmed and styled into plaits, while Killop's had been cut short, and his beard had been shaved off. For the first time since his chin had started sprouting hairs, he was bare-faced. Not trusted with a razor-blade, a slave now came in every few days, with an armed escort, to freshly shave him.

Kallie had looked startled when she had first seen him short-haired and beardless, while Bridget had laughed. He had stared back at them, open-mouthed. Seeing the women scrubbed up in their clean, fitted clothes, they looked beautiful.

He had grown used to his appearance, but wondered what other Kellach would think of them looking like Rahain servants. Would his sister even recognise him? Would he want her to?

A bell rang as he was about to leave the bathroom and he paused, waiting. One bell meant that the captives were to stay clear of the central hallway, as the guards were about to open up the gate.

A few moments later, the bell rang twice, signifying that they were allowed to move freely around their quarters again. Killop opened the bathroom door, and saw Simiona walking across the hallway.

'Good morning, Killop,' she said.

'Morning, Simi,' he replied. 'You're early.'

'Yes,' she said. 'I wanted to catch you before Professor Geolaid gets here for today's lessons.'

He walked with her into the common room, where Bridget and Kallie sat. They looked up, breaking off their conversation.

Simiona eyed the sullen expressions, and raised an eyebrow. She looked at Killop, who shrugged.

'What's going on?' said the Rahain. 'Did you have a fight?'

'Not that I know of,' Killop said.

Kallie looked away, folding her arms.

'Bridget?' asked Simiona.

The Brig woman looked at Kallie for guidance, but she kept her eyes downwards.

'Killop talks in his sleep,' Bridget said at last. 'Apparently.'

'What did I say?' he asked, remembering vague impressions of his dream, a sinking feeling in his stomach.

Bridget cleared her throat. 'This morning,' she said, her cheeks red, 'Kallie heard you call out for Daphne; you know, that Holdings woman we met ages ago.'

Killop's face paled. It had been Daphne in his dream? Shit.

'I, I'm sorry,' he stammered. 'I don't remember any dream about her.'

'I can tell when you're lying,' Kallie said, keeping her head down.

'I'm not lying.'

The room fell into an uncomfortable silence.

'Well,' Simiona said, blushing, 'I don't really know what to say to that. There was something I was going to tell you, but I'm not sure that I should any more.'

'You'll have to tell us now,' Bridget muttered.

'It involves this Daphne Holdfast,' Simiona said, avoiding the captives' eyes. 'I heard a couple of days ago that she had been to the academy, asking questions about you.'

'A few days ago?' Bridget asked.

'No, sorry,' Simiona said, 'I only heard about it then, apparently this happened about a third ago, not long after you'd moved here. She just missed you by a day or two.'

'That's a pity,' Bridget said. 'I'd quite like to have seen her again.'

Kallie glared at her.

Bridget shrugged. 'It's not my fault your man dreams about her.'

'I don't dream about her,' Killop said.

'Let's just eat breakfast,' Simiona said. 'We have a long day ahead.'

'A long day of boring writing,' Bridget grumbled, picking up a handful of olives from a bowl.

'Your progress has been amazing, Bridget,' Simiona said, grinning. 'Neither I, nor Professor Geolaid, have seen anything like it. And you, Kallie,' she said, turning to face her, 'I was hoping for the next verses of the Lay of the Bear and the Hunter. I had questions about the brother and sister in it. Can I ask, are they meant to be twins?'

'No,' Kallie lied. On this topic, and anything to do with the Mages of Pyre, they all avoided the truth. The Rahain seemed to be in ignorance of the crucial position of twins within Kellach Brigdomin society, and displayed much confusion surrounding their mages' abilities. From what they had said, it was as though they believed that fire mages could create fire, as well as control it. They also appeared completely unaware of the existence of spark mages, and how they were twinned with fire mages. The captives had all privately agreed that they would avoid helping the Rahain in these matters, and had become proficient liars when crafting their tales and songs for transcription.

'Just brother and sister,' Kallie said.

Simiona nodded.

'Killop,' she said. 'Another day's reading for you.'

'Great,' he said. 'More children's stories about Toam and Tyella.'

'It's what every Rahain child uses to learn how to read,' Simiona said.

'Every child?' he asked.

'Apart from the majority of slaves, and the peasants,' Simiona said, blushing. 'Sometimes I forget how lucky I am.'

'Lucky?' Bridget said. 'You're a fucking slave, Simi, just like us.'

'It's different for me,' she said, her tongue flickering. 'I was born a slave, and this, believe me, is the best it gets. Some of my previous masters...' She shuddered.

Killop gazed at the young Rahain woman, as she closed her eyes for a moment.

'Whereas you,' she said, opening them again, 'knew freedom all your lives, until the soldiers came and took you away.'

'It was a bit more complicated than that,' Killop said.

'Was it?' Simiona shot back. 'I know next to nothing about the war to conquer your lands. I've heard the propaganda, of course, about the noble and valiant Rahain army, and their glorious victories, but I doubt if every second word of that was true. So tell me, what was it like?'

'A nightmare,' Kallie said.

Killop looked at the floor, memories flooding him. What could he say to Simiona, that could make her understand what they had been through?

'The Rahain took everything they could,' Bridget said. 'Destroyed everything else.'

'I'm sorry,' Simiona whispered.

The bell rang once, breaking into the sombre silence of the common room.

'That will be the professor,' Simiona said.

They waited for the bell to ring twice, then stood, and went into the hall.

'Good morning, everyone,' Professor Geolaid greeted them, pausing by the door to the classroom. Her long, flowing black robes swung as she turned. She noted the downcast looks on their faces.

'Oh dear,' she said. 'And what have you been talking about this morning?'

'The war, professor,' said Simiona.

Geolaid's expression darkened.

'Stupid girl,' she glowered at her. 'The war is not an appropriate topic for you to be discussing with the Kellach Brigdomin. Am I understood, slave?'

'Yes, professor. My apologies.'

Without another word, Geolaid strode into the classroom.

'Didn't mean to get you into trouble,' Bridget said.

Killop felt ire on Simiona's behalf. Geolaid treated her as just another slave, and often spoke to her out of turn, humiliating her when she offered a contrary opinion, and constantly playing down her role in the work they were doing. The professor spoke to them, the reputedly savage barbarians, with more respect than she did Simiona.

'She feels threatened by you,' he said. 'She can't stand that you know more than her.'

'The professor is an eminent and accomplished scholar,' Simiona said, 'for whom I have complete respect.'

Bridget sniggered as they turned and walked into the classroom.

The morning dragged for Killop, as so many of them did. He had to read out loud, and answer questions about little Toam and Tyella's trip to their uncle's farm, while Bridget shook her head at him in silent mirth. She had passed this stage a half third previously. While he was still stuck on children's books, she had progressed to more advanced literary works on history and science, and her knowledge was expanding rapidly. She was also assisting with transcribing the songs that Kallie knew, or rather the songs that she and Kallie twisted, and partly created, as they spun their own versions for the Rahain to record.

Geolaid remained in a bad mood throughout, snapping at them, and making a fuss over every mistake Killop made. She left them over lunchtime, returning to her own comfortable rooms beyond the second gate, where she lived.

Simiona, who had been relentlessly bullied by the professor all morning, also went to her own room to lie down, complaining of a headache.

After lunch Geolaid returned, her face grim.

'Stay seated,' she said to them as she entered the classroom. 'I apologise for my temper this morning. I lost a very good friend of mine during the war in your lands, and hearing about it reminded me of a commission that I have been asked to undertake by the patron of this academy. A commission I have been putting off.'

The captives waited for her to continue.

'Councillor Laodoc,' she said, 'has asked me to produce a written record of the conflict, from your point of view. We must document everything you saw, and everything you remember about the war. The councillor wishes this to be a major part of the book he is intending to publish, and the thought of it stirred up some sad memories for me. As it will do for you too, I'm sure.'

'Is that why you took this job?' Bridget said. 'Because of your friend?'

'Yes, partly, I admit,' she said. 'To come face to face with the people that killed my... never mind. Not that I meant you personally killed him, of course.'

'What happened?' said Killop, feeling sorry for her. Aside from bullying Simiona, she didn't seem to be a bad person, and, excepting other slaves, she was one of the only Rahain who seemed to treat the Kellach as people, rather than mindless savages. 'Maybe if you tell us, then it won't seem so bad.'

Kallie gave him a scathing glance.

'Maybe,' Geolaid said, resting her elbows on the desk in front of her. 'My friend, he was not a soldier.' She paused. 'He was a skilled worker of metal, and had taken on a contract as an armourer in the forces sent to the tribal lands. I mean, the Kellach Brigdomin lands. Half a year in, he was with the army when there was a large battle with the Kellach warriors. The warriors attacked the baggage train at the rear of the Rahain army, and slaughtered everyone there, slaves mostly, but also the merchants, smiths, carpenters, cooks, doctors. And the armourers.'

Killop, Kallie and Bridget shared a glance, but Geolaid was paying them no attention.

'It was massacres like that one,' Geolaid said, 'that really turned the Rahain people against you. At the start of the war, there was some sympathy here for your plight, but when word of the atrocities came through...'

The captives rose to their feet in outrage, and Geolaid took a nervous step backwards, her hands rising instinctively.

'You destroyed our country,' Bridget shouted, 'and complain because we fucking fought back?'

'I saw Rahain soldiers cut down old folk that would be no good as slaves!' Kallie cried.

'And they murdered our chief in cold blood,' Killop said, pointing at Geolaid, 'when he tried to negotiate.'

Simiona walked in at that moment, and Killop realised he must have been too enraged to hear the bell ringing.

'Everyone, please!' she called out, her voice high.

Killop glanced from her to Geolaid, who looked terrified and ready to bolt for the door. Killop sat back down into his chair, and after a moment, first Bridget, and then Kallie, joined him.

Geolaid gazed over them, her expression calming.

'I see that this will be a testing time for us all,' she said. 'There will be no classes this afternoon. Instead, I want you to think about your threatening behaviour just now, and reflect upon the fact that I have the authority to send you back to the clearing-house if I feel that your temperament is not conducive to an atmosphere of learning.'

She paused to gather her composure, and left the classroom.

'What did she mean?' Killop asked, as the double bell sounded a few moments later.

Simiona walked over and sat down by the captives. 'She said, if you lose your temper again, you're going back to the slave pits.'

'Is that true?' said Bridget. 'Can she do that?'

'My master would never allow it,' she said. 'He has all kinds of plans for you. What did the professor say that angered you all?'

'Some bullshit about how we were the bad guys in the war,' Bridget snapped.

'And,' Killop said, 'about how we killed some Rahain who weren't soldiers, during a battle.'

'Oh?' Simiona said. 'The battle where the professor's friend died? I remember hearing about it at the time. You, I mean the Kellach warriors, attacked the baggage camp, to distract the Rahain army while you burned their mangonels.'

'Their what?' said Killop.

'Stone-throwers,' Bridget muttered. 'Six of them.'

'You know of this battle?' Simiona asked.

Killop suppressed a curse. Was she talking about Marchside, where he had led a company in an attack of the rear camp of the Rahain? Where he had personally cut down many non-combatants, while his sister Keira had torched the giant stone-throwing machines? Had he killed Geolaid's friend?

'We've heard of it,' Kallie said.

'Many of the peasants here in the capital rioted when the news arrived,' Simiona said, 'demanding the army take revenge for the atrocity. There was a tangible feeling of anger in the air, a taste of which has recently returned, after the terrorist attack on the coal depot.'

'What attack?' Bridget said.

'Apparently a rogue fire mage is leading a band of renegades in the Kellach territories,' Simiona said, a wild light in her eyes. 'They attacked a massive mining operation, killed hundreds, and burned the entire place to the ground.'

The captives stared at her in stunned silence.

'They're sure it was a fire mage?' Killop asked, keeping his racing nerves under control.

'Yes,' Simiona replied. 'She was seen by one of the survivors.'

'She?'

'A woman, yes.' She arched her eyebrows. 'What's got into you lot?'

They said nothing. Killop sat back, in shock. Was his twin sister still out there, fighting?

'Killop,' Simiona said, studying him, 'do you know a female fire mage?'

He opened his mouth to answer.

'We knew loads of them,' Kallie said. 'Every village had one. They all died in the war, as far as we know.'

Simiona glanced from one captive to the other. 'You never talk about the fire mages,' she said. 'I would be very interested in hearing about them.'

Killop stared at the floor, while Bridget and Kallie remained silent.

'That's all right,' Simiona said, a hurt expression on her face. She got to her feet. 'I'll see you all tomorrow, then.'

'Bye, Simi,' Bridget said.

The captives watched her leave the classroom.

'For fucksake, Killop,' Kallie said. 'You were going to tell her about Keira.'

'No, I wasn't.'

She glared at him. 'You're a liar. I could see you opening your mouth, about to tell that Rahain cow everything.'

'Simiona's not a cow.'

'She's one of them.'

'But she's a slave, like us,' he said. 'She had nothing to do with the war. It's not her fault.'

'So you fancy her too, do you? Do you dream about her as well?'

Killop bit his tongue.

'And,' Kallie went on, 'the way you were fawning over Geolaid. "You can tell us, professor, it'll make you feel better." It's like you've forgotten what those bastards did to us. Some nice food, a comfy bed, and a set of clean clothes was all it took, and yer a happy wee slave.'

Killop sat in silence, his face dark.

Kallie stood. 'It's funny,' she said. 'I saved your life at Marchside, while you were slaughtering the carpenters and cooks. And the armourers. If you had died there, then all I would remember of you was that you were a hero, and my lover.'

She walked to the door.

'Want me to come?' said Bridget.

Kallie shook her head, and left the classroom.

Killop and Bridget sat in silence. He went over Kallie's words. She was right about some of what she had said. He did feel empathy with some of the Rahain, especially other slaves like Simiona, and the four that did their cleaning and cooking. How could he hold them responsible for what had happened to the Kell? Kallie hated them with a passion, and without exception, but Killop's hatred had been diluted by seeing signs of kindness and vulnerability in some of them, and he was incapable of hating Simiona just because she was Rahain.

Had he been about to tell the Rahain slave about his sister, when such information could prove to be dangerous for them if Simiona chose to repeat it? If the renegade fire mage was Keira, then the Rahain authorities would no doubt be very interested to learn that her twin brother was in custody in the capital city. He had to be more careful; Kallie had been right about that.

'She's wrong, you know,' Bridget said, 'about you dying at Marchside. She didn't mean it. It was you that pulled me through these last few thirds, and there's no way Kallie would still be around if you hadn't taken care of her.' She paused.

'Is there a "but" coming, Bridget?'

'But,' she said, 'you've got to watch you don't get too close to them. I agree with you about Simi; she's not a cow, but that doesn't mean we should trust her with our secrets. She's been a slave all her life, her loyalty is to Laodoc, and she'd betray us if he ordered her to. She'd hate herself for it, but she'd still do it.'

'I know,' he said. 'I get it. I'll be more careful.'

Bridget nodded. 'Now all you've got to do,' she said, 'is stop dreaming about Daphne Holdfast.'

CHAPTER 13
WAYLAID

R ahain Capital, Rahain Republic – 25th Day, Last Third
Autumn 504

Laodoc glanced up from his book as the waiter approached.

'Your tea, Councillor.'

'Thank you, my man.'

He watched as the servant arranged the cups, spoons, bowls, and a teapot painted with little yellow flowers onto the table in front of him. As the waiter departed, Laodoc stole another surreptitious glance around the busy café. Tea from the Holdings had become very fashionable in Rahain over the preceding thirds, and teashops like the one he was sitting in had sprung up all over the city. This was Laodoc's first time in such a place, the location for the lunch date having been selected by his younger son.

Laodoc cursed under his breath. He should have had someone show him what to do, he thought, worried he was going to look like an amateur. At home, he had steadfastly refused to drink, or serve, the strange foreign brew, finding it risible that anyone would pay to burn their throats with scalding liquid.

There was an almost ritual-like quality to the manner in which the other café patrons went about preparing their tea, involving pouring, sieving and stirring in a precise order. He looked down at the table, his eye catching the little bowl of brown crystalline sugar, another item imported from the bountiful plains of the Holdings Realm. The Rahain upper classes couldn't get enough of the stuff, and when it had first arrived it had sent the nobility into a sweet delirium, distracting them from the growing troubles within the republic.

'There you are, father.'

He looked up to see his uniformed younger son approach, a weary smile on his handsome face.

'Commander Likiat,' Laodoc said, standing, and shaking his son's hand. 'It's wonderful to see you, my boy.'

'Sorry I'm late,' Likiat said, as he sat. 'Took a bit longer than I'd hoped to file my reports.'

'It's no trouble,' Laodoc said. 'Tea?'

'That would be marvellous.'

Laodoc poured, holding the metal sieve over each steaming cup in turn. 'Sugar?'

'Two spoons, please.'

His son loosened the buttons on his tight army jacket, and sighed. 'This is the first chance I've had to relax in a while.'

Laodoc stayed quiet, passing his son a cup, and stirring some sugar into his own.

'You can say it, father.'

'Say what?'

'I told you so.'

Laodoc chewed his lip.

'You were right, father,' Likiat went on. 'The campaign against the Kellach rebels has been, well, not a complete disaster but, as you probably guessed, I'm back in the capital to request extra funding, and more troops. A lot more troops.'

'Then the rumours we heard...?'

'Are all true, I'm afraid,' Likiat said. 'Chasing bands of renegades over the mountains all autumn, it was like hunting ghosts. And that damned fire mage. Ambushing and burning our supplies faster than we could fly them in. Hitting the mines, our camps and forts. We nearly caught her on three occasions, and each time I lost hundreds of soldiers, incinerated. I even saw her, once. It's the same mage that burned our artillery at the battle of Marchside, I'm sure of it. I thought we'd got her under the temple to their fire god, but she must have slipped away.'

Likiat tailed off, staring into the distance.

'I offered my resignation, of course,' he went on. 'The High Senate refused to accept it. They said that out of the officer class I have the most experience of the occupied lands, and I must finish what I started. So I told them I needed another forty thousand soldiers.'

Laodoc gasped. 'And what did they say to that?'

'They're going to vote on it, tomorrow,' Likiat said, 'and then, if the High Senate approves, it'll be the City Council's turn.'

His son looked at him, his eyes dark.

'Will you speak against me again, father?'

Laodoc sipped his tea. 'Yes.'

His son glared at him.

'Because I must,' Laodoc said. 'Because I believe that this expedition serves nobody. However, I will temper my language this time. I will say that your actions have been brave and noble, and no blame or fault accrues to you. You did your duty, as any loyal and diligent Rahain should. But, having said that, it is time to admit we are over-stretched, and pull back.'

'No, father,' Likiat said. 'It's time to do what we should have done in the first place. Eliminate the savages, eradicate them completely from the entire peninsula. We were too quick to withdraw the army at the end of the war, while ragged bands of barbarians still lurked in the high mountain passes. We were so greedy to begin mining, we left ourselves vulnerable to terrorist attack.'

'My son,' Laodoc said, selecting his words with care, 'are you suggesting that we kill all of the native people that remain in Kellach Brigdomin? The children? The old folk?'

'They are vermin!' Likiat snapped back. 'You must not think of them as people. They understand nothing of civilisation or law, or common decency. Maybe if they had remained up in their mountain caves, and allowed us to carry on the work of progress in peace, we could have ignored them, and permitted them to live. But, father, the atrocities they have carried out!' He banged his fist on the table, rattling the delicate teacups. 'They barred the doors of a sleeping block for requisitioned miners, and burned the place to the ground, slaughtering five hundred defenceless serviles in their beds! Serviles who had never wronged them, and who had looked to their betters to protect them.'

He lowered his eyes. 'We were thrashed. Well, not again, father. If the senate approves my suggestion tomorrow, then I intend to put an end to the rebellion – and make an end of the Kellach Brigdomin.'

'Remember,' Laodoc said, 'that nearly two hundred thousand of these savages are currently enslaved here in Rahain. We've had to draft many more brigades of peasantry to guard them, to cover our losses on the peninsula. If the Kellach slaves learn of what is happening to their homeland, there may not be enough soldiers here to prevent them from rising up.'

Laodoc felt a twinge of guilt for not voicing his true feelings, and for disguising his disgust at his son's plan. Let Likiat think his objections were purely pragmatic, let him not suspect his growing fondness for the three Kellach slaves in his mansion.

'Perhaps you have a point, father,' Likiat muttered. 'The troubles affecting the city came as a surprise to me, I'll admit. I can understand the need to keep sufficient troops here, to quell the current unrest among the lower classes.'

'Maybe,' Laodoc said, 'if you were to reduce the quantity of troops in your request to say, twenty thousand, and limit your offensive to the north-eastern quadrant of the peninsula, Kell as I believe it's called, you could secure the mines there, and get the coal flowing in. Then you would be a hero to the under classes in the city; the man who stopped them freezing over winter.'

'And what about the mage?'

'It sounds like she will come to you, if you restart the mines. Set a trap for her.'

Likiat looked thoughtful. 'And afterwards,' he said, 'once the peasants here in the city have been pacified by the heating being turned back on again, I can request the additional forces. By that time the mage will have been captured or killed, and I can clean up the rest of the peninsula in no time.'

He looked Laodoc in the eye.

'Thank you, father,' he said. 'Sound advice. For a moment I thought you had gone soft on me, but I was forgetting how long you've been in politics. Will you vote for the proposal, if I amend it as you suggest?'

'Of course,' Laodoc said, groaning inwardly, having caught himself in his own trap. This would take some explaining to Pleonim's Liberals, and Niuma would probably punch him in the face for supporting the import of coal from Kellach. Also, he was making a fortune from his shares in the Grey Mountain coal mines, the value of which would again plummet if supplies started to arrive from the occupied peninsula. He realised that none of it mattered, if he had just stopped his son from slaughtering a hundred thousand Kellach Brigdomin civilians.

Across the table from him, Likiat smiled, and sipped his tea.

'Have you noted everything down?' Laodoc asked, as his carriage was pulled through the city.

'I think so, master,' Simiona said, checking her hand-written list. 'Matching set of cups, bowls, saucers and a teapot. Silver spoons, steel strainers, and orders for tea and sugar from Douanna's trading house, all to be delivered before Winter's Day.'

'I heard that Lady Douanna is back in town,' Laodoc said. 'If you happen to bump into her when you are making the order, be a dear, and remember to ask if that fierce Holdings woman still works for her. Inquire if she would like to visit us, to see how our Kellach are doing. I think she may well be pleasantly surprised.'

'Yes, master,' Simiona said, a tiny frown at the edge of her lips.

'Don't you like her?' Laodoc asked. 'I wouldn't be at all surprised of course, considering the way she spoke to me last summer.'

'It's not that, master,' Simiona said. 'It's just that Killop and Kallie have been getting on together so well recently.'

Laodoc's tongue flickered in confusion. 'And what does the Holdings woman have to do with that?'

'Apparently,' Simiona went on, her cheeks reddening, 'that time Miss Daphne visited, she and Killop made some sort of connection. According to Bridget, who is the only one of the three who will talk about it, they stared at each other for several minutes, and Kallie got jealous and angry. The two of them argued for thirds afterwards, and even fell out about it for a while.'

'Interesting,' Laodoc said, pursing his lips. 'Tell me, Simiona, are you attracted to Killop?'

The slave's cheeks flushed even deeper.

'No, master!' she cried. 'I mean, he's good-looking, I can see that, just as I can see that Kallie is very beautiful. But the Kellach are so different from us, I could never think of them in that way.'

'And yet Killop and the Holdings woman were capable of staring at each other with carnal desire?'

'Yes, well that's what Bridget said.'

'Do you want to know something very strange, Simiona?'

She nodded.

'The five sub-continents that came together in the Collision,' he said. 'All different, yes? Different species of birds, mammals and so on?'

'Yes, master.'

'However, did you know that the large, mammalian creatures the Holdings call cows, also exist on the Kellach peninsula? And that's not all. The cereal crops, wheat and barley, are also found in both places, even though they are at the opposite ends of the continent.'

Simiona raised an eyebrow.

As she was about to speak, the carriage jolted to a halt, and shouts were heard out on the street.

'Whatever is it now?' Laodoc muttered, opening the shutters on the side of the carriage, and peering through the window at the crowd outside.

'Get down, master!' Simiona screamed, pulling Laodoc by the arm. They fell to the floor of the carriage as a rock smashed through the window, sending jagged fragments of glass showering over Laodoc and the slave.

'My master is a city councillor!' he heard Beoloth call out from the driver's bench, amid the roar of angry voices surrounding them. The carriage shuddered as more stones thudded against it. Laodoc curled up in terror as Simiona huddled next to him, keening lowly. The door of the carriage was yanked open, and arms reached in. Hands grabbed hold of Laodoc's coat, and he was pulled out and flung to the ground.

'Gold-tongued bastard!' someone shouted, his accent low and coarse. 'Kill him!'

'Torture the shit out of him first!' a woman cried.

'Hold on!' an older voice called out. 'Calm yourselves. If this old boy really is a city councillor, we can use him to bargain for food and fuel. He'll be worth nothing to us dead.'

Laodoc opened his eyes, his hands trembling. He had urinated, and he noticed that the seat of his trousers felt warm and wet. To his left Simiona was swaying back and forth, her eyes wide in terror, while Beoloth lay prone to his right, unconscious from a blow to his head, blood trickling from his left temple.

'Urgh!' the woman laughed. 'He's gone and pissed himself.'

'Who are you?' Laodoc said, his voice shaky, as he pulled himself into a sitting position, his back against a carriage wheel. There were about a dozen peasants in front of him, armed with clubs and long knives.

'Are you a councillor, then?' a man asked.

'I am,' he whispered.

'Which party?' asked another.

'The Liberals.'

'We probably shouldn't kill him,' the older one said. 'Aren't the

Liberals meant to be on our side? Didn't they vote for the heating fuel to be shared with our districts?'

'I was hoping he was a Conservative,' the woman said, looking disappointed. 'Then we could have eaten him.'

'We should still string the bastard up!' another butted in. 'All politicians are the same. Doesn't matter what colour you paint gaien-dung, it's still shit under the surface.'

A younger man ran over from the right. 'Soldiers,' he cried, 'coming up the road!'

'Let's get out of here!' the older man shouted.

As the peasants started to scatter, one approached.

He spat on Simiona. 'Fucking slut, whoring yourself out to these gold-tongued bastards.' He pulled back his right foot to kick her.

An impotent fury rose up in Laodoc, as Simiona raised her arms to shield her face.

'Don't touch her!' Laodoc tried to shout.

The man turned towards him, a mocking grin on his face. He pulled a knife from his belt.

The first crossbow bolt took him in the throat, the second and third buried themselves deep in his chest. He flew backwards, landing sprawled out on the cobbled road.

'Encircle the carriage!' an officer yelled, as soldiers ran up to where Laodoc sat, their crossbows trained on the fleeing peasantry.

'Councillor!' the young lieutenant shouted. 'Are you injured?'

The officer ran over to him, placing her hand on Laodoc's shoulder.

'A few cuts and bruises only,' he replied, his voice high and reedy. 'Thanks to your timely arrival. Help me to stand would you, my dear.'

The lieutenant offered her hand, and assisted Laodoc as he gingerly stood. His heart was racing, and he felt out of breath. Simiona also stumbled to her feet.

'Thank you, master,' she whispered, clutching his arm.

Laodoc frowned. He had done nothing to deserve any thanks. He looked at the slave, who was glancing over at the body of the dead peasant. The thought of her being hurt appalled him, and he felt himself getting angry again just thinking of the way that peasant had spoken to her. What would he have done if the man had attacked her with the knife? He grimaced in pain.

Simiona frowned at him. 'Are you all right?'

He cared for her, he realised. Not in the way insinuated by that filthy peasant, but as he loved his own sons. Except she needed him, depended on him for every detail of her servile existence, whereas his pig-headed sons required him for nothing. He also knew that she could never love him in return, not while he was her owner, and she a possession. Yet he longed for her love, as a father craves his children's love, while knowing he had no right to expect or demand it.

'Just a little shaken up,' he said, his hand brushing some loose strands of hair from her face. He started to cry.

'I think the councillor might be in shock,' the officer said to Simiona. 'Let's get him back into the carriage. We shall escort you home.'

'Thank you, Lieutenant,' Simiona said. She took Laodoc's hand.

He remained silent, not trusting himself to speak. Caring about one of his slaves. How Stoelica and his sons would laugh.

The lieutenant sat with them on the way home, once the broken glass had been swept from the carriage floor.

'Armed bands of belligerent peasants have been waylaying the nobility with ever more frequency,' she was saying, as Simiona nodded. 'The relative light and warmth of the caverns in these quarters attracts them, and then they come face to face with their betters, and are filled with rage and jealousy. We've had road blocks set up around most of the areas where the nobility live, but there are so many tunnels, and we haven't enough soldiers, frankly, to keep them all out.'

Laodoc sighed, as the young officer spoke on. His tremors were subsiding, but he felt nauseous, and had a raging headache behind his temples. He was too old for this excitement, and he yearned for a cup of tea, despite only having his first sip of the stuff a few hours before. He gazed out of the smashed carriage window, watching the soldiers march alongside them.

The tunnel opened up into an enormous cavern, close to where he lived. Ahead, a soldier from a different detachment was holding up the traffic. As their carriage lurched to a halt, Laodoc saw the reason why.

Approaching along a road from the left was a long procession of chained Kellach slaves, walking four abreast. Simiona let out a stifled gasp, and the lieutenant quietened, and they watched the slaves march along the road ahead of them.

There were dozens of soldiers on duty, with crossbows trained on each side of the column, and pikes at the rear to urge the slaves on. The Kellach were in a pitiable state, ragged, filthy, with long red weals down their skin from repeated flogging. They were emaciated, and many were covered in sores, suffering the effects of malnutrition, parasitic infestation and infection. Laodoc blinked as he forced an emotional distance in his mind, trying not to see what was plainly evident before his eyes, trying to recall the way he had previously viewed these people, as savages. Animals. Dumb brutes. It was no good. He closed his eyes, overwhelmed by the intrusion into his mind of a vision of Killop, Kallie and Bridget in that slave procession, and he bowed his head, screwing his eyes shut, and biting his lip.

Laodoc clung onto his composure. He was a gentleman of Rahain, he told himself, unaccustomed to displaying his emotions in public.

After an eternity, the carriage lurched forwards, and he opened his eyes. The young officer was looking out of the window, while Simiona was gazing up at him, a sad smile on her face.

'I think,' he said, forcing calmness into his voice, 'that our little brush with the peasants has left me feeling rather dizzy.'

'I would recommend, sir,' the officer said, 'that you retain a small bodyguard when venturing outside for the immediate future. I know many of your station who have taken such precautions.'

'Yes, perhaps that would be a sensible idea.'

As the officer continued to talk about possible arrangements of guards, Laodoc's thoughts drifted back to Killop. What a perfect body-guard he would make. His size alone would put off all but the most desperate of freezing and hungry peasants. He would become the talk of the city, of course. A councillor with a Kellach bodyguard? Would he be praised or mocked? More importantly, would Killop do it? Would he try to escape if he knew that Kallie and Bridget remained locked up in the secure area of the mansion while he was out?

He needed to test his idea.

A hint of a smile edged its way back onto his lips, as he thought of the perfect way.

CHAPTER 14
SILVERSTREAM

Silverstream, Rahain Republic – 26th Day, Last Third Autumn 504

Shella pulled her coat around her, the heavy flakes swirling through the air blocking her view of the others on the hillside.

'Damn cold,' she heard Pavu curse ahead of her, as they climbed the rough slope. 'Damn snow.'

It had been a shock when it had arrived a few days before, snow being unknown in the Rakanese wetlands. At first some had thought it another ash-fall, but with the volcano scores of miles behind them, Shella had known better. When it had started to land, many had cried and leapt like children, as they discovered the flakes to be merely frozen water, and drinkable.

The novelty had worn off for Shella, as she trudged up the steep hill. The snow lightened, and passed away, as they reached the summit. The sun was halfway up the eastern sky, and was shining through a gap in the clouds, transforming the snow-covered valley below into a sheet of dazzling white, dotted with the dark marks of hundreds of tents. The trees that had once stood in this valley had been felled for firewood, and Shella could make out the smudges of stump clusters near the fast-flowing stream that rushed through the middle of the camp.

'Quite a sight, boss,' Pavu said. 'We've made it.'

Shella shook her head. 'Let's just see what Rijon has to say, once he's done his sighting.'

She knew the valley would be hard to leave. It had been the first fertile, green place they had seen since crossing the basalt desert, with grass, woodlands, and the bright little river. It had seemed like paradise to many, who were starting to look upon it as home.

But it was too small. The trees had been cut down, and the local wildlife hunted to scarcity. More importantly, the water supply was nowhere near sufficient for the three hundred thousand refugees that had survived the desert, half the number that had left Arakhanah the previous summer. Looking down upon the densely inhabited camp, Shella realised that Obli had guessed right, when she had spoken on the day the volcano had nearly destroyed them all. It had also been the day when Shella had assumed temporary control of the migration, as Obli was incapacitated by her head injury for almost a third. Even after she had recovered, she continued to delegate to Shella much of the day to day running of the marches and camps, acknowledging her sister's undoubted expertise.

Not that Shella had ever felt like an expert in anything, except the dark art of killing. During Obli's absence, a hand-picked cadre of brutalised mages had accompanied Shella on her endless tours around the camps, quelling trouble and ruthlessly keeping order. And somehow, it had worked. The people had picked themselves up from the barren rock of the desert every morning, and kept walking. Day after day, through agonies of dust and thirst until, finally, they had crawled out into this valley. Three hundred thousand corpses littered their path back to Arakhanah, desiccated and discarded like a painful sloughing off of skin, but the survivors still stood, their dreams of a new home nearly fulfilled.

Obli was now like a goddess to the migrants, who said prayers daily for her health, and lined up for hours to get even the merest glimpse of her passing. In contrast, Shella was looked upon with terror, and her mages vilified and hated. Shella marvelled at the way her sister seemed to bear none of the responsibility or blame for the ruthlessness of the mage cadre, despite being the one who had given the orders.

She glanced at the black-robed Holdings man next to her. 'You ready, Rijon?'

'I am, madam mage.'

Although she still mistrusted him, she had grown to respect the Holdings man's strength of will, and the hardiness he had displayed throughout the migration. She had never heard him complain about hunger, or exhaustion, and he had never once refused to perform a sighting for them.

Shella remembered his previous vision, and the reaction he had provoked, when he had smiled and told them that they were only a day's march from the valley where they now camped. The news had almost caused a stampede, as the people's desperation threatened to turn into mass hysteria. In the end, the leaders had stepped aside, and let them run.

'The view is excellent from up here,' Rijon went on, sitting on a rock. 'Do you see that ridge on the horizon, to the south-west?' He pointed. 'That is the northern end of the great Tahrana Valley that runs between the Grey Mountains and the uplands where the Rahain have their underground cities. I don't think you want to go in that direction. Directly to the south, all our information tells us that the land lies empty, and there is a place where two tributaries join, forming a wide river that flows all the way to the sea-cliffs. I doubt my abilities will stretch as far as seeing to that distance, but if I can locate the northern tributary river, which runs from the Grey Mountains somewhere ahead, that will give you a target to aim for.'

Shella sat down next to him. His eyes glazed over, and his mouth opened, as he entered his sighting trance. She pulled a small flask from a pocket in her winter coat, and drank some of the nasty spirits that Sami had procured for her. She grimaced, but the liquid warmed her, and took the edge off the bitter wind.

The guards on the hilltop with them were standing around in small groups, looking bored. She had left her mages at the camp, seeing no need to bring them all the way up the wind-blasted rock. Pavu stamped his feet, and rubbed his gloved hands together.

'It's so cold,' he said.

'Wow, I have a genius for a brother,' Shella replied. 'Maybe we could train you to perform some tricks for our entertainment.'

Pavu scowled. 'Why must you always be like that?'

'I guess it amuses me,' she said, shrugging. 'At least I can choose when to be a sarcastic bitch. You're stuck with being stupid.'

He walked off, huffing.

Shella chuckled to herself, just as Rijon came out of his trance. He gasped, his head lolling forwards, and Shella held his arm to stop him falling off the rock. She offered him a flask of water, which he took without speaking. He drank, then retched the water back up again, holding onto his stomach in pain.

'I would sell my grandmother for a cup of tea and a cigarette,' he groaned.

'I have a bag of fire-roasted ants.'

Rijon retched again, shaking his head in disgust. She laughed.

'How you can eat insects, is beyond me,' he said.

She shrugged. 'They're tasty.'

'Anyway,' he said, shaking his head. 'Bad news, I'm afraid. No sign of the northern tributary yet, for at least five days' march. I can take another look then.'

Shella swore.

'On the bright side,' he said, 'there are several other streams along the way, and plenty of forestland filled with furry things to hunt, birds to net, and, no doubt, lots of insects for you to enjoy.'

She nodded.

'May I ask what you're planning?' he said, sipping from the water flask.

'Simple, really,' she said. 'I've amalgamated all of the remaining districts into twenty new ones, and intend on sending them south one by one, each leaving a few days after the previous one, and taking a slightly different route. It'll take more than a third to get them all moving, but hopefully by the time the last one leaves, the first will already be at this great river you keep talking about.'

'I would imagine so,' he replied. 'I estimate it is about fifteen to twenty days south of here.'

'Then I shall have scouts sent out today,' she said. 'The sooner we get there the better. We'll need to set up spawning pools as soon as the first settlers reach the river, to get ready for the flood of children about to arrive.'

He raised an eyebrow.

'There will be tens of thousands of women down there who will be pregnant,' she said, looking at him like he was stupid.

'What?' he replied. 'Already? But we've only been here a few days, surely there hasn't been enough time.'

'What are you talking about?' she asked. 'Are you an idiot? Most of them will have been pregnant since before the migration even started. In fact every pregnant woman in the city without a licence probably joined the march.'

Rijon looked at a complete loss. 'I don't understand, there have been no births that I know of throughout the migration, and I have yet to see a woman that looked pregnant anywhere in the camp.'

Shella frowned. She had assumed that pregnancy was pregnancy, and that it was the same everywhere.

'Rakanese women,' she said, 'can become pregnant, but if they don't feel the time is right for having children, then they can hold it in abeyance, until they're ready to go ahead.'

'Abeyance?'

'Yes. I don't know how else to say it, like in storage, waiting? It can also happen without the woman knowing it, if her body is under stress.'

'Like, say, crossing a volcanic desert?'

'Exactly,' she replied. 'Then their bodies can switch it back on again, once the stress has gone. Who knows how many women down there are pregnant and don't even know it yet.'

'Is there no indication that they are with child?'

'Well, your period stops, that's usually a bit of a giveaway,' she said, noticing the Holdings man frown. 'But out in the desert, many might have put that down to exhaustion, or hunger and thirst, and not realised it was because they were in abeyance.'

'How long can this state last?'

'About a year or so,' she said. 'Then, if the woman still doesn't want to spawn, or if their bodies are still under stress, the embryos are reabsorbed back into her body.'

'In the Holdings,' he said, 'things are much simpler. A woman becomes pregnant, then, if she carries to full term, a baby is born nine thirds later. There are no spawning pools in the Holdings either. These I do know about. What is it? Four thirds of pregnancy followed by a further five in the pool?'

'Yeah,' she said, relieved he wasn't completely ignorant. 'That's about right.'

'And our women,' Rijon went on, 'only carry one child at a time, or occasionally two, whereas for you...'

'A dozen is about average,' she said. 'Although numbers in the high-teens are not uncommon.'

He shook his head.

'Come on,' she said, as she saw Pavu approach. 'Let's go before our asses freeze to this rock.'

Back at the camp, she went straight to her tent, and finished writing up her plans, while Jayki and Braga waited outside. She gathered up the paperwork once it was completed, and left the tent. She looked around, noticing the camp was quieter than usual, but also that there was a low roar of noise from down by the stream.

'What's going on?' she said.

'Executions, we heard, miss,' Jayki replied.

More rioters? Strange, she thought. The camp had seemed peaceful since they had arrived.

They passed a pair of militia and entered the main command tent. They were stopped by half a dozen guards at the inner entrance to Obli's meeting hall.

'Lady Kanawara is indisposed at present,' one of them said.

'What?' Shella replied.

The tent flap opened, and Dannu came out. 'We will be ready for you in just a few minutes, mage sister,' she said. 'Are those your orders? May I?' She reached out and took the plans from Shella's hands.

'What's going on?' said Shella.

'A bit of necessary business,' said Dannu. 'We won't keep you waiting long, I promise.' She slipped back through the tent flap.

Shella considered brushing the guards aside, and entering anyway, but hesitated. She could kill them any time she wanted. They knew it. Yet there they stood, creating a solid barrier in front of Obli's chambers.

She tapped her foot as she waited, her paranoia conjuring visions of what could be happening inside.

After what seemed like hours, the tent flap was opened wide, and the guards parted.

Shella strode in, glancing around, not knowing what to expect, but everything seemed in its usual place. Obli sat on the raised chair that Shella refused to call a throne. She was dressed in white, and looked radiant. Dannu and Tehna stood to either side, along with other men and women of the court, while soldiers lined the walls.

'Mage Kanawara,' Obli said, smiling.

'Sister,' she replied, hiding a smirk.

'We have wondrous news,' Obli went on. 'We wish to announce to the Migration that I am with child! The discovery of this fertile land has triggered my pregnancy, the surest sign yet that the gods are with us, and that this country is where we are destined to make our home.'

Shella smothered a sigh, not altogether surprised. 'Congratulations!' she beamed.

'Thank you, high mage,' Obli said. 'We shall proclaim a day's holiday to allow the camp to celebrate the news. And then,' she said, holding up Shella's plans, 'we will follow the instructions that you have described here.'

'You approve of what I proposed? Sending each new district out one at a time?'

'Yes,' Obli said. 'It is a fine plan. It's what you're good at of course, the details. I have just one or two alterations to make, and it'll be ready.'

'Alterations?' Shella said, noticing Dannu and Tehna glance at each other.

'Yes,' Obli replied. 'In particular, regarding the disposition of your mage cadre.'

'You don't like the idea of splitting them up?'

Obli paused, and in a split second the atmosphere in the room grew cold. The guards on either side stilled in readiness as if at an unspoken command.

'Do you remember the advice you gave me a while back?' Obli said. 'And the warning? I told you not to worry, that I would take care of it. And today, I have.'

'What?'

'Yes,' Obli went on. 'You warned me about how dangerous the other high level flow mages were, and I have seen the truth with my own eyes, how your mages have destroyed the lives of hundreds of our Rakanese youth.'

'Rioters,' Shella gasped, feeling like she had been punched. 'At your command.'

'Well, now it must end,' Obli said. 'Has ended. What happened in the basalt desert was terrible and tragic, and although it may have seemed necessary at the time, history will judge it, judge us, as barbaric. But we have passed through the desert, and entered a new age. No more must the people live in perpetual fear, cowering from the sight of the dark-robed mages of death. I could not allow the risk that one of them would harm any of the spawning pools. Imagine the damage they could do, with a flick of their wrist!'

'What have you done?'

'What needed to be done, sister,' Obli said. 'I have removed the threat. The people no longer have to live in fear.'

'You killed all the mages?'

'Of course not,' Obli said. 'Do you take me for a fool? Only the high level flow mages, those with the power to take lives. Every other mage is perfectly safe; we'll need the lower mages to maintain the spawning pools and keep the water fresh...'

'And me, sister?' Shella said.

'What about you?'

'I too have killed. And have the power to kill again. Are you going to execute me?'

'Don't be ridiculous, sister,' Obli laughed. 'I trust you.'

Obli looked down on her, and her laugh faded, her face darkening.

'But no more killing, mage sister,' Obli whispered, leaning forward, her eyes narrow. 'Do you understand?'

'Yes, Obli.'

'Good,' Obli smiled. 'The day after tomorrow's celebrations then, the first new district will depart for the south, and I shall accompany them. You, mage sister, will remain behind, ensuring that everyone leaves on time. This is a great day, sister, the first of a new era.'

'Yes, my lady,' Shella said, her mouth dry.

'That is all,' Obli stated, sitting back on her throne.

Shella nodded, fighting the urge to run. No one met her eyes as she walked across the meeting chamber, and she knew they would be talking about her the moment she left.

'Miss,' Braga said as she came back outside. He had a guilty look in his eyes.

'Did you two know?'

'Heard a rumour, miss,' Jayki said as they started to walk back to her tent. The inner circle was still quiet, and the low roar of voices over by the river had decreased since she had last been outside.

'How did it happen?' she said.

Her guards looked at each other. Braga shrugged. 'Soldiers surrounded them while they were having breakfast this morning,' he said. 'The guy ropes were cut, and the tent was collapsed on top of them, and then guards clambered over with knives and spears, stabbing them through the canvas. They took down all eleven of your high mages, miss.'

'Seventeen guards were killed,' said Jayki, 'when Mage Cano managed to crawl out from under the tent, before she was shot down with arrows.'

They reached Shella's tent. 'Why am I still alive?' she said.

'Miss?' Braga said.

'You are Lady Kanawara's sister, miss,' said Jayki.

'I want to see them.'

'Who, miss?' asked Braga.

'My mages,' she said, fighting back her growing anger, and her tears.

'I don't think that's a sensible idea, miss.'

'Why?'

'Because, miss,' Jayki said, 'if the people see you, they will rip you to pieces with their bare hands. They know you survived the mage cull, and hate you more than they hated the other mages put together. They won't come looking for you up here, out of respect for her ladyship, but if you go out into the camp...'

'But you'll protect me,' she said, looking them in the eye. 'Won't you?'

'Sorry, miss,' Braga said, lowering his gaze. 'New orders. We are to guard you so long as you remain here, but if you leave the inner circle, then you're on your own.'

Shella walked into her tent while he was still speaking, not able to stand any more of it.

She had been betrayed, so utterly and thoroughly betrayed. Used by her sister to carry out her dirty work, and when those services had no longer been required, Obli had slain the very monsters she had created. And now Shella was her prisoner.

She wanted to lie down in a dark room, shut herself off from everything, and curl up into the smallest ball she could make.

'Hi, sis,' said Sami, perched on a chair in her tent's living area, Clodi sitting next to him.

'What are you two clowns doing in my tent?' she said. 'And why are all those boxes here?' She pointed to a pile of trunks and crates to the side.

'Obli has put us in with you,' Clodi said.

'What?'

'To prevent you from escaping,' Sami said, flushing.

Shella laughed. 'I'm not sure how you two could stop me.'

'We're not here to stop you,' Sami said. 'Obli will have us executed if you leave.'

Shella collapsed into a chair, her heart racing.

'Then you know what happened?'

'About your mages, yes,' Sami said. 'Sorry.'

She saw Clodi start to cry, as she often did. She really should have stayed at home.

'We watched them being executed,' Sami went on, avoiding Shella's eyes. 'Obli made us. The people, sis, you should have heard the noise they made when Obli had the bodies hung up by the river, so everyone could see. The rage in their eyes.' He shuddered. 'I doubt there's much left of them by now.'

Clodi's tears flowed stronger, and she lowered her head into her hands. Sami put a hand on her shoulder.

'But she spared me,' Shella said. 'I don't understand why.'

'She needs you, Shella,' Sami said. 'She depends on you for so much. You practically ran the entire migration, from the moment we assembled in Newmarsh district back in the summer. Every plan, every order, every detail, has had your fingers all over them. And once Obli reaches the great river, she'll need you again. Who do you think is going to be organising this new nation of hers?'

'But that's fucking ridiculous!' Shella cried. 'There must be dozens, hundreds of migrants who used to work in council planning, or local government back in the city, who are a thousand times better qualified than me.'

'That's probably true, sis, but none of them are called Kanawara. Obli is setting up a monarchy, I'm sure of it.'

Shella snorted.

'Come on, sis,' Sami said. 'Remember when you suggested setting up a council made up of representatives from all the districts, to take over the running of some of the camps? Obli over-ruled you, she said that the migration needed unified leadership, not a squabbling assembly. She promised that she would set up a council once we had crossed the desert. Well? Has she?'

Shella said nothing.

'And look at those who hold the power,' he went on. 'Lady Kanawara, our holy leader. Pavukanawara, commander of the militia. Priestess Tehnakanawara, responsible for the cult of Obli worshippers. Herald Dannukanawara, in charge of access to the throne room. And, of course, Mage Kanawara, Obli's loyal second-in-command, organising everything from the shadows behind the throne. A terrible weapon, too, if need be. Obli's personal killer.'

'Shut up, Sami.'

'She's not going to give up her grip on power,' Sami said, ignoring her. 'Not after it cost us so much to get here.' He jerked his thumb at Clodi. 'At least she and I have roles in the family now. Royal Hostages Samikanawara and Clodikanawara. Obli has found a use for us at last! If only Klebo had made it. He could have been court jester.'

'What have we done, Sami?' Shella asked. 'How could it have gone so wrong?'

Before he could answer, Braga stuck his head round the tent flap.

'Miss,' he said, 'that Holdings priest is here to see you.'

'Let him in,' she said. She wiped her face with a sleeve to conceal her tears. 'Sami, find us a bottle of something nasty.'

'Yes, sis,' he replied, getting up and rummaging in a crate.

'Madam mage,' Rijon said, entering. He looked calm, but there were faint worry lines on his forehead, a notable emotional signal from a man so usually closed.

'Rijon,' she said. 'Come in. Sit down.'

He took a seat as Sami set down a bottle of clear spirits onto the table, along with four glasses.

'Madam,' he began.

'Save it,' Shella said. 'Drink first.'

Sami poured for them all.

'It is against my religion to drink alcohol,' Rijon said.

'Cut the crap,' Shella said. 'I've seen you with that little flask you carry, when you think no one's looking.'

He picked up a glass and shrugged. 'I am a sinner.'

'Aren't we all.'

They clinked glasses together, and drank. Clodi coughed, while Sami patted her back. Rijon, to his credit, looked like he had tasted worse.

He put down his empty glass. 'I have drunk,' he said. 'Now you speak. Why have you executed your high mages?'

Shella laughed. 'Me? Obli did it while we were freezing our asses off up the mountain this morning. She didn't include me in her plans.'

'Why would she do it?' Rijon said, shaking his head. 'They were the most powerful force you had.'

'Fear,' Shella replied. 'Obli feared them, the dark mages of death, she called them. The people feared them. Everyone feared them.'

'And the Rahain would have feared them too,' Rijon muttered, his face darkening.

'What?'

'You Rakanese,' he sighed. 'So wise in some ways, and so naïve in others.'

Shella sat, waiting for him to continue, as he poured himself another drink, and took a sip.

'I would guess,' he said, 'that your people have never been in a war?'

'A what?'

CHAPTER 15
SUMMONS

R ahain Capital, Rahain Republic – 30th Day, First Third
Winter 504

Daphne turned on the hot water tap, letting steam fill the small bathroom. Despite the scalding temperature, she cleaned the blood from her fingers and face.

She dried herself on a towel, and pulled on the long black cloak that she had taken from the man's wardrobe. Her shielded left arm fitted easily into the ample sleeve, and the hood was big enough to hide her face. She picked up her boots, having wiped away the tendrils of gore that had been stuck to the soles, and turned the tap off.

Placing her fingers on the door handle, she paused. Keenweed was pumping through her veins, instilling her with an alert and emotionless calm, but even so, she dreaded what she was about to see.

She pushed the door open, and almost vomited.

This killing had been different.

For the first time, she had lost control. Rage had possessed Daphne, transforming her into a frenzied blur of knives, spinning, slashing, stabbing, over and over, continuing long after the old politician was dead.

Barefoot, she tip-toed across the bedroom carpet, avoiding the coagulating pools of blood and grey coils of spilled intestines. The head was almost completely severed from its body, and the torso was lying exposed and open, raggedly hacked apart.

Had she done this?

Had she rid the world of a monster, only to put a new one in its place?

Douanna had been pleased and impressed with her work when she had visited over the Winter's Day holiday. Three names, three corpses. She had paid Daphne, and provided her with two more names. The first had been a Patriot senator, who had repeatedly proposed blockading the Holding's possessions in the Plateau, and provoking them into a war. Daphne had disposed of her easily, as simple as a push off of a building, an event that many in the city believed had been an accident, or perhaps suicide.

The second target lay dead on the carpet before her. Douanna had smiled when she had described the senator to Daphne, understanding full well that she would relish the death of such a man.

He was one of the biggest slave dealers in the whole of Rahain, which would have been reason enough for the Holdings woman, but his greed was insatiable, and he made even more profit from running illicit dens where otherwise respectable Rahain citizens could go, if they had heard the whispered rumours. In these back alley cellars and rundown old tenements, Rahain nobles could amuse themselves with slaves in an astonishing variety of ways. Torture, rape, murder, watching slaves beat each other to death, all could be bought and paid for.

She had followed him earlier that night, as he had sneaked his way through the dark streets from his home in one of the richest districts of the city, all the way to a large, decrepit house near one of the slave-slums. Despite a shadowy dread in the pit of her stomach, she had sneaked into the building after him.

A few minutes later she was back outside, throwing up in the street.

Daphne had gone back to his house to await his return, her mind growing colder and her rage burning like a blue flame within her.

When he had arrived some hours later, she felt her conscious, moral mind retreat, and her trained fighting instincts take over. He had been armed with a knife, and had put up the hardest struggle of any she had killed so far, but his efforts had been in vain. Powered by rage, battle-vision and keenweed, Daphne had burst through his guard in a second. She had vague images of slamming her left wrist guard into his throat, pinning him in place, while her right arm repeatedly rammed a blade into his groin, but most of the fight was hazy in her memory.

Looking down at the corpse, she felt sorry, not for the dead senator, but for the part of herself that she had lost forever.

Three hours later, Daphne was sitting at her favourite café for breakfast. She had ordered coffee, toasted ryebread with eggs and ham, and a glass of brandy. She sat alone, smoking a cigarette, her food untouched. She should have gone back to Douanna's mansion, but she had been having trouble sleeping since she had witnessed the children clinging onto their dead father, and she was running low on dullweed.

The coffee tasted burnt and stale, but had still cost her a fortune. It didn't matter. Douanna's word had been true, and she had paid Daphne a huge sum for the work she had done. Five bad men and women.

She couldn't do it any more.

Douanna wasn't due back in the city for another third or so, but when she arrived, Daphne would tell her that she was finished. If that meant she had to leave Rahain, then so be it. She had long grown to hate the place. Hate what it had done to her, what it had turned her into. Not that she felt those she had killed had deserved mercy, it was her own soul that had been hurt and sullied. If it had made any difference to the Rahain government she might have been able to forgive herself, but the same parties were in power, and the same policies were still being pursued.

She longed for a friend to talk to, to share her pain. The old servant in Douanna's house was polite enough, but his loyalties lay firmly with his mistress. She missed her old cavalry colleagues Chane and Weir, and smiled at the thought of them, even though the time they had spent together in the Sanang forest had been as hard as any she had experienced. It was Killop that she yearned for still. Even though they hadn't shared a single word, she continued to think of him, continued to wish hopelessly.

'Miss Daphne Holdfast?' someone asked her. A voice she recognised. The voice of a young Holdings man.

'I think you already know the answer to that.'

'We're here, miss, to escort you to the Embassy of the Holdings Realm.'

She looked up. Six soldiers, all in Holdings army uniforms. At their head was the man who had approached her when she had first arrived in the capital, to inform her that she was still wanted by the Realm authorities.

She was sluggish from the brandy, and the lack of sleep, but knew she could take them all if she had to. She checked the door, and loosened her cloak.

'Am I under arrest?'

'No, miss,' the young man said, eyeing her up and down.

'So you're asking me to come, voluntarily?' she said, lighting another cigarette.

'Yes, miss.'

'Six of you?'

The young man smiled. 'Showing an appropriate level of respect, I would say.'

As she looked at the Holdings soldiers, she caught the eyes of two of them clouding over almost imperceptibly. She smiled to herself. Battle-vision.

'All right,' she said. 'Let me finish my breakfast first.'

While the troopers stood around waiting, she drank her coffee, then downed what was left of the brandy. She took a last draw of her cigarette, and stood.

There was a carriage lined up outside the café, and the young man gestured for Daphne to board. He climbed in after her, and the others took up their positions, hanging onto the outside railings.

As the gaien lumbered off, Daphne observed the young man sitting opposite her. He was good-looking in a boyish way, short-haired, clean-shaven, and smart in his uniform. He looked confident, although he was regarding her with a certain amount of wariness.

'What's your name, Lieutenant?' she said.

'Getherin,' he replied, 'of Hold Liant.'

Minor aristocracy from the western plains, she thought. Back in the Holdings, her family would have looked down on him, and her father would have considered this man to be an unworthy suitor for his youngest daughter.

She caught him looking at her.

'What's this about then?' she asked.

'The ambassador wishes to speak with you.'

'Now?' she said. 'After I've been in the city for half a year?'

'I'm sure the ambassador will explain everything.'

She wondered what the young man thought of her. Throughout her life, she had never been considered dangerous. She had always been one of the good girls at school, and then at university. At the academy she had shown promise, and had impressed the combat instructors, but was still regarded as a lightweight by her peers, there only because of her father.

Now, after all she had been through in Sanang, the Holdings, and Rahain, Daphne Holdfast required six guards just to politely ask her to come to the embassy. She saw Getherin glance at her again. That wasn't the way he had looked at her when she had first arrived, she noticed.

'Would you care for some tea, miss?' the butler asked, as Daphne waited in the ambassador's plush greeting room. Lieutenant Getherin sat a few feet away, holding his officer's cap on his knees. The carriage had pulled into a small courtyard in the shadow of the High Senate complex, home to the comfortable and spacious Holdings embassy, the only diplomatic mission in Rahain from any of the other nations on the continent.

'Do you have any coffee?'

'I'm afraid not, miss,' he replied, frowning.

'Tea it is, then.'

As the butler set out cups and saucers on the tea-stand, the doors to the embassy's private quarters opened wide, and the ambassador strode in, flanked by consular officials. A pair of guards entered behind them, and took up positions by the door.

Getherin stood. Daphne waited, watching.

'Ambassador Quentin of Hold Terras,' the female official to his left announced.

Daphne rose to her feet.

'Miss Daphne Holdfast,' Getherin said, introducing her.

The ambassador approached. She had seen him several times before, but only from a distance. He was tall, with skin the colour of roasted coffee. His short hair was receding, and his forehead wrinkled with something approaching trepidation, as he held out his hand.

She took it, and they shook.

'Please sit,' he said.

They all found comfortable seats by a roaring fire set into the south wall of the chamber. The butler served tea, and Daphne found herself enjoying it.

'Made properly, at least,' she nodded to the butler. 'Unlike the savages around here.'

The butler smothered a smile.

'Quite,' the ambassador said.

She turned her gaze to him.

'I have news,' he said, looking her in the eye. 'Tragic news of profound importance for the Holdings.'

She leaned forward, her smile vanished. Let it not be father.

'Her Majesty the Queen is dead,' the ambassador said. 'Succumbed at last to her long... illness.'

The pause told her everything.

'Mages have sent word,' he went on. 'Prince Guilliam is now our Lord and King, may the Creator preserve his reign. He was crowned a half-third ago, on the fifteenth day of the first third of winter, in the year five hundred and four.'

Daphne's face fell, feeling a sadness for the queen that was as unexpected as it was sudden.

'The queen's passing marks the end of an era in the Holdings,' the ambassador said, choosing his words with care. 'Change is afoot. Already we have heard that His Royal Highness has taken steps to end the war in Sanang, a most popular decision with his subjects. His Majesty has also announced that his court will be moving south, to take up residence in Plateau City, which will become the new capital of the Holdings Realm.'

'And the church?' Daphne said.

'We all know that King Guilliam is a most pious man,' he replied, 'but there have been no major changes in religious policy thus far. A high priest has been sent out to join our embassy here, to offer advice, and guidance.'

'However, Miss Holdfast,' he went on, 'I am delighted to inform you there is also news that affects you personally. In her Majesty's will were certain acts and proclamations, and among them, was a full pardon for yourself.'

Daphne's mouth opened in surprise.

'Congratulations, miss,' the ambassador said. 'You are no longer wanted by the authorities, and it was with some pleasure that I tore up your arrest warrant yesterday when the news arrived.'

'Then,' Daphne said, 'I can go back? I can go home?'

Quentin sighed. 'I would strongly recommend against it. While you are under no threat of arrest, there are still many in the Holdings who wish you harm. Perhaps if you give it more time.'

She closed her eyes, and hung her head.

'One day, miss, I'm sure,' the ambassador said. 'Your new status as a free subject of the Realm brings other privileges. For example, the embassy is now happy to act as an intermediary with your father, allowing a transfer of Holdfast credit to you here in Rahain. You can access this fund as of today. Your father has deposited the equivalent of two million ahanes to use as you see fit.'

She raised her head again, smiling at the thought of her father reaching out to her in the only way he knew how, through money. He must have made a fortune in the last Sanang campaign.

'You are suddenly a rather wealthy young woman,' Quentin said.

And one now free of Douanna, she realised.

'Tell me,' she said, 'how does a subject of the Realm gain the legal protection of its embassy?'

The ambassador smiled. 'Is it possible that our trains of thought are converging?'

'Tell me what you mean and I'll answer.'

'I will,' he replied. 'But first...' He waved his hand to his officials to leave, and waited until they had departed.

'It's simple,' he said, leaning forward in his chair. 'To gain diplomatic immunity, you come and work for us.'

'Doing what?' she said, her eyes narrowing.

'Well,' he said, rubbing his chest, 'I would hazard that it would be the same line of work that you are currently doing.'

'And what do you know of that?' she cried, her mind racing, her body preparing itself.

'Please, miss!' Quentin said, rising from his chair and holding his palms out. 'No need to be alarmed. You will come to no harm here, I swear.'

Daphne realised that she had half got to her feet, her right fist clenched, and her teeth bared. Getherin's hand had gone to the sword hilt by his waist, while the guards by the door were poised to rush over.

She sat, running a hand over her face.

'Apologies,' she muttered.

Quentin sat back down. 'The truth is, miss,' he said, 'that we don't know exactly what it is that you do, except that you seem to be very good at it. I have my suspicions. No evidence, though. Of course, as a wanted fugitive, it was my duty to have your movements monitored, and reported back to the Realm. It had been a fairly easy task to keep track of you while you were accompanying Lady Douanna, but once she had returned to Jade Falls, you became a most frightful nuisance to follow. It was a running joke here at the embassy, betting on how long each of our agents could track you before you slipped away.'

'If you suspected something, then why didn't you report me?'

'Understand this, miss,' Quentin said. 'My loyalty is to the Holdings, and no one else. If some harm were to come to the enemies of the Realm, then why would I intervene?'

Daphne sipped her tea.

'We can have a more frank discussion if you agree to join us,' Quentin said. 'Until then, I don't think I should say too much more about what I think you may, or may not, have been up to recently. We would require you to cease your employment with Lady Douanna, of course. Would that be a problem?'

'No,' she replied. 'Our relationship is purely business. Look; I'll need some time to think it over, and to take care of a few things. I also have several conditions.'

'I would have expected no less, Miss Holdfast.'

'First, I would need an apartment,' she said. 'Without a Rahain sponsor I'm not allowed to rent or buy property, and would require you to do so on my behalf. I was thinking of somewhere like Appleyard Cavern, central, comfortable, but not too ostentatious. An apartment with a balcony overlooking the orchards, from where I could see the sky.'

'You have excellent taste,' he said. 'I can have an agent start looking for you immediately. Under a false name, of course, there must be no documents connecting you to the state apparatus of the Realm. Your name will not be mentioned by us in any correspondence with the government of the Holdings. If you agree to work for us, then you would not be paid, well, not officially. However, if we found you a suitable place to live, and furnished it, provided servants and so on, then would you accept that in lieu of payment?'

'If you drop the servants and throw in a regular supply of coffee and tobacco, then we may have a deal,' she replied.

Quentin shook his head in mock sadness. 'Coffee? Really?' he laughed. 'And your next condition?'

'I need you to organise the transport of a horse,' she said, 'from Jade Falls to here. Then find me a place I can keep him, somewhere close to my new apartment.'

'I'm sure that can be arranged,' Quentin said. 'Leave the details with the clerk at the front desk. Anything else?'

'Yes,' Daphne said, lowering her voice. 'I won't kill for you, not unless it's absolutely necessary.'

Quentin sat back in his chair, nodding.

There was a knock at the door, and a messenger entered. Quentin waved her over, and she leaned down and handed the ambassador an envelope. He waited until she had departed before opening it.

His face paled as he read the note. A slight tremor shook him, and he handed the paper to Getherin.

The young lieutenant scanned it.

'Let her read it,' Quentin said, and Getherin passed her the note.

The words on the document described the most gruesome and bloody murder of a prominent member of the High Senate from the Patriot Party, whose body had been discovered that morning by servants coming to awaken him.

'Before we agree anything formally, I must know this,' the ambassador said. 'Will the Rahain authorities find anything to connect you to this incident?'

'No,' she said. 'Why would they?'

Getherin looked over at her, a smile forming on the edge of his lips.

Jorge had been the last man she had slept with, she remembered ruefully, and that had been nearly two years before, in the final days before setting off to join the war with the Sanang. Two years. In just over a third she was going to be twenty-three.

She glanced across the table at Getherin as he refilled her glass with red wine. His apartment's small balcony overlooked a courtyard, which lay dark and quiet beneath them, the lamps dimmed for the night. The air had a chill in it despite the flow of warmth coming from the cavern's heating grilles, and she shivered.

'Here's to working together,' he said, raising his wine.

She raised hers, and the glasses clinked. He smiled as she met his eyes. He had been trying to impress her all evening, with tales of the inner workings of Rahain, most of which she already knew, though she had kept quiet about that.

He had hinted at knowing a lot more. This, she told herself, was the reason she had come back to his apartment, after they had shared dinner in an expensive restaurant. It was also the reason she had spiked his wine with a touch of dreamweed, which tended to loosen people up.

'You were talking about the Patriots,' she reminded him. 'About how you think they're less likely to attack the Holdings now.'

'Yes,' he said. 'But not so much because of the assassinations, though this latest one will put fear into their cold lizard hearts. No, it's something else.' He paused, looking unsure of himself.

'It's all right,' she said, lighting a cigarette. 'I can wait until the ambassador tells me himself.'

'No,' he replied. 'You're right. The ambassador will tell you anyway, so there's no real harm in me mentioning it to you now.' He looked across the table at her. 'This really is secret, though, you mustn't tell anyone.'

'Of course not.'

He leaned across the shadows of the balcony towards her. 'Hundreds of thousands of Rakanese migrants have crossed the border into Rahain territory. There is a Holdings mage-priest accompanying them, sent by our embassy over there. He has made contact with us, and shared a vision with the ambassador here in the city. Hundreds of thousands, Daphne! They crossed over the lava fields all the way from Arakhanah!'

'Why?'

'To settle,' he said, smiling in bemusement.

'In Rahain? Uninvited?'

'Can you imagine what the lizards are going to do?'

'It depends,' she shrugged. 'Have the Rakanese brought an army?'

'No,' he replied. 'They're all civilians.'

She shook her head, leaning her right arm over the balcony rail. She gazed out into the dark courtyard, smoking. She remembered Douanna's husband describing the Rakanese with contempt and disdain, and he was supposedly one of the more enlightened ones.

'What could make hundreds of thousands decide to get up and leave?'

He shrugged. 'Over-crowding? Secretary Joley mentioned a theory to do with migrating toads.'

'Where are they now?'

'Still close to the border, but moving south towards the Vaharin River,' he said. 'That's where they plan to settle, according to the mage.'

'Do the Rahain know yet?'

'The Rakanese must have been seen by now,' he replied, lighting a cigarette. 'If the senate don't know already, they will soon.'

'It'll certainly keep them occupied,' she smiled. 'They've already got two hundred thousand Kellach slaves, who knows where they'll fit the same number of Rakanese.'

'How can you joke about it, Daphne?' he said. 'Have you seen the condition of the Kellach slaves? It sickens me, it truly does.'

Her face darkened. 'Sorry.'

'Ending slavery in Rahain is something I could fight for,' Getherin said, as he finished his glass of wine. 'The treatment of some of them defies imagining.'

Daphne said nothing, trying not to think of the sights she had witnessed in the dead senator's illegal den.

'There are only a few lucky ones,' he went on, slurring his words. 'Or so I am told. Apparently a Liberal councillor is keeping three slaves hidden away in his mansion. He wants everyone to believe that the Kellach are there for scientific research, but the rumour is that he's become fond of them.'

Daphne froze. She had not heard about any of this from Douanna.

'Would that be Councillor Laodoc?'

'Ahh,' he said. 'You know him?'

'Not really,' she said, getting up. 'Excuse me for a moment.'

She entered the apartment, walked to the small bathroom, and locked the door.

Breathing heavily, she leaned against the sink, closing her eyes.

Killop.

He was alive, and in the city.

She knew where Laodoc lived, had even scouted it a few times while prowling at night, though she had never seen any sign that the Kellach Brigdomin slaves were inside. She could be there in under an hour, she thought, then remembered that Getherin was waiting for her on the balcony.

She needed to think of an excuse, anything so she could get out of the apartment as quickly as possible. Killop was out there, and she couldn't wait any longer.

CHAPTER 16
SLATEFORD

S lateford, Rahain Republic – 9th Day, Second Third Winter 504
Killop gazed rapt out of the small round window at the snow covered mountains as they drifted by. During his last experience of being transported in a wooden cylinder, carried aloft by four of the great flying lizards, he had been crammed in with hundreds of other slaves from his homeland, bound for captivity in Rahain.

This time, he was more comfortable.

Laodoc had chartered a luxurious carriage to travel the eighty miles to an estate he owned up on the surface. He had arranged for Simiona and Killop to accompany him, along with the four guards necessary whenever transporting Kellach slaves. They had attached his shackles to an iron ring embedded into the inside wall of the carriage, but had left him alone throughout the flight, preferring to play cards and bicker. He had got to know them in the time he had been staying in the councillor's mansion, nearly half a year now, and although he was still wary of them, he also felt some sympathy for the soldiers. He knew that he had killed dozens of them in the war, maybe more. He didn't regret it for an instant, he would have killed them all if it had saved Kell, but he also knew that, given freedom and a proper education, most of the slave soldiers would probably turn out to be decent people.

He caught Simiona glancing over at him, and he smiled at her. She grinned back. She was unshackled, of course, except for the delicate silver chain around her neck, and she looked as excited as he felt to be getting out into the open air.

Killop had mentioned to Laodoc his desire for a glimpse of the sky and sun, and the old man had come good, selecting him for this trip up the high mountain valley to the councillor's estate. He was in store for some heavy work. The large country house in the middle of the estate had been unoccupied for some time, and was apparently in dire need of some repairs. Laodoc had told stories of the happy times he had spent there in the past, when his boys had been younger, and he had still been married to Stoelica.

Simiona was sitting on a large trunk, listening while Laodoc pointed out some of the sights below.

'Master,' Beoloth called out, from where he was standing by the front window of the carriage. 'We're almost at Slateford Estate. The pilots will be landing us in a few minutes.'

'Everybody hold on,' Laodoc said, as he pulled a belt around his waist. Killop turned to the little window by his side, and watched as the land hurtled towards them. He felt a pulling motion in his stomach, and closed his eyes just as the earth rose up, and the craft bumped down, skidding to a gentle halt after a few metres.

The hinged side doors were unlocked, and they swung down to create a ramp onto the grass. A guard unlocked Killop's chains from the iron ring, and pointed over to the stacked crates and trunks.

Killop nodded, and began ferrying the cargo out of the carriage, while the guards sat about, and Laodoc and Simiona continued their conversation on the grass. The pilots set their beasts loose so they could stretch their wings for a while, and watched from atop the roof as Killop worked.

There were patches of snow in the shady corners of the grove where they had landed. The sky was overcast, and another fall looked likely. The chill breeze on Killop's face felt serene, and he could smell the soil, the grass, and the trees. It was almost like being at home.

The pilots recalled their beasts as Killop shifted the last of the luggage onto the open ground in front of the carriage.

Simiona offered him a flask of water. He wiped the sweat from his face and drank.

She smirked. 'I feel just awful that you did all the work.'

He looked around at the dozen or so heavy crates and trunks.

'I'll let you carry them to the house,' he snorted, 'if it'll make you feel any better.'

'I'd love to,' she said, 'only Beoloth's gone to fetch a wagon.'

'Well, you can help me load.'

Laodoc strode over, a long overcoat shielding him from the sharp wind.

'Come, Simi,' he said. 'Let's walk to the house. I'm sure Killop won't mind waiting for the wagon.'

'Yes, master,' she smiled, cocking an eye at the Kell slave.

He scowled back, making her laugh as she and Laodoc strolled off along the path through the glade.

As they disappeared from view, Killop heard the pilots call from the roof of the carriage, and he saw that each of the beasts had been re-tethered to the vessel. Their wings beat in unison, and the carriage rose into the air. It circled overhead for a couple of turns, then sped off north-east, back to the Rahain capital.

Killop sat on a trunk. The four guards were crouching together over a small fire they had built, struggling to light it, the sharp wind blowing out the matches they were using. He knew he could simply walk over and spark it up for them, use the mage skills he had possessed since his teenage years. He smiled at the thought that he would ever betray the secret of his powers to the Rahain. From everything he had witnessed and heard, it was clear they remained in complete ignorance of the power of a fire mage's twin, and he wasn't about to enlighten them.

It was a long day for Killop, the hardest physical labour that he had undertaken in some time. He felt muscles he hadn't used in thirds ache at the effort of loading and unloading, then carrying, all of the luggage for Laodoc's stay. He had blisters from the shackles on his wrists and ankles, but still felt satisfied when he had finished, once the last crate had been stowed away in a small cottage close to the country house.

The large mansion was almost derelict, as far as Killop could see. It looked like it hadn't seen use in at least two decades. Its windows were broken, and boarded up, and ivy had been allowed to grow wild, and completely covered the western side of the mansion. The roof was missing slates, and the nests of birds flown north for the winter hung from the eaves.

'The old house is not quite how I remembered it,' Laodoc said, joining him outside the cottage. It was getting dark already, a gloomy winter's afternoon. The heavy clouds clustered overhead, and the first flakes were starting to fall.

'Going to need a lot of work,' Killop said.

'Indeed,' Laodoc said. 'I'll have to bring a team of workers up here for a couple of thirds, at least. I think now this visit shall be more of a survey, rather than a patch-up job. Let's see exactly how much needs done, and then I can decide what's what. In the interim, we shall be lodging here, in the cottage. It's rather small, but it will only be myself, Simiona and you who'll be staying.'

'Where are the guards going to sleep?'

'I've sent Beoloth and the guards away on the wagon to the nearest village,' Laodoc said, looking up at the sky as the snow began to get thicker. 'I can't have them sleeping rough in weather like this, and there's no room for them in the cottage. I gave them a modest purse of ahanes, and told them to go and enjoy themselves for the night.'

Killop frowned. What was the old man up to?

'Come inside,' Laodoc said. 'Simiona is preparing some dinner for us.'

Killop followed the old man into the cottage. The room where he had carried most of the luggage was on the left, while down the hall were three bedrooms and a bathroom. To the right was the main living space, a long room, with a kitchen at one end, and comfortable chairs by a fireplace at the other.

Simiona was busy setting plates onto the dining table in the centre of the room, while pots and pans bubbled on the stoves behind her. A crate had been opened, and ransacked for supplies. As well as food, Killop noticed that a plentiful amount of wine and brandy had also been unpacked.

'Before we eat...' Laodoc began, then paused. Killop turned to face him, and saw that the old man was holding up a key in his hand. 'I trust Simiona,' he said, 'and she wears no shackles.'

Laodoc hesitated, as if having second thoughts.

Killop remained standing, watching the old man.

'No,' Laodoc said. 'I told myself I would do this, and I shall.'

He stepped forward, and unlocked the chains on Killop's wrists. They fell heavily onto the thick rug covering the polished floorboards. Laodoc handed Killop the key.

'Unlock your ankles,' he said.

Killop nodded, bending over to release the shackles at his feet. He noticed that Simiona was watching from the dining table, her eyes wide.

'I do not think you will try to escape,' Laodoc said. 'I do not believe you would abandon Kallie and Bridget, but I would like to hear you say it.'

Killop freed his ankles, and picked up the pile of chains. How easy it would be to push the old Rahain aside, load up with supplies, and disappear into the frozen mountain ranges, where they would never find him. He had survived in far colder temperatures than that, and he could hunt, and fish in the small streams. But without Kallie and Bridget, what would be the point? And what would happen to them if he fled?

'I will not escape.'

Laodoc smiled. 'Thank you,' he said. 'Now put those chains away, then go and take a bath; hot water has been drawn for you. Dinner will be ready in twenty minutes.'

'The Patriots have gone a little mad,' Laodoc said, as he poured himself a third brandy. 'That's the only logical explanation.'

Killop pushed his empty plate to the side, feeling pleasantly full, and picked up his wineglass.

'Thanks for dinner, Simi,' he said.

'You can make it tomorrow evening,' she smiled, then turned to Laodoc. 'How many soldiers are they going to ask for?'

'Ruellap tells me that they wish to requisition another sixty thousand servile troops,' Laodoc sighed, shaking his head. 'On top of the additional twenty thousand that we recently voted to send to Kellach Brigdomin. They'll have to strip the farms and factories of workers to meet that quota. It'll be worse than what it was like during the Kellach campaign.'

'Sorry to have caused you so many difficulties,' Killop said, raising an eyebrow at the old man. He didn't dislike Laodoc, but there was such a gulf of understanding between them that he wasn't sure they would ever see eye to eye, even if he wasn't a slave.

'But,' Killop went on, before Laodoc could respond, 'surely there's an easier way? Why don't you send diplomats to these Rakanese, and ask them what they want? If your reports are right, and they have no army, then what threat can they be to you?'

'I agree with you, Killop,' Laodoc said. 'That is roughly what I advised the Liberal Party to say, but they are scared of the reaction from the peasants if they appear to be too soft on these foreign invaders.'

'Invaders?' Killop snorted. 'Hardly.'

'That is what the lower classes believe,' Laodoc shrugged, sipping his brandy at the same time. 'They are fearful that the Rakanese, who breed like flies so it's told, will settle, and then spread everywhere over the whole of Rahain like an infection. The peasants are repulsed by the

Rakanese, and hold them in the highest contempt. You should hear some of the names they are being called.'

'Frogs and toads are among the more polite ones,' Simiona said.

'So what are the Liberals going to do, then?' Killop asked. 'Abstain?'

'That's the most likely outcome, I'm afraid,' Laodoc replied.

'Cowards,' Killop muttered. 'Some of these Liberals seem to know in their hearts what the right thing is, but they seldom do it.'

'All is not yet lost,' Laodoc said. 'If I can work on the Merchants, I may be able to persuade them to vote for my proposal, and if they do, then the Liberals will sniff an opportunity to defeat the war coalition. I'm sure they would fall into line.'

'The Merchants?' Killop asked, then nodded. 'You're right. Those greedy bastards couldn't care less about the rubbish the Patriots say, about how it's the destiny of the Rahain to rule the world. They only care about making a profit, and if you can convince them that there's money to be made out of the Rakanese...'

'Exactly,' Laodoc said. 'Their eyes will water at the thought of picking up some of the contracts that could be on offer if we take a more friendly approach. Trade, cheap labour, a building boom.'

Killop nodded. The old man wasn't all bad, he thought. At least he tried.

'So what are the Patriots proposing to do with sixty thousand troops?' said Simiona. 'If they get them?'

'Blockade the eastern entrance to Tahrana Valley,' Laodoc replied. 'Prevent the Rakanese getting near the city entrances, or the tunnel being built through the Grey Mountains. I think that's as far as the plan goes. I haven't seen the proposal myself, and I spoke with my son for only a moment.'

'I think the Rahain will attack,' Killop said. 'Kill the fighters, and enslave the rest.'

'Right now, I think the senate just wants them to leave,' Laodoc said, 'and go somewhere far away. But if they're still here by spring, then I fear you may be correct.'

Simiona leaned over the table, her wineglass held precariously in her left hand. She was looking a little drunk, Killop thought. He glanced at his full glass of wine. He was wary of drinking in Laodoc's company, unwilling to put himself into a position where he would say or do something stupid or reckless. He picked up his drink. He should relax, it was only the three of them present. The guards were far away, and would stay away, if the blizzard raging outside made the roads impassable for a few days. He drank the wine, emptying the glass. So sour, he thought, grimacing.

'It's funny,' Simiona smirked. 'A councillor taking advice on politics from a barbarian slave.'

Laodoc's face darkened. He rose to his feet and clenched his fists, and looked for a moment like he was going to strike her. Killop tensed.

'I'm sorry, master,' Simiona cried out. 'It was just a stupid remark! I shouldn't be drinking.'

Laodoc stared at her, furious. Killop coughed, and the old man turned his glare onto him.

'You wouldn't be angry,' Killop said, holding his stare, 'if we weren't slaves. This is how slavery poisons everything. It kills friendship, throttles love.'

Laodoc blinked at him, and his tongue flickered as he stood speechless for a moment.

The old man sat, relaxed, and picked up his brandy glass, finding it empty. 'Simiona, I apologise. You are correct of course, I do value his opinion.' He poured himself another drink. 'Slavery,' he sighed.

Killop and Simiona remained quiet, waiting for him to continue, but the old man sat in silence, sipping his brandy.

After a moment, Laodoc stood again.

'If you two will excuse me,' he said, making his way unsteadily to the door. 'I require a short visit to the bathroom.'

Once he had left, Simiona got to her feet. 'Help me clear the dishes away,' she said.

Killop carried the plates and cutlery over to the sink, as Simiona put the kettle on the stove to make tea.

'I am such an idiot,' she muttered. 'I should never have said that to him.'

Killop chuckled.

'It's all right for you,' she snapped at him. 'He never gets angry with you. With me it's all happy, call me Laodoc one minute, then shut up you slave the next.'

'I'm sorry,' he said, still smiling, as he filled the sink with hot water. 'You're right. It's the same with Geolaid as well. Sometimes they don't take you seriously. But with me, well it probably helps being a lot bigger than them.'

'And being a man.'

'Do you think that makes a difference?' he said. 'The Rahain don't seem to bother about that.'

'No?' she said, placing cups onto a tea tray. 'I saw the way Geolaid looked at me the first time she saw me. The same way they all do. They think I'm only favoured by Laodoc because I must be sleeping with him.'

Killop looked over his shoulder as he washed the dishes. 'So, he's never tried...?'

'Never,' she said. 'I admit, when he first bought me, I suspected much the same. After all, that was what I was used to back then. That's why I have to watch what I say when I'm around him. I sometimes forget how lucky I am. I take it for granted.'

They walked to the fireplace at the far end of the room, where Simiona set the tray down onto a little table. There were comfortable looking armchairs arranged in a half circle, and Killop moved them closer to the hearth, then began to tend the fire, feeding in some of the wood that had been piled next to it.

He heard Laodoc come back into the room. The old man stopped by the dining table to collect the bottle of brandy and some glasses.

He staggered over to the fire and sat in the nearest chair, as Simiona poured the hot tea.

'Lots of sugar, if you please, Simi,' he smiled.

'Yes, master,' she said. 'Killop, do you want some?'

'No thanks,' he replied. 'If I want my tongue burnt, I'll stick it in the fire.'

Laodoc laughed. 'Exactly what I used to think, my boy.'

My boy? Killop thought, keeping his face even. The old man was getting confused, forgetting the line between master and slave.

'What I would do for an ale,' Killop said instead, sitting in one of the chairs. Simiona handed him his refilled wineglass, and sat between him and Laodoc, the fire now roaring warmly.

'Simi mentioned that you had a sister,' Laodoc said.

'Yes.'

'Do you know if she lives?' the old Rahain said, looking melancholy.

'How could I?' Killop said. 'She was alive when I was captured, but I've not seen her since.'

Laodoc nodded.

'Simi,' Killop said. 'What about you? You've never spoken of any family.'

She glanced away, while Laodoc flushed.

'What is it?' Killop asked. 'Did I say something wrong?'

There was a long, uncomfortable silence, broken by Laodoc.

'You can tell him.'

Simiona raised her head, but remained silent, her eyes unsure.

'Go on,' the old man said.

'In Rahain,' she said, 'slave children are not brought up by their families. It doesn't matter if their parents were slaves, or if a peasant family is selling one of their unwanted babies. The child is taken away and raised with other slaves. I remember living in a big house, in the cellar, with dozens of other children.' She went quiet, paling at the memory.

'What was it like?' Killop said.

'Please, Killop,' she said, tears forming in her eyes. 'I don't want to talk about it.'

He sat back, his heart breaking for her. He glanced over at Laodoc, and saw the old man cringing with shame.

'And what do you think of this... system?' Killop asked him, as Simiona wept.

Laodoc glowered. 'I don't think that you are in any position to lecture me on my culture's traditions.'

'I wasn't lecturing you,' Killop said. 'Just asking a question. Interesting that you called it a tradition. Isn't that the word used to justify doing something that otherwise makes no rational sense?'

'You think quoting my own words back at me is so very clever, don't you?'

'You're changing the subject,' Killop said. 'I asked you for your thoughts on the bringing up of slave children.'

'The rules are in place for a reason,' Laodoc spat, his tongue flickering. 'Remove one of them, and the whole structure of society would fall apart.'

'And that excuses such cruelty?' Killop said. 'It makes me sick.'

'She's a possession!' Laodoc shouted. 'I own her! I do not have to justify anything, especially to another slave.'

'A possession?' Killop said. 'What, like a gaien? Or a pig?'

Laodoc stood, his face convulsed with rage.

'You can call her a possession,' Killop said, 'but I know the truth. You love Simiona like she was your daughter.' He heard her gasp, and Laodoc's expression changed from rage to surprise. 'You wish she was your daughter.'

The old Rahain fell back into his chair, and put his head in his hands.

Killop looked at Simiona. The young slave woman was staring at Laodoc, pity and sadness etched on her face. She got up and went over to him, laying a hand on the old man's shoulder.

'What are the rules for freeing slaves?' Killop asked. 'There must be some mechanism.'

Laodoc didn't answer.

'It only applies,' Simiona said, 'to those who were not born into slavery. They can sometimes revert to their previous, free state, if someone pays off their bondage.'

'Sorry to hear it, Simi,' he said, 'but does that mean I can be freed?'

She shook her head. 'The Kellach are a special case. You're all owned by the government, and are not allowed to be bought privately. Our master holds only your requisition papers.'

'Simi?' Laodoc said. 'Would you please help me get to bed?'

'Of course, master,' she said, holding out her hand. Laodoc took it, and he pulled himself to his feet.

'Good night, my boy,' the old man slurred.

'Good night, Laodoc.'

He watched as Simiona guided Laodoc from the room. He put down his wineglass, and picked up the brandy. He shook his head as he thought of the old Rahain. He was a good man at heart, but so blinded by the arrogant assumptions by which the Rahain elite lived their lives. It was so obvious to Killop that slavery was wrong, and yet it must seem obvious to Laodoc that it was a necessary part of society.

Killop poured himself a large brandy, and drained the glass.

He wondered if he could somehow engineer bringing Kallie and Bridget up to the cottage. It was the best possibility of escape that he could see, the only one in fact, that he had seen.

Killop looked at the door.

He could just get up, and walk out into the blizzard. He could pack a bag, and take a few of the fine kitchen knives that lay on the drying rack by the sink. A little bit of snow didn't bother him. He could be free in five minutes.

'That's him asleep,' he heard Simiona say, as she came back in. She caught his expression.

'Thinking of running?' she said, picking up her wineglass.

'Don't you?'

She laughed as if he were joking. 'In this weather?'

'You'd be all right in a heavy coat,' he said. 'I'd look after you. We take the food, and some clothes; we could be gone in moments.'

She sat, her expression dropping. She looked scared.

'Please, Killop,' she said. 'Don't say such things. I cannot hope, do you understand? I cannot allow myself to hope. It would break me.'

They sat in silence for a few minutes, while Killop began feeling the effects of the brandy. May as well get thoroughly drunk, he thought, pouring himself another measure.

'I couldn't run away,' he said. 'Not without Kallie and Bridget.'

'It's nice to see you and Kallie happy again,' she said, sipping her wine.

He smiled, thinking about Kallie. She had been improving over the thirds, though she was still depressed and withdrawn at times, and her hatred of the Rahain hadn't dimmed.

'No more dreams of Daphne?' Simiona asked.

'One or two,' he said. 'Don't tell Kallie, though.'

'I won't,' Simiona said. She looked thoughtful for a moment. 'It might be a mistake to tell you this, but I've seen her recently.'

'Who? Daphne?'

'Yes,' she said. 'I spotted her a few nights ago, in the cavern where we live. I was going up to speak to her, but she'd vanished by the time I'd walked over.'

'What was she doing?'

'I don't know,' she said. 'It looked like she was watching the mansion.'

Killop didn't know how he felt. Did he want to see her again, after all the trouble it had caused five thirds before? He had been lying to Simiona earlier. He had dreamed about Daphne countless times since meeting her. He gave his days to Kallie, but his nights belonged to the Holdings woman.

'Have you heard the latest about the Kellach terrorist?' Simiona said, interrupting his thoughts.

'No,' he said, draining another glass, his head swimming.

'She's been running rings around Laodoc's son,' she grinned. 'There's still not a single mine open, and she brought down an entire supply convoy, sent it falling from the sky, on fire, into the ocean.'

'Sounds like you admire her.'

'I think she's wonderful,' she said. 'Finally, someone is standing up to the idiots in charge of this country. She is a hero, noble and honourable.'

'Honourable?' he slurred. 'It's clear you've never met my sister...'

Simiona opened her mouth in shock.

'I knew you were keeping something from me!' she cried, as his heart sank. 'She's your sister, Killop! The fire mage is your sister!'

He shook his head, cursing under his breath.

'Don't worry,' she said, looking at him with a new kind of respect. 'I swear on my life that I'll never betray this to anyone, not Laodoc, not anyone.'

He prayed to Pyre that she was telling the truth.

CHAPTER 17
RENDERED

Rahain Capital, Rahain Republic – 23rd Day, Last Third Winter 504

'Fellow councillors,' Ziane said, his low voice booming out across the chamber. 'The issue before us is clear. A third of a million migrants are squatting on our doorstep, founding a new settlement, or more accurately, a slum, a pit of mud and squalor, and filth, all within a few days' march of our fair and ancient cities. They are polluting the Vaharin River, and blocking the Tahrana Valley. Are we to just sit here, and allow them to swarm over our land like locusts, while we prevaricate, wring our hands, and do nothing?'

The Conservative paused, as his colleagues in the war coalition shouted 'No!'.

'Our Liberal cousins over there,' Ziane pointed at the benches where Laodoc sat, 'tell us that we should appease this horde of interlopers, trade with them, and, in fact, although they hesitate to say it out loud, allow them to settle in our Republic! What, I ask you, will the other peoples of this continent think when they hear of this capitulation, this craven weakness? Will they respect us? Will they fear us, as they should? No, they will laugh at us! Blockade the Rakanese, I say, continue to cut them off entirely until they either leave, or starve.'

The chamber echoed with roars of approval as the old politician sat, his colleagues slapping his back.

Several councillors stood, Laodoc among them, trying to catch the lord speaker's eye.

The nod went to a Patriot called Kaeotip, the replacement for the councillor who had died in his bath the previous autumn. Laodoc sat again.

'My esteemed fellow councillor speaks wisely,' she began, 'but, in my view, does not go nearly far enough. If we merely continue to blockade the amphibians' camp, as he suggests, then there is a high chance they will revolt, and we will have to fight them. And if that is the case, and an armed conflict is inevitable, then we should choose the time and setting of the clash ourselves, rather than wait for them to get desperate. I see, across the chamber, some sceptical glances in my direction, at the thought that these parasites might be up for a fight. But I ask you this, if they came in peace, as some suggest, then where are their children, where are their old folk? Every last one of them, all three hundred thousand, is of fighting age, of military age. They did not come in peace! They filled up their own miserable land, and now they have come for ours! I propose that we demand the High Senate orders a general mobilisation, and an all-out assault on the migrant camp as quickly as can be arranged. We must purge this infestation from our flesh before it is too late!'

She sat, amid uproar. Over half of the members were on their feet, shouting and pointing across the chamber. Laodoc looked over at the benches of the Merchant Party, many of whom were sweating. He chewed his lip, wondering if they would keep their nerve. For many days, he had been working on them, meeting each councillor individually, trying to persuade them to vote for his proposal, and running through the vast potential profits to be made if they traded with the immigrants, rather than vilified them.

Several had pledged their votes to him, but in the volatile atmosphere of the debating chamber, the Merchants looked like they were feeling the pressure. With thirty-four Liberal votes secure, Laodoc needed nearly all of the twenty Merchants to swing his way.

The High Senate had already voted to continue the blockade, so in many ways the posturing of the Patriots in the City Council was needless, however his own proposal offered something more practical. The High Senate would find it hard to stop the council from sending its own trade mission to the Rakanese, and there was a chance that, by the time the legal means had been found to stop them, it would be too late, and peaceful trade would have begun.

It was risky, Laodoc knew. His fellow Liberals were queasy at the thought of alienating the mass of peasants, for whom hatred of the Rakanese was passionate and heartfelt, and had only agreed to support him if he could guarantee that the Merchants would do the same. His old Hedgers, he thought, were the most likely to vote alongside him, their nose for a profitable deal out-weighing any thought of public approbation.

He remembered the thrill he had felt leading his small party through countless tight sessions of the council, their eleven votes often making the difference between victory and defeat. Every other party had courted him, and complimented his acumen, until he had believed himself invincible.

Now, his stomach was tight, his throat dry, and he felt old, and tired.

Laodoc rose to his feet as the lord speaker gazed around, and he got the nod.

'Lord Speaker,' he said, lifting his voice to fill the room. 'Our nation is at a crossroads. We have conquered the Kellach lands, and we control half the Plateau. Our armed forces are the greatest the world has ever seen. We are feared, and respected, as we should be, just as my fellow councillor remarked earlier. Now, the whole world watches us, to see what we will do, what actions we shall take, when faced with this unexpected challenge. They all look for the Rahain to show leadership, but among too many of us, our natural reaction is fear, and alarm, and we are tempted to lash out.'

He paused, scanning the room. Many were shaking their heads and muttering at him on the opposite benches.

'There is another way,' he said, 'where everyone benefits. We should seize this opportunity, lease the land to the Rakanese, and trade with them.' Shouts were now ringing through the chamber at his words. 'Prosperity and peace,' Laodoc shouted over the increasing noise. 'Make of the Rakanese an ally, a trading partner. We don't use or value the land where they have camped...' He paused again, drowned out by the roar of disapproval coming from the war coalition benches.

The lord speaker banged his fist, shouting for silence.

'You will allow the councillor to finish,' he called out, 'or you will be ejected from this chamber.'

The room quietened.

'I propose,' Laodoc said, 'that the city sends a trade mission to the Rakanese camp, to talk with their leaders, and discuss a treaty.'

A loud chorus of boos echoed out, along with a few mocking laughs among the more confident Patriots. Laodoc sat.

'Your proposal is noted,' the lord speaker said. 'Does it have a seconder?'

Wyenna, the veteran Liberal, rose, and nodded.

'Thank you,' the lord speaker said. 'And a dissenter?'

Ruellap stood. As soon as they saw him, the others from the war coalition who had got up sat back down again.

'Lord Speaker,' Laodoc's elder son said, 'there is a word for what we have just heard, although it won't pass my lips in this chamber. At this very moment, fellow councillors, down in the Tahrana Valley there are eighty thousand Rahain soldiers defending this Republic against a swarm of migrants four times their number! While our brave armed forces hold the line against this tide of wanton criminality and lawlessness, there are others in this chamber who would go behind the back of the most noble High Senate, the highest authority in this Republic, and cravenly seek to treat with the enemy.

'For let us make no mistake,' he went on. 'The Rakanese are our enemy. If we do not demonstrate to them that this is our country, if we seek instead to appease them, then they will take full advantage. Does anyone here seriously believe, that if we allow them to settle, then more will not come? It is in their nature, part of their amphibian heritage. Another mass wave will follow the first one, as sure as night follows day, until they fill up our land, as they have filled up their own. Every river, every spring and mountain lake, every stream and every well, the degenerate Rakanese will befoul and despoil, with their breeding spawn, and their filth. They will outbreed us in a few generations, and when our ancient caverns are filled to overflowing, and our granaries empty, they will move on to the next victim. Such will be our fate, if we show weakness now, and such a fate we shall deserve, if we betray our nation and act like slaves, rather than the mage-blood of Rahain.

'Yes,' he continued, to a silent chamber, 'they are our enemy. And those who seek to treat with the enemy? Well, there's that word again, the word I will not pollute my lips with. Any in this chamber who may be tempted to add their vote in support of this proposal should beware that they, in turn, are not tarred with the same word.'

Laodoc glanced over at the merchants. Their leader turned to him, and shook her head.

Next to him Pleonim sighed.

'Sorry, old man,' he whispered. 'Not this time.'

'I, however, trust in the High Senate's judgement,' Ruellap said, 'and favour the continuation of the blockade. Furthermore, in order to place this great and noble chamber above any hint of suspicion, I now counter propose a ban on any and all contact between the city and the Rakanese.'

'Thank you,' the lord speaker said. 'A seconder?'

He nodded at one of the many conservatives who stood.

'A vote is called,' the lord speaker said. 'Those in favour of the proposal from Councillor Laodoc raise your hands.'

Laodoc raised his hand, along with Wyenna, who shrugged at him, and six of his ex-Hedgers.

'And those in favour of Councillor Ruellap's counter-proposal?'

A forest of hands went up on the opposite benches.

'Councillor Ruellap's counter-proposal is hereby carried by fifty-four votes to eight,' the lord speaker announced. 'And it is therefore and with immediate effect, declared a criminal offence to initiate or take part in, any and all contact or communication with the Rakanese camp, and any person therein. The clerks of the council will pass this decree to the jurists, who will appropriately compose and publish said decree in due course. This session is now ended, see you all in the bar.'

Laodoc remained seated as the rest of the councillors got to their feet and made their way across the marble floor to the great doors, which were being swung open. Most ignored him as they filed past, although he received mumbled apologies from a few Liberals who shuffled by.

'You are still an eloquent speaker, father,' Ruellap said as he approached. 'It's just a pity that the content is so lacking.'

'We missed an opportunity today, son,' Laodoc said. 'One that may not come again. One that we may well regret not taking, if things escalate.'

'That is for the High Senate to decide,' his son said, sitting down next to him. 'I understand, father, that you think you are trying to do the right thing, but we cannot allow a mass influx of foreigners to over-whelm us.'

'We out-number them ten to one.'

'Yes,' Ruellap replied, raising an eyebrow at him. 'For now, we do. But for how long? We know they multiply like flies. Tell me, where does it end? Where would you draw the line, father? Five hundred thousand? A million? Three million?'

'How about you tell me where you think it ends, son? With the starvation and destitution of three hundred thousand refugees, according to the august High Senate's grand plan. Or would you prefer, like Kaeotip, to send the troops in to slaughter them?'

Ruellap scowled. 'No, father, I happen not to agree with what she proposes. What I want,' he said, 'is for them all to leave.'

'Back over the volcanic wastes?'

'If necessary, yes.'

'Where countless more would die?'

'Since when, father,' Ruellap snorted, 'have the lives of amphibians mattered more to you than those of your own blood here in Rahain? Have you grown soft in the head? Please don't tell me that the rumours are actually true!'

'What rumours?'

'The ones that tell how you keep three Kellach Brigdomin slaves in your house, despite the provisions of the Slave Bill prohibiting this.'

'They are part of the academy's research!' Laodoc cried. 'They live, heavily guarded, on academy grounds, under the close supervision of Professor Geolaid.'

'In your house?'

'The northern wing, which I have leased out to the new faculty.'

Ruellap smiled.

'Come and see for yourself, if you don't believe me,' Laodoc said, folding his arms.

'I might just do that, father,' he replied. 'Come on, I'll buy you a drink.'

They stood, and walked to the door.

As they entered the crowded bar, everyone turned to look at them, and began to applaud and cheer. Laodoc was about to sidle off to allow his son to bask in the acclaim, when he felt a tug on his sleeve.

'Father,' Ruellap whispered, looking puzzled but amused. 'They are applauding you!'

Laodoc turned, and looked at the councillors cheering. His son was right. The accolades were aimed at him.

'My friends,' he said, 'whatever has come over you?'

Ziane strode forward, beaming, and thrust a glass of sparkling wine into Laodoc's hand. The old conservative then turned to face the crowded councillors.

'Most honourable colleagues,' Ziane beamed, 'it appears we have caught our friend Laodoc unawares. Shall I tell him the news?'

The councillors cheered their approval.

Ziane grinned as they quietened down.

'A messenger has arrived,' he proclaimed, 'all the way from our distant Kellach domains, bearing the joyous news that the renegade fire mage has at last been captured, and is on her way here to the capital, in chains!'

The whole bar roared, councillors from all parties shouting and stamping their feet, grins on every face, drinks in every hand.

'That is indeed wonderful news,' Laodoc called out, 'but the congratulations surely belong with Commander Likiat?'

Ziane gestured to the crowd, who hushed themselves again.

'Your most honourable and valorous son,' he said, 'has expressly stated that the credit for the mage's capture is yours, and that he couldn't have accomplished it without your advice.'

Laodoc staggered as his other son thumped his back.

'A cheer for Councillor Laodoc!' Ruellap shouted.

The crowd cheered again, and surged forward to surround Laodoc, his earlier humiliation subsumed into a jubilant wave of congratulations.

Laodoc felt oddly deflated as he stood waiting for Beoloth to bring his carriage round to the steps of the council building. After an hour of back-slapping, free drinks and patriotic fervour, he still felt hollow from his earlier defeat. There was also a pain in his heart when he remembered the speech his son had made against him. Ruellap had practically accused him of being a traitor, in front of the entire chamber. He knew it was just rhetoric, and that he himself had used such hyperbole many times in the past, but it still hurt.

'May I speak with you, Councillor?'

He turned. It was the trader, Douanna, whom he hadn't seen in thirds.

'Good evening, my lady,' he said, forcing a smile. 'I am at your service, of course. However, it is a little late, so perhaps an appointment in the morning...?'

He broke off as his carriage arrived, and Beoloth opened the door.

'It won't take long,' Douanna murmured, as she walked down the steps beside him. 'We could talk on the way.'

She held out her hand.

Sighing inwardly, he took it, and helped her into the carriage.

'Home,' he called up to Beoloth as he boarded, settling into a seat opposite Douanna.

'I listened to the speeches this evening,' she said, as the carriage lurched off. 'Yours was rather interesting. However, before we get to that, I do believe that some hearty congratulations are in order. That nasty little fire mage, caught like a weasel in a net! You may not know this, but I recently invested a rather large sum in the Kellach Brigdomin mines, and with this savage in chains at last, I may actually get to see a profit before I grow too old to enjoy it. I owe you my thanks, as it was all down to your plan, I believe.'

'My son was too generous with his praise,' he said. 'I may have had the initial thought, but the real planning and execution, that was Commander Likiat's doing.'

'You're far too old for false modesty, Laodoc, old chap,' she said, smiling. 'Anyway, I daresay that this success will do you no harm whatsoever, when you decide to campaign for the High Senate.'

'I wouldn't be so sure of that,' he said. 'It may be over-shadowed somewhat in the collective memory by my other son virtually accusing me of treachery.'

She shook her head. She was quite good-looking, now that he thought of it.

'I do admire your boy,' she said. 'A fine young fellow. Although I find some of his politics to be rather, immature and short-sighted. A trait he shares with his fellow Patriots, and a good few members of the other parties as well.'

Laodoc smiled.

'Your speech, on the other hand?' She paused. 'Quite visionary, I thought. To look past the fear and panicked reaction at the arrival of the Rakanese migrants, and instead see ahead to the future.' She caught his eye and smiled. 'A future that involves us making a lot of money.'

'Thank you,' he said. 'Unfortunately, as I'm sure you are aware, the council also passed a decree prohibiting all contact with the refugees, and they remain cut off by our army.'

Douanna sighed, and sat back into her seat.

'There will be loopholes,' she said. 'There always are. Hold tight for now, and wait for the law to be published. See if they remember to add in clauses about the use of third party intermediaries, or free agents, or holding companies. There will be something in there we can use.'

He gazed back at her, intrigued.

The carriage shuddered to a halt.

She sighed. 'I can only stay for one drink.'

Laodoc stammered. 'I would be delighted if you would join me.'

He got out, and held Douanna's hand as she stepped gracefully down.

They walked through the quiet mansion. It was close to midnight, and Laodoc knew the Kellach would be locked up in the northern wing, as they would have been all day, with him busy at the council. He led the way to his study, where he seated Douanna in a comfortable armchair, and poured two glasses of brandy.

'Thank you,' she said, taking her drink.

'Do you know anything,' she said, 'about the skills the Rakanese mages possess?'

'A little, I think,' he replied, sipping his brandy. 'They control water, don't they? Similar to our power over rock.'

'Indeed,' she said, 'that is their most famous ability. However, it's a little known fact here in Rahain, that some of their mages have a different skill altogether. At the lower end, they can turn raw clay into bricks. These mages will no doubt be hard at work in the Rakanese encampment, turning out bricks for walls, and houses and so on.'

'Fascinating,' he said.

'Not really,' she replied, narrowing her eyes. 'Do you think I'm here to discuss bricks?'

Her frown cracked into a smile. 'Just teasing,' she said. 'No, it's the upper end of these mages' powers that interests me. These few have the ability to transform coal into diamonds.'

Laodoc spluttered, some of his brandy going up his nose.

'Somewhat more fascinating than bricks, wouldn't you agree?' she chuckled, as she waited for him to compose himself.

'What do you think, then, old chap?' she went on. 'Could we put our heads together, and take a close look at the new law once it's published?'

He pondered. He knew Douanna's motives for wanting to contact the Rakanese were different from his, but what did it matter? She had trade contacts, money and brains, and needed him solely for his position in the council. But if he could use her calculating avarice to open up a channel to the Rakanese leadership, it might be worth the risk.

There was a knock at the door.

'Enter,' he called.

The door opened, and Simiona walked in.

'Apologies for interrupting, master, my lady,' she said, her eyes lowered. 'I saw the light on, and wondered if you required anything?'

Laodoc heard Douanna stifle a laugh.

'Not just now, thank you,' he replied. 'Though I do have a letter I need you to deliver first thing in the morning.'

'Of course, master. How was your day?' she asked, blushing a little, no doubt due to Douanna's presence.

'Oh, it was fine.'

'What was I saying about false modesty?' Douanna laughed. She turned to Simiona. 'No, girl, your master's day was better than merely "fine". Councillor Laodoc won a standing ovation from the entire chamber this evening.'

'Then you won the vote?'

'Unfortunately not,' he said, his features reddening. 'No, the uh, ovation was for something else.' He found himself cheering up at the thought that he had assisted in the capture of the notorious killer and terrorist. He smiled.

'What was it?' she asked.

'It was to honour my small part in the arrest of the infamous Kellach fire mage.'

For a brief second Simiona's face contorted in fear and alarm. Poor dear, he thought, she has been romanticising these rebels, no doubt lapping up the exaggerated tales he had overheard Bridget spinning her.

'Please excuse me, master!' Simiona cried, her voice strained.

'Of course,' he replied, as she fled the room.

'Strange girl,' Douanna said, after watching Simiona leave.

'I think she may have had a little crush on the Kellach rebel,' Laodoc smiled. 'She is at a most impressionable age.'

'I daresay,' Douanna said, before turning back to him. 'So, do you think you would be interested in exploring the new law when it is published?'

'That sounds prudent,' he replied. 'Although we would have to proceed cautiously.'

'Of course,' she beamed. 'Just think. Coal into diamonds.'

CHAPTER 18
AT THE RIVER

Rakanese Camp, Rahain Republic – 23rd Day, Last Third Winter 504

'Quit whining, Clodi,' Shella snapped, as they trailed along the muddy track by the base of a low hill. 'We're nearly there. In a few minutes we'll be able to see the city.'

Though she had never been there, Shella felt like she knew every detail of the place, having been supplied with continually updated plans and maps while she had been working in the camp at Silverstream. It took seven days for a runner to travel between the two camps, as one steadily grew, while the other emptied. As soon as Obli had arrived at the great river and declared it to be the location of their new city, she had been sending messengers back up north to Shella on a daily basis, and the flow mage had planned out every detail from a distance.

As Obli had ordered, she had remained behind until the last of the new districts, Juniper Grove, had set out. At first she had been terrified, thinking that at any moment assassins would come for her, and she had spent many restless nights, despite having Jayki and Braga sleeping outside her tent. They were the only guards that she trusted, and she was paranoid that some of the others might secretly be under orders from Obli to do away with her. However, as the days had passed, and more districts departed Silverstream camp, her fear had dwindled away, replaced with a burning anger at what her sister had done.

Growing slowly in confidence, she had decided to bend the rules in a few areas, and had permitted those most reluctant to leave the right to remain. From each district there had been a few objectors, who had petitioned her to be allowed to settle there. Consequently, ten thousand Rakanese were now building a permanent township at Silverstream. She had relocated them several miles up the small river, to be away from the heavily polluted ground where they had first camped, while recycling everything salvageable from the heaps of detritus left behind. Shella had also endowed them with a democratic constitution, with daily morning assemblies, and an elected council. There had been no explicit rules forbidding this, but she had kept the details from her sister nevertheless.

Her conscience felt clearer at least. She had not been ordered to kill anyone since her mages had been executed, and had instead buried herself in work, not only taking charge of the regular departures of the districts southwards, but also the layout and planning of the new city.

Shella looked up as she marched with Sami and Clodi at the rear of the Juniper Grove column. The majority of the civilians were already out of sight round the bend in the track, shielded by the hillside.

She stopped.

'Let's get a better view,' she grinned, nodding at her guards. 'Up the hill; come on!'

Before anyone could protest, Shella started racing up the grassy slope. The others followed, and she could hear Clodi shouting 'Wait!' as she ran.

She reached the summit, out of breath, and put her hands on her knees.

Below her, to the south, lay the great river, shining and glistening in the sunlight of a late winter's afternoon. On either side was a broad, flat plain, that had been grassy meadows and boggy fens, until the arrival of the Rakanese. Now, the entire vista was shaded in browns and reds, from the mud and bricks of the new city. Walls and buildings were being constructed east and west along the riverside. One bridge across had already been completed, resting its length upon a dozen brick piers, while a further four were under construction. The northern bank was the busiest, and was fully occupied from the foot of the hillside where she was standing, for the entire mile down to the edge of the river. Thousands of boots had churned up any land not yet built upon into acres of thick, wet mud. Brown-smeared tents poked up from among half-finished brick walls, and a steady hum of vibrant life rose to her ears.

'By all the demons!' Sami cried next to her, staring open-mouthed. 'Akhanawarah City.'

'What a mess!' Clodi said. 'Why are there no roads?'

'We need to build lots more drainage canals,' Shella said, scanning the city below them. She pointed. 'One there, linking possibly to a series of pools over there. Or the mud'll never dry out. Canals first, Clodi, then dry roads.'

'Do you ever stop working, Shella?' Sami smirked. 'Can you not just enjoy the view?'

'I must admit,' she went on, ignoring him, 'Obli chose well. This is a great site. The way the valley keeps broadening to the south-east means we'll be able to expand that way whenever we need to. This range of hills we're standing on will absorb most of the bad weather from the north. It'll be a fine summer down there. Not as hot as we're used to, but pleasant enough.'

She glanced at Sami. 'The only thing I don't like,' she said, 'is the name.'

'Miss!' she heard Braga shout. She turned to see her guards waving, and pointing down to a company of soldiers, who had come from around the base of the hill, and who were looking in her direction.

'What's up?' she asked, as she approached Braga and Jayki, though she could guess the answer.

'That lot,' Jayki muttered, thumbing at the soldiers below. 'They're not too happy about you running off like that.'

'And why the fuck would they care?'

'They're here for you, miss,' Braga said.

'They knew you were about to arrive in the city,' said Jayki.

'Ahh!' she said, putting on a fake grin. 'My guard of honour!'

Braga looked away, chuckling.

'Something like that,' Jayki said, spitting onto the grass.

Sami and Clodi joined them.

'Not house arrest again?' Sami groaned.

'Looks like it,' Shella said. 'Holiday's over.'

Clodi sighed, and they set off back down the hill.

'Welcome to your new home, mage sister!' Dannu greeted them as they emerged from an arched passageway into a small courtyard in the centre of a finished block of tenements.

Shella took off the long cloak she had been given to wear by the soldiers, ostensibly to protect her from the mud, but the more likely reason, she knew, was to make sure her identity had been kept hidden from the people they had passed in the streets.

Nearly two hundred soldiers, just to escort her. And these soldiers looked, and behaved, differently from the rough militia she had known throughout the migration. They were dressed smarter, and were a lot more disciplined than before. They were still armed with clubs and bows, however, with metals being so scarce among the migrants.

'Hi, Dannu,' Shella said. 'Where's Obli?'

'Her Highness is busy, I'm afraid,' Dannu replied. 'Her afternoons are taken up with hearing petitions from her subjects. She has given me the honour of greeting the arrival of our high mage to Akhanawarah. And of course, to you Sami, and to you Clodi, welcome.'

'Are we going to be living in an apartment here?' Clodi asked, looking up at the towering edifice surrounding them.

'This whole building,' Dannu said, sweeping her arm across, 'has been assigned to High Mage Shellakanawara, for use as living quarters, and for your work.' She glanced at Shella. 'There are map rooms, offices, and all of the archives have been moved here, as well as enough books to make up a small library. Her Highness made it one of her top priorities to have this building completed and ready for your arrival.'

'Generous of her,' Shella said. 'Am I allowed to leave it?'

'No,' Dannu said. 'You are not. Under pain of immediate arrest and execution without trial or appeal. And the same goes for you two.' She looked at Sami and Clodi. 'Do you understand?'

Shella grunted.

'I'll take that as a yes,' Dannu said. 'Everything you require is in this building. The top floors have been made over into your private quarters.'

She gestured to a burly looking soldier to her left.

'This is Officer Tanni of the city wardens,' Dannu said. 'She is in command. She has an entire company of wardens at her disposal, to see to your protection. Anything you need, and anyone who visits, goes through her.'

'What about these two fools?' Shella said, nodding at Braga and Jayki. 'Do I get to keep them?'

'They may remain here with you, if you wish,' Officer Tanni said.

'Bad luck, boys,' Shella muttered.

Braga chuckled.

'Take a few days to unpack your things and get settled in,' Dannu said, 'and then you can start interviewing for clerks and assistants.'

'So this is my life, then?' Shella said. 'Sure, it's comfortable, but it's still a prison.'

'You should be grateful you have your life!' Dannu snapped at her. 'Half of her Highness's counsellors argued for your immediate execution, before you could take a step inside the city, polluting it with the taint of death.'

'How rude,' she said. 'And I thought they all loved me.'

Dannu narrowed her eyes. 'I will leave you now, sister,' she said. 'Pass on word through Officer Tanni here if you require anything. Farewell.'

Shella stood in silence, her arms folded, as Dannu walked away.

'High Mage?' Tanni said, coughing.

'Yeah?'

'Shall I show you to your rooms?'

'Go on, then,' Shella muttered. May as well get used to her new life, she thought. Secluded and isolated, the dark mage alone in her tower. She would have to get herself a long black cape, with a hood, and cultivate her cackle.

'What you're suggesting, Shella,' Rijon said, putting down his cup of rice wine, 'is treasonous. You're advocating the overthrow of your sister.'

Shella shrugged. She looked over the table at the Holdings mage, his face in the shadow of the library's small lamp. He had become her friend over the thirds, and had been a great help to her while she had been in Silverstream, supplying her with information from his numerous sightings of the new city.

'I want democracy back,' she said. 'No offence, but this monarchy crap is not for us. The city is bursting with new ideas and energy, and all Obli does is squash everyone down. This new ban on unauthorised assemblies, enforced by her uniformed thugs, is turning the people against her. If they decide to rise up and knock Obli off her stupid throne, there will be anarchy. All I'm suggesting is that we need to be prepared.'

'Who have you contacted so far?'

'No one,' she replied. 'Tanni's wardens are too thorough about who comes in and out. It might be some time before they get lazy. That's why I am asking you this favour. You won't be searched when you leave.'

'I like you, Shella,' he smiled, while shaking his head at the same time, 'you know I do, but this feels like crossing a line. I am forbidden from interfering in the internal power struggles of other nations. If I take these letters out for you, then...' He sipped his drink.

'I understand,' she said. 'Was worth a try. I would use one of the guards, but I don't trust any of them, and Jayki and Braga are routinely searched whenever they pass through the gates. I must admit, Obli's got me well trapped here. Wardens on every floor, to "protect" me, but really all spying, and telling their tales to Tanni.'

'What about the staff you've hired?'

'They're still new to me,' she said. 'They might all be spies, though some seem decent enough. Polli, my office assistant, I'm fairly sure of. And Bowda, I trust him. Anyone in this city who admits that they used to be an agent for the Spawn Control Board has got to be honest. As for my loyal siblings, Sami spends half his days drunk, and sleeping with anyone he can afford, while Clodi barely comes out of her room. I'm not exactly best placed to start a coup.' She took a drink. 'Yet.'

He sighed.

'Give me the letters,' he said, reaching out his hand.

'Thanks,' she grinned, passing him the bundle before he could change his mind.

'Who are they for?'

'Names and addresses are on a slip inside,' she said. 'Just a few people who I'm sure would prefer a return to democracy. District community leaders, old union bosses, a couple of the craft guilds.'

He nodded, and slipped the package into his robes.

'Now,' he said, 'do you want to hear the report of my sighting?'

'Sure.'

'The new heralds your sister sent got as far as the great palisade the Rahain have constructed across the valley,' he said, 'but their attempt at getting a message across ended the same way as the others. As soon as they got to within fifty yards of the wall, the Rahain started shooting at them.'

Shella shook her head as she drank.

'I saw bolts hit the ground just feet in front of where the Rakanese heralds stood. They had no choice in the end, but to turn around.'

'It doesn't make any sense,' Shella said. 'How did Obli take it?'

'She used the same words you just did,' he said, smiling.

'Well, she's right for once,' Shella said. 'Why won't the Rahain speak to us?'

'Their government is split,' he said. 'I have spoken with our embassy in the Rahain capital, and they tell me that the High Senate keep voting to maintain the blockade because they don't know what else to do. There's a noisy minority who want to get the army to attack, but so far the government has been restraining them.'

'Attack?' Shella said. 'Why would they attack? We see their flying snakes every couple of days, circling overhead, watching us. I can understand why they're curious, but they must realise by now that we're no threat to them.'

'Curious?' Rijon laughed. 'They have close to a hundred thousand soldiers dug in behind ditches and a great big wall just over twenty miles from here. I would hazard that they are a little more than curious. Your priority has got to be building the army.'

She shook her head. 'You know that none of that stuff is my responsibility any more. I'm only in charge of the civil crap, sewerage, drainage canals, housing, roads, and all that.'

'And Pavu...?'

'Is a fucking idiot,' she said. 'It's okay, you can say it. Obli's keeping it quiet, but she made him hire all these old hands from the district constabulary, then put them in charge. Pavu's leadership of the glorious armed forces of Akhanawarah is pure fantasy. He gets to wear all the shiny medals, and the big hat, but he's not in charge of making any grown-up decisions.'

'So you have retired police constables responsible for your defences?'

'They're the most qualified people we've got.'

'And no metal for arms or armour?'

'Yes,' Shella sighed. 'That is a problem.'

'There was one last thing in my vision,' he said, after a pause.

'Something I left out of the report I gave to her Highness. I wanted to talk it through with you first.'

'Now I'm intrigued.'

'South of the blockade,' he said, 'maybe forty miles from the river, I saw a small group of travellers, heading this way.'

'Who?'

'I'm a well-travelled man,' he said. 'Of the five peoples on this continent, there is only one that I've never seen before. Until now.'

Shella thought. She knew of the Holdings to the north, and the Rahain to the south, but her knowledge of the lands to the far west was limited.

'The monkey people?'

'If by that you mean the Sanang,' he said, 'then no. Before coming to Arakhanah, I was posted to the great forest lands, where our people were at war with the Sanang.' He looked unhappy at the memory. 'I saw them, and would recognise them again. The people I saw were not from Sanang.'

She picked up her glass of rice wine, waiting for him to continue.

'Have you ever heard of the Southern Mountain Tribes?' he asked.

'The giants?' she laughed. 'That scary old bedtime story?'

'They are rather tall,' he said, 'but not quite giants. The Kellach Brigdomin is their proper name.'

'What are they doing so close to us?'

'That,' Rijon said, 'is what I intend to find out. I know from my embassy contacts that the Rahain ended a war with these tribes a while back, and that there are many thousands of them in Rahain, as slaves.'

'What's that word again?'

Rijon sighed. 'Remember I told you,' he said, 'about how the Rahain have a custom, where people can own other people, and get them to do whatever they want?'

'I thought you were making that up,' she said. 'But how could the Rahain have them as slaves? How could they force giants to do what they want?'

'With spears at their backs,' Rijon replied, 'and crossbows aimed at their hearts, I imagine. They are mostly chained up, working in the mines, or helping to dig the great tunnel through the mountains. This group may well have escaped, and fled this way.'

He refilled his drink.

'Tomorrow,' he said, 'I'm going to take a little trip. Discover what this group are up to.'

She raised an eyebrow.

He smiled. 'After I have your letters delivered, of course.'

A few nights later, as Shella was amending a proposal for a new canal to link two of the spawning pools, Jayki knocked and came into her office.

He was wearing civilian clothes, his old militia company having been disbanded, and so Shella had hired him and Braga as her personal guards and errand-runners.

'What is it?' she said, relieved to break the tedium of her work.

'It's Father Rijon, miss,' he said. 'He wants you to come down to the courtyard.'

'At this hour?' she said. 'It's past midnight.'

As she got to her feet, Jayki showed her the cudgel he had hidden beneath his cloak. 'He also told me to bring this.'

Shella and Jayki left her office and went down the four flights to the ground floor, picking up a sleepy Braga on the way. At the bottom of the stairwell, in a passageway leading to the courtyard, Rijon was standing in the shadows. The dim light from a couple of torches flickered overhead through the heavy echo of rain.

'What are you up to?' she asked him. 'Sneaking about in the dark?'

'I have them.'

'Who?'

'The travellers I told you about,' he said, restrained excitement in his words. 'The Kellach Brigdomin.'

'Why are you doing bringing them here?'

He laughed. 'They have come in search of you. All the way from the southern tribal lands. For you, Shella.'

'What?'

'I'll let them tell you the details,' he said. 'They speak Rahain, in fact one of their group is a Rahain. I hope you remember all I taught you?'

'Just about,' she said, 'it's been a while since we practised. How did you get them all the way here?'

'Hid them in the bottom of a river barge, and from there into the back of a wagon. We were lucky with the weather. Most people are sheltering indoors out of this rainstorm.'

'And they're looking for me?' she asked again. 'Really?'

Jayki stepped forward. 'How do we know they're not assassins, sent by Queen Obli?'

'They know nothing of her Highness,' Rijon replied, 'or in fact anything about your people, except that they are searching for a Rakanese high mage. They showed me a drawing of your likeness.'

'A drawing?' she snorted. 'Might not even be me, then.'

'It does look like you,' he said, 'and you are the only high mage. Also, their leader said that one of the Kellach Brigdomin mages put your image into his head, along with the image of a Holdings woman he is also looking for. He said he would recognise you as soon as he saw you.'

'Okay,' she said, 'but what am I supposed to do with them? How do we get them past Tanni's wardens at the gate?'

'Just get them upstairs as quickly as possible, and you'll see. As for the wardens,' Rijon smiled, 'I'll deal with them.'

He turned and strode down the passageway towards the courtyard, leaving Shella staring. Braga and Jayki shrugged at each other, then ran after him.

Shella followed. As she rushed out into the courtyard, she felt the heavy rain soak her through. Rivulets were streaming across the brick cobbles set into the ground. She saw Rijon standing in the middle of the open space, grimacing, water pouring down his hood. Ahead of him, six wardens lay flat out on their backs, leaving the gate unguarded.

'What have you done?' Shella cried.

'Quiet!' he said. 'They're only sleeping. We've got about ten minutes before they awaken.'

He pointed at the gate. 'Get it open. The wagon is out on the street.'

Braga and Jayki ran to the gate, stepping over the bodies of the unconscious guards. They unbarred the large wooden doors and pulled them open.

Shella walked through. She was tempted for a moment to run for it, but so strong was her desire to see her sister overthrown that she knew she couldn't leave.

She saw the big wagon, backed up against a wall, the rain bouncing off its canvas covering. The street was dark, and the only noise was coming from the hammering rainfall. The ropes were slick in her hands as she undid the fastenings at the back of the wagon. She pulled open the flap, and peered inside. Six large figures were hunched over in the cramped darkness of the wagon's interior. Eyes gazed back at her from under their hoods.

'Follow me,' she said in Rahain.

Without looking to see if she was obeyed, Shella turned and ran back through the mud to the gate. Jayki stood there, scanning up and down the street. Next to him, Braga's mouth dropped open, as he looked over Shella's shoulder.

She kept going, and arrived back into the courtyard.

The guards were still out cold, and she rushed past them, all the way to the passage leading to the stairwell.

There she turned, and her heart nearly stopped. Five giants were hurtling their way through the rain towards her, each at least two feet taller than she was, and all well-built. As they ground to a halt a few paces in front of her, she noticed there was a sixth member of the group, who was shorter than the others, more the same scale as Rijon. A Rahain.

One of the giants moved to pull back his hood.

'Not yet,' she said. 'Come on.'

She turned, and ran towards the stairs. She led them up three flights to where a whole wing was unoccupied. They were remarkably quiet, she thought. She had expected them to be lumbering and noisy, but they moved with an easy stealth.

She unlocked the door to an empty apartment, and shepherded them all in, while she waited at the entrance. A few moments later, Rijon, Jayki and Braga appeared at the top of the stairs.

'Gate's all locked up again, miss,' Braga said, his hair and clothes dripping water onto the floor.

'And the wardens?'

'We propped them up against the wall,' Jayki said, 'so they wouldn't drown in the rain.'

'What will they remember?' she asked. 'When they wake up?'

'Nothing,' Rijon said, 'except that they suddenly felt very sleepy.'

'That's a good trick.'

'Yes,' he said, 'but performing it on six minds at once may have over-taxed me for a while.'

She nodded, putting her hand onto the door handle.

'Ready?' she said, and opened the door.

She went inside, into darkness, the others following.

She gestured to Jayki to light some lamps, and as he did so, she made out the figures in the room. They were sitting around a table, their long cloaks discarded and lying in a pile. There were four men, including the Rahain. The three male giants were all bearded. Two were dark-haired, while one had long red braids. There were also two female giants, tall and muscled, one with blonde hair, the other dark. All of the giants were armoured in leather, plate and mail, and were armed with swords, axes, knives and bows, both long and crossbows. Each also carried a shield almost as big as she was, slung over their backs. Shella had never seen so many weapons in one place before.

'Boys,' she said to Jayki and Braga. 'Kitchens. Go get them some food and drink. As much as you can carry.'

They looked up at the giants.

'Don't worry,' she said, 'if they want to kill me, it won't make much difference if you two are here or not.'

They looked a little hurt at this, but obeyed her, and left the room. Rijon had removed his cloak, and was lighting the wood in the fireplace.

She swallowed her nervousness and walked up to the giants. Kellach Brigdomin, she reminded herself.

'I'm Shella,' she said in Rahain.

They stared at her. One of them stood. He was the slightest of the males, but looked the most authoritative.

Shella approached him, craning her neck upwards.

Towering over her, the man stared down at her face, and nodded.

He said something, his voice a throaty guttural rumble, the words unintelligible to her, and his companions also nodded, some looking relieved. The red-haired male smiled at her.

'Who are you?' she asked them.

'I am Kylon,' their leader said. 'We've travelled a whole season. Looking for you.'

'For me? Why?'

'We have a mage who sees the future,' he said. 'He saw you in mine.'

'He saw me?'

'He saw you. He told me I needed to find you, to protect you from what's going to happen.'

'What's going to happen?' she said, scarcely believing that she had said the words. No one could see into the future, she knew this, yet the man in front of her held her mesmerised.

'He didn't say,' he replied. 'All I know is that I'm here to save you from it.'

She stared up at him. He was handsome, in a rough and massive kind of way, though his eyes held a troubled well of pain.

'You are the one,' Kylon said, 'and we pledge our lives to you.'

CHAPTER 19
DREAMS OF KILLOP

Rahain Capital, Rahain Republic – 24th Day, Last Third Winter 504

As Daphne lay sleeping in bed, her dreaming mind escaped through a tiny opening under her left eyelid, and the vision skills she possessed but barely knew how to control stretched their wings and took flight. Her dream-vision rose up from her head, and shot out of the window, between the slats in the shutters. Picking up speed, her vision flew along deserted tunnels, through caverns, bouncing from fixed point to fixed point, as she observed the dark, sleeping city.

A small part of her consciousness remained lucid, and watched as her sight raced through the underground streets, always heading in the same direction, until it came to a halt in front of a large, barred window.

Killop's room.

She had looked in here once before, not long after Getherin had told her the Kellach were still in the city. What she had seen then had crushed her hopes. Killop, it had been obvious, was with the red-haired woman, Kallie, and they had seemed happy together.

She had vowed then that she would never look in Killop's bedroom again, in case she saw something that she would never be able to unsee, and she had kept that promise, though she had been tempted at times.

But there she was again, her dream-vision having guided her to that point.

Her vision pushed through the glass, and entered the small, sparsely furnished room. She saw a single figure lying in the bed, and relaxed. Approaching, she realised it was Kallie and, in an instant, she pulled her vision back outside.

Where was he? she thought, as her sight followed the line of the building around to the other side. She stopped, seeing a light on in the big room where the Kellach ate and spent time together.

She pushed through the glass, and glanced around.

At a table, with just a single lamp lit, Killop was sitting talking to Simiona, who looked upset. Daphne could hear nothing. At this point, her conscious mind would have pulled back, but in her dream-state, her powers felt no moral qualms, and instead she pushed her vision into Simiona's mind, remaining silent, so that the Rahain would not feel her presence.

She felt a powerful surge as Simiona's emotions washed over her: fear, anxiety, pity, frustration, loneliness.

'I can't believe it,' she heard Killop say, the first time she had ever heard him speak, and it was through another's ears.

'I'm sorry, Killop,' Simiona said, 'but that's what he told me. She's been captured.'

Who's been captured? Daphne thought. *Who are they talking about?*

'How could they have taken her alive?'

'He didn't say,' Simiona said, 'but she's on her way here, to the capital.'

Now we're getting somewhere, Daphne thought. *It must be the Kellach terrorist.*

'Are they going to put her on trial?'

'I don't know,' she said.

'My sister would never have gone down without a fight.'

What? His sister?

Daphne's vision zipped back all the way to her head in a flash, a feeling so nauseating and disorientating that she rolled right off the bed.

She hit the wooden floorboards with a thud, and retched.

'The Kellach terrorist is his sister,' she groaned, dizzy and weak, her eyes closed. 'Killop's sister.'

'Are you all right?' a man's voice said. Getherin. That's right, she thought, she was in Getherin's apartment. She groaned. Already she was starting to forget the entire dream. She retched again. Was it a dream? Had she just used her vision in her sleep? It seemed she had, if the pain in her guts and the throbbing headache were any judge.

'Daphne, are you all right?' Getherin repeated. 'Here, take my hand.'

She opened her eyes, her sight blurry. In the faint candlelight, she saw the outline of his body, lying on the bed above her, his hand lowered. She took it.

He pulled her up onto the mattress, and she lay on her back, her head spinning.

'Bad dreams?' he said.

'I think so.'

'You called out.'

'Did I?' She couldn't remember speaking, her mind was too groggy. 'What did I say?'

'Oh, nothing interesting,' he said. 'Just ramblings. Best go back to sleep.'

She relaxed into his arms, and he blew the candle out.

Getherin had gone when she next awoke, the light from the morning streetlamps shining through the shutters.

Her vision-induced aches had passed, but she still felt anxious about what had happened. Had she really used a combination of line, range and inner-vision? She guessed that she should be able to use range-vision, lying as it did on the scale between two skills she knew she possessed, but she had never attempted it in her waking life.

She would have to practise, she realised, feeling quite excited. Range-vision would expand the limits of what she could see from a few miles to dozens, or even hundreds, if she was good at it.

She washed and dressed, and put the kettle on to make coffee, using a supply that she kept in one of Getherin's kitchen cupboards.

It was while she was on her second cigarette, relaxing out on the balcony in the morning air, that she remembered what Killop had said.

The terrorist, the one the Rahain had just caught. She's his sister.

There was one way to test if it had been a dream or not, she thought, as she left Getherin's apartment. She kept to the shadows on her way to the embassy. There was a bustle about the senate cavern that morning, a lively air to the officials and politicians hurrying about their business.

'Good morning, Miss Holdfast,' Brookes said as she came into the main reception.

'Good morning,' Daphne replied. 'Could I borrow one of those newspapers, please?'

'Of course, take your pick,' Brookes said, gesturing to the pile on the desk in front of her.

Daphne took a quick look at the front pages. They were all variations on the same theme: KELLACH MAGE CAPTURED!, their headlines screamed.

Before she could begin to digest the implications, she heard Joley behind her.

'Do you have a minute?' the ambassador's secretary asked, his face sour.

Daphne nodded, and followed the man to his office, where he closed the door.

'This won't take long,' he said, 'but I have to ask you. Have you mentioned to anyone at all that you're working for the embassy?'

'No,' she replied. 'No one that doesn't already work here.'

'Are you quite sure?'

'Of course I'm sure. I think I would remember that.'

'Very well, miss,' he said, 'but I had to ask.'

'Why?'

'Unfortunately,' he sighed, 'it seems that your status as an embassy employee has become public knowledge.'

'What does that mean?'

'Don't worry, you still have a job,' he said, 'but some of the work you'd been scheduled to carry out will have to be re-assigned to someone else. You're not much use as a secret agent if everyone knows your secret. It also means that there are certain rules you will have to follow, if you are a public face and representative of the embassy, but on the bright side, at least you will be able to come in by the main entrance now.'

'Do I get to keep the house?'

'Of course,' Joley said. 'The ambassador is a man of his word.'

'Thank him for me.'

'I will.'

'So,' Daphne said, 'do you think there's a leak in the embassy?'

Joley narrowed his eyes. 'We have our suspicions.'

'Anything I can do to help?'

'We can handle it, thank you,' he said. 'Now, I have something for you to do today.'

He pulled a letter from his desk drawer.

'This arrived for you this morning,' he said. 'It seems that even Councillor Laodoc knows how to find you.'

He passed her the letter, and she scanned it. It was an invitation to visit his art faculty, to inspect the progress being made into the research on the Kellach Brigdomin.

Daphne felt a weight in the pit of her stomach. Only a short while before, she would have been excited about the prospect of visiting Killop, but after the previous night's dream, the thought made her queasy.

'I think today would be the perfect day for a visit,' Joley said. 'The ambassador is very curious about what the Rahain have been doing with those three Kellach slaves, and this seems a good opportunity to find out. May I ask why he chose you, Miss Holdfast?'

'I visited them once before.'

'Really?' Joley asked, looking amused. 'How did that go?'

'I screamed in the councillor's face about his treatment of the slaves.'

'Well, this time,' he said, raising his eyebrows, 'as a representative of the embassy...'

'Yes, I get it. I'll restrain myself.'

'Jolly good,' he said. 'Get yourself along there then, and take a good look around. Ask lots of questions. Then write it all up and hand it in. Should be an easy enough day for you.'

'Daphne!' Simiona cried as she entered the front hall of Laodoc's mansion. 'How good to see you again!'

The Holdings woman muttered her thanks to the doorman, and shook Simiona's hand.

'Wasn't sure you'd remember me.'

'Of course we do,' Simiona replied. 'It was I who delivered the invitation for you to come. Master Laodoc is most looking forward to showing you around.'

Damn, Daphne thought, as she realised that she would have to act surprised, when in fact she already knew most details about the house, and how the Kellach were living. She was impressed, however, she wouldn't have to fake that. Despite the fact that they were still legally slaves, Laodoc seemed to give them as much freedom as he was able.

'Tea?' Simiona asked.

Daphne opened her mouth to speak.

'But I heard you prefer coffee,' Simiona said, smiling.

'You have some?'

'We do,' she said. 'I think my master might be trying to impress you.

Especially once he found out you were working for the Holdings embassy.'

She led Daphne through the carpeted halls and corridors, until they came to a door. Simiona knocked, and entered.

Daphne followed her into a small office, where Laodoc was seated behind an old wooden desk. There was a coffee pot and three cups on a table nearby.

'Ahh, Lady Holdfast,' Laodoc exclaimed as he saw her, rising to his feet. 'Greetings.'

'And to you, Councillor,' she replied, bowing. 'And many thanks for your kind invitation. Although, one tiny thing. My dear mother is the only Lady Holdfast, I am merely a miss.'

'My humblest apologies, miss,' he said, his tongue flickering. 'And, of course, congratulations on your new post at the Embassy of the Realm of the Holdings. What was your title there, again...?'

'Liaison Officer,' she said. 'Just a polite term for the person the embassy sends out when they want to talk to someone. Officially.'

'So this could be termed an official visit?' he said. 'And I wouldn't be abusing the truth if I happened to mention it as such in the council chamber?'

'That would be acceptable,' Daphne said. 'I'm here in a personal capacity, but also on behalf of the ambassador.'

They paused as Simiona set out cups of coffee in front of them, along with a bowl of sugar.

'I confess,' Laodoc said, as he scanned the table, 'I have never tasted coffee before. Tea, I have come to hold dear to my heart, so I have high hopes, I admit.'

Daphne spooned in three sugars, and picked up her cup.

'It's a more unforgiving drink than tea,' she said, taking a sip. 'Excellent,' she said. 'Best I've had since Sanang. Whoever made this should be complimented.'

Laodoc smiled. 'Simiona made it,' he said, as the girl blushed and looked down at her feet. 'I had her go out and learn from a café, then she came back and has been experimenting for days.' He sighed. 'It's been costing me a fortune, to be honest.'

Daphne laughed.

Laodoc took a sip, then sucked his cheeks in, a sour expression on his face.

'Yes,' he said. 'Unforgiving. Quite.'

Simiona passed him a cup of tea. 'I had this ready just in case, master.'

Daphne watched as Laodoc smiled and gave his slave a look. A look that reminded her of the way her own father looked at her, with love, and a fierce pride.

Simiona beamed.

***

'Naturally,' Laodoc said, as they stood next to a solid set of steel bars blocking a passageway, 'security is our highest priority, and this gate is the first of two that completely seal off the faculty from the rest of the mansion. In fact, once we pass this gate, then legally we are on academy grounds.'

He signalled to the guards, who swung the gate open.

Laodoc went through, followed by Simiona and Daphne. They had just come from the office of Professor Geolaid, after having been subjected to a lecture by her about the progress they had been making. Daphne had enjoyed the parts about Kellach history, and what they had reported about the recent conflict, but had been bored by the lists of animals, trees and every other difference in nature that existed between the Rahain and the Kellach lands. Laodoc had joined the professor in pointing out to her the strange fact that the Holdings and the Kellach peninsula shared a few animals and plants, but she hadn't found it particularly impressive.

'This,' Laodoc said, as they turned a corner in the passageway, 'is where the guards are billeted, in these rooms on the right. Opposite is the kitchen, the servants' quarters, and Simiona's office.'

Daphne nodded.

Laodoc gestured to a guard, who pulled on a cord. A bell rang once, and the guards at the end of the corridor unlocked and opened a barred gate.

'And here we are at last,' Laodoc said, as they passed through into a small hallway, with an atrium skylight overhead. 'This is where the Kellach live. These are their private rooms, and on this side is their common room, and the teaching room.'

She heard the gate lock behind her, and the bell rang twice.

A door on the left opened, and Bridget strode out.

'Daphne,' she nodded, smirking.

The Holdings woman stood amazed for a moment. Bridget looked fit and healthy, her skin and hair were nothing like the last time they had met, when the prisoner had stretched out her arm through the bars of her cage in supplication.

'You look well,' Daphne said.

'Bored, mostly,' she replied, laughing. She approached and gave Daphne a firm hug that nearly cracked her spine, and she felt glad her left arm had its protective armour on.

Bridget walked with them as Daphne was shown round the facilities.

'It's all very impressive, Councillor,' she said, as they sat at the large table in the common room. 'You really have done a most wonderful job here.'

'Too kind, thank you,' Laodoc said, flushing.

Simiona was sitting a little uncomfortably.

Daphne said nothing, and the silence stretched.

'If you're wondering,' Bridget said, her face reddening, 'where Killop and Kallie are, they uh, thought it best if they stayed in their room.'

'I think they are maybe feeling unwell,' Laodoc blustered.

Bridget smirked, and shrugged.

Daphne ignored Laodoc, and turned to face Bridget. 'May I ask why?'

Bridget looked at her for a moment.

'Killop,' she began. 'He... was having dreams. About you.'

Daphne felt her heart break.

'Tell him I do too,' she said, lowering her face.

'I don't really see how that would help, to be honest,' Bridget said. 'Look; we all saw the way you stared at each other when you met before. It was obvious what you were both thinking. Do you want to risk that again? It took them thirds to get over it last time. Sorry.'

She felt embarrassed, humiliated even, and wished she had kept her mouth shut. Of course Bridget was right. What would she do if she saw Killop? Throw herself at him? She had to remember she worked for the embassy now.

The others around the table remained silent as she regained her composure.

'You're right, Bridget,' she said. 'I apologise.'

Laodoc breathed a little sigh of relief.

'It's been a most wonderful tour,' Daphne said, smothering her feelings. 'Instructive and inspiring. My report back to the embassy will be a positive one, I assure you.'

'Thank you, miss,' Laodoc said. 'Would it be possible to obtain a copy once it has been prepared?'

'I'll have one sent over as soon as it's ready,' she replied, standing.

'Excellent,' he said. 'I look forward to it. Come, let me escort you to your carriage.'

'Bye,' said Bridget, looking at Daphne with her big, sad eyes.

'Good bye, Bridget,' she said, following Laodoc out.

'Thank you for joining me at such short notice, my dear,' Douanna said, smiling as a servant poured more tea, 'but I just had to tell you my news.'

Daphne forced a smile onto her face, and nodded, while Douanna composed herself.

'I'm to be made a city councillor!' she exclaimed, causing a couple of heads in the busy café to turn.

'Congratulations,' Daphne said, wondering if that was what she had been angling for since the beginning. 'Which party have you joined?'

'Oh, I'll be loosely associating myself with some representatives from the Merchant Party,' she said, 'but I'll be free to vote as I see fit. I won't be tied to a single group.'

'Is that normal?' Daphne said. 'I thought new councillors always came from the party that had a vacancy?'

'Usually, yes,' she replied. 'I however, demanded certain conditions, and they were met.'

'I knew you were rich, but...'

'Come now, Daphne, don't be vulgar,' Douanna said. 'Money had nothing to do with it. I merely happened to come into possession of a certain rather valuable piece of information. The High Senate was most grateful.'

'Really? And what was that?'

'Well,' Douanna replied, lowering her voice, 'it turns out that the barbarian fire mage, you know the one who was recently captured, has a brother.' She paused, studying Daphne's reaction, a flicker of amusement in the corners of her eyes. Daphne felt her blood race, but kept her expression neutral. 'A brother,' Douanna went on, 'who happens to be in this city, living as a slave. And, oh Daphne, you'll never believe it, but he's one of the slaves in Councillor Laodoc's academy.'

Daphne said nothing, her throat dry, her heart pounding.

Douanna sat back, and sipped her tea.

'My dear Daphne,' she said, 'at least try to look surprised. Don't worry, I won't let on to anyone that you knew. It can be our secret.'

'You told the High Senate?'

'Of course I told them,' Douanna said. 'It was my civic and patriotic duty. And, just about now, unless I'm much mistaken, several detachments of soldiers should be storming Laodoc's mansion. They would have done it earlier, but I asked them to wait until you had left. I didn't want you getting mixed up in all that unpleasantness.' She shook her head. 'Just imagine. A councillor, harbouring the brother of a notorious murderer and terrorist! And to think that only last night I almost made a deal with him.'

'Do you think he knew?'

'Maybe, maybe not,' Douanna shrugged. 'He's a fool or a traitor, either way he's finished. I'll tell you someone who did know however, that pretty little slave girl of his. I made certain the senate knew of her involvement. We cannot tolerate sedition amongst the servile classes.'

'What will happen to her?'

'Oh, best not to think about that,' Douanna said, pulling a face. 'Punishments meted out to slaves for crimes against the state tend to be rather gruesome.'

Daphne jumped to her feet, her anger exploding. Several café patrons turned to look, and she forced herself not to shout. She unclenched her right fist.

'Oh Daphne, you're no fun,' Douanna said, smiling. 'Leaving already, when you haven't even asked me how I came by this information?'

Daphne sat, but said nothing.

'That mean expression on your face is most unattractive,' Douanna said. 'I hope you made more of an effort for Getherin.'

Daphne's eyes narrowed.

Douanna laughed, her tongue flickering in amusement. 'You have only yourself to blame, my dear,' she said. 'After all, it was you who first asked me to speak with him, and so I did. If it's any comfort, he was in my pay long before you two got together romantically. I was looking for someone inside your embassy, and there he was. He had debts, and some odd, expensive habits, and I had the money. It was a perfect match. And then you started sleeping with him! I couldn't believe my luck when he told me.'

'I'll kill him.'

'Sorry, my dear, but you're too late,' Douanna said, mock-sadly. 'Apparently embassy investigators discovered there was a leak, and closed in on him this morning. Killed trying to escape, I believe. Practically his final act in my service was to inform me about Killop and the terrorist.' She sighed. 'I'll miss him. Who will tell me all your gossip now?'

Daphne seethed, her battle-vision flickering in and out like a coiled spring. She weighed it up. Not there. Not in a crowded place. She forced herself to relax, and stood.

'Thank you for the tea,' she said. 'I will of course kill you if I see you again.'

She walked away, hearing the sound of gentle laughter behind her.

She reached the street and started to run, her emotions racing. She wasn't aware of where she was going, passing streets and busy squares, until she realised that she was heading for the central cavern, towards the High Senate.

Where Killop would have been taken.

She hesitated, and ducked into a side street. She leaned against the wall and threw up. Her rage boiled over and she almost punched the wall in frustration, with only the memory of her crippled left arm stopping her.

What was she going to do? Rescue them on her own?

No, she thought, but she could find them.

She walked back onto the main street, and continued towards the High Senate. When she got close enough, she slipped around the back of a tall building, and climbed to the roof. She found a sheltered spot, and lay down.

If she could find him in her dream, then perhaps she could do it again.

She focused on one of the many spires that towered up from the domed chambers of the High Senate, and used her line-vision to pull her sight up there in an instant. Now where? Just relax, she told herself, where would they take the Kellach? Think.

She looked around. The jumble of domes and arches piled up below her. She noticed a small open window, on the gallery of a squat dome.

All right, she thought, let's try range-vision. She focussed on the window, and tried to repeat the same step that she took when initiating line-vision. Her sight shot out, but at the same time she felt an overwhelming sense of dizziness and disorientation. She lost the sense of up or down, or back or forward, her sight spun and whirled, the light of the small window flickering past with each revolution. She felt panic surge through her.

Back, she willed, back. In an instant her sight returned to her body. She closed her eyes in pain, and vomited sour cups of tea down the tiled roof of the building where she lay.

Her head felt like it was going to burst, and blood was coming from her nose. Almost blind, she crawled across the roof, and staggered down the steps, pulling her hood over her face, and keeping her head down.

Daphne tried not to stumble too often on her long walk home, defeated, and in agony. Killop was gone, and Kallie and Bridget. Laodoc too, though he had probably known nothing about the fire mage. And Simiona? Tears came to her eyes as she thought of the young Rahain.

Once home, she went straight to her room, collapsed onto her bed, and curled up into a ball. Every part of her ached, her teeth and ears pounded in agony, and nausea soaked through her in waves.

Maybe not everything had been a total loss, Daphne grimaced, as she remembered her experiment with range-vision. She had managed it, she thought, though the price had been high, and it would take a lot of practice before she would be able to control it. She had to master her new skill, were she to rescue Killop.

She would also need to see her new weed dealer again soon.

CHAPTER 20
KEIRA, FIRE MAGE

Rahain Capital, Rahain Republic – 24th Day, Last Third Winter 504

'You can come out now, ya great big cowards,' Bridget shouted, as she thumped on Killop's bedroom door. 'The scary woman's gone.'

Kallie glanced at Killop, smiling weakly.

'Come on in,' he shouted to Bridget.

She opened the door, sauntered over and sat down at the table next to them, a smirk on the edge of her lips.

'How'd it go?'

'Fine,' she said. 'We gave her a tour of the place, all very civilised.'

'And Laodoc?' Kallie asked. 'Was he angry?'

'A bit annoyed,' Bridget replied. 'But he hid it well. You did tell him that you'd be staying in your room, so at least he knew in advance.'

'Did she ask where we were?' said Killop, avoiding her name.

'Aye,' she said. 'Of course. Only natural. You come to inspect three specimens, to make sure they're being well treated, and you're only shown the one, then you're going to ask.'

'What did you say?' Kallie asked.

'Laodoc told her you were both feeling sick.'

'Did she believe it?'

'Aye, I think so,' Bridget said. 'Anyway, that was right before she left.'

Killop felt a surge of disappointment. He tried to keep his expression even, as if he wasn't really interested in talking about Daphne.

'Never mind her,' Bridget went on. 'Killop, did you remember to speak to Laodoc about getting us up to that place in the mountains? It's been over a third since you went. I'd love to see it in spring.'

'Aye,' he said, 'but he's so wrapped up in the whole Rakanese business that I couldn't pin him down. I don't think he's even seen any builders yet.'

Bridget sighed.

'I need to get out of here,' she groaned. 'We go up to the mountain estate together, and then we make a run for it. But it needs to be soon. This place is doing my fucking head in.'

There was a loud crashing sound, as if several windows had been smashed, and then angry shouts echoed up from outside.

The prisoners looked at each other, then got up and walked through the hall to the common room. They went up to the far window, and looked down onto the front of the mansion.

Killop swore. Dozens of soldiers were moving through the courtyard, and into the house by the front doors, which were lying on the ground, their hinges broken.

'What's going on?' Bridget hissed. 'Are they coming for us?'

'Why in Pyre's name would they?' Kallie asked. 'Why now? We've been here for thirds.'

Killop stayed silent, his mouth dry. Had he been stupid to believe that Simiona wouldn't tell anyone? But why had she come to let him know about Keira's arrest, if she was going to betray him?

They heard shouts ringing out from the halls and corridors of the mansion, as the soldiers spread through the building.

'Look!' Kallie called out. Killop turned back to the window, and saw Laodoc being escorted down the wide steps at the front of the mansion, a soldier gripping each arm. The old man looked terrified and was glancing about in confusion. The soldiers bundled him into a waiting carriage, which lumbered off as soon as the door was closed.

'Why have they arrested him?' Bridget asked. 'What's that poor old bastard ever done?'

Another wagon arrived, this one with a large steel cage upon its flat bed. The three captives then gasped as they saw Simiona being brought out of the house next, being dragged by the hair. Soldiers pushed her down the steps in front of the entrance, and in between two ranks of guards, who lashed out, kicking, and clubbing her with crossbow butts as she was dragged along.

'Bastards,' Bridget whispered. Killop looked away, a bitter sickness growing inside him.

'What will we do?' Kallie asked.

Killop looked around the room for anything he could use as a weapon.

'We fight,' he said.

'Aye,' Bridget nodded.

Killop pushed the heavy dining table over, and kicked off one of the thick wooden legs. Kallie hurled a wall-mirror to the floor, smashing it. She ripped off a thick piece of the curtains, and wrapped the fabric round her hand, then picked up a long shard of glass. Bridget armed herself with a foot-long bronze candlestick from the mantelpiece.

Killop looked at the two young women, standing prepared to fight. He tried to think of the right words to say.

'You ready?' he said.

Bridget raised an eyebrow and squinted at Kallie. 'Inspirational speech.'

Kallie laughed, and went to the door. She opened it a crack and peered out.

'I can hear them in the corridor,' she said. 'They're ordering Laodoc's guards to put down their weapons and surrender. Wait, there they are, they're coming to the gate.'

'This is an order for the Kellach Brigdomin slave known as Killop,' a voice called. 'Come out and surrender.'

Killop stepped back in surprise. They wanted him? His heart sank as he realised they must have found out about Keira. He almost cursed Simiona, before he remembered how he had last seen her.

'Come and take him!' Kallie cried.

'The lives of the two female slaves will be spared if the male Killop surrenders,' the voice shouted.

'Go fuck yourselves!' Bridget yelled back.

'They're opening the gate,' Kallie said from the door.

'Let's go!' cried Killop. 'Get into them!'

He charged out into the hallway, just as the first Rahain soldiers were rushing through the gate. They held spears, but hesitated for a second too long, and Killop crashed into them, clubbing heads with the table leg, swinging it two-handed.

Rahain troops poured into the small hallway, filling it up until it became a sea of surging bodies. Some soldiers carried ropes, which they threw over Killop's frame, while hands snatched at him from all directions. He lashed out at the crowd as they pressed closer around him. A rope was looped round his wrist, wrenching the table leg from his grasp, so he used his free fist to beat down those pushed up next to him. He could hear Bridget shouting, but lost sight of her, and Kallie, as the tremendous crush of bodies tightened around him. He felt a rope land over his shoulders, and then tighten round his neck, constricting his breathing. He swung his elbows, cracking one Rahain in the face and knocking him unconscious, but the soldier didn't move, held upright by all the other bodies crammed into the hallway.

'Alive!' he heard someone shout. 'Take him alive!'

Gradually, Killop was pulled beneath the wave of Rahain, and forced to the ground. He heard the final breath of a soldier who had got trapped beneath him, as his ribcage was crushed by the weight. His view darkened, as the Rahain trampling him blocked out the light, and his eyes started to close. He pulled his free hand up to tug at the noose round his neck, as boots stamped down on him. He heard a scream. Bridget? He lost consciousness.

He came to, his swollen and bleeding face pressed down against the dirty wooden floor of a wagon. He was wrapped in chains, and lying on his side. He ached all over, and his breath came in painful rasps from his bruised throat. He opened his eyes a crack, and saw crossbows aimed at his body, by soldiers who sat on the benches to either side of him. He felt the unsteady rocking motion of the wagon as it lurched along the road. The Rahain must have separated them, he realised, remembering the steel cage.

He closed his eyes, his mind foggy, and concentrated on staying alive.

'Look at the condition of him!' a man shouted.

'We brought in the captive alive, sir,' a woman replied. 'As ordered. He resisted arrest.'

Killop felt hands prod his ribs, then feel his arms. He lay motionless on the ground, chains digging into his skin.

'Will he live?' the man asked.

'Oh yes,' said a male voice much closer to him, as hands moved down his legs. 'He'll be fine, no broken limbs. These Kellach are tough, my lord. I've seen some of them survive wounds that would have killed any Rahain. And they recover a lot faster than us as well. This one should be back on his feet in a couple of days.'

'Thank you, doctor,' the first man said, audibly relieved. 'And to you, Lieutenant, my thanks also.'

'Sir.'

'And the other Kellach?'

'Also captured, sir,' she replied. 'Both females sustained injuries in the struggle.'

'Fighters, eh?'

'Yes, sir.'

'And where are they now?'

'We put them in with the fire mage's servant,' she said. 'Doctors are looking at them now.'

'Good,' he said. 'Make sure at least one of them lives. We'll need them to persuade this savage here to do as he's told.'

'Yes, sir.'

'Get him inside then,' he said. 'Shackle him to the wall, then take these chains off. Make sure he has food and water. I'll be back shortly. I have to check on Councillor Laodoc, see how the old boy's liking his new accommodation.'

Killop heard movement, then hands reached out and lifted him. He was carried for a moment, then placed down onto a bed of straw. He felt his wrists and ankles be fitted with new shackles, and then the other chains were cut from him. His ribs eased out, sending excruciating bolts of pain through his chest.

Footsteps backed away from him, and a gate swung shut, its hinges grating.

He opened his eyes.

Outside the bars of his cell, a lamp was burning, illuminating a small guardroom where four soldiers stood in the flickering shadows, crossbows slung across their shoulders.

On the stone floor next to him lay a jug of water, and a plate with a chunk of ryebread.

The Rahain soldiers watched as he crawled across the straw. He splashed water over his bloody face, then drank. He picked up the half-loaf, and sat, his back against the wall, eating slowly, his jaw bruised and swollen. He felt too numb to even begin trying to work out what had happened. His future had been wiped clean again, and whatever occurred, there would be no going back to the life they had led at the mansion. It had to be Keira. They were going to use him, to get to her. Why? What did they want with her? Surely they would just execute her, somewhere out in public, where all the peasants could watch.

He remembered that Kallie and Bridget had been hurt, but at least they had survived. Had Simiona?

Killop hung his head. Taken alive again.

Guards changed shift, more food arrived, and the hours passed. Occasionally the female officer would come in to check everything was fine, but no one spoke to Killop. The sleep and meals had done him some good, and he could feel his strength returning.

After maybe a day, Killop was awoken by a shout.

He sat up, opening his eyes.

Two dark-robed men and the officer were standing on the other side of the bars from his narrow cell.

'Do you understand me?' the taller, older man said. The younger to his right was glaring at Killop in suspicion and loathing.

'I do,' he replied, remaining seated on the straw.

The two Rahain men stared at him for a while, contempt emanating from them. The officer kept her face impassive.

'What is your name?' the old man asked. 'Your full Kellach Brigdomin name?'

'I'm not Kellach Brigdomin, you ignorant shite,' he replied. 'I'm Kell.'

'We have your friends in custody,' the old man said. 'Know that we have no qualms about hurting them if it makes you do as we say.'

'How do I know they're alive?'

'Will you confirm,' he went on, ignoring him, 'that your full name is Killop ae Kellan ae Kell?'

Killop remained silent.

The old man nodded. 'Very well,' he said. 'The screams you'll shortly be hearing will be coming from one of your friends. We will return later, after you've had some time to think.'

He glared back at them, a storm of emotions raging through him, but remained silent. Defiance fought with resignation. They already knew he was Keira's brother, otherwise he would not be there. Getting him to admit it was just a formality. But yielding to them felt bitter.

'I will tell you my name,' he said, as they were turning for the door, 'if you let me see that my friends are unharmed.'

'They will be unharmed if you cooperate,' the Rahain replied. He talked with the others for a moment, and then the officer unlocked and swung open a wooden door leading to a passageway. Down it ran a series of cells, and Killop got to his feet to look.

The officer gathered some guards, and they opened up a cell at the far end of the passageway. With crossbows and spears, they first led out Kallie, then Bridget, who was being supported by another woman. All three were standing, though Bridget looked hurt, her face and chest bandaged, and Kallie's arm was in a sling. They were squinting up the corridor towards him, but there was a lamp directly above where they stood, and he doubted they could see him.

The guards pushed them back into their cell, and the door was closed.

Killop smiled.

Then it hit him. That had been Lacey, standing with Kallie, and helping to prop up Bridget. Lacey, his sister's personal fire-starter. Pyre's bollocks, they really had captured Keira.

'There,' the old man said. 'You have seen them. Unharmed. Now, confirm for us your name.'

Killop remained standing, looking down at the three Rahain on the other side of the bars.

'I am Killop ae Kellan ae Kell,' he said, 'and one day my sister will burn you all.'

More days passed, and Killop was left alone, excepting the constant presence of the guards.

With plenty of regular food, he was healing, and his ribs were giving him less pain. He tried to exercise, working his bruised and strained muscles, and thought about Kallie, Keira and Bridget. And Simiona, all the women in his life. He had let them down. How much simpler everything would have been if he had been killed, as he had intended, in the last battle under the Fire Mountain. Simiona and

Laodoc would never have been arrested, and the Rahain would not have leverage over Keira. Then he remembered Kallie and Bridget. He believed that Bridget would have survived without him, but Kallie? But what had been the point of saving her, if it had led to this?

At first he had listened to the guards talk, but they had kept their conversations to discussing how much they had drunk the previous night, and on the outcome of the bets they had placed on the staged gaien fights. He had tried talking to them, but once they had got over their initial surprise that he could speak Rahain, they had ignored him, and had begun to speak in whispers so he couldn't overhear.

Killop tried to judge the passage of time by the guards' shift changes, and on around the fourth day, a different group of officials entered, bringing with them Laodoc. The old man was not in chains, but looked frail and ill, his face grey, and his yellow eyes sunken.

Killop stood as they approached.

One of the robed men pointed at him.

'Will you confirm that this was your slave?' he asked Laodoc.

Laodoc nodded.

'Councillor,' the man said, 'we require a verbal response from you.'

'I confirm it,' he whispered.

'And do you swear,' the man continued, 'that you had no knowledge that this slave was a close relative of the most wanted terrorist in Rahain, Keira the Kellach fire mage?'

'I swear.'

'And do you now denounce him?'

'I do,' Laodoc said, keeping his eyes lowered.

'Very good, Councillor,' the man said. 'Barring some paperwork, I hope to see your release come through by the end of today.'

He gestured to a pair of guards.

'Take the councillor back to his cell.'

Killop said nothing as the old Rahain was led out of the room.

'Slave,' the robed man called to him. 'Do you confirm...?'

'The old man knew nothing,' Killop said. 'Do you think I would tell a councillor?'

'And Professor Geolaid?'

'The same,' Killop replied.

'What about the slave?'

'She's innocent,' he said. 'She would never betray her master.'

The man nodded.

'Where is she?' Killop asked.

The Rahain ignored him. He looked to his colleagues. 'It's time.'

The officer flicked her hand, and a dozen more soldiers trooped into the room, half with crossbows, half with pikes. The officer held up a large hood, and threw it through the bars.

'Put it on,' she commanded.

'How about you tell me what's happening first?' he said, leaving the hood where it lay on the straw in front of him.

The robed man nodded at the officer.

'We're going to escort you out of this cell,' she said. 'Your sister has requested that she be allowed to talk with you alone.'

'What is it that you want her to do?' he asked. 'Why haven't you executed her? And me, for that matter?'

'None of that is your concern,' the robed man said. 'We will meet your sister's condition. You will not be harmed.'

Killop picked up the hood, and pulled it over his head. He then stood with his arms out-stretched. The cell was unlocked, and his shackles unbolted from the wall. He felt a pike jab his back, and he started walking.

'Ye can take off the hood.'

He tried to reach with his hands, but the chains had been fastened to the wall, and he couldn't move them. He shook his head instead, and the hood slid to the ground.

'Keira!' he cried, looking across the shadows of the cell to where his sister had been chained to the opposite wall.

'Wee brother,' she said, smirking. She looked well, though the signs of fading bruises and lesions were evident, even in the half-darkness. 'When they told me you were alive,' she said, 'I didn't believe it. I said, there's no way my wee brother would get captured. No fucking way. And yet here you are, hair all cut off, and with a face as smooth as a bairn's arse. Well, there's fuck all I can say about it; they got me too.'

She shook her head, and spat onto the straw.

'Why have they not killed me?' she said.

'I've been wondering that myself.'

'The bastards said they would cut you up into small pieces if I didn't cooperate.'

'They're using the exact same line on me,' he said. 'They've got Kallie and Bridget. And I saw Lacey as well.'

Keira laughed. 'She's still alive? Listen; she's not the only one.' Her expression turned serious. 'Ma and Da, Killop.'

Killop gasped. 'How?'

'After the war,' Keira said, 'most of the lizard soldiers cleared out, and all these slave miners moved in, taking over the whole of the north. We spent most of last spring in Domm, with all the survivors in the deep glens down there. People were coming in from all corners, Brig, Lach, and Kell. Ma and Da found me. They just arrived at my tent one morning. They'd heard all about the Mage of Pyre, and realised it must be their crazy daughter, and walked all the way from Kell.'

They shared a laugh. Killop had long thought his parents dead, and the news of their safety seemed to restore a chunk of his life that he hadn't realised had been missing.

'Tell me,' he said. 'How did you get captured?'

'Lizards led us right into a trap,' she sighed. 'And I had no Kalayne to warn me.'

'Kalayne?' Killop said. 'What was that old bastard doing there?'

'He wasn't there, ya numpty, that's the point,' she said. 'He left with Kylon in search of the frog-folk thirds back. He'd been helping me fight the Rahain, using his mage sightings to tell me how everything was laid out before we went in and kicked the shit out of them. He would have seen the trap that got me. They had machines that threw great nets made out of chains, then hundreds of soldiers with cross-bows came out of nowhere. It was like the bastards were only after me, they just ignored everyone else.' She shook her head again. 'Dozens of them jumped me, wrapped me up in chain nets, then dragged me into one of their flying wagons. We were up into the air within seconds. I hadn't seen at first, but wee Lacey must have chased after me, and jumped on board right before we took off. The last I saw, the lizards were beating the crap out of her. Stupid wee cow; she should have stayed in Kell.'

'You were captured in Kell?'

She smiled. 'Aye. A few squads of us left Domm and went north at the end of spring. That's when we started hitting them.' She laughed.

'We heard about the raids,' he said. 'You're famous.'

'About fucking time.'

He rattled his chains. 'If my hands were closer together,' he said. 'I'd spark you.'

'Thanks, wee brother,' she said, 'but there would be no point. There's fuck all to burn in here. By the time the stones got red hot, we'd both be roasted. Ye know, I think the lizards have finally figured out that I can't make fire from nothing.'

'I thought they might, eventually,' Killop said. 'They still know nothing about what I can do, though, we didn't tell them anything about that.'

'Speak with them much, did ye?'

'Aye,' he said. 'A bit. They're not all evil, Keira, just the ones in charge. One of the Rahain slaves was a good friend to us.'

She snorted, and was silent for a moment.

'What happened to the others in our old squad?' she said. 'Conal?'

Killop shook his head. 'Me, Kallie and Bridget got arrested for trouble-making, and they separated us from the rest of the captives. When I last saw them, both Conal and Koreen were still alive, but Pyre knows where they are now.'

'Kelly?'

'She died well.'

'Shit,' Keira spat. 'Old Tornface. She always said she'd never be a slave. Mind you, so did I.'

'We're not slaves, Keira,' he said. 'We're prisoners.'

'Thing is,' she said, 'this whole year that's passed, I've been living, thinking you were dead. When I fought, when I slaughtered the lizards, burning whole buildings full of the bastards to the ground, I was doing it in revenge for you. Not just you, of course, for all of Kell, but mostly for you. I'd just about got used to you being dead, and now? Fucksake, Killop; I don't want to lose you again.'

'Listen, Keira,' he whispered. 'If they want to use you to do something, something wrong, then don't think of me. Do what's right; don't carry out their evil for them.'

Keira lowered her face.

'What the fuck is evil, anyway?' she said. 'I've done so much bad shit in my life that others could use that word about me. Is killing unarmed slaves evil? Then I'm already guilty, brother.'

There was a bang at the door, and it opened. Guards filed in, their crossbows level.

'Don't worry about me, Killop,' she said, as soldiers filled the cell. 'Just stay alive, and keep the others alive too. I'll come for you once I get out of here.'

Guards put the hood back over Killop's head.

'They made a big mistake by not killing me,' Keira shouted, as he was led out of the cell. 'Stupid wee arseholes! I'm going to burn this fucking world to the ground, wee brother. Just you wait and see.'

CHAPTER 21
THE BEAR AND THE BLOODY HEM

Rahain Capital, Rahain Republic – 14th Day, First Third Spring 505

Laodoc sat alone.

Having wept for days, he now felt numb, and stared at the painted pattern on the living-room wall, an untouched cup of tea sitting cold on the table next to him.

The house was quiet, and seemed too big, just as it had after his divorce. With the Kellach and most of the servants gone, it was nearly empty. He hadn't gone up to the northern wing since the raid, not wanting to witness the broken and scattered furniture, or see any of the meagre possessions that his captives had once owned.

His captives. His slaves. Killop had looked at him with pity as he had been forced to mumble his humiliating denunciation in the cell-block under the High Senate. Somehow that had made it worse. It would have been easier to have faced his anger.

He kept his left fist clenched, his ragged fingernails cutting into his palm. A couple of servants had suggested that he take a bath, or look to his personal hygiene, but he had ignored them. His unopened mail sat neglected in a growing pile on the table next to the stale cup of tea, added to whenever the post arrived, though the quantity of letters had declined since his arrest. People, he knew, would be distancing themselves from him, despite the official judgement pronouncing his innocence in the whole affair. They would be laughing at him, the softhearted old fool who had been deceived by his own slaves. He almost wished that he had known that the terrorist was Killop's sister.

Simiona had known.

Laodoc lowered his head and started to cry again. He cursed aloud. He knew he should never think of her, as it was the sure route to tears. He closed his eyes, unable to blot out his last sight of her, lying dead on the dirty cell floor where she had been flung by the guards once they had finished with her. From the adjoining cell he had howled his grief, reaching out in vain towards her broken body, his arm stretching through the bars. His fingers had managed to grasp a torn and bloody piece of the hem of her dress, but her skin had lain just out of reach.

He had never desired the death of anyone before in his life, but he wanted to kill those guards. Watch their mocking eyes close forever.

'Master?'

It was Beoloth, one of the few remaining servants.

Laodoc knew he should respond, but couldn't summon the will to lift his head.

'Master,' Beoloth went on. 'Your son Commander Likiat is here to see you. He's waiting in the hall. What should I tell him?'

His son. The valiant and noble hero, captor of the savage terrorist.

'Will I ask him to come back later?' Beoloth suggested.

Laodoc said nothing.

'That's what I'll do, then,' Beoloth said, then he shuffled out of the room.

Laodoc heard the door close, and then moments later the sound of a raised voice came echoing in from the hall.

The door swung open, and Laodoc looked up.

His son, in full uniform, was striding into the room. Behind him, Beoloth stood, shrugging.

'Dear me, father,' Likiat said, gazing around in disapproval. 'Sitting here moping all day? It won't do, you know.'

He gestured to Beoloth.

'Servant,' he called. 'Fetch us some food, and wine; one of the better bottles.' He pulled up a chair, and sat opposite Laodoc at the small table.

Laodoc said nothing.

As Beoloth scurried off, Likiat gazed at his father, shaking his head.

'Let's see what we can salvage from this mess, shall we?'

'Why do you care?' Laodoc rasped, his mouth dry.

'Part of me doesn't, you old fool,' his son said. 'What were you playing at, living here with Kellach slaves as if they were members of your own family? You're a laughing stock to the entire city; they even made fun of you in the High Senate. Ruellap and I are coming under a lot of pressure, we...'

'So you and your brother are worried for your own reputations. I see.'

'Yes,' he snapped. 'To be frank, we are. Ruellap's career could take a real knock over this, and I'm getting tired of being asked if I knew about the damned slave, as if that was the only way I could have captured the mage. It's all meant as a big joke of course, but this is the sort of thing that sticks.'

They waited as Beoloth came back in and poured wine into two glasses. He also placed a large platter of food before them.

'That will be all, servant,' Likiat said.

Beoloth retreated, a look of relief on his face.

'What do you want me to do?' Laodoc said.

Likiat poked about the food for a moment, and took a sip of wine.

'Go to the City Council, father,' he said. 'Apologise, admit you were wrong, and announce your immediate retirement. The moment you do so, the other councillors will forget all about your foolishness, and rally round. Once they're sure you're going, it'll all be back-slapping, and "for he's a jolly good fellow". Then retire to Slateford Estate, and let the rest of us move on.'

Laodoc sat in silence. Giving up seemed the easiest thing in the world to do.

'How did they find out?' he said. 'No one ever told me that.'

Likiat looked annoyed at the change of subject, and took another drink.

'Apparently one of your slaves, the girl, was overheard talking about it,' he said after a while, as he picked at a leg of roast poultry. 'So they examined the dossier that I compiled during my first tour against the mage. I had included a section on what we knew about her personal life at the time, and the name of her brother was in there. Once they saw it was the same name as one of your Kellach slaves, they moved in.'

'Who overheard her?'

'I don't know the details,' Likiat said, 'but it's no secret that the information was brought to the High Senate's attention by the merchant, Lady Douanna.'

Laodoc stirred.

'It was her?' he hissed, his eyes narrowing, and tongue flickering. 'She betrayed me?'

'Betrayed is a little strong, father,' he said, raising an eyebrow at the change in Laodoc's demeanour. 'She did her duty, and was well rewarded for her trouble, elevated all the way to the ranks of the City Council.'

'Are the Kellach going to be executed?'

'No, I don't think so,' Likiat replied. 'I heard that your old slave is the only thing the barbarian mage cares about. He's being held as a hostage to his sister's good behaviour.'

Laodoc looked up. 'Why?' he said. 'What do they want with her?'

'To be honest, I don't know,' Likiat said, 'but I can think of a few things a fire mage with her power could do for us. I've seen her in action, more than once. She is incredible, father. If it turns out that her brother is what we need to keep her under control, then I'm sure he'll have a long life ahead of him in the cells under the Tyrant's Tower.'

Laodoc said nothing.

Likiat put down his glass. 'If that reassures you, then what about my suggestion? Will you go to the council?'

'Yes, son,' Laodoc replied. 'I think I will.'

Likiat smiled. 'Good,' he said. 'Can I tell Ruellap?'

'Yes, though I will need a little time to put my affairs in order. Tell him I'll speak by third's end.'

'I'll do that, father,' he said, rising. 'Thank you.'

Laodoc nodded to his son, and watched as he left the sitting room.

For the first time since his release, he felt moved to act, to do something. He relaxed his left hand, sore with cramp, and uncurled his clenched fist. He looked down at the small piece of fabric on his palm, stained with the blood of someone he had loved more than his own sons.

'I will avenge you,' he whispered.

Professor Geolaid had left most of her personal belongings behind, such was her haste to be gone from Laodoc's mansion the moment she had been released from questioning. The old man had not seen her since, and this was the first time he had been up to the professor's old rooms to look over the damage caused by the guards and investigators.

Geolaid's office had been ransacked, and every piece of written research had been confiscated by the authorities. Laodoc gazed over the empty bookshelves and over-turned furniture. Now that he had the vague beginnings of a plan, he tried to distance himself from the loss of the work of half a year, and went through to the professor's old living quarters.

He opened the doors of a wardrobe, and pulled out a grey academic robe with a long hood. He needed something unobtrusive, showing status, but without anyone suspecting he was a city councillor. A thrill raced through him. It had been years since he had walked anywhere in the city, having travelled exclusively by carriage like every other noble. He pulled the grey cloak around him.

He left Geolaid's apartment, and stepped out back into the passageway. To his left was the first gate, which led to the Kellach's old quarters. It lay open and undamaged, his guards having surrendered as soon as they had been challenged. He steeled himself, and entered the old faculty. He saw no sign of any disturbance until he turned the corner, and looked down towards the second gate. Everything here had been turned over, from the slaves' room to the guards' billets. Simiona's office had been sacked and, from the empty boxes lying scattered on the floor, more research documents had been confiscated. Her own work, he realised, sadness welling through him. Her precious research probably now lay with Geolaid's documents, gathering dust in a storage vault, unread until it rotted.

Laodoc paused, shaking his head as he forced down the tears.

He went through the second gate, to the Kellach's small hallway. There was blood on the floor here, from more than one person, and everywhere were signs of a fierce struggle. They hadn't gone down easily, he thought.

He lost himself for a while, wandering the rooms where his slaves had lived. He left everything where it was, and was going to take nothing, until he went into Kallie's room. Like the others, it was sparsely furnished, and there was little in the way of personal items. On her bedside table, he noticed a small model of an animal. He picked it up. It was made of wood, and was of a great beast, a mammal, rising up on its hind paws. Its powerful forelimbs ended in claws, and sharp teeth had been carved into its savage jaws.

A bear, he thought. He had heard the Kellach talk of such a beast, that had roamed the high mountains of their homeland.

He put it into his pocket, next to the scrap of Simiona's dress.

The way was long, and the streets were not as Laodoc had remembered them. Beggars lined the roads, and out-of-work peasants lingered at every corner and tunnel entrance. With so much of the budget going to the maintenance of the blockade against the Rakanese encampment, many civil works had been cancelled, and food was being rationed for the lower classes. At least winter was over, he thought, and no one was freezing to death any more.

He was accosted several times by people shoving begging bowls at him, but he wasn't recognised by any of the slaves or peasants on the streets. None of them knew the faces of their rulers, he realised. The elite kept themselves insulated from the masses, living in guarded caverns and travelling in windowless carriages. There were a few soldiers around, out on patrol, eyeing the populace, their rapid-fire crossbows level and primed.

He had to stop twice to ask for directions, and hours had passed before he found the main entrance to Appleyard Caverns. Its gate was open during the daytime, and the few guards present let him pass after a cursory glance at his academic credentials. It was a beautiful place, he thought as he came out into the large cavern. There were several sky windows letting in real sunlight, and below, on tiered terraces and platforms, small orchards were laid out beneath the main apertures in the cavern roof. Each apple tree was showing the early signs of spring, with tiny green buds appearing at the tips of their whip-like branches.

He found the address that Simiona had obtained for him before the raid, and climbed the outside steps to a high apartment, built on a single level on a ledge jutting out from the cavern's side, under one of the sky openings.

He gathered his breath at the top, and knocked.

The door swung open.

Laodoc stepped back in surprise, and waited, but there was no sound from within.

'Hello?' he called out into the dark hallway.

He hesitated. It would be bad manners to enter someone's house uninvited, but he had been walking for hours, and to turn back seemed ridiculous. He summoned his courage, and entered the house, closing the door behind him.

'Hello?' he called out again, and started to walk towards a dim light at the end of the hall.

The place stank of a strange, acrid smoke. Laodoc passed the dark kitchen, which was littered with empty bottles of wine and piles of unwashed plates and dishes. His eyes started to water a little from the pungent fumes in the air, as he reached the door from where the light was seeping. He knocked. After a moment with no reply, he turned the handle and went inside.

Daphne was sitting cross-legged on the floor, her head tilted backwards, her eyes staring upwards into the distance. Next to her were empty coffee cups, glasses of half-drunk wine, and full ashtrays.

The room was unfurnished, except for a bed, two chairs and a table, upon which lay a pile of books, and more used cups. There was an opening in the ceiling, through which the edge of a sky window allowed a glimpse of the afternoon clouds.

Laodoc stood for a while, watching the young brown-skinned woman. Was she ill? Should he go for help?

She spasmed, and he jumped in fright. She fell over onto the floor, curled up in a ball, then retched down the rug, a thin brown stream of sick.

'Miss Daphne!' Laodoc cried, and knelt down beside her. He put his hand on her left shoulder and, faster than his eye could follow, she whipped out her right hand and gripped his wrist, squeezing it.

'Owww!' he yelled, letting go of her shoulder. Keeping a firm hold of his wrist, Daphne spun on the floor into a squatting position, pulling her armour-plated left arm back to strike.

The rage on her face changed to surprise.

'You!' she hissed. 'What in the Creator's name are you doing here?'

She pushed him away, releasing his arm at the same time, so that he fell backwards onto the floor.

As he scrambled to his knees, she rooted around the ashtrays, until she found a half-burnt white stick. She placed the unburned end in her mouth, and lit a match. She held it to the stick, inhaled, then sat on the rug, blowing out a thick cloud of smoke.

'Can you make coffee?' she asked.

He shook his head, coughing, as the smoke enveloped him.

'Wine it is, then,' she said. She picked up a bottle, and poured a large measure into a dirty glass. She downed it in one gulp, then sighed.

'Miss?' he said, sitting across from her on the carpet. 'Are you well? What are you doing?'

'Practising,' she said. 'Getting better, too...'

'Are you quite yourself?'

She raised an eyebrow at him, then gazed around the room, as if seeing it for the first time.

'I guess this must seem strange to you,' she said. 'Why are you here?'

'I came to ask you a few questions,' he said, realising from her glowering expression that it had probably been the wrong thing to say. 'Your door was open!'

She refilled her glass, and smoked her white stick.

'A few questions about what?' she said. 'Have you come from the council? Where are your guards? You can't arrest me; I work for the embassy.'

Laodoc got to his feet.

'May I sit at the table?' he said. 'I'm too old to be conducting conversations from the floor.'

She nodded, and continued to watch him as he pulled out a chair and sat.

'I have not come from the council,' he said. 'I am here in my own capacity.'

'How did you get my address?'

'Simiona.'

Daphne's eyes widened. 'Is she...?'

'They killed her,' Laodoc said, his throat catching. He paused, blinking to stop the tears.

'I'm sorry,' Daphne whispered, lowering her eyes.

'I was betrayed,' he spat, his grief turning to anger, 'by an acquaintance of yours. Lady Douanna.'

'Yes,' she replied. 'I know. She told me.'

He glared at her.

Daphne leant over, and picked up a different smoke-stick from a pile, putting down the one she had been using.

She lit it, and seemed to withdraw into herself, her eyes growing distant.

'It was my fault,' she said, her voice barely a whisper.

'How?' he rasped. He leaned forward, tensing.

'I'm a Holdings mage,' she said. 'I used my vision in a dream to see Killop talk about his sister to Simiona, and I blurted it out to one of Douanna's spies.'

'You saw Killop in a dream?'

'I used my vision powers. You must know how they work. Don't you study that sort of thing?'

Holdings mages, he thought, could they see things happening far away? He tried to remember what he had read about it, but he had been so taken up with the Kellach recently, that he had spent no time researching the other peoples of the world.

He shook his head.

'Well, you'll just have to believe me,' she said, drinking more wine from where she sat on the floor.

'Why were you watching Killop?' he said.

She snorted. 'You heard me argue with Bridget, didn't you?' she said. 'Killop and I dreamt about each other. If I'd seen him that day, I don't know what I would have done. Well,' she laughed, 'I have a pretty good idea.'

'You're in love with him?'

'Was,' she said. 'He's probably dead by now.'

'He is alive, Miss Daphne,' Laodoc replied, fixing her with his eyes.

She blinked, and put down the smoke-stick.

'How do you know?'

'My son captured the terrorist, remember?' he said. 'Both Killop and his mage sister are being kept alive.'

'Your son, Commander Likiat, told you this?'

'He did,' Laodoc replied. 'Under the Tyrant's Tower, he said. That's where Killop is being held.'

An enormous smile spread over Daphne's face.

Laodoc watched her, nodding. He could use this woman. He had come to find out as much as he could about Lady Douanna's background and habits, but may have found a potential ally. True, she held only a lowly position at the Holdings embassy, and he didn't know what else she might be capable of, beyond over-hearing conversations in her dreams, if that was what she had really done.

'And what are your feelings towards Lady Douanna?' he asked her.

'If you're thinking of revenge,' she said, 'you'll have to wait in line behind me. As soon as I've broken Killop out of prison, I intend to deal with Douanna.'

Laodoc let out a laugh before he could stop himself.

'My dear miss,' he said, as she glowered back at him, 'the Tyrant's Tower is one of the most heavily guarded parts of the High Senate complex. You would need fifty soldiers the size of Killop to break in.'

She picked up her wineglass, and smiled. 'But you're not opposed to the idea in principle?'

'Miss,' he said, 'if it were possible to free Killop, and Kallie and Bridget, then I would give anything. I am ruined, Miss Daphne, humiliated. My own son said I was a laughing stock who should retire. No, I will settle for revenge on Lady Douanna, for the Kellach, but also for Simi, who should not have died. Not like that.' He broke off, closing his eyes.

'Describe the tower for me,' he heard Daphne say.

'Miss!' he cried. 'It is useless, one cannot...'

'Describe it for me!'

Laodoc wiped away his tears, and gazed at her.

'I've been practising for nearly twenty days,' she said. 'It took me fourteen to see as far as the High Senate building.'

He stared at her, his mouth opening.

She looked up, and pointed at the opening in the ceiling. 'There's a point on the cavern wall,' she said, 'from where I can see right down to the fourth boulevard, and from there I can get to just about anywhere in the city. I've been all over the High Senate, searching, and getting an overview of the place. I have seen several towers. Describe for me the one where Killop is.'

Laodoc was dumbfounded for a moment, as he tried to digest the power claimed by the woman sitting on the floor in front of him.

'It's squat,' he said. 'Square, with dark stone, flecked in gold and grey. It has three pinnacles, one taller than the other two. It has, em, it is in the north-western part of the complex...'

'Yes,' she nodded. 'Near the Onyx Entrance.'

'It is, yes!' he cried, an almost hysterical laugh coming from his mouth.

'I know the one,' she smiled. 'And the cells?'

'I was blindfolded when taken there, but I believe the prison lies two storeys below ground level, in the foundations of the tower.'

'Good enough,' she said. 'Now, I'll be gone for a bit, so make yourself at home, and bring some fresh wine or coffee or, sod it, even tea would be nice. I'll be needing it after this.'

Before he had time to reply, she fixed her gaze on the opening in the room's ceiling, and her eyes went blank.

CHAPTER 22
SHELLA, FLOW MAGE

Akhanawarah City, Rahain Republic – 24th Day, First Third Spring 505

'But, Shella,' Clodi said, 'why can't they stay?'

'Shit, Clodi,' Shella said, 'I've already told you they can, if we can find space for them.'

Clodi pouted as she reclined on a long couch. Her new red and gold gown shimmered in the bright morning sunlight streaming through the tall windows in Shella's private reception room. 'You let Sami's friends move in.'

'That was when the building was half-empty! Now we're packing them in six to a room.'

'But they're in danger, Shella,' Clodi said. 'They don't feel safe in the city any more.'

'So they say, but I have to prioritise. Political dissidents first, those on the wardens' wanted list. We can't provide a refuge for everyone.'

'Aren't you worried?' Sami chuckled, a glass of rice spirits in his hand, despite the early hour.

'About what?'

'That Obli wants you to gather her enemies here,' he said, 'so she can arrest them all at once?'

Shella smiled. 'You dope, Sami,' she said. 'Obli has, what, ten days until she's due? Have you ever seen a pregnant Rakanese woman who has ten days to go?'

'Well, no.'

'That's because they can't get out of bed, never mind rule a fucking city.'

Shella and Clodi shared a knowing smirk at their brother.

'And Dannu,' Shella went on, 'is completely clueless. She doesn't know the first thing about governing. This is our best, maybe our only opportunity. If it works, then by the time Obli has given birth, and is capable of going back to work as our beloved queen, then the assemblies and courts will be up and running, and there won't be a thing she can do about it.'

'I hardly think Pavu will just stand by and watch, while you reconstitute democracy,' said Sami.

'He'll do nothing. Kylon and the others scare him shitless.'

'Yes,' Sami said, 'but there are only six of them, against thousands of wardens and police.'

'Remember that six of them were enough to clear the upper floors of Tanni's wardens. They haven't dared come up here in a third. And anyway, I've been recruiting...'

From behind Shella's left shoulder, Polli cleared her throat.

'Don't mind her,' Shella said to Sami. 'She still doesn't trust either of you. Thinks you might go running off to Dannu or Pavu with the plan.'

She caught her young assistant's eye for a moment, and smiled at her. Polli was turning out to be an invaluable help, clever and loyal. Maybe a little too loyal at times.

Clodi and Sami laughed as Polli glowered at them.

Shella grinned at her siblings. Polli was probably right. She shouldn't be telling Sami and Clodi too much, but it had been good to see the two of them starting to relax after being withdrawn for so long. The atmosphere in the mage's tenement had changed overnight with the arrival of the Kellach Brigdomin. The wardens had scattered, terrified, once Shella had ordered Kylon to clear them out. Tanni's forces still occupied the ground floor, which meant they also had control over the main gate, but they had left Shella and the others alone since that night.

Dissidents had started flocking to the tenement, once word had got out that she had taken over the upper floors, and she had found jobs and rooms for them all, until the place was bursting at the seams.

Officially everyone had a role in the public services, managing the construction of canals, roads and housing, and administering a hundred other projects, but Shella had also given the brightest and most experienced the task of designing a new constitution, one that could be implemented quickly. It would retain Obli as monarch, but reduce her powers, and elected officials would take over the running of the government.

She had cultivated a network of contacts throughout the city, all of whom now awaited her signal. There was a thirst in the half-built settlement for the restoration of democracy. Pavu's brutal and officious wardens had become loathed by the general populace, who, if her spies were correct, would support her if she acted. There was still a residue of ill-feeling directed towards her personally, due to the dark powers she possessed, but the memory of the harsh times they had shared in the Basalt Desert was changing all the time, as each survivor re-imagined their own role in what was fast becoming a founding mythology. Thanks partly to the discreet whispering campaign she had been waging, Shella was now being remembered for her heroic role in rescuing the migration during the violent volcanic eruption, while Obli, who had been adored by the masses at the time, was being portrayed as a tyrant, obsessed with her rule.

There was a knock at the main doors, and Bedig entered. He was the tallest of Kylon's crew, a member of the Brig clan. Long braids of red hair hung down his back, over the steel and leather armour he always wore. It was all cleaned up and polished now, as was he. The handsome young Brig ran Shella's new hand-picked squads of Rakanese guards, all recruited from trusted sources.

With him walked Bowda, her cunning spymaster and general plotter. His features were gaunt and severe, and his black robes made him appear sinister. It was an effect Shella was sure he played up to, and one he had probably learned from his days as an agent for the Spawn Control Board back in Arakhanah.

'Good morning, you two,' Shella called to them, as they approached the circle of couches and chairs.

'Morning, mage,' Bedig grunted, as he sat. There was a long, low table next to the couches, filled with plates and bowls of food, and cups and jugs. While Bowda remained standing, Bedig poured himself a glass of pressed fruit juice. In the Rakanese tradition, everyone helped themselves, and Shella had not hired any servants, unlike the new royal court.

'Anything to report?' Shella asked.

Bowda glanced at Sami and Clodi, then shared a raised eyebrow with Polli.

'Fine,' Shella sighed. She turned to her siblings. 'You two, scram for now. Let the grown-ups talk.'

Shella noticed a smirk on Polli's lips as Sami and Clodi huffed and tutted their way to the door.

As soon as they were gone, Bowda sat, and took a cup of rice wine.

'High Mage,' he said, 'if I may begin?'

She nodded.

'We may have made a breakthrough in our plans to infiltrate the wardens,' he said, a dark look in his eye. 'A small group of sergeants, all veterans from before, and none of them too happy about the way things have been going.'

'Where are they based?'

'Over by the eastern clay-pits.'

'And you've made contact?'

'Just last night,' he said. 'They want full immunity if they come over to our side, and they want to keep their jobs, and their apartments.'

'Is that all?'

Bowda shrugged. 'They've sensed the mood of the people, and

know it might turn ugly at any moment. If it does, it'll be the wardens the mobs will target first.'

'Okay,' she said; 'we can agree to that. Get them to give us a list of every company they think will remain loyal to Dannu and Pavu.'

Bowda nodded, and drank his wine.

'Bedig?' she said.

The young Brig smiled at her, his red beard trimmed short. They were brutes, she thought, but quite pleasing to look at.

'The night passed peacefully, mage,' Bedig said. 'Nothing from the patrols. Klai's got the fourth squad at the west stairs today, and Kilynn has the fifth over on the east side. Usual crowds outside. Tanni's lot are keeping them quiet.'

Shella smiled to herself. Not so long ago, any mob outside her house would have been calling for her head. Now, they were here to beg for jobs, or favours.

'Thanks, boys,' she said. 'Polli, what's on for today? And sit, girl. I can't keep craning my neck to look at you.'

Her young assistant came round from behind her shoulder, and sat on the couch to her left.

'High Mage,' she said, her eyes sharp, 'you have a meeting this morning with the planning heads to discuss the next ten-day work schedules, then the property team are due to arrive over lunch, they want to present their proposals for the housing extension in Garden District. I've kept an hour free after that for you to sign off your correspondence, and then...'

'Enough!' cried Shella. 'It's probably better if you just let me know on an hourly basis. That way I won't want to kill myself.'

'As you wish, High Mage.'

The main doors opened again, and two more men entered. She smiled at Kylon and Rijon, feeling a twinge of pride at the calibre of allies she had attracted.

'Good morning, lads,' she said. 'Sit yourselves down.'

She waited as they each took a seat. She noticed Bowda eye the Holdings priest with a touch of suspicion, or maybe jealousy.

Kylon was dressed in black, trimmed in silver, and looked as brooding as he usually did. In the early days, Shella had teased him endlessly, trying to make him smile, but she had long given it up as a waste of time.

'Good morning Mage Shella,' Rijon said. 'I have a report for you, from the Holdings embassy in Rahain, if you'd like to hear it?'

'Sure, Rijon,' she replied, reclining and picking up a glass.

'I was in contact with them last night,' he said. 'They informed me that the Rahain delegation has been sent out, and should be arriving here this afternoon.'

'What?' Shella cried, sitting up. 'Already? I thought the senate had just decided the other day?'

'It only takes a few hours to travel to the Rahain front lines when you go by winged gaien,' Rijon said. 'The delegates flew out yesterday morning, with orders to approach Akhanawarah City today.'

'Shit,' she muttered. 'They'll go straight to the palace, only to find Dannu minding the shop.'

They all watched her.

'Bowda,' she said, 'make sure I hear of it as soon as the Rahain approach the city. Bedig, have every squad standing by all day, ready to assemble in the central courtyard at my order. No, wait; we can't all go.' She took a sip of orange juice. 'Leave two squads, along with Klai and Kilynn. The rest will be coming with me.'

'Aye, mage,' Bedig said, standing. 'I'll get to it.' He nodded to her, then to Kylon, who grunted.

Bowda also stood, and the pair walked together from the room.

'Unlikely friends,' Rijon said as they left.

'Bedig gets on with everybody,' Shella shrugged. 'He's a happy lad.'

'Bedig watched,' Kylon said, in a low voice, 'as the Rahain murdered his mother and father, and led him and his twin brother off in chains.'

Shella raised her eyebrow. 'What happened to his brother?'

'Still a slave,' he replied. 'Or dead. Bedig walks each day weighed down with the shame of having left him behind while he escaped. I told him not to despair, that the knowledge that he was free would sustain his enslaved brother in his darker moments.'

She gazed at him. 'You're in a grim mood this morning.'

Rijon shrugged. 'He's angry that there's still no news of the Kellach Brigdomin fire mage the Rahain captured,' he said. 'The Holdings embassy has intelligence that states she is still alive, but nothing else has been heard of her.'

'If the Rahain had executed your friend,' Shella said, 'I'm sure we would have heard. After all, didn't they parade her through the streets a while back? If they were going to kill her, it would have been then.'

Kylon said nothing.

She looked at the Kell warrior, a low pulse of anger rippling outward from him.

'You really hate the Rahain, don't you?' she said.

'Of course not,' he said. 'They're just people, like you, and me. Most of them are kept in chains of ignorance and servitude. Their leaders have enslaved them, just as they have my people. As they intend to do to you.'

'They have done nothing to us,' she said. 'They're not affecting us in any way.'

'Then why are we sitting here, none of us Rahain, yet all speaking their language? It is but a first step. The Rahain wish us all to be slaves.'

'There you go again,' she said, 'with your forecasts of doom. Look; the Rahain have been sitting behind their damn wall for nearly two thirds now. If they were going to attack, surely they would have done so before we had built so much of the city. If they'd attacked when we were all still living in tents... but they didn't. And now they're sending a delegation. At last, they want to talk to us. So long as it's not Dannu they end up meeting.'

Kylon shook his head.

'You really intend to speak with them?' said Rijon.

'Of course,' she said. 'Who else? Dannu? Pavu? Don't make me laugh. Maybe Obli at her finest could have faced up to them, but she happens to be a little busy at the moment. No, it has to be me.'

'I'm not sure I should be present.'

'You're probably right,' she said. 'You can stay here, or head back to your consular office.'

She glanced at Kylon. 'You're coming, though.'

'Aye.'

The message arrived as Shella was sitting down to lunch, the members of the property management team settled and ready to begin their presentation.

'The Rahain delegation has been spotted, miss,' Jayki whispered in her ear, 'entering the western districts.'

She stood. 'Apologies all, but you'll have to excuse me.'

'But, High Mage,' one protested, 'it's taken days to organise this meeting, surely you can spare us five minutes?'

'Nope,' she said. 'See Polli, and reschedule.'

She walked to the door before anyone else could complain.

'How many?' she asked Jayki, as they hurried towards her private rooms.

'Two carriages,' he said, 'and about twenty guards.'

'Okay. Alert Bedig, tell him it's almost time.'

'Yes, miss,' Jayki said, then turned for the stairwell.

She went through to her personal office. Polli looked up from the desk.

'They're here,' Shella said, without stopping. 'Fetch Kylon and Bowda.'

Shella entered her own rooms, and got changed. She pulled on a set of long black robes, and was just finishing her hair when Polli knocked, and entered.

'We're ready, High Mage,' she said, bowing.

Shella swept back out into the office. Kylon stood waiting, fully armed and armoured, towering beside Bowda, whose stoop made him appear shorter than he was.

'All in black, I see,' Shella said. 'Good. At least we've made an effort to look the part.'

'The dark mage and her minions,' Bowda cackled, rubbing his hands together.

'Come on then, my minions,' Shella said. 'We need to save the city from Dannu.'

They hurried down the stairwell to the eastern guardroom, where Bedig had assembled all but two of the new squads.

Leah, the Lach archer, and Baoryn, the Rahain renegade, were also waiting, and were talking with Jayki and Braga. Everyone was armed.

They stilled when she entered, and turned to face her.

'We're going to the palace,' she said. Eyes blinked, and faces looked surprised. She realised with a start that several of them probably thought that the coup was about to begin. Maybe it was.

She turned on her heels and went down the hall to the stairs. Descending, she came out into the open air of the tenement courtyard. She strode towards the main gates, then stopped a few paces away, watched by a handful of Tanni's wardens on duty.

Behind her she heard her company move in and fill the courtyard, and she felt Kylon's presence at her right elbow.

'Wardens!' she called out. 'Move aside, I command you.'

The guards looked around, heavily out-numbered by Shella's force.

Kylon nodded, and Baoryn stepped forward, a crossbow in his hands. The renegade Rahain walked towards the wardens, motioning for them to put down their spears, and move to the side.

'Stop!'

Shella turned her head to see Tanni running from a door to the right, a dozen wardens filing out behind her.

'High Mage!' she panted, as she came to a halt before her.

'Listen carefully, Officer Tanni,' Shella said. 'I'm going to the palace, to meet the Rahain delegation.'

'But my orders...'

'Were given by the queen, who is presently not at liberty to amend them,' Shella said. 'As she surely would, if she knew that the future of the city was depending on the diplomatic skills of Herald Dannukanawara. Don't you agree?'

Tanni looked at a loss for a moment, and Shella could see the woman weighing up her options.

'I'll be expecting you to escort us there, of course,' Shella said, smiling. 'For our protection.'

The warden pursed her lips, and nodded.

'Open the gates!' Shella called out, and soldiers from her company ran forwards to remove the bar, and pull the doors wide.

'After you,' Shella said to Tanni.

'Form up!' the officer shouted, and led her wardens through the arched tunnel gates. Shella followed, with Polli and Bowda at each shoulder, and Kylon and Baoryn to either side. Behind her, Bedig, Leah, Jayki and Braga each led a squad.

They moved out onto the street, where the usual crowd was standing. The wardens had pushed them back from the road, and they lined the pavements, each straining to catch a glimpse of the dark mage emerging from her internal exile.

Though the palace was only a few hundred yards away, across the main square in the centre of the city, their passage was slow, as more crowds gathered, curious to see what was happening. Groups of wardens closed in as lines of excited people clustered on either side.

'Are you ready, High Mage?' Bowda whispered to her.

She swallowed, keeping her nerves down. This was turning into something she should have foreseen. She had intended to meet the Rahain, then return to her tenement and carry on as before, but her symbolic act of walking the streets, in disobedience of the only order she had ever been given, was setting off her plans early.

'We might need to alert our contacts,' she whispered back.

'I did so an hour ago, High Mage,' he replied.

She chuckled.

She heard her name called out, and it turned into a chant, repeated by thousands as she walked to the palace gates. Shella flushed. Being an object of adulation felt alien and uncomfortable, and she avoided eye contact with any of the cheering public. At the same time however, she couldn't hold back the surge of pride that rippled through her.

In the vast, walled off gardens at the front of the palace, Shella could see the carriages the Rahain had brought with them. Each had a pair of enormous reptiles harnessed at their front. They stared at her, with piercing yellow eyes.

'Gaien,' she heard Baoryn mutter, as they left the crowds behind them, and passed through into the gardens. She looked over at the renegade Rahain, Kylon's most loyal soldier. She had heard the Kell warrior had protected Baoryn's life when he had been captured, and had refused to allow anyone to touch him.

Ahead, she saw that her company had come to a halt. Tanni was speaking and gesturing to the wardens guarding the main entrance to the palace buildings.

'You four,' Shella whispered to those closest to her. 'With me.'

While everyone's attention was on the palace gates, Shella slipped through the orchard to the left of the main path, and made her way round the side of the palace. She knew the layout well, having designed it while in Silverstream many thirds before, and she found the small postern door by the main audience hall.

It was unguarded.

'In here,' she said, opening it. She watched as Polli, Bowda, Kylon and Baoryn went in, and then followed them into the dark passageway.

She put a finger to her lips, and went through another door. They emerged into the shadows under a large arched balcony which ran around the walls of the main audience hall. Afternoon sunshine from clerestory windows flooded the central area of the chamber. At the far end, Dannu was standing next to the empty throne, Pavu a few steps to her right. Courtiers, advisors and wardens stood to either side.

The Rahain were gathered before the throne. Three men and a woman were standing out in front of a group of about twenty Rahain soldiers, all armed with the same type of crossbow that Baoryn carried. The four delegates were dressed in rich robes, and were listening as Dannu talked.

'We need to get closer,' Shella whispered.

She led her small group through the shadows created by the arched supports of the balcony, until Dannu became more audible.

'...and wish to welcome them into our city,' she finished, in Rakanese. A young man to her left, dressed as a royal courtier, began translating for the Rahain delegates.

It was an awkward speech, honouring the visit of the Rahain as if greeting a friendly neighbour.

When he had finished, one of the Rahain stepped forward.

'Now that the diplomatic pleasantries are over,' he said, 'we can get straight to the point. The Rahain Republic, for whom we are authorised to speak, hereby demands the immediate evacuation of all Rakanese illegal immigrants from its territory. We are also authorised to inform you, that if no signal or confirmation is received by us that you fully intend to comply with this demand, then there will be consequences.'

Dannu stood calmly while this was said, waiting for her translator to begin.

Shella edged closer, until they were almost level with the delegation. There was a warden in the archway ahead of her, but he was absorbed in watching the Rahain, and didn't notice them sneak up.

She watched Dannu's expression change as the words of the delegate were translated.

'What consequences?' Dannu asked, her voice calm, but Shella could see her hands shake.

'The armed forces of the republic will redouble the blockade,' the Rahain replied, without waiting for a translation. 'To fully encircle the Rakanese encampment. We will declare a state of siege, madam.'

'But why?' Dannu cried, when the words were translated for her.

This time the Rahain waited, so they could hear the question. They laughed when the young Rakanese translator spoke.

'You Rakanese,' the Rahain delegate said, contempt rising in his voice, 'are a parasitic growth, feeding off the body of the Rahain

Republic. Your race does not belong here, your people will never belong here. This is Rahain!'

'Not any more!' Shella said, stepping out from the shadows, her comrades close behind. 'You had your chance to make demands,' she said, pausing as she saw Bowda instruct the courtier to translate her words back to Rakanese. 'And instead you built a wall and sat behind it for thirds.'

She circled the delegates, her black robes swaying. She could see them staring at her, and at her retinue, especially Kylon and Baoryn, their tongues flickering.

'And now it's too late,' she said. 'The city is built. We cannot evacuate, for this is our home.'

'You stole the land!' one of the Rahain shouted, his yellow eyes gleaming.

'You weren't using it, and now we are. If you threaten us, we will stand up to you. If you attack us, we will defend this city with our lives, and yours.'

The entire room fell silent. Shella could feel the eye of every Rakanese on her.

'We're not afraid of you,' she said, 'but we need not be enemies. We could be friends, trading partners, allies even.'

'Friends?' one of the Rahain said. 'While you openly flaunt a runaway slave and a deserter in our faces? We demand that they are handed over to us at once!'

Kylon and Baoryn reacted first, both going into a crouching stance, their hands poised by their weapons. The Rahain soldiers reached for their crossbows.

'Stop!' cried Shella. 'If you try to take these men, there will be a bloodbath, and none of you will be returning to Rahain.'

'We could kill every one of you in this room in a minute,' said one of the Rahain.

Shella narrowed her eyes. 'Try it.'

The Rahain delegates stared at her, and she stared back, her teeth bared. One of them gestured to a squad of Rahain soldiers, who levelled their crossbows at Shella's group.

'Arrest them!' the Rahain delegate shouted.

Shella raised her right arm, and swept her hand across the line of soldiers.

Ten Rahain heads erupted in a roar of blood, as pieces of brain and skull flew across the hall, much of it hitting the delegates. Cries of horror echoed through the air.

Shella staggered back, nearly falling. She swore as she realised how badly she had misjudged Rahain physiology. She had killed ten soldiers, when she had only intended to give them mild concussions.

'The rest of you,' she heard Bowda shout, 'lay down your weapons!'

The other squad of Rahain soldiers pulled their crossbows off and threw them to the floor.

The delegates, dripping in blood, stared at her, terrified.

'I am High Mage Shellakanawara, and in the absence of Queen Oblikanawara, I rule this city,' she said. 'You will return to your republic, now that you understand how we deal with threats. And now that you've seen our power.'

She gestured for them to leave, and they fled from the hall. As the doors opened to let them out, her own soldiers ran in, fanning out through the room.

'Clean that up,' she said to a group of palace wardens staring openmouthed at the corpses of the ten dead Rahain. 'Kylon, gather their weapons.' She glanced up at her siblings as she walked towards the throne. 'Dannu, Pavu, you're both fired.'

She turned at the top of the raised dais.

'Obli is still the queen,' she announced to the room, as a hundred faces gazed up at her, 'but I'm in charge for now, with Bowda and Polli as my first ministers. Orders have been sent out to organise assemblies and elections, and as my first act I intend to restore democracy.'

There was a loud cheer from her soldiers, and a few nervous looks from some of the assembled courtiers.

'I also intend to build an army,' she said, 'to defend this city from the maelstrom that will soon assail it. This is our home, and I will lay our enemies out in heaps if they try to take it from us!'

There was another cheer. This time many wardens joined in. As she took in the applause, she noticed Kylon frowning.

'You might have told me you were going to do that,' he whispered.

She smiled, her heart pounding. 'Just nod and play along.'

CHAPTER 23
THE WOMAN FROM THE PROPHECY

R ahain Capital, Rahain Republic – 26th Day, First Third
Spring 505

Daphne punched the leather bag with her right fist, her body
streaming with sweat. She kept her left arm raised, its skin-tight
armour glistening.

Her feet danced, as she struck again, and again, keeping her focus,
allowing just enough battle-vision to weigh and guide her punches.
Confident that she had mastered range-vision enough to attempt to
free Killop, she had pulled back from the hours of mental practice, and
was getting herself fit again, after so many days of physical inactivity.
She still ranged out once a day, for thirty minutes or so each morning,
just to check that Killop hadn't been moved from his cell, and that he
was still being reasonably well-treated. She had resisted entering his
mind, it seemed like a violation, and had restricted herself to watching
him in silence, before checking and re-checking her planned route in
and out of the dungeons under the Tyrant's Tower.

She had quit alcohol and dullweed, and had cut down on her keenweed intake, smoking just enough to assist with her visions. Without it,
she guessed it might have taken her thirds instead of days to learn how
to range.

Or maybe she was just a natural, she thought, as she slugged the leather bag with all her strength.

Just a few more days, and she would be ready.

She stopped, her heightened hearing catching a noise coming from the front of the apartment.

She pulled a towel around her shoulders, and left her makeshift gym. As she made her way up the long hall, she heard a loud banging on her door. She hoped it wasn't an official visit, dressed as she was in a pair of shorts and a vest, and covered in sweat.

She opened the door. Outside were three people from the Holdings embassy, a man in consular robes, accompanied by two guards.

'Good morning, Dale,' Daphne said.

'Ah, Miss Holdfast,' he replied, looking her up and down. 'I was about to give up. Are you well?'

'Much better, thank you,' she said, remembering she had told them that she was sick. 'Just getting back into shape before reporting for work.'

'Good, good,' he nodded. 'Secretary Joley will be most pleased. I apologise for coming round uninvited, but I'm afraid the ambassador has requested your presence. If you are fully recovered, of course.'

'What for?'

'I'll explain on the way.'

'Come in, then,' she frowned. 'I'll need to take a quick shower first.'

'Of course, miss,' he said, entering her apartment. 'We can wait.'

'Tell me what you know of the Rakanese, Miss Holdfast,' Dale asked her, as their carriage lurched through the tunnels of the city.

'Not much,' she said, 'except there's a third of a million of them squatting by a river to the east. And that we have an agent with them.'

'Who told you that?'

She looked away. 'Getherin.'

Dale nodded. 'Of course,' he said. 'I never got the chance, miss, to ask how you were feeling after that unfortunate business.'

'Still angry that I didn't see it,' she said, continuing to look out of the window.

'Not to worry, miss,' Dale said. 'You weren't the only one he fooled.'

'Yes, but I was the only one sleeping with him.'

'I suppose,' he said. 'You know, we never did discover who his contact was among the Rahain...'

'I've already told Joley everything I know.'

'Of course, miss,' he spluttered. 'I wasn't implying...'

'Anyway, Dale, the Rakanese?'

'Yes,' he said. 'Getherin was correct, we do have an agent working with the Rakanese leadership, which means that the Rahain also know. Of course, we'd never admit it, or let them know how we keep in contact with him. Officially, we have had no dealings with the Rakanese. Until now.'

'What's changed?'

'There was an incident,' he said. 'And now, talk of war.'

'War?'

'A couple of days ago,' he said, 'some representatives of the High Senate went out to the Rakanese camp, to present their terms...'

'They have terms?'

'Hmm, quite,' Dale replied. 'Basically, leave or else, that was the sum total of it. And that's when it got ugly, according to the delegates. The initial reports are a little confused, but it seems that the Rakanese were harbouring some deserters or fugitives from the Rahain army, and when the senators demanded that they be handed over, the Rakanese refused.'

'Was there a fight?'

'If so,' he said, 'it was a little one-sided. It turns out the Rakanese have a high mage, and she killed ten of the Rahain guards with a wave of her hand.'

Daphne gasped.

'The Patriots are calling it an act of war,' Dale went on, 'and the

Conservatives look likely to back them if they call for sterner action to be taken. A full-blown siege looks certain at this stage. The ambassador decided that a final attempt to secure peace should be made, and offered his services to the Rahain as an intermediary. Somewhat to his surprise, they agreed.'

Daphne noticed that the road they were taking was leading to the surface, away from the central caverns.

'Where are we going?'

'Winged gaien are standing by, ready to depart,' he said. 'We shall be leaving as soon as both of us are on board.'

'We're flying to the Rakanese camp?'

'We are, along with the ambassador.'

Her heart sank. 'Why me?' she said. 'What good will I be? I'm not a negotiator, and I know nothing of the Rakanese.'

'The ambassador requested you specifically.'

'Yes, but why?'

Dale shrugged. 'To be honest, miss, I think the news of their high mage has put everyone on edge. You're coming along to watch the ambassador's back in case they try anything. You're the most skilled operative we have in that respect.'

She scowled at him.

'Don't take offence, miss,' he said, shaking his head. 'Only a very few in the embassy are aware of the extent of your abilities, and what use you've put them to. The Rahain did discover that you were an agent, thanks to Getherin, but they remain ignorant of what you can do. Luckily, you didn't confide that to him.'

She stared out of the window, not replying.

They reached the surface, where a cloudy spring morning greeted them. A large cylindrical carriage was on the grass, its flying beasts tethered and hovering above. Dale escorted her across the grass and up the ramp. She saw Ambassador Quentin seated by a table next to Shayba, one of his closest aides. She noticed that the two guards from before had not come aboard, and there was no one else present in the carriage.

'Miss Holdfast,' Quentin said, 'so good to see you well again. Take a seat, we are about to depart.'

She and Dale took the bench opposite the ambassador and Shayba, and strapped themselves in. They were positioned next to a large, circular window, and they watched as the craft lifted into the air.

'Has she been briefed?' Quentin asked Dale, as they soared upwards.

'She has, my lord,' Dale replied, 'concerning where we are going, and why. She is also aware we have an agent working for us there.'

'Good,' he nodded. 'It'll be a long trip,' he said to Daphne. 'We won't reach the Rahain lines until past nightfall. We'll rest there, and visit the Rakanese settlement tomorrow.'

'Shall we see their high mage?' she asked, her annoyance starting to give way to curiosity.

'I sincerely hope so,' Quentin replied, 'as she appears to be in charge for the moment. Fortunately for us, our agent has long been close to her, and is now one of her nearest and most trusted advisors. He has vouched for our safety, as long as we make no threatening gestures.'

'Is she dangerous?'

'Very, it seems,' he said. 'She eliminated half of the Rahain delegation's guards in a second, which is why I felt it prudent to leave ours behind when we visit. What we know of this mage, Shella as she is called, is that until now her mage powers have been reined in by her sister, the queen. However, the queen is currently with child, and the high mage has taken control in her absence.'

'Is she their only mage with such powers?'

Quentin looked around the table.

'Absolute secrecy is required here,' he said to them all. 'The Rahain must not be allowed to discover the truth in this matter. As far as they are concerned, I am happy for them to believe that the Rakanese have a whole company of such mages. However, the plain truth is that she's the only one left.'

'What happened to the others?'

'The queen had them executed,' Quentin said. 'They were becoming too powerful, too dangerous.'

'If they can kill ten soldiers with a flick of the hand,' Dale said, 'she may have had a point.'

'Maybe so,' Quentin replied, 'but, for whatever reason, she didn't execute her own sister, and now she's the only one remaining.'

'The Rahain will go for the siege, then,' Daphne said. 'They won't want to risk a frontal assault if they fear there may be Rakanese mages waiting for them.'

'Exactly,' Quentin said. 'A siege buys us all a little time. I'm under no illusions that the Rakanese will leave this land willingly. From what our agent has said, they suffered enough getting here. No, the best we can hope for is that the Rakanese sit tight, and do not provoke the Rahain to attack.'

'Why are the Holdings getting involved?' Daphne asked.

'New directives from the Realm,' he said. 'The church and crown wish for there to be peace and unity among the peoples of this continent, and have instructed us to make every effort to that end.'

'Noble of them.'

'The Creator wishes it so,' the ambassador said.

'I'm sure he does.'

The stop-over in the Rahain fortress was awkward and uncomfortable, with troops and supplies bustling through the crowded area behind the walls and ramparts of the blockade.

Another forty thousand soldiers were in the midst of arriving, as the Rahain prepared to extend the lines of their siege closer to the city. The traffic moved all night, and none of the Holdings delegation got much sleep. In the morning, a gaien wagon was prepared for them, and they set out across the flat grasslands beyond the Rahain lines.

After a few hours they came to a river on their left, and found a barge waiting for them.

A Holdings man was standing on the bank, gesturing to the crew on the boat. He turned as he saw them approach.

Daphne squinted through the mid-morning light as she got out of the carriage, onto a muddy track leading to the river, the sun in her eyes.

That man, she thought, *I've seen him before.*

She froze. Then ran.

'You!' she cried, as she pulled near. He turned to see who had called out, and saw her. His face opened in shock as she swung her right fist and cracked him on the chin. 'Bastard!' she shouted as he fell, landing on his backside in the mud.

Dale appeared at her side, pulling her back.

'Miss Holdfast!' the ambassador shouted. 'Desist at once!'

Rijon sat in the mud, looking up at her. His shock had turned to a broad smile, and he started to laugh.

'You survived Sanang, I see,' he said.

She took a step back, as Dale gripped her right arm.

'Most of my company didn't,' she said.

The smile vanished from Rijon's face, and he looked down.

The ambassador arrived.

'What's going on?' he cried.

'You never told me that Captain Daphne Holdfast was working for you,' Rijon said, still sitting in the mud.

'I'm not a captain any more,' she said. 'They threw me out of the army, right before they sentenced me to death.'

'It was a bad business,' Rijon said, getting to his feet. 'One I'd rather pretend never happened.'

She heard a low laugh, coming from the right. She looked over and saw a large Kellach warrior stride towards them. Daphne opened her mouth in surprise. She was fair-haired, with blonde braids, wearing a long coat of chain mail, and had a longbow slung over her shoulder. She was taller than Kallie, and stronger built than Bridget.

'Now that was funny,' the Kellach said in clipped Rahain. She slapped Rijon on the back, nearly toppling him over again, then turned to face Daphne.

'Who are you?' she said.

Rijon frowned. 'The introductions will have to wait, Leah. The high mage is expecting us.'

The warrior stopped, and looked over at him.

'Aye,' she nodded. 'Let's get back.'

'Everybody, onto the boat, please,' Rijon said. 'My lord, if you would,' he said to Quentin, extending his arm.

'Thank you,' the ambassador said, letting Rijon escort him.

Daphne remained where she was, watching the others step onto the barge.

'Are you all right?' asked Dale.

She said nothing.

Dale looked at her, then back at the barge.

'Are you going to be able to deal with Rijon?' he said. 'I don't know what history the two of you share, but can you keep it private for the duration of this trip, at least?'

Daphne thought back to the fort in Sanang, and the last time she had seen Rijon. It already seemed like a different life, one from long ago, and though she had always sworn she would kill him if she ever saw him again, she realised that if she was going to attempt to rescue Killop, she would need to stay out of trouble, and get on with her job.

'I'll be fine,' she said, and they walked to the barge.

On board, Daphne got her first look at the Rakanese. There were six of them, all punting the long barge down the river. They were short, she thought. She was a few inches taller than them, and she was below average Holdings height. They had big eyes which made them look like astonished children, and were olive-skinned, halfway between her chocolate brown, and the milky white of the Kellach.

Their bodies were lithe and lean, and they handled the boat expertly, at home on the water, while the Holdings folk looked queasy, and gripped the handrails.

They came to the confluence with another tributary, and the river widened. The Rakanese piloted the craft out into the middle of the water, where the current bore them swiftly along, past fields and gentle hills.

'How far is the camp?' Daphne asked Leah, who stood to her right.

'It's not a camp,' the Kellach said; 'it's the biggest city I've ever seen.'

Rijon smiled. 'I thought you only had villages and goats where you're from?'

'Cheeky bastard,' she said. 'We had a few towns as well. Our largest used to have thirty thousand people living there. This is way bigger.'

'But how could it be called a city?' Daphne said. 'They only got here a few thirds ago.'

'The Rakanese,' Rijon said, 'are fast builders, whatever else you might say about them. Most of the three hundred thousand migrants are already out of their tents and living in brick housing. They have also constructed a network of canals, linking everywhere in the city, and countless bridges and pools. These are not savages you're about to face.'

'I never said they were,' Daphne replied. 'I don't have any opinion of the Rakanese, as it happens. I'm in complete ignorance of them.'

'Then what are you doing here?' Rijon said. 'What use do you have on this trip?'

'If I get an opportunity,' she said, 'I'll be happy to show you.'

Leah laughed.

Rijon looked at her sideways. 'Be careful, Daphne,' he said. 'I have no doubt that you have become powerful; I can see it in your eyes.' He paused, staring at her, and she felt his gaze bore through her. 'At least up to inner,' he muttered, blinking and looking away. 'Possibly beyond.'

He laughed to himself, shaking his head.

'Look,' Leah said, pointing.

Daphne peered up the river, and saw the tops of buildings appear over the long grass. Before long, the river banks were crowded with structures, with canals and subsidiary channels dug in every direction. Quays and wharves had been built, and graceful bridges spanned the river at its widest, as the barge pulled its way through the new city of the Rakanese. Brick towered upon brick, and the housing blocks soared into the sky on either side. The noise and smell also hit her, and the multitudes of life. People worked, and stood, and haggled, and talked, and were everywhere she looked.

'No,' she said, 'not a camp.'

'That is the palace of Queen Oblikanawara,' Rijon said, as the carriage pulled into a large square.

'But we're not going there, you said?' the ambassador asked.

'No,' Rijon replied. 'The queen is confined to her labour within. High Mage Shellakanawara prefers to work out of that building there.'

He pointed across the square, to a large brick tenement block, several storeys high.

As their carriage approached, Daphne saw that the building was ringed with black-clad soldiers, who were keeping back the masses pressing against them.

'I assume she's expecting us?' asked Shayba.

'Yes, ma'am, she is,' Rijon said.

The soldiers cleared a path for them, and their carriage was pulled under an archway and into a large courtyard. More soldiers were awaiting them, along with another two Kellach warriors, one male, one female, each with long black hair.

'Is there an explanation regarding these Kellach Brigdomin?' the ambassador asked as their carriage halted.

'There is, my lord,' Rijon said. 'Some of the details surrounding their presence trouble me. However, it can wait for a more private moment.'

The ambassador nodded. Daphne pretended not to hear, and stepped down into the courtyard.

She pulled on a slender thread of battle, and took in the positions of everyone around her. She stood behind Quentin, and gauged every possible threat. She saw Rijon glance at her, and knew he could tell she was drawing on her vision.

They were led into the building, and up several flights of stairs, until Quentin had to pause for breath near the top. Daphne strode over to Rijon as they waited.

'A truce for now,' she said to him.

He nodded. 'I would appreciate that.'

'What's she like?' Daphne asked. 'The mage?'

'She's amazing,' Rijon said. 'She organised the migration, then designed and built the city. She is also ruthless in her desire to protect the people.'

'It sounds like you're in love with her.'

'I am, a little bit,' he said. 'You needn't worry, though. As you can imagine, Daphne, I'm not one to allow emotion to interfere with my duty. Or my orders.'

'Three of us made it out of Sanang,' she said, keeping her voice calm. 'Three, from the entire company. After you followed your orders.'

'As I said, it was a bad business,' he replied. 'It's a hard thing, to sacrifice your own troops for the greater good, and not a decision I myself could have made. My orders came from the top, and I knew my duty, as much as I hated doing it.' He looked down. 'For what it's worth, Daphne, I'm sorry. And believe me, it gladdens my soul to see you alive, and in such good shape.'

He smiled at her, and she looked away, frowning.

The party continued to the top of the stairs when the ambassador had recovered. As well as the five from the Holdings, a squad of black-uniformed Rakanese soldiers marched with them. The door opened to a large reception room, with couches surrounding a long low table.

On the opposite side of the table, near the centre, reclined a woman, dressed in a long black gown. She had a black band on her brow, and her long dark hair tumbled down over her bare shoulders. She looked up with her big eyes, as she beheld the Holdings delegates.

'High Mage Shellakanawara,' Rijon said in the Rahain tongue, as they approached the table, 'I am pleased and honoured to introduce to you His Lordship the Exalted Ambassador of the Holdings Realm to the Rahain Republic, Lord Quentin of Hold Terras.'

The woman smiled. 'I'm not sure I'll remember all that,' she said. 'Will Quentin suffice?'

'Certainly, High Mage,' the ambassador bowed.

'And these are the ambassador's aides,' Rijon continued. 'Lady Shayba of Hold Elance, Mister Dale of Hold Anster, and Miss Daphne of Hold Fast.'

'Just the four of you?' Shella said. 'No guards?'

'We are here as friends, High Mage,' Quentin said. 'Friends do not bring guards.'

'Of course,' she laughed. 'Sit, all of you. Eat, drink. Already I'm liking you more than the Rahain.'

Daphne sat to Quentin's left, where she had a good view of the ambassador, though she didn't think the mage looked likely to attack. She scanned the other Rakanese at the table, as a glass of cool water was placed in front of her by Dale. A young woman sat to Shella's left, and a man to her right, both also dressed in black.

'Rijon tells me,' Shella said, addressing them across the table, 'that you're acting as intermediaries between ourselves and the Rahain Republic. If you have come to ask us to leave this city, then I'm afraid you'll be disappointed.'

'It is our duty to find a way to peace,' Quentin said.

'And have you found one?' she asked. 'If so, then please let me in on the secret. You must know the Rahain well, Ambassador. Tell me, are they a peaceful nation?'

Quentin smiled. 'I'm sure the Kellach Brigdomin among you will have told you something of the nature of the Rahain Republic, as regards foreigners. And war. We left the Rahain lines this morning, where tens of thousands of reinforcements are arriving, and are preparing to encircle this city completely, unless you evacuate these lands.'

'That would be a pity,' she said. 'These are beautiful lands, which, as I'm sure you know, were neglected and unused until we arrived here.

The Rahain don't seem to like living in these low-lying river areas. They prefer mountains, don't they? We could always swap some land with them. To the west of Arakhanah City is the range we call the Forbidden Mountains, which separates our homeland from the high plateau beyond. As our name for them would suggest, we have no interest in these hills, finding them useless, barren and rather unsightly. We could allow the Rahain to take their pick of an area of similar size to this new settlement, say twenty square miles. How does that sound?'

'High Mage,' Quentin said, 'I do not believe the Rahain would take such an offer seriously.'

'I do not believe so either,' she replied, smiling, 'but it will give you something to take back to them, so your mission doesn't look a complete failure.'

Daphne smiled.

'I would also like you to take back some gifts,' she went on, 'for yourselves and for our mutual neighbour, a selection of our best produce and finest crafts, as a token of our desire for friendship and peace.'

'Thank you, High Mage,' he said. 'Is there also a message to go with these gifts, and the offer of a land swap?'

'Indeed there is, Lord Quentin of Hold Terras,' she replied. 'Inform the Rahain government that, if they want this land back, then they will have to come and take it from us. Did you look around when you arrived? If we can build a city in such a short time, then how quickly do you think I can build an army? How quickly do you think I can have my soldiers armed, trained and ready to fight? This city will be the mass grave of the Rahain if they try to enter.'

Quentin nodded. 'And if they place you under siege, High Mage?'

Shella laughed. 'Six hundred thousand of our people set out from Arakhanah last summer, and we left half that number lying dead from hunger and thirst along the way. We're better equipped to survive a siege than the Rahain. I've already begun moving the majority of food production to within our defensive perimeter, and am fortifying the water supplies and stores. I have three hundred thousand skilled workers in this city, and we are united in our will and purpose. We shall outlast any siege, and still be living comfortably when the besiegers have given up and gone home. Tell me, Quentin, how much money is the blockade costing the Rahain? How long will their coffers hold out while funding such an extensive siege?'

The ambassador smiled. 'I have no answers, High Mage,' he said, 'but will pass on your message, in full.'

'For that I thank you,' Shella said. She swung her legs off the couch and stood. 'And now, if you will kindly excuse me, I have some pressing engagements. Please stay and have some lunch before you depart. Rijon, with me.'

She left the room, flanked by her aides, while Rijon rose and followed her.

With the Rakanese guards lining the walls, the small group of Holdings around the table looked at each other.

'That went about as well as I could have expected,' Quentin said.

Dale shrugged. 'We're still alive.'

'She seems to know what she's doing,' Daphne said. 'Rijon told me that she was responsible for organising and designing the city.'

'He was correct,' Shayba said. 'She would be a useful ally.'

'She won't be much use to us once the Rahain surround them,' Quentin muttered. 'We'll need to keep Rijon here for a bit longer, that's clear.'

'Remember, Ambassador,' Shayba said, 'Father Rijon works for the church, not you.'

'I don't trust him,' Daphne said.

'Yes,' Shayba said. 'We saw that quite clearly by the river bank, thank you. Be careful, miss. Father Rijon's connections go to the very top, and his own powers are... considerable.'

'I'm already on rather bad terms with the prophet,' Daphne said. 'Rijon doesn't scare me.'

She caught Dale smiling at her. Just then, the main doors of the room opened, and a big Kellach warrior walked in. He was slighter than the other males she had seen, and had long jet-black hair. He glanced over at the long table, where the Holdings delegates sat, then paused, and turned to a guard. They spoke for a moment, then the man approached them.

'Greetings, Holdings folk,' he said in a low voice, as he looked at them. 'I was on my way to see the high mage, I thought she was in here. I am Kylon, from Kell, I was...' He stopped as his glance fell on Daphne. 'You?' he said, his eyes widening.

'Do I know you?' Daphne asked, caught by the man's gaze.

'Come,' he said. 'We must speak alone.'

He turned, and without waiting to see if she followed, started to walk from the room.

Daphne glanced at Quentin.

'Go,' he said, 'but be careful, and don't be long.'

She got up and walked after Kylon. He led her to a small room, with a tall window overlooking the city. He closed the door, and turned to look at her.

'Do you know me?' she said.

'A Kell mage named Kalayne put your image into my head, along with Shella's, to guide me,' the warrior said, staring at her with his troubled eyes. 'You are Killop's dark-skinned woman from the prophecy.'

'You know Killop?'

'Aye,' he said, 'and unlike Keira, I've always believed he's still alive.'

'He is,' she said. 'I saw him two days ago.'

Kylon smiled, and she saw how young he was. Probably the same age she was.

'Where is he?' he asked her.

'In prison.'

'Then how did you see him?'

'I used my mage powers,' she said. 'Do you know what Holdings mages can do?'

'Aye,' he replied. 'I've seen Rijon do it often enough.'

'Good,' she said. 'Then you believe me. Now, tell me about the prophecy.'

'The mage I mentioned, Kalayne, he saw the future,' Kylon said. 'He saw you and Killop together. He also told me I would meet you, more than once.'

'He saw me and Killop together?'

'Aye. Tell me, have you ever met Kallie? Is she still alive?'

'Yes,' she said. 'Also in prison.'

'And Keira?'

Daphne shook her head. 'The fire mage? The Rahain move her around a lot. I don't know where she is right now.'

Kylon swore, and a dark look touched his face.

'I should be in the Rahain capital,' he groaned, clenching his fists. 'Not out here. This is not my fight. My place is with Keira.'

Just as her place was with Killop. Her feelings for him, so sudden and passionate, had been prophesied. It was destiny. She smiled and looked up at Kylon.

'Do you want me to send a message to Killop for you?'

'You can use your powers to do that?'

'I could,' she said, 'but I won't need to. As soon as I get back to Rahain, I'm breaking him out.'

CHAPTER 24
DAPHNE, VISION MAGE

Rahain Capital, Rahain Republic – 2nd Day, Second Third Spring 505

Killop had nothing to do but think about Keira, and imagine what the Rahain intended to do with her.

The day before, she had been hauled in front of his cell for a second, brief, meeting.

Whatever they had ordered her to do, she must have demanded that she be allowed to see him again, which meant, well, he didn't know what it meant, but it couldn't be good. She had looked exhausted but defiant, still insistent that she was going to escape, and that she would come for him when she did. Killop had barely time to say anything, before she had been dragged away again, her chains scraping against the ground.

Apart from his sister, a few others had come to see him. Officers went by now and again to check he was all right, and a small number of well-dressed nobles had come to gawk.

He had lost count of the number of days he had been imprisoned in the small, dark, windowless cell. When food was brought to him he ate, and when he was tired he slept, lying on a dirty, straw-filled mattress. The chains attached to his wrists and ankles had rubbed his skin raw, and then the healed tissue had been rubbed raw again, over and over. He still had scarring from his previous time in chains, and it would probably never fade. A single lamp in the passageway outside his cell provided the only light, its cold blue flame flickering through the bars.

He heard the door at the end of the corridor open, and the guards outside the cell snapped their heels to attention. As footsteps grew nearer, Killop got to his feet.

'Prisoner,' a guard called through the bars. 'Stand back, you have a visitor.'

Killop rolled his shoulders, and waited.

A man dressed in an officer's uniform approached the bars from the left. He looked at Killop with a critical eye.

'Have you come to say anything,' Killop said, 'or just stare like the others?'

The man's tongue flickered. 'Tomorrow,' he said, 'I'm being posted to the Rakanese front, but before leaving the city, I wanted to lay eyes upon the slave that ruined my father.'

'You are Likiat.'

'I am.'

'You captured my sister.'

'Yes.'

'A mistake.'

Likiat frowned. 'Looking at the ripples it set off, I might be inclined to agree. It was supposed to elevate my father. Instead, it brought him low. Now he sits in mourning, wasting his tears on a dead slave and a captured savage.'

'Your father's a good man,' Killop said.

'He's soft in the head and unfit to be a councillor,' Likiat said. 'He has proved that, by loving slaves.'

Killop said nothing.

'You will never leave this cell, do you know that?' Likiat went on. 'Have they told you that? Do you understand? You'll be kept alive, but you'll never leave.'

He gestured to a guard, and strode back down the corridor, the door slamming shut behind him.

That, Killop thought as he sat back down, was the longest conversation he had enjoyed in many days.

He dreamed he was back in Kell. The land was empty of people, and the heavy grey clouds loomed over the wet grass and tumbling hills. Someone was looking for him. They called his name, but their voice was lost in the cold wind as it scoured the forsaken countryside. He was running, he realised, his feet stumbling over the rocks and turf that were barely visible in the fading light. Thunder rumbled through the bank of dark clouds.

Killop! the voice cried again, and this time he recognised it. His heart pounded, and he stopped running.

Killop, she said. *You are dreaming.*

She appeared before him. She was standing on the grassy hillside, the wind blowing through her dark hair, her green eyes shining. He had never seen anything so beautiful.

'You seem more real now,' he said to her, 'than when I dreamt of you before.'

That's because I'm in your mind, she smiled. *I know I shouldn't have entered without asking, but I need to speak with you.*

Killop laughed. 'Are you dreaming too?'

No, she replied. *I'm standing about twenty yards from your cell.*

Killop woke with a start and sat up, sweating. His cell was silent, and dark, except for the faint blue light from the corridor. He shook his head. She had seemed so real, as if she had really been in his head.

I'm still inside your head, Killop, she said, and he could hear the smile in her voice.

'How are you doing this?'

Using my mage skills, she said. *I'm here to rescue you.*

He knew she wasn't lying. Without any rational justification, he knew he could rely on her. A surge of emotions swept through him, surprise, anticipation, and the slow building of an animal longing for her, an ache in his heart. She was so close, so near. He imagined touching her...

Stop, Killop, she said. *I can't concentrate when you feel like that.*

'Daphne,' he whispered.

Listen to me, she said. *I need you to distract the two guards outside your door. Can you do that?*

'Aye.'

I'll be with you soon, Killop, she said. He felt her leave his mind, and the gap she left seemed enormous, as if part of himself had also gone.

He rolled off the mattress and onto the stone floor.

'Guards!' he called out. 'Help me! Help!'

Within moments, two soldiers appeared in front of the bars, their crossbows slung over their shoulders.

Killop clutched at his throat. 'I'm choking; please help!'

The two soldiers looked at each other, then there was a blur of movement behind them, and they fell, collapsing to the ground.

In their place stood Daphne, dressed in black. She leaned a long wooden stave against the wall, and took a set of keys from a pocket.

Killop pushed himself to his feet and waited, watching her as she fitted a key into the door of the cell. Her hair was tied back, and he noticed she was holding her left arm out, as if it were injured. He took in every detail of her face, she was just as beautiful as he had remembered from his dream. Nervous anticipation grew within him.

The cell door swung open, and Daphne entered, reaching for another, smaller key. She crouched down, and unlocked the shackles from his ankles, as he stood motionless, his heart racing, and his desire for her growing more intense with every second. He felt her hand brush his leg as she stood up. He held out his hands, his eyes never leaving her, and she unlocked his right wrist, then his left. The chains fell to the floor with a clattering thud.

She gazed up at him, and their eyes met for the first time since all those thirds before, back in Laodoc's academy. He had never wanted anyone more than he wanted her at that moment, and his desire filled him, pushing out all other thoughts.

He touched her face, his palm against her cheek, and with his other hand pulled her by the waist towards him. Her face tilted up, she closed her eyes and they kissed, while he held her body close to his. She put her arm around his neck. He tasted her, smelled her, drowned himself in her.

Killop started to pull her clothes loose.

'Ow!' she yelled, as he tugged at her sleeve. 'Careful with the arm,' she whispered, but a smile was on her lips, and as she looked up at him he could see his desire mirrored in her own eyes.

They kissed again, and pulled each other down onto the mattress.

He held her close, while she rested her head on his chest, her hair tangled over him. He had never felt so alive. His mind was spinning. He kissed her. This was the woman he was meant to be with, he knew with a fierce certainty.

'I love you, Daphne,' he said. 'I have since the moment I saw you.'

'Me too,' she whispered, smiling. 'But we have to go.'

He started to remember where he was, where they were, lying in his dark cell, with the door wide open.

She rolled off him, and started to gather her clothes. He watched as she pulled her black tunic over her left arm, which was encased in an armoured, close-fitting shell made of dark stone framed in metal. It ended at her wrist, and her left hand was bare, the fingers withered and twisted.

'Old injury,' she said, noticing his gaze as she finished dressing. 'I usually keep the armour on to protect it. Does it bother you?'

Killop shrugged. 'It's part of you.'

She tied her hair back, and went to the door.

He forced himself to stand, and got dressed.

'How did you get here?'

She shrugged as she glanced out of the door. 'It's what I'm good at,' she said, stepping out into the corridor.

Who was this woman? What did he really know about her? He stood in a daze, barely able to believe what had happened.

'Help me,' she called from the passageway, and he went out to find her dragging one of the soldiers towards the cell.

'Are they dead?' he asked, picking up the ankles of the other guard.

'Just a little concussed,' she said. They hauled the two guards into the cell, then stripped them of weapons. Each had a sword, which felt more like a long knife in Killop's hands, and a crossbow.

'Do you know how to work these?' Daphne said.

'Aye,' he said. 'Plenty of practice in the war.'

'Take them both, then,' she said. She fastened a scabbard across her left shoulder, and slung the sword over her back.

'Do you have a plan?' he asked.

'Yes,' she laughed. 'Do you think I would have come without one?'

'I don't know what to think,' he said. 'I haven't the first idea what's going on. I feel like I'm dreaming. Who are you, Daphne?'

'I'm a woman who loves you,' she said. 'But you'd better wake up quick, because I'm going to need you if we're getting out of here alive.'

They left the cell, and Daphne picked up the wooden stave from where she had placed it against the wall, spinning it in her right hand.

'Ready?' she asked.

He nodded, and they started to walk towards the door at the end of the corridor.

'Wait,' he said.

She turned.

'The others,' he whispered. 'We can't leave them.'

'Of course not,' she said. 'We're getting them out too.'

They looked at each other in silence, in the blue flame of the corridor's only lamp.

'I'll tell Kallie,' he said, 'once we're free of here.'

'What is she to you now?'

'I care about her,' Killop said. 'She seems tough, but she's vulnerable, and has been through a lot.'

If Daphne was satisfied with this answer, she didn't show it. She turned again, and they made their way in silence. Killop tried to clear his mind, but his emotions were in turmoil, and he didn't know how he felt about Kallie at that moment. Did he love her? Part of him was relieved at the thought that their relationship was ending, but mostly he felt the heavy hand of guilt weighing down on him. He had betrayed her. He had abandoned himself to Daphne, for just a few precious minutes, but it was enough. He didn't feel like the same man he had been an hour before. When he looked at Daphne, his heart soared, but it didn't seem real. He groaned. If they managed to rescue Kallie, she would sense that something had changed, yet he didn't regret a single moment.

Daphne raised her hand for him to stop, and crouched down, to peer through the keyhole.

'Two guards to the right of the door,' she whispered. 'Stay here.'

She got back to her feet, tensed herself, then threw the door open. She leapt out, and swung her stave in a double arc. Killop heard two dull clangs, followed by the sound of bodies falling to the ground.

He walked into the corridor, and saw Daphne standing over two unconscious guards, her stave twirling in her fingers.

She smiled at him, then motioned for him to help her. They pulled the two soldiers back into the first passageway, took their swords, then closed the door.

'This way,' she said, as she led him to the left. There were blue-flamed lamps every ten yards or so, and they walked in silence down the stone corridor.

'Not many guards tonight,' she said. 'Most are up in the city, dealing with the latest riot.'

'There are riots?'

'The peasants again,' she said. 'More being press-ganged into the army, and more shortages.'

They paused when they came to a crossroads.

'The way is clear,' she whispered, and they set off again.

'Can you see round corners?' he said. 'As well as enter people's dreams?'

'I'm a vision mage,' she said.

They came to a door, and she crouched by the keyhole.

'Guardroom,' she breathed. 'Eight of them inside, sleeping.'

They padded to the next door.

'This is the one,' she whispered, opening it. They went through into another corridor, this one short, and coming to a dead end ten yards ahead of them. Running down the walls were barred doors, three on each side. Daphne pulled out her set of keys.

At the first door, Bridget sprang to her feet, and rushed over from her mattress.

'What the fuck?' she cried. 'You two! I mean, Pyre's tits!'

'Good to see you too, Bridget,' Daphne smiled through the bars. 'We've come to rescue you.'

Killop heard a noise from the cell door behind him, and turned. Kallie was standing by the bars, looking sleepy and bemused.

'Are we getting out of here?' she asked.

'Who's there?' came a voice from a third cell.

'It's Killop!' Bridget said. 'And Daphne; they've come for us.'

'Daphne?' Kallie said, peering through the bars into the darkness.

Daphne found the right key, and the door swung open. Bridget ran through and jumped into Killop's arms, a broad smile on her face, while Daphne moved down to Lacey's cell.

Killop laughed, and put Bridget down.

'Here,' he said, handing her one of the crossbows.

'Fucking beauty,' she grinned. 'Armed at last.'

'Hi, I'm Lacey,' Killop heard the Lach woman say, as Daphne opened her door.

'Hi, Lacey, I'm Daphne.'

'So I already heard,' Lacey replied, stepping out into the corridor, and staring down at the Holdings woman. 'You're the one that Killop was dreaming about? What are you doing here? I notice you freed him first. Why? Did he make you come for us?'

'Lacey, shut up!' Bridget said. 'We can argue this shit when we're out of here.'

Lacey looked from Daphne to Killop, a knowing smirk on her face.

Daphne ignored her, and went to Kallie's door.

Kallie stepped back, waiting.

As the door swung open, the corridor fell silent. Killop looked from woman to woman. Lacey had a slight scowl on her lips, while Bridget glanced at Kallie, her eyes wide.

'Thank you, Daphne,' Kallie said, as she came out.

'Kallie,' said Daphne. 'Sword?'

'Aye,' she said, taking the offered weapon.

Lacey held out her hand, and Killop passed her the other crossbow.

'What's the plan?' said Bridget.

'We're getting out the same way I got in,' Daphne said. 'It'll be a tight squeeze in places, but there are hidden tunnels and passageways riddling this part of the cavern. It'll take us a few hours, and we'll come out somewhere by the Tile Market, where I have a wagon waiting.'

'And how do you know all this?' Lacey said.

'I have been over every inch of this tower, and all the tunnels that lie beneath it.'

Lacey stepped closer to Daphne, and glared down at her. Daphne looked small, surrounded by the three tall clanswomen, but stood her ground.

'How?' Lacey repeated.

'I'm a mage,' Daphne said, looking her in the eye. 'I can see things.'

'Kallie,' Killop said; 'do you remember Kalayne? How he could see things that were far away? She can do the same.'

'Kalayne?' Daphne said.

'A mage from Kell,' said Killop. 'He has the same seeing powers as you.'

Daphne crinkled her brows in confusion. 'Wait,' she said; 'is he the one who can see into the future?'

'Aye,' Killop said. 'How did you know that?'

'He prophesises,' Kallie said, staring at Daphne.

Daphne held her stare. 'I know about the prophecy,' she said. 'Kylon told me.'

The atmosphere in the corridor froze. Bridget looked incredulous, Lacey sceptical.

'You spoke to Kylon?' Killop said. 'Did you go into his dreams?'

'No,' she said. 'I met him. He's in the Rakanese city, protecting their mage leader.'

'What the fuck's he doing out there?' Bridget cried.

'Quiet,' Killop said. 'There are guards sleeping in the next room.'

'There was another prophecy,' said Lacey, frowning. 'Kalayne said he had a vision of Kylon with the Rakanese, so Keira sent him off there, to save their mage from some catastrophe that's supposed to happen. I thought it was stupid. We lost Kylon, Kalayne, and one of our best squads, all on some pointless mission. If Kalayne had still been there, Keira and I would never have been captured.'

Killop noticed that Daphne and Kallie were still staring at each other, paying no attention to the others. Pyre's bollocks. This wasn't going to be easy.

There was a sound from the main corridor outside, and Daphne's attention snapped back to the door. She drew the sword from the scabbard on her back, and moved up the passageway.

'Well done, Bridget,' Lacey scowled.

'Crossbows,' Daphne whispered, pointing at Bridget and Lacey. 'Cover me.'

She stole to the door, peering through the crack.

'Two of them,' she breathed. 'Come to see what the noise is about.'

She leaned by the wall next to the door, her sword held level by her head.

The door opened, and the Rahain guards walked through.

Before they could take in the scene in front of them, Daphne's blade flashed out, slicing each through their throats.

Lacey's crossbow went thrum a moment later, catching one of the guards in the chest as he fell. He flew backwards, crashing into the back wall. Lacey shrugged, as the others glared at her. They heard raised voices, coming from the room next door.

'Shit,' Bridget groaned. 'The rest are coming.'

Daphne dashed out into the corridor, and disappeared to the left.

'Where's she going?' Lacey said.

There was a cry from the corridor, and more shouting, and Killop ran to the door. He burst through, to see Daphne carving her way through half a dozen Rahain soldiers, her blade whipping out, as she spun, ducked and rolled.

Killop stood, awestruck. He felt the others join him at the door, also watching the slaughter. What Daphne was doing was impossible. Her speed was mesmerising, her movements fluid. She was using her left arm to shield, block, and also as a weapon, while the sword in her right hand slashed through the leather armour of the guards like it was paper.

'Look at her go!' Bridget whispered.

They watched enthralled as Daphne rammed the end of her blade into the eye socket of the last living soldier. She leapt up, and used his falling body to pull the blade out as she landed.

'Fucking bravo, Daphne!' Bridget shouted and clapped, a grin splitting her face. Kallie and Lacey looked on, saying nothing.

Daphne sheathed her sword, blood streaked across her.

'Come on,' she said. 'There will be guards down from the floors above in an hour or so. We'd best be out of here by then.'

They followed her as she led them through more corridors, where they dodged a pair of half-sleeping guards at a junction. They took the paths that led downwards, and continued deeper into the bowels of the tower. It grew dark, and Daphne stopped. She began rooting about in a pile of debris by the rough entrance to another tunnel.

She pulled a satchel from the heap of rubbish, out of which she took a torch and a flint set.

The others waited in the shadows as she tried to light the torch.

'Damn it,' Daphne muttered. 'It's got damp down here.'

Killop stepped forward.

'Don't do it,' Kallie said. 'She's not one of us.'

'She trusts us,' he replied. 'I trust her.'

He knelt by Daphne, and took the torch in his left hand. He looked at his right, his palm and fingers dirty and scarred. It had been a long time, he thought. Not since the Rahain had arrived at Fire Mountain, and he had allowed Keira to use his powers to destroy a flying beast. He smiled at the memory, and focused, letting energy gather in the space between his hands.

Blue lightning sparks flew out of his fingertips, leaping the gaps between the digits on each hand. He threw the sparks at the end of the torch, and it burst into flames. He eased his power off, and sat, grimacing. He handed the lit torch to Daphne, and took a moment to steady himself.

'You shouldn't have done that,' Lacey said. 'Our secrets are not for other folk to know.'

Killop looked up. Daphne crouched next to him, her face open with surprise, as she stared at the burning torch in her hands.

'Lead us out of here,' Killop said.

Daphne nodded, and stood. 'Follow me,' she said, and started down the tunnel.

The clansfolk followed Daphne down the dark, rough tunnel. The way was hard going, with the roof low and sharp, and Killop had to stoop to avoid scraping his head. He was soon disorientated, as they made their way through the warren under the High Senate complex.

After what seemed an hour, Daphne raised her hand, and they halted. She leant the half-burnt torch against a rock, and reached into the satchel. She took out a flask of water, and passed it to Bridget.

'Drink,' she said. 'We're nearly there.'

As the others rested, Daphne approached Killop. He looked at her in the dim light. She appeared calm and composed on the surface, but her eyes were troubled.

'They don't like me,' she whispered.

'Why do you think that?'

Daphne smiled. 'I don't care,' she said. 'Them not liking me. But it'll complicate things, when we get to the surface.'

'What are you two whispering about?' Lacey asked.

Kallie and Bridget also turned to look.

'We were talking about what to do,' Daphne said. 'About the plan. About how you not liking me might make things difficult.'

'Ha!' Lacey smirked. 'Who doesn't like you?'

'Well,' Daphne replied, 'you, for a start. And Kallie. I don't think Bridget minds one way or the other.'

Lacey's face went red.

'You're right,' Kallie said. 'I don't like you. I know why you're here. I know what you want.'

Bridget sighed. 'Can we not leave this until we're out of here? And you're wrong, Daphne; I do like you, despite you having a crazy crush on my best friend's partner. I had hoped you'd got the message last time we spoke, but at the same time, if you weren't still after him, we'd all be back in our cells.'

'Thanks, Bridget,' Daphne said. 'I think.'

'The prophecy was wrong,' Kallie said. 'It said I would be reborn when the fire goddess returned. Well, Keira is here, somewhere in the city, and nothing's changed. If that prophecy's wrong, then so is the one about you and Killop.'

Daphne said nothing.

'Tell her, Killop!' Kallie cried. 'Tell her she's delusional!'

'I'm with Bridget on this,' he said. 'Let's get out of here first, talk it through later.'

Kallie stared at him, shaking her head.

'You can talk about it all you like when you get to the surface,' Daphne said, 'but I won't be there.'

Killop turned to her, but she kept her gaze averted.

'By now,' she went on, 'your escape will have been noticed, and guards will soon be swarming through these caverns, hunting you. The path up to the surface is there, to the right. That low tunnel. You can take the torch, I have another. I'll stay here to cover your tracks, and will lead your pursuers in the opposite direction. I know a dozen other ways out of these tunnels.'

Her voice had been steady throughout, though Killop could feel the pain in her words.

'Alright,' Lacey said. 'How far is it to the wagon?'

'About another ten minutes from here,' Daphne replied. 'Stick to the path. It rises steeply, so be careful. When you get to the wagon, go straight into the back, then knock on the front rail three times. I've already paid the driver, he'll be waiting for the signal. The wagon will take you all the way to the open air, by the Gate of Pillars. From there, you can flee into the countryside.'

Bridget hugged her. 'Thank you, Daphne.'

'Take care, Bridget,' Daphne whispered, her voice hoarse.

Kallie picked up the lit torch, and nodded at Daphne.

'Let's go,' Lacey said.

'One moment,' Daphne said. She took her spare torch from the satchel, and lit it off the brand in Kallie's hand.

Kallie, Lacey and Bridget moved to the tunnel's low entrance.

'Killop?' asked Kallie.

His feet felt frozen to the ground. He looked from Kallie to Daphne. Daphne leaned in close to him.

'Go,' she whispered. 'Our love survived us being apart before, it will again. Go.'

He stared at her, feeling like he was dreaming, his heart aching.

'I'll find my sister, then I'll come for you,' he said.

'Killop!' Bridget called.

He nodded to Daphne, then turned and joined the others, leaving the Holdings woman standing alone in the dark tunnel, a solitary tear rolling down her cheek.

CHAPTER 25
RADICAL

Rahain Capital, Rahain Republic – 5th Day, Second Third Spring 505

'Careful with that box,' Laodoc called out. 'It has many old and fragile books in it.'

'Apologies, Councillor,' the porter muttered, struggling under the weight.

Beoloth approached.

'Is this the last of it?' Laodoc asked him, as he watched his possessions being loaded up onto the wagons parked outside the front of his mansion.

'Almost, my lord.'

'Good,' he said, rubbing his hands together. 'Once they've finished, tell the workers they can stop for lunch before setting off for Slateford.'

'I will, my lord,' Beoloth said, remaining where he was.

'Was there something else?'

'Yes, my lord,' Beoloth said. 'Some visitors have arrived from the High Senate. They want to ask you some questions.'

'Really?' Laodoc said. 'I wonder what that could be about. Where are they?'

'I showed them to the green room, my lord.'

'I shall go and speak to them,' Laodoc nodded. 'You can finish up here.'

Laodoc walked back to the mansion. He suppressed a nervous grin, and felt that he could even burst out laughing if he wasn't careful. Daphne Holdfast had been true to her word, and had freed the Kellach captives. She had then informed Laodoc in a highly unorthodox manner, by entering his mind to communicate with him. He chuckled. A most interesting young lady.

He composed his features as he walked to the green room, making sure his face was appropriately sombre. He entered, to see three officials standing by the bay window. One was in a uniform he recognised from the time of his own arrest, that of a state investigator, and the other two fellows were his guards.

'Good morning,' Laodoc said, 'and please forgive the lack of refreshments. As you can see, I'm preparing to make a move up to my hillside estate.'

'An interesting time to be leaving the city, Councillor,' the investigator said.

'The second third of spring?' Laodoc replied. 'Why is that interesting?'

The investigator studied him.

'So, what can I do for you?' Laodoc said.

'A few nights ago,' the investigator began, 'four Kellach Brigdomin prisoners escaped from the cells under the Tyrant's Tower.'

'Impossible!' Laodoc cried. 'Isn't that the most heavily guarded part of the High Senate?'

'It is, yes.'

'Oh dear, how embarrassing for you,' Laodoc said. 'Have you come to warn me that my life may be in danger from these fugitives? I thank you for your concern, but why would they bother with me?'

'Three of the slaves used to live here,' the investigator said, 'as part of your so-called academy.'

'So-called?' Laodoc said. 'Sir, I am grievously offended. My political career may be in tatters, but I am still proud of my academic achievements. Did you ever read the research I produced on the fascinating subject of the gestational cycle of the copper-horned gaien? It really has much to recommend it...'

'Councillor,' the investigator said, 'please account for your whereabouts at the time of the escape.'

'That, I'm afraid, I cannot do.'

'And why is that?'

'Because you haven't told me when it was,' Laodoc replied. 'A "few nights ago" is a little vague. You weren't trying to trick me now, were you?'

'Councillor,' the man frowned, 'where were you on the night of the second day of the second third of spring?'

'Ahh, three nights ago,' Laodoc smiled. 'Now, let me see...' He put his hand to his chin. 'Yes, I remember; three nights ago I stayed over at the residence of a Professor Helliur. She and I are old friends, and we had dinner and a few drinks. A lovely woman. When you question her, be sure to mention I said that.'

'Thank you, Councillor,' the man said. He gestured to the two guards. 'We will leave you now. The slaves had help to escape, and we believe that whoever provided that assistance must have had inside knowledge of the layout of the tower. If you hear anything, please let us know.'

Laodoc watched in silence as they walked to the door. As soon as they were gone he sighed.

Fools, he thought, they knew nothing. It felt odd not to care about getting caught, and he would have liked to have seen their faces if he had told them he had known what had happened. He couldn't though. Daphne had kept her side of the bargain, and he would never betray her.

His mood slumped as he walked back through the deserted house, its remaining furniture all covered in dust sheets, and the shutters up on most of the windows. Memories of Simiona were in every room. Here was where she had assisted him each morning in the running of the household, there, where the skirting was loose, was where she had once tripped and skinned her knee. He stopped when he got to the front door. His legs felt heavy, and his spirits were low. Outside, the workers were sitting in the shade, eating their ryebread lunch. Behind them, the line of wagons stood loaded, and ready to go.

'Well done, Beoloth,' he said, forcing cheerfulness into his voice.

'Thank you, my lord.'

'Good luck on the road,' Laodoc said. 'I will follow you up to Slateford in a few days. Take good care of the wagons, and make sure the porters and guards are well paid on arrival.'

'Yes, my lord.'

'I'd best be off,' he said. 'I have a few things to say at the City Council.'

Laodoc was not looking forward to retiring. He knew he had determined to do so, but dreaded the speech he would have to make, with all the insincere apologies, cringing and hand-wringing it would involve. Most of all, he hated the idea that the other councillors would then offer their own speeches, just as dishonest as his own, in which they would applaud his integrity, while pretending to respect him, and reduce their animosity to the level of a great game. After that, he would probably have to spend time with them in the bar, acting as if they were all good friends, when he hated almost every one of them.

But then it would be over, and he could retreat back to his house, and get ready to move into retirement at Slateford.

He was greeted on the front steps of the council by a Conservative politician with a smug smile, and he guessed that Ruellap must have told everyone about his impending announcement.

Inside the entrance doors, he saw Pleonim and Wyenna. He sighed, knowing it would be bad manners to avoid his Liberal colleagues.

They nodded at him as he approached.

'Good afternoon,' he said.

'My dear Laodoc,' Pleonim said. 'Good to have you back, old chap. Our side has missed you over the last third. And your vote.'

'Would it have made any difference to a single debate?' Laodoc asked.

'No,' Pleonim said. 'The war coalition are tighter than ever. No one's breaking ranks. They're going to push for a general city-wide mobilisation this evening.'

Laodoc gasped. 'More troops?'

'The High Senate believe that the hundred and twenty thousand already requisitioned isn't enough for a complete circumvallation of the Rakanese camp,' Pleonim said. 'They think another thirty to forty thousand should do it. They have also decreed that the City Council shall be responsible for fulfilling the requisition.'

'And where is the council supposed to get all those new soldiers?'

'Farms, factories, wherever they can find them,' Wyenna said. 'And the High Senate also want to summon every mage under fifty that hasn't already been called up.'

'Well, at least I'm too old for that,' Laodoc said. 'But really, every mage? If I recall the numbers correctly, the army only required a score of mages for the entire campaign in Kellach Brigdomin.'

'Yes,' Pleonim said, 'but the Kellach peninsula is actually just a long mountain range, where one mage could create an earthquake on his own, while the Rakanese have settled on a flood-plain. It's just clay and soil, no bedrock close to the surface. It's going to require a considerable effort to generate an earthquake if they decide they need to.'

'If they decide they need to?'

'They would have already done it if they could,' Wyenna said. 'The day after the guards were killed by the Rakanese mage, the High Senate almost voted to obliterate the entire camp, and would have, had the migrants built on rock instead. They came that close to destruction.'

Laodoc stared at them. 'Our leaders are insane.'

Pleonim laughed as if he had been joking. 'Well,' he said, 'you'll be out of it soon enough. Off to enjoy a comfortable retirement in the countryside.'

'I still can't believe you're going,' Wyenna said, 'just when we needed you the most.'

'Thank you, Wyenna,' he said, smiling, 'though you are probably the only one who thinks so.'

'You'd be surprised,' she muttered.

They strolled together towards the debating chamber, while other councillors nodded to Laodoc as they passed.

'This feels a little disconcerting,' he said. 'None of the usual scowls. I almost miss them.'

They took their seats by the other Liberals, many of whom stood to let Laodoc pass. A few looked at him with a sense of disappointment, others with mild contempt.

The lord speaker banged his fist for silence.

'This session is now commenced,' he called out. 'Who is looking to speak?'

A dozen councillors stood, but as was tradition, Ziane, the longest-serving in the chamber, was given the nod.

'My fellow councillors,' he cried, 'the crisis our beloved Republic currently faces is one that requires a singular dedication, a steadfast and unyielding will, and, yes, sacrifice. We know from yesterday's reports that our mighty army, whose soldiers valiantly protect us from the murderous Rakanese hordes, are moving into position around the gigantic slum the migrants have thrown up. We also know, that to encircle the Rakanese completely, a further requisition of troops will be required. The High Senate have handed us here in this chamber the honour of ensuring that this requisition is fulfilled.

'Therefore I ask you, should we falter now, after so much effort and gold have already been expended in holding back the migrant tide? Or do we rally, as the capital city of this nation, and rise to face the challenge? This is the making of us. This is when we show the world that we do not give up when times get tough.

'So therefore, I now propose that we set this great and proud city on a complete war footing, placing its population and resources under the direct control of a new committee made up of city councillors, to requisition the required troops, mages and supplies necessary to ensure the siege of the Rakanese is speedily brought to a successful conclusion.'

He sat, to generous applause and shouts of approval.

'Your proposal is noted,' the lord speaker said. 'I shall hold the vote over until we have heard from some others.' He looked around, as several quickly got to their feet.

Yaelli, from the Merchant Party, got the nod. Next to her, Laodoc saw Douanna sitting. She was beautifully dressed in rich robes, and exuded serene confidence. Laodoc bit his tongue, his heart burning in silent rage. No doubt she would have already noticed his presence, and was probably looking forward to his retirement speech. He wondered if she would talk to him in the bar afterwards, in some pretence of friendship, and he felt almost physically sick at the prospect. His hand went into his left pocket, his fingers finding the small scrap of torn fabric.

'Fellow councillors,' Yaelli said, 'the parlous state of the city's coffers demands that we act with a certain prudence. Production is down, trade is down, taxes are up, and our economy is stretched and fragile. In short, we are all feeling the squeeze. While I agree with the necessity of everything my esteemed colleague has just proposed, I would ask that we add an amendment, to limit the emergency committee's requisition and mobilisation powers to a single third, upon completion of which, the law will automatically lapse, unless we vote again on that date to continue it. This is a wholly precautionary measure, to allow this august chamber to sensibly evaluate the powers of the new committee, and modify them if necessary.'

Yaelli sat, to a smattering of light applause.

'That's it?' Laodoc whispered to Wyenna. 'That's all the Merchants are asking for? The siege must be costing them a fortune.'

'They're too browbeaten to put up any resistance,' she replied. 'And if you think that's bad, just listen to what our own party is about to propose.'

She quietened, just as the Liberal Nueillin was selected to speak.

'My fellow councillors,' she said, 'we here on these opposition benches will not stand in the way of the will of the council, and will not vote against such emergency measures as proposed. We will, however, be offering our support to the amendment from the Merchant Party. An automatic expiry date for the suggested committee will give everyone time for reflection.'

She sat, her contribution almost ignored by the ranks of Patriots and Conservatives, who were chatting amongst themselves.

Wyenna gave a told-you-so smirk to Laodoc, who sat in silence, as anger built within him.

'This is what it's been like,' she whispered, 'ever since you were arrested.'

Ziane rose to speak again.

'Lord Speaker,' he said, 'I am happy to humbly yield to Councillor Yaelli's amendment, and incorporate it into my own proposal.'

'Very well,' the lord speaker said. 'Is there a dissenter?'

No one rose.

'Councillor Ziane's proposal,' the lord speaker boomed out, 'as amended by Councillor Yaelli, is therefore carried without dissent. Private property laws in the city are hereby suspended for one third, and all productive capacity and means are now under the direct control of this council, until a standing requisition and mobilisation committee can be established. The debate to discuss said committee's remit and membership will be held as the first item of business at tomorrow's session. Please come prepared.'

He looked out over the councillors, as they began gossiping about who should be on the committee.

'This session continues,' he called out. 'Who is looking to speak?'

Laodoc rose, along with a dozen others, among them Ziane.

When the veteran Conservative saw Laodoc standing, he smiled, nodded, and returned to his seat. Taking his cue, the others started to sit as well. The lord speaker pretended to examine his fingernails until Laodoc was the only one left on his feet. The speaker smiled, and gave him the nod.

'Thank you, Lord Speaker,' Laodoc said, taking some time to gaze at the expectant faces around the chamber. 'It has truly been a privilege, and a great honour, to serve in this fine institution, alongside such noble and excellent colleagues, both on this side of the chamber, and on the other.'

There was much smiling and nodding, and many councillors settled down to listen.

'There are too many names to mention each one individually,' he continued, 'but my highest praise and respect is extended to Councillor Ziane, the father of this chamber. It will not be long, I believe, before his talents take him all the way to the High Senate.' There was applause, and a beaming Ziane got his back thoroughly slapped by his fellows. 'And, of course,' Laodoc went on, 'what kind of father would I be, if I failed to commend the excellent performance of my own son, Councillor Ruellap. A man with a great future ahead of him, if only he can avoid his old man's mistakes.'

There was generous laughter at this. Laodoc noticed that while the Patriots and Conservatives were lapping it up, many Merchants and Liberals were frowning. He paused, surprised. He had assumed everyone wanted him to go. He looked over the Merchant benches. Some of his old Hedgers were shaking their heads at him, while Douanna sat in their midst, grinning.

His mind went blank, his mouth dry and sour. Killop was free, and that was good, but Simi was still dead, and nothing could change that.

'I have, unfortunately,' he began again, 'made several mistakes. Not many get the opportunity to stand in front of their peers and colleagues, and apologise for their errors, and so I count myself fortunate that I am able to do so today.'

The chamber quietened.

'I have three apologies to make,' Laodoc said, with all eyes upon him. 'The first is to the slaves of Rahain. What arrogance, to imagine that almost one half of the population should be owned by the other half.' The faces of the councillors changed to puzzlement. 'What stupidity, to deny almost half the population any say in their own lives, to cut short their potential, and treat them as if they were gaien. Or worse.'

Some voices started to call out against him, but most sat still in silence, hoping the old man would rant for a minute, then retire.

'I apologise to all the slaves of Rahain,' Laodoc proclaimed, 'for centuries of abuse, cruelty and degradation at the hands of people like myself. For those who say that it is our tradition, I say, take a look at the other nations on this continent. The Holdings are every bit as civilised as ourselves, and they see no need for slavery. In fact, they despise it, and rightly so. The Kellach Brigdomin did not even know the word for slavery before we invaded them, though I'm sure they are well acquainted with its meaning now. Even the Rakanese see slavery as beneath them. We should join the ranks of the truly civilised, and utterly and irreversibly abolish slavery.'

The looks of anger and contempt came from across the council chamber, as all pretence at listening politely was abandoned.

'My second apology is to those Kellach Brigdomin I just mentioned,' Laodoc went on, 'or, as I should more correctly state, the Kell, the Lach, the Brig, and the Domm. We committed a savage and barbaric act of unprovoked aggression on one of our neighbours, so we could open up a few more coal mines. Is it any wonder the other nations fear us? Or hate us? Release the Kellach captives, I say! Give each one an apology and a bag of gold, and let them return to their lands, or stay here, if they prefer.'

The noise in the chamber increased, as did the level of anger aimed at him. He revelled in it, enjoying the hatred rolling in waves from the Patriots and Conservative ranks. Even Douanna looked annoyed.

'Let him finish!' the lord speaker shouted.

'My third, and final apology,' Laodoc shouted through the noise as the lord speaker banged his fist.

'I said let him finish,' the lord speaker roared, 'or face immediate ejection from this chamber!'

The noise died down.

'My thanks, Lord Speaker, as always,' Laodoc said. His chest swelled with pride, and he held his head high. 'As I was saying, my third apology is to the Rakanese, who came here, barefoot and starving, having endured unimaginable torment crossing the Basalt Desert. It was a poignant and beautiful opportunity, for us Rahain as a nation, to prove to the others that we were not savages, no matter the crimes we had committed against the Kellach Brigdomin. It was a chance to redeem ourselves, and make a new ally.

'Instead, we built a wall, and plotted to annihilate a third of a million refugees. We are savages.'

There was uproar. Several councillors from the Patriot Party got to their feet, threatening him, and shouting. Pleonim, sitting to his side, stared up at him open-mouthed. Wyenna was smiling however, and nodding, urging him to continue.

The lord speaker whispered to a clerk of the chamber, who ran to the door. Moments later, a dozen guards trooped in, and formed up before the speaker's platform.

The chamber quietened again.

The lord speaker nodded. 'I trust that you can all see these soldiers standing here? Good. Next to speak out of line shall be escorted from the premises.' He turned to Laodoc. 'Councillor, am I to assume that you have nearly reached the conclusion of your peroration?'

'Indeed,' Laodoc replied. 'I am almost there.'

'Then,' the lord speaker waved at him, 'please continue.'

'I have a few more words, directed to those sat here,' Laodoc said, looking over the crowd of councillors. 'I will not waste my breath on the Patriots, abhorrent as they are, and opposed to everything I stand for. There is also little hope for the Conservatives, ridden as they are with fear, apathy, loathing and a smug self-satisfaction. Maybe once that oaf Ziane has gone, there might be hope for some fresh thinking, but until then...'

A few Liberals laughed, as the veteran Conservative sat fuming.

'To the Merchants, however,' Laodoc said, turning to them, 'I say this. Why are you continuing to follow a policy that is ruining you? The folly of the Patriots, and the fear of the Conservatives, is bankrupting this country. Are there any of you, sitting here today, whose businesses are not suffering? What will it take before you realise that you are the fools of this whole game?

'And,' he turned to the Liberals, 'to my own party, I simply shake my head in sorrow. A friend once said to me that he believed the Liberals knew in their hearts what to do, but they were cowards who could not find the courage to stand by their ideals. Your pathetic capitulation today has confirmed for me the truth of this opinion.

'It is with a sad heart, therefore,' Laodoc said, as the chamber sat in seething silence, 'that I announce my resignation from the Liberal Party.'

The faces stared at him, waiting.

'I do not intend to retire,' he proclaimed, to gasps of disbelief and cries of rage. 'Instead,' he went on, as pandemonium erupted, 'I will start my own party, based on the principles I have espoused in this speech...' He paused, as the volume of noise grew too loud to be over-heard. Several Patriots were rushing across the floor towards him, while a few Liberals gathered round protectively. He saw the lord speaker shouting at the guards, and they barged their way through the crowd.

Wyenna grabbed his arm.

'Come on!' she shouted.

The guards reached them, and formed a ring around Laodoc, as punches flew. Two of his old Hedgers were attacking a Patriot who had been trying to grab a Liberal, who, oblivious, was shouting insults at the Conservatives.

'Order!' the lord speaker bellowed out. 'Councillor Laodoc is hereby suspended for three days for provoking a disturbance. Guards, please escort him from this chamber, and off the premises. This session is now ended.'

The guards started moving, pushing anyone who got in their way, as Laodoc was bundled from the council. The heavy doors of the chamber glided shut behind them, and the noise died away.

Wyenna was still holding on to his arm, and was looking up at him with a mischievous grin.

'That was amazing,' she said, as they were marched through the long halls to the main entrance. 'I don't think I've ever seen Ziane that angry. Did you plan the whole thing?'

He shook his head. 'I walked in here today fully convinced I was going to retire. But, standing up there, seeing how pleased my enemies were by the prospect, I simply couldn't do it.'

'And are you serious about a new party?'

'I am.'

'Do you want any help?'

'Are you offering to become my first member?'

'I am.'

Laodoc laughed. 'Then welcome to the Radical Party.'

CHAPTER 26
THE HEIGHTS

A khanawarah City, Rahain Republic – 16th Day, Second Third Spring 505

Shella peered through the device Kylon called the lizardeye as she lay among the boulders dotting the dusty brown hillside, watching as ranks of Rahain soldiers marched through fields a little over a mile away. Above the lines of troops, the morning sun was starting to appear over the horizon.

'Shit,' she said. 'That's us completely surrounded then. They've closed off the eastern gap.'

She passed the viewing-tube to Polli, who lay next to her.

As her assistant took her turn to look, Kylon turned to Shella.

'We can still get through their lines over the northern hills,' he said, 'if we keep the numbers low. Their pickets are thinly spread in places.'

'Not much good for bringing in wagons of supplies, though,' Shella replied. 'Since they dammed the river, the road east was our main way of bringing food in.'

'Then we'll have to eat less,' Kylon shrugged.

'That'll go down well,' she snorted. 'Another cut in rations, so soon after the last one? How long can the Rahain keep this up? There must be over a hundred thousand of the bastards out there.'

'Not losing confidence?'

'No,' she replied. 'We're still going to win. But it's going to get messy.'

'It already is.'

She nodded.

'They've stopped,' Polli said. 'Looks like they're forming a front line.'

'Give me that,' Shella snapped, grabbing the lizardeye.

Her assistant was right. The Rahain soldiers had halted two hundred yards in front of the city's eastern defences, and were digging along a line a mile and a half in length, all the way from the hillside to the river.

She sighed, then turned to her right.

'Might as well check out the southern front while we're up here,' she said.

She scanned past the buildings clustered on the southern bank, and out to the fields beyond, now churned into acres of thick mud by days of incessant catapult fire. She had built her defensive lines out past the rice-fields, and the smaller orchards that lay on the drier ground to the west. Ten thousand labourers had been working in shifts on the whole line down there, building a thick maze of ditches, trenches, brick walls, pits, canals and palisades, but the Rahain army had arrived before it could be completed. The makeshift fortifications had served their purpose however, as two full divisions of Rahain troops had been enticed in, only to become bogged down in the muddy and confused front lines.

In her attempt to protect the main food-producing areas within the defensive perimeter, she had unwittingly created a vast sea of mud, some four miles long and two deep, pounded day and night by Rahain throwing machines. It hadn't done much good for the food supply, but it had created an effective defensive barrier. If there was a full-scale assault from that direction, the Rahain would drown in the mud by the thousand.

From the hillside she could see a constant but low-level bustle of violent activity, as archers shot crossbows from hidden locations deep in the mud, hitting exposed soldiers on both sides. There was a fight going on over the possession of a small brick bunker, while, all around, enormous boulders smashed into the ripped-up earth, gouging great holes that soon filled with water.

The stream that had fed the rice-fields was still flowing down from the southern hills, but it disappeared into a hundred channels as it passed through the frontlines, saturating the whole area between the Rahain army and the river.

The river itself, however, was dry.

It had been eight days since Shella had first noticed that the level of the river was falling. Three days after that, it had ceased altogether. Shella had ordered every cistern filled, and every sluice gate closed, to preserve all they had. Several wells had also been constructed, reaching down through thick layers of clay to the water table beneath. It was tight, but with strict rationing, and some luck with the weather, there should be enough for everyone.

The spawn pools had been prioritised, and each had their own dedicated wells, including one in the palace, where Queen Obli was now the proud mother of nine royal spawn, whom she fed daily while they swam in the warmth of the pool. The queen had not left the palace since before her spawning, and had made no public comment about the newly elected democratic government of the city.

Shella lowered the lizardeye.

'What now, Commander?' asked Polli.

'Best report to the ministry,' she said, turning to go.

'I liked it better when you were in charge,' Kylon muttered, as he followed her down the hill. 'Those idiots your people elected are already making a mess of things.'

'Democracy is shit,' Shella said. 'Only marginally less shit than the alternatives. And, I'm still the high mage, and the commander of the new army, and of all the defences, so it's not like I've sunk back into blissful obscurity.'

At the bottom of the hill was a new food silo, ringed by housing that was thickly occupied despite being only half-finished. There were a few tents left over from when all domestic building had ceased, and work on the defensive lines and fortified positions had begun.

Her brown-uniformed soldiers, volunteers in her new army, guarded the silo, each with a short bow, a flint-tipped pike and a shield. With the entire city focussed on war production, weapons had been constructed in their thousands, supplemented by every Rahain crossbow or sword they could get their hands on. There were now fifty thousand in uniform, five divisions, each assigned to a sector of the city, two on the more densely populated northern bank, and three engaged in the skirmishing on the mudflats making up their southern flank. Hundreds more men and women were joining up daily, and were rushed through a harsh five-day training programme devised by the Kellach Brigdomin. If they were lucky, they got the northern bank, if not, the mud.

They saluted her as she passed the silo, and she nodded back.

She had given away her power, but she knew she could take it back any time she needed to.

'I'm pretty sure Leah fancies you,' Shella said, her glass of rice-sprits held out in her right hand.

'She doesn't,' Kylon muttered.

'Well,' Shella went on. 'What about Kilynn? I mean, I know she never seems to leave her brother's side... What's all that about?' She squinted at Kylon, but he ignored her. 'Anyway, I'm sure she'd make a good lover for you.'

'She wouldn't.'

'Look, I know you're pining for your locked-up fire mage,' Shella said, leaning over the side of her chair towards him. 'But I worry about you, not getting any.'

'What about you?' he growled back at her. 'I've not seen any evidence of you "getting any" either.'

Her face drooped.

'You're right,' she said, taking a drink. 'No man will come near me. Afraid of what I might do to them if I lose my temper.'

'It's a pity,' he said. 'You're a fine-looking woman, you know, for one of the wee folk.'

'If that's an attempt at a come on,' she said, laughing, 'then I'm totally up for it. I promise I'll try not to kill you.'

'You have that in common with Keira,' he said. 'The ability to kill effortlessly. I often wondered what she might do if she lost it with me while a fire was burning close by.'

'Talking about your girlfriend is a real turn-off,' Shella said. 'I've changed my mind, you're too vulgar for me. And much too hairy.'

'Then I guess we'll both have to remain alone. Your loss,' he muttered, turning his head away.

'Ha!' she shrieked. 'Caught you smiling!'

He turned back to face her, the smile transforming his face. She saw how young he was, and how handsome, in his gigantic way.

'You're a strange woman, Shella,' he said, shaking his head.

'And you're a mysterious man,' she shot back. 'I must have told you a hundred stories about my family, and life, while you've said almost nothing. And don't say it's part of your tradition or anything, because I've heard the others tell their own tales. You talk about your woman Keira often enough, but you never say anything about yourself.'

His smile vanished, and his dour expression returned. He shrugged, and turned from her.

She swore. Why did she have to do that? Could she not just have enjoyed the moment with him?

There was a knock at the door.

'Yeah?' she called out, sitting back into her chair, while Kylon brooded next to her.

The door opened, and Bowda entered.

'Mage Commander,' he said. 'Apologies for interrupting at this late hour, but there is an urgent report from the hill-scouts, stating that several companies of Rahain soldiers have been seen on top of the northern range.'

She put down her glass and stood.

'Numbers?'

'The messages are confused,' Bowda said. 'A few thousand is my best guess.'

'Have you summoned the staff?'

'Yes, ma'am.'

'Let's go, then,' she said, walking to the door. 'Kylon, move your hairy ass.'

She walked to her command office, where the generals of the two northern divisions were already waiting, along with several other staff officers. She had transferred the retired police officers back to their old jobs, and had promoted rapidly through the ranks. Their inexperience was painful to behold, but Shella had thrown in anyone with a spark of potential to become the officers of her army.

'Polli,' she said. 'Report.'

Her chief of staff stepped forward a pace.

'Latest accounts from the northern hills say that the Rahain flew in four waves of troop-carriers, dropping them off over a three-mile stretch of the ridge.'

'We must prepare the city defences, Commander,' General Darra said, her brow creased, 'for imminent attack.'

'There can't be more than a few thousand of them,' Shella said. 'They're not going to attack. Polli, where they landed, does it overlook the city?'

'It does, Commander,' she replied. 'They are positioned directly above the northern bank.'

'Then they probably want to dig in, and fly their catapults up there,' Shella said. 'So they can hit us down here. Well, we're not going to let them. General Darra, assemble your division, and have them ready to move out, to re-take the northern heights.'

'Move out?' she said. 'All of them? At night?'

'Would you prefer to wake up to the sound of ten-tonne boulders landing on the northern bank? Yes, all of them, and yes, at night. Spread them over a five-mile front, and march them up the fucking hill, General Darra. Do you understand?'

'Yes, Commander.'

'General Barri,' she said, walking towards her other northern officer. 'You remain here, split between guarding the western and eastern fronts. All new recruits are assigned to you until further notice. Kylon, what do you think?'

'If we hit them fast enough,' he shrugged, 'before they can get settled.'

'Good enough for me,' she said. 'Go get Bedig, Leah and Baoryn.'

'Are you joining the assault, High Mage?' Bowda asked, as he watched Kylon leave the room.

'Yes,' she replied. 'If speed and surprise are needed, I should be at the front.'

She turned to the officers and staff.

'I'm departing as soon as Kylon's crew get here,' she said, her heart racing at the prospect. 'We shall be first up the hill, with any hill-scouts we pick up along the way. General Darra, you will be close behind. Get them up that hill as fast as you can, then envelop the Rahain from both flanks. We must push them off the ridge, tonight.'

'No quarter to be given,' she whispered as they ran up the barren hillside in the pitch black of night. They hadn't found any of the hill-scouts, who were probably wandering lost in the darkness, but the Kellach Brigdomin seemed to possess an uncanny ability to see at night, and they led her half-stumbling towards the Rahain positions.

They came up over a small ridge, and the torches of a Rahain camp shone before them. Shella heard Leah notch her longbow, as Kylon crouched and gestured for them to stop. Shella stared at the busy camp. There was a row of fires, and in the light at least four dozen soldiers were digging trenches along the top of the ridge.

'How far away can you use your powers?' Kylon whispered.

Shella closed her eyes and reached out with her mage skill, feeling for the fluids inside the Rahain bodies a hundred paces away.

'About half this distance?' she guessed.

He pulled the shield from over his shoulder, and nodded for the others to do the same. 'Leah, you're with Shella,' he said. 'Cover her until she's close enough. Baoryn, you're on Bedig and me. We'll circle round and distract them from the other side, you rush them from here once we're engaged.'

'Okay,' she said.

'Everyone,' Kylon whispered. 'Silence on the approach. Let's get this done quietly, we don't want to alert the whole hill. Ready?'

They all nodded.

Shella and Leah stayed crouched, while the others started running away to the left through the darkness.

'Now we wait,' Leah said.

'No shit.'

'You stay behind me when we run, okay?' Leah went on. 'Yell at me when you're in range.'

A shout came from the far edge of the camp, and Shella saw Rahain soldiers stop and look about in confusion.

'Now!' Leah cried, and launched herself into a sprint, her shield held out in front.

Shella got up and ran as fast as she could, her feet almost tripping over the loose stones in the dark. Leah was racing ahead, Shella panting and stumbling behind.

'Stop!' Shella called, but not loudly enough, and Leah continued, unhearing.

'Stop!' she shrieked, this time so loudly that half the camp turned to look.

Leah halted, and knelt down onto the rocky ground, her shield propped up against her left shoulder, her head down. Shella kept running, as Rahain soldiers reached for their crossbows. Sweat was pouring into her eyes. She dived to the ground just behind Leah, as several crossbow bolts flew past. One struck Leah's shield, punching its steel head an inch through the thick wood.

Shella crawled the last few yards, and took shelter behind Leah as more crossbow bolts whistled through the air.

'What fucking took you?' Leah scowled.

Shella picked some grass from her mouth, and wiped the dirt from her hands. She peered around the edge of the shield. At least twenty Rahain were in their half-dug trench. They had abandoned their shovels, and all held crossbows.

She reached out with her power, but not too quickly. The last time, in the palace, she had assumed that Rahain bodies were similar to those of the Rakanese, and she had been spectacularly wrong. This time she took a moment to feel out the pathways of the fluids flowing through the flesh of the soldiers.

'They're so fragile,' she whispered.

'Hurry the fuck up!' Leah grunted.

Shella smiled. Their hearts, she thought. They're weak.

She swept her hand in an arc, and Leah jumped back in alarm, as all twenty Rahain soldiers convulsed for a second, then collapsed.

'Come on,' Shella smiled, getting up. Now that she knew how easy it was to kill Rahain, she was eager to do it again.

She walked through the camp. As Rahain troops fled in panic, she flicked her finger out.

Head, she pointed at one, who fell, his eyes bleeding.

Lungs, at another, who instantly drowned.

Leah caught up with her, and watched her back as she stalked the camp, killing any soldier that entered her line of sight.

She pointed at another, finger raised. She stopped. Baoryn.

The renegade Rahain's face went white, and Shella laughed.

Kylon moved into the light, looking around at the scene of carnage. His gaze lingered on the corpse of a soldier that Shella had killed by forcing his guts out through his rectum.

'Pretty fucked up, Shella.'

'Oh dear,' she said. 'Does Kylon disapprove? Does Kylon only want me to kill Rahain while leaving their bodies unblemished?'

'What Kylon wants,' he growled, 'is none of your concern. Are you enjoying this?'

'No!' she cried. 'I make jokes, but the truth is I hate it, I hate killing.' She waved her arms at the scattered bodies. 'All this was just so I could work out the easiest way to kill as many of them as possible. Their bodies are not like ours, and I was... experimenting. Luckily for those with a weak disposition, a simple heart attack seems to require the least effort.'

Kylon nodded, but his eyes were unconvinced.

Shella's stomach churned. She felt nauseous, not from all the death, but from the realisation that Kylon was right. She had enjoyed killing the Rahain soldiers. Their lives had been nothing to her, and she had thrilled inside at thinking up new ways to destroy them.

Heart attacks only from now on, she thought. And no more jokes.

'Let's work our way along the ridge,' Kylon said, and they set off.

Shella soon lost count of the Rahain slain by her hand. Kylon's crew were in the thick of it too, fending off attacks, while swathes fell to the power of the dark mage. She felt like she had been up on the hill for hours when they heard the first sign of Darra's division approaching.

Shella found the nearest officer.

'Captain,' she called.

'Commander!' the captain shouted, as her soldiers arrived behind her. 'What are our orders?'

'Advance to the nearest trenches,' Shella cried, pointing. 'Leave enough to secure them, then send messengers up and down the line, telling everyone else to do the same. We're going to occupy the entire ridge. Companies coming up from behind, direct to the east, the Rahain have been cleared for a mile to the west of here.'

'Cleared? How?'

'She killed them all,' Leah muttered.

'There's plenty left for everyone,' Shella said.

The captain looked away.

'Have you seen General Darra?' Shella asked. 'Where was she in relation to your company?'

'About half a mile to the east, Commander.'

Shella nodded at Leah. 'Let's go find her.'

Shella and Darra pored over the map in silence, as the dawn light spread its way into the command tent. Shella was spent. She had used her powers for hours on end, and felt like she had aged a year in a night. In the end, she had had to retire to their makeshift command post, and let her soldiers take over the struggle in the more traditional manner. Traditional for the Rahain, she thought. For the Rakanese, this was the first pitched battle in their known history. It had been a painful birth into the world of war. Well organised Rahain crossbow detachments, dug into their hillside redoubts, had held out against much higher numbers of Rakanese, slaughtering them as they had charged up the steep slopes.

A messenger appeared at the entrance.

'Commander, General Darra,' he nodded. 'Major Grego reports that all Rahain resistance has now ended. He reports that he has taken four hundred and ten prisoners, and sustained losses to his own battalion of two hundred and ninety-three.'

Shella nodded at the young man. 'Thank you, soldier.'

He smiled. 'We won, Commander.'

'Yeah.'

As he left, Darra removed the last red token from the map, replacing it with a black one.

'That makes it about three thousand casualties altogether, Commander.'

'It had to be done, General,' Shella said. 'We couldn't allow them to take the heights. And now we hold them.'

'But such losses,' she replied. 'Three out of every ten.'

'Think of the slaughter,' Shella said, 'had the Rahain managed to get a hundred catapults up here, each firing day and night into the heart of the city. Imagine it, every citizen down below living in terror, their houses pulverised into rubble. It was a high price I know, and the loss of every soldier is painful, but they did their duty and protected the city. They are heroes. You, General Darra, are a hero. You commanded the Rakanese army to its very first victory in its very first battle, and saved the city.'

Darra nodded, but her eyes were empty.

'I'm heading down the hill,' Shella said. 'You're in command up here. Finish the work the Rahain started, and get the trenches linked up. I'll make sure you're supplied by this evening.'

'Do you think the Rahain will be back?'

'I'm sure they will,' Shella said. 'They'll no doubt send their flying snakes over in the morning to take a look. Then they'll have to decide if they think it's worth another assault. If you can ensure the division is securely dug in along the whole ridge, then that might be enough to dissuade them.'

Shella kicked the chair next to her, and Kylon grunted from where he sprawled.

'Battle's over,' she said. 'Let's go.'

'You look tired, Commander,' Polli said, as she gave her a glass of water.

'It was a tough night.'

'A fine victory, though,' Bowda said, a rare smile on his face. 'The entire city stayed awake last night, watching the army march up the hill, and then waiting for news. We beat them! We beat the Rahain!'

'Try not to sound so surprised.'

'I am surprised,' he said, chuckling. 'An inexperienced, barely trained division, climbing a hill in darkness to fight the world's most powerful army? The shock the Rahain generals must be feeling round about now, when they hear the news. Two thousand Rahain troops killed or captured, while the same number retreated ignominiously! Ha!'

'Yeah, well hopefully it'll teach them to stay behind their lines from now on,' Shella replied, Bowda's gloating setting her nerves on edge.

Shella looked around. 'Where's Rijon? I wanted to ask him if he could contact the Holdings for me. I think they would be very interested to hear about last night's events.'

'Ahhh,' Bowda sighed, looking away.

'What do you mean "ahhh"?' Shella snapped. 'Where is he?'

'He's gone, Commander,' Polli said.

'Gone?'

She sat, a wave of exhaustion overcoming her.

'Yes, Commander,' Polli said. 'We sent someone to his office last night, but he wasn't there, and all of his things were missing. I went to his apartment myself, but...'

'Shit.'

'Don't worry, Commander,' Bowda said. 'We don't need him. The Holdings were never likely to come to our rescue, and we can now see the enemy with our own eyes. Rijon was useful, but he was never one of us.'

'The Holdings must have ordered him to evacuate,' Shella said. 'He thought they might have to at some point, if they believed that the situation had become untenable. In other words, they think we're fucked.'

Her advisors looked at each other.

'Perhaps they'd gotten wind of the plan to assault the heights, and assumed its success?' Bowda suggested.

'Yes,' Polli said. 'Rijon probably expected the city to be under bombardment this morning.'

Shella sighed, and closed her eyes, a dull feeling of dread creeping through her.

CHAPTER 27
KISSED

R ahain Capital, Rahain Republic – 16th Day, Second Third
Spring 505

'Sorry, Jamie,' Daphne whispered. 'I should have visited more often.'

The horse returned her gaze with its big brown eyes, as she brushed its flank.

'I'll take you out for a good run soon,' she said, 'then you can stretch your legs. You must be so bored here.'

She glanced around the old gaien stables, and shook her head. She should have left Jamie in Plateau City, and never brought him to Rahain. The caverns were no place for a horse. Using some of the money her father had transferred, she had rented this small private building, close to one of the city's great gates, and had fitted it out for Jamie to live in. She had also employed an old Rahain man to look after the stables, but had found little opportunity to visit. She missed the liberating feeling of being on a horse, and wished she was riding over the open plains with him, to anywhere but there.

The old man was sitting on a wooden bench, smiling toothlessly as he watched her groom the horse's soft brown hair. He was doing an adequate job, Daphne thought, though she was over-paying him.

'Are you taking him out into the courtyard twice a day?'

'Yes, ma'am,' he grinned. 'Just as you said. Morning and evening, before I give him his feed.'

She lifted up a foreleg, and examined the hoof. The shoe had some signs of wear, but was still secure and sound.

'They make sparks on the cobblestones,' the old man said. 'I showed the grandchildren a while back, they were amazed to see an animal with metal shoes.'

'You've brought people here?'

The old man's smile dropped. 'Yes, ma'am,' he said. 'Only a couple of times, when I was watching my girl's little ones while she was out looking for work. I couldn't leave them in the house all by themselves, and I needed to feed Jamie. I'm sorry if I did wrong.'

Daphne's anger seeped away. With the money she was paying him, the old peasant was probably supporting his entire family, and she saw the fear in his eyes that he might lose his job.

'Did the children like him?'

'Oh, yes,' the old man replied, his smile returning. 'They were very excited. But don't worry ma'am, I made sure they stood well back, and didn't touch.'

Daphne smiled back. 'You can let them stroke him,' she said, 'if they're very careful. But remember, only from the front, where he can see them.'

The old man nodded, relief putting the colour back into his face.

Daphne reached into her bag, and counted out a handful of gold ahanes.

'This is a little bonus,' she said, giving him the money. 'Jamie's in a fine condition. There will be more if he's as well cared for next time I visit.'

'Thank you, ma'am,' he gulped, as he gazed at the gold in his hands.

She kissed Jamie's head. 'See you soon, boy.' She nodded at the old man, and left the stables.

She pulled her hood up over her head as she walked along the backstreets running parallel to the main road, not wishing to draw any attention to herself. She had been keeping her head down ever since breaking the Kellach out of the Tyrant's Tower, and had sent a message to the embassy to say that she would not be back at work for a while. She knew they would come and find her if they needed to. She was confident that she had left no clue behind that would lead the Rahain to her, but she worried about Douanna, who well understood what Daphne was capable of.

She heard the sounds of another disturbance, coming from the direction of the main road. More rioting peasants, she thought to herself. There were shortages of almost everything, food, fuel, water, clothes, and a hundred other essentials, with the economic might of the capital focussed on the siege of the Rakanese city.

She paused as she reached a crossroads. On one side a thin line of soldiers were standing, their shields formed into a solid wall, while on the other side of the road a mob threw stones at them, their faces covered and hooded.

Daphne dashed up a side alley, and climbed onto the roof of a nearby workshop to get a better view. She scampered across the tiles, leaping the short distances separating the buildings, and looked down. The soldiers were retreating, heavily outnumbered by the rioters.

They're losing control of the city, she thought. Street by street, district by district, the peasants were forcing the armed representatives of the state to withdraw, preventing them from carrying out more requisitions, whether of conscripted troops, or taxable supplies.

Perhaps by accident, one of the soldiers fired his crossbow, and a rioter fell. The mob roared and charged. Some of the soldiers turned and fled, those that didn't were engulfed in seconds, trampled under the roiling wave of rioters. Daphne leaped across the street above the screams, landing on the roof opposite, and kept running.

She cleared her head as she sped across the buildings, drawing on a steady stream of battle-vision to aid her steps. Her mind turned to Killop. She missed him, ached for him, but smiled all the same at the memory of their moments together in his cell. She wondered where he was. The Rahain had been keeping quiet about their escape, but she was sure she would have heard something if they had been recaptured. She thought of him travelling with three other women, and if he would tell them the truth about what had happened. Even if he didn't, she felt confident that he would stay faithful to her, no matter how long it took before they were together again. 'I will come for you,' he had said to her. But how?

Something was wrong. Something was out of place, Daphne knew, as she stared across Appleyard Cavern in the direction of her apartment. The front door was closed, and appeared normal. She looked down the side of the low building. The shutters were all pulled shut, and locked. Just as she was starting to think she was being paranoid, she noticed that the latch on the fourth window along was sitting at a funny angle, and her nerves jangled.

She leapt across to a neighbouring roof, and scaled the next-door apartment block. It was one of the highest in the cavern, and from its flat roof, she was able to jump and pull herself up by the edge of a huge sky window. She landed onto the grass on the hillside, blinking in the warm afternoon sunshine. There were several people out enjoying the weather, basking in the light, or having a picnic lunch. A few turned to glance at her, but most weren't paying any attention, and she got up and brushed herself down.

Use the stairs next time, she told herself. And remember, it's the middle of the day.

She strolled over to the aperture that was positioned above her own apartment, feeling the spring sun on her skin, and missing the scorching heat of her homeland.

'Nicest day of the year so far, wouldn't you say, miss?'

She turned. A man was sitting on the grass near the sky window, his jacket neatly folded by his side.

'I wouldn't know,' she said. 'I don't get out much.'

'A pity.'

She smiled. 'Now, if you'll excuse me.'

She dropped over the side of the aperture, falling six yards through the air, and landed on her own roof with a soft thud. She ran to the large vent over her vision room, unlatched it and jumped down, hitting the carpet, and rolling to the side.

She knew her noisy arrival would have ruined any chance of surprise, so she grabbed a knife from under a cushion and sprinted to the door. She surged her battle-vision to its fullest extent, and threw it open, then ran, taking in every detail as she went. Her eyes went to a tiny mark on the handle of her bedroom, and she burst through the door, using the armour protecting her left arm to batter it open.

There was a flash of movement to her right, and she swivelled as a knife slashed an inch from her face. She ducked, and threw herself upwards, ramming her knife into the chest of a woman dressed in black.

She scanned the rest of the room in an instant and, finding it empty, relaxed her vision. She staggered, dizzy from such a short but intense burst. She sat, and glanced around. The dead intruder lay bleeding by the door to her left. The rest of her room had been ransacked. Clothes were lying scattered across the furniture and floor, and her bedside table was on its side. Dirty coffee cups and ashtrays lay staining the rug.

She leaned over, and looked at the floor where the bedside table had stood. It was undisturbed. She smiled, and pulled at the edge of a loose wooden slat, lifting it up. After removing two more cut floorboards, she pulled out a bag, and then a box.

She got up, and took down a much larger bag from a shelf. Into it she threw the box and the other bag, and then hunted out some clothes, and stuffed them in too. She hefted the bag over her right shoulder, lit a cigarette, and walked back out into the hall.

She ducked, but the crossbow bolt was swifter than she, and it tore through the skin of her neck below the right ear, removing an inch of flesh before embedding itself in the wall behind her. She stumbled, dropping the bag, her right hand going up to her neck, the blood pumping out.

She pulled on battle-vision as she fell, drawing it in until the screaming pain subsided. She opened her eyes. The man from the hillside stood a few yards away, calmly reloading his weapon.

She reached across the floor, picked up her smouldering cigarette, and flicked it up into his face. As he spluttered away the sparks, she sprang at him, launching herself with all she had. She knocked him over, and they landed on the floor. His hands grabbed her by the throat, and he squeezed, blood from her neck wound seeping between his fingers. She rolled, until she was on top of him, and tried to pull herself away, but he was stronger, and kept his grip, and she started to choke and gasp for air. Her right hand scrambled across the floor blindly, feeling for anything to use as a weapon, as her sight started to fade.

She pulled her left arm over, wrenching it as far as she could, the pain almost unbearable. She started to lose consciousness. She heard the man laugh, as her right hand tried to pull his fingers away from her throat.

The last thing she remembered was clicking a catch with her left thumb, and the sound of another bolt being loosed.

Daphne awoke on the floor, pain burning every part of her body. Her breath was coming in rasps and wheezes, and her neck ached.

She opened her eyes. Inches from her face was the man from the hillside, a black dart sticking out of his right ear. She pushed herself up onto her knees, and looked round. Aside from the dead man on her floor, everything else seemed to be in place. She reached out with her right hand and grabbed hold of the end of the black dart. Placing her foot against the side of the man's head, she plucked it out, and dropped it into her pocket. She picked up her bag, and stumbled to the kitchen.

Stupid, so stupid, she muttered to herself, as she washed the blood from her face in the sink. There was a small hand mirror, and she examined her neck. The bolt wound was red and raw, but had stopped bleeding, while livid weals showed up where the man's fingers had been. She tied a dish-towel around her throat, then pulled her hood up over her head.

The pain was excruciating, but she tried to ignore it, and went to the back of her apartment, where a small door led out onto the garden. The lamps in the cavern had been dimmed for early evening. At the rear of the garden was a small service and ventilation shaft that she never used, keeping it as an escape route, though one she hadn't imagined she would ever need. She removed the plant pot that hid the entrance, and crawled through.

She steeled herself, and began the slow journey through the tight service tunnels that honeycombed the rock between caverns, until she was far from her apartment. Over many thirds, she had laid down supplies at various points in this little-known network, and she stopped when she reached a large and comfortable niche carved out of the rock, where she had previously stowed a lamp, an assortment of weapons and blankets, and plenty of food and water.

She lit the lamp, and pulled a blanket over her shoulders. She found a jug of water, removed the stopper that was keeping it fresh, and drank. She opened her bag, and took out the small box.

At last, she thought. She removed a stick of mixed dullweed and dreamweed, and lit it. The pain subsided as she inhaled, and she sighed as the narcotics took effect.

Too close, she thought. That had been too close. Having always worked alone, she felt foolish not to have guessed that there might have been a second assassin working alongside the first, and he had nearly got her. It had to be Douanna who had sent them. But why now, after so long?

She remembered the dart, and took it from her pocket. She wiped the blood away, and examined it. The tip had been bent and blunted by the impact with the side of the man's head, but it could still do damage, so she slotted it back into the bow mechanism built into the protective shell on the underside of her left arm. The drugs had also lessened the pain in her crippled limb, after she had strained it to be able to shoot the assassin. Her elbow was burning, and it felt as if she may have fractured the joint. She hoped it was just the muscles, and not the badly-fused bones. The idea of re-living the pain she had previously endured was unthinkable, and she shed a tear of self-pity. She had seen Killop look at her arm, when she had been getting dressed in his cell. Before that night he probably hadn't known she was crippled. The first time he had seen her, she had been wearing a long cloak, and she wondered if he minded. She wouldn't blame him if he thought her arm was disgusting, after all, that's what she thought of it. A horrible, twisted, withered limb.

She shook her head and told herself to snap out of it. Her guts churned, and she threw up the water she had drunk. She unwrapped the vomit-dripping blanket from around her shoulders, and threw it to the side. Turning the lamp down low, she curled up into a ball, and fell into the oblivion of sleep.

She awoke sore and hungry, but her self-pity had fled, and she felt ready to act. She made up some breakfast, and smoked a little dull-weed, just enough to numb the pain from her neck and arm, then lit up a keenweed stick, and pulled on a tiny amount of battle. She changed her clothes, and stretched out her limbs, performing her usual morning exercises within the cramped confines of the tunnel, while she planned her next move.

A large part of her just wanted to get Jamie and ride out of the city, but she needed her money, and supposed it was only polite to let the embassy know she was leaving. She nearly lost her newfound composure when she realised that she had no idea where to go. Killop could have gone anywhere, in any direction. Would he come back to the city to begin his hunt for his sister, or stay hidden in the mountains? Why had he told her that he would find her? Why had they not thought of something more precise? And now he could be a hundred miles away.

One step at a time, she thought. First, the embassy.

She got a surprise when she emerged from a service tunnel to see that the lamps were set to early evening, and she realised that she must have slept for the whole day. She made her way through the tunnels to the gigantic central cavern where the embassy was located, and switched to travelling along the rooftops, as night approached.

There was a huge armed presence in the cavern, clustered around the main roads leading to the City Council and High Senate buildings, and there were no peasants to be seen anywhere on the streets. She reached the small side alley that ran by one wall of the embassy, and dropped to the ground. The Holdings guard on duty jumped as she approached, his spear held out.

'It's only me,' she said, pulling her hood back a little so he could see her face.

'Miss Holdfast!' the guard cried, while looking up and down the street. 'You best come inside.' He unlocked and opened the side door to the embassy, and ushered her through.

The reception was closed for the night, and most of the building lay in darkness. She knew that Joley lived inside the embassy, and headed towards his office. The lights were on, seeping out under the door into the dark corridor.

She knocked once, and entered.

Secretary Joley looked up from his desk, and put down his pen.

'Ahh, Miss Holdfast,' he said, 'I was wondering when you'd turn up.'

She walked over and sat down in one of his armchairs.

'Are you hurt?' he said, glancing at her makeshift bandage.

'Crossbow bolt kissed my neck.'

Joley leaned back, and pulled a rope attached to the rear wall of his office. A distant bell rang.

'What happened?' he said, getting a bottle of brandy from a cabinet next to his desk.

'Two assassins,' she said, watching him pour. He handed her a glass.

'Assassins?' he said. 'Not soldiers?'

'They were definitely assassins,' she said. 'Why would soldiers try to kill me?'

'There's a warrant out for you.'

'I thought they couldn't arrest anyone who worked at the embassy.'

'Technically, they can't.' Joley said, shrugging, and picking up his glass. 'Their warrant states that they want to question you, not arrest you. Frankly, I'm not convinced that the new Requisition and Mobilisation Committee cares too much about the difference. All normal legal procedures have been suspended, now that the City Council has declared martial law, and the damned committee are making up the rules as they go along.'

'They sent soldiers here to get me?'

'They did,' Joley said. 'Of course, we told them the truth, which was that we had no idea where you were.'

'Thank you,' she said, sipping her brandy.

There was a knock at the door, and a guard entered.

'Sir?' he said, standing to attention.

'Sergeant,' Joley nodded, 'please wake the doctor, and bring her here. No fuss, and no noise.'

'Yes, sir,' he replied, and left.

Joley sat back in his chair, studying her.

'Are you going to tell me why the Rahain authorities wish to question you?' he said. 'I have all kinds of theories.'

'I'm sorry,' she said, 'but no. The information would only endanger you, and the embassy.'

A choked, half-laugh came from him. 'Really? That bad, eh?'

'It would probably be best if I left the capital.'

'Perhaps,' he said. 'After all, you do seem to be slipping a little. Whatever you did, you must have left some trace behind that has led the authorities to you, and then you allow a couple of assassins to almost turn you into a pincushion. Also, I'm afraid that you wouldn't be able to stay here in the embassy. We wouldn't hand you over to the

Rahain authorities, but if they were to discover we were sheltering you, it could create difficulties for all of us.'

'I understand,' she said. 'I'll be on my way as soon as I get my gold.'

'Of course,' Joley said, standing. 'I'll collect it for you now. Wait here for the doctor, I'll be back shortly.'

Daphne remained at the embassy for several hours, as her wounds were tended to, and she received her saddlebags of gold. When she was ready to leave, she stopped off in the embassy kitchens for a bowl of soup, and ate alone, her bags packed beside her.

What Joley had told her seemed to confirm her earlier suspicions. It must have been Douanna who had sent the assassins. She would worry what Daphne might say if she was picked up and questioned, and had decided to eliminate the risk. By eliminating Daphne.

The kitchen door opened, and a Holdings man dressed in priestly robes entered the room.

She put down her spoon.

'Miss Daphne Holdfast,' the priest said, 'I've been waiting to speak with you. I am Father Ghorley, sent by the church to assist the embassy here in Rahain.'

'By assist,' she said, pushing her bowl aside and lighting a cigarette, 'I assume you mean "tell them what to do"?'

He shrugged. 'I ensure they keep to the tenets of our faith, and follow the instructions of the church. I arrived just a few days ago. As I said, I have been waiting to speak with you.'

He sat opposite her at the kitchen table, and poured himself a glass of water.

'Come to remind me that I'm still unwelcome in my homeland?' she said.

He smiled, nearly laughed, she thought.

'During my journey here,' he said, looking her in the eye, 'I was contacted by the Lord Vicar, and the leadership of the church. They, in turn, had been in communion with the Creator.'

He paused.

She smoked.

'The Creator himself!' the priest cried. 'He has passed on his word to the holy church, and his word, Miss Daphne Holdfast, concerns you.' He pointed at her.

'Me?' she frowned. 'The Creator spoke of me?'

'He did,' Ghorley said, grinning. 'He has been watching you closely, Miss Daphne. He has observed the way you fight, and approves of the progress you have made with your vision gifts.'

'Really?' Daphne snorted.

Ghorley glanced around. 'He also witnessed you rescue the four Kellach Brigdomin slaves.'

Daphne sat up. 'I didn't think the embassy knew about that.'

'They don't,' he said, shaking his head. 'The church has access to a level of intelligence that goes far beyond what a mere ambassador knows, Miss Daphne. The Creator sees all, and when he passes on his word, we listen.'

'But why has he been watching me?'

'He remembers you, Daphne,' Ghorley said, his smile returning. 'He recalls talking with you in the Sanang forest, and wishes to remind you that you made a deal with him.'

Damn, she thought, trying to recall what she had promised. She had lived for so long with the belief that she had been hallucinating, that the details of her encounter with the Creator were confused. Could it be true? Had she really talked to a god?

'The Creator has a task for you, Daphne,' Ghorley said, his eyes sparkling, 'one that he has asked us to assist you with. All embassy resources will be placed at your disposal. Furthermore, if you complete this task, then all past misunderstandings will be forgotten, and the church will welcome you back to the Holdings gladly. His Majesty, King Guilliam has also personally interceded, to send you an assurance that your safety would be guaranteed.'

Daphne shrugged. 'Forgive me if I'm sceptical, but I've been made promises by the church before.'

Ghorley sighed. 'May I speak frankly? The church's betrayal of you and your company was a grievous mistake, which is deeply regretted. The Creator has shown us our error, but he has also pointed the way to our mutual redemption. Accept this task, Daphne, complete it, and you can return home.'

'Where you would expect me to work for you?' she said. 'Like Rijon?'

'If you like,' he said. 'It's up to you. The Creator has ordered us to help you, not force you into working for us. Of course, with the powers you possess, we would certainly be keen to recruit you.'

Daphne shook her head. Could she work for the church to get back home? Did she want to go home? She knew her family would be there, and she longed to see them, but what about Killop? Helping the church went against her every instinct, but did she have a choice?

'Do you know where the freed Kellach captives are?' she asked.

'No,' he said. 'The last information I had was that they were seen disappearing into the mountains north of here. If you wish, I can make further enquiries, but it may take some time.'

'Do that, please.'

He smiled. 'May I therefore assume that you are willing to perform the task the Creator has asked of you?'

He held out his hand. Daphne hesitated for a moment, then took it, and they shook.

'Excellent,' he smiled. 'Now, if you'll come with me, I have a safe house nearby where you can stay for a few days, while you prepare.'

She stood.

'What's the task?'

'A mission of mercy, Miss Daphne,' Father Ghorley said, clasping his fingers together. 'We need you to go back into the Rakanese camp.'

CHAPTER 28
DISTRACTED

Mountains north of Rahain Capital, Rahain Republic – 18th Day, Second Third Spring 505

Killop watched her from the shadows of the gaien stables, keeping his distance.

Kallie was at the well, drawing a bucket of water, pulling in the rope. Her long red hair fell down her back, shining in the morning sun. Her skin was pale, having been underground for so long. She bent her back, straining against the weight of the heavy bucket as she hauled it up. Around her in the farm courtyard, spring flowers sprouted between the uneven flagstones, coming up to her knees in a burst of colours, blues, yellows, pinks and green.

For a long time, Killop had believed that his future would be intertwined with Kallie's. Hearing the prophecy hadn't changed that, as he had flatly refused to believe that dark-skinned folk existed. Even after seeing Daphne in Laodoc's academy, he had thought that his love for Kallie would win, and that what he was feeling about Daphne was just an illusion, a temporary infatuation. Kallie was his one, his soul mate, and yet, as he gazed at her from the shadows, he knew his passion for her had gone. As if a switch had been turned off in his mind, he understood that he was no longer in love with her.

He loved Daphne. His desire for her tore at his mind, and a nervous anger rose in his guts at the thought of not seeing her again. Part of him wanted to go straight back to the city for her, but he had to find Keira first, and free her from the Rahain. Daphne would have to wait.

On the first evening following their escape, while they had huddled under some trees from the cold rain, Killop had told Kallie what had happened between him and Daphne.

Though she had sworn enough at the time, she hadn't spoken to him since, and acted as if he wasn't there most of the time, while he had fallen into a well of guilt and awkwardness. He had said and done nothing against the barbs that Lacey threw at him, once Kallie had told the others, and had spent the next few days saying as little as possible, as they had wound their way up the narrow, wooded valleys leading through the mountains.

'It's not polite to stare,' said a voice to his left, 'especially at the woman you cheated on.'

'Hi, Bridget,' he muttered.

They watched as Kallie lifted the full bucket, and poured its contents into a pair of smaller ones taken from the barn, the water droplets sparkling in the sunlight amid the wild flowers.

'She's beautiful,' Bridget said.

'Aye.'

'And you fucked it up,' Bridget said, shaking her head. 'Silly boy.'

'You find anything?' he said, changing the subject.

'Aye,' she said. 'No gaien, though. Same as the last place, all the fields are empty. The beasts must have been rounded up for the Rakanese siege.'

'Any food?'

'Aye,' she said. 'A few sealed tubs of supplies, cornmeal, some salty old pork. Nothing too exciting, but enough for a few days.'

Killop watched as Kallie picked up the two smaller buckets, and started walking back towards the cottage.

'Killop,' Bridget said, 'do we have a plan?'

He shrugged.

'Somehow that fails to instil me with confidence.'

'I don't know,' he said. 'Beyond getting away, I hadn't thought further than that.'

'Well you'd better fucking start,' she hissed. 'The lizards will be out looking for us, they won't want to lose their leverage over Keira. If we keep heading in the direction we're going in, then we'll run into them sooner or later. This whole region, between the capital and Tahrana City, is just one gaien ranch after another, with pig farms, vineyards and other estates dotted about. We need to go somewhere quieter.'

'Where?'

'Didn't you look at any maps while we were at the mansion?'

'A couple,' he said. 'None of here, though.'

She thought for a moment. 'I don't know,' she said. 'It depends what we want to do. Are we staying in Rahain, or going back to Kellach Brigdomin?'

He looked at her, narrowing his eyes. 'You're using their word for us?'

'It's just easier to say,' she shrugged. 'It's not important. What we should be doing...' She tailed off, her attention caught by something.

'Shit,' she muttered, staring upwards.

Killop followed her line of sight, pausing when he saw a black dot in the sky.

'Winged gaien,' she scowled.

'Think they've seen us?'

'How would I know?'

They stayed where they were, crouched in the shadows of the stables, waiting for the flying beast to pass. Once it had disappeared over the horizon to the north-east, they scampered back to the cottage.

Kallie and Lacey were inside. Lacey was scrubbing clothes in a bucket, while Kallie was filling small water canisters. Neither looked up as Bridget and Killop entered.

'No fires again today,' Bridget said. 'Flying lizards are about.'

Kallie nodded.

'I found us some food,' Bridget went on.

'More pig fat?' Lacey spat.

'Probably,' Bridget said. 'Haven't opened all the tubs yet. Some definitely stink of it.'

'We got better food in prison,' Lacey muttered.

'You go and fucking find some then,' Bridget snapped, taking a seat by the cold fireplace, and filling a cup of water from one of Kallie's buckets.

'Food is your job,' Lacey said.

Bridget sighed.

'I look after our clothes and weapons,' Lacey went on, though they had been through this before. 'Kallie gets the water, and you get the food.'

The room sat in expectant silence.

'Oh,' Lacey continued, 'and Killop gets to be an arsehole, a job he excels at.'

She grinned at him, then went back to washing the clothes.

Killop said nothing.

He glanced around the room. Lacey was scowling as she held a skirt against a washboard, scrubbing it. Kallie was keeping her head low, careful not to catch his eye, as she tightened the stoppers on their water canisters. Bridget looked at him. He knew that she wanted him to lead them, resume his old position as their squad leader, but his tongue seemed stuck inside his mouth.

He shook his head, and Bridget nodded.

'We need to decide what to do,' she said to the room. 'We need to talk about where we should go.'

No one else said anything, but both Lacey and Kallie glanced up at the young Brig woman.

'Here are our choices,' she said. 'We could try to get back to Kell, and Brig and Lach. Link up with the warriors Lacey knows, and join in the fight.'

'Or just go home,' Kallie said.

'Aye, maybe,' Bridget said. 'We could decide that once we got there. Or, we stay here, in Rahain, though doing what, I don't know. The lizards are looking for us, and maybe they'll be watching the roads to Kellach, thinking that's where we're most likely to go, so we could stay here instead, for a while.'

'Here?' Lacey said, looking around the room. 'In this cottage?'

'No, donkey-brain,' Bridget said. 'Much too busy round here. We'd probably be best heading east, if we want to avoid the lizards, hide out in the forests over there.'

'How do you know that?' Lacey asked.

'Pyre's arse,' Bridget said. 'Am I the only one that's looked at a fucking map?'

'I read the maps,' Kallie said.

Bridget nodded.

'What about Rainsby?' Lacey said.

'You heard of that place?' Bridget asked.

'Met some folk who went there,' Lacey replied, looking pleased. 'They didn't like it, came back. They said that thousands of the clans-folk are living there. Others have moved all the way up to the new city being built north of the inland sea. We could go that way.'

'Aye,' Bridget said. 'We could, though, again, I don't know what we'd do when we got there.'

'We could...' Killop began. As soon as he spoke, Lacey's bottom lip turned into a sneer, and Kallie looked away. 'We could look for Keira and Kylon.'

'First,' Bridget said, a pained expression on her face, 'we have no idea where your sister's being held, although you can guarantee it'll be the most heavily guarded place in the country. Second, Kylon happens to be stuck in a city that's being besieged by over a hundred thousand lizard soldiers. I mean, I'd love it if we could just snap our fingers and rescue them both, but we can't all be like...'

She paused, her face reddening.

Killop's tongue remained frozen, and he lowered his eyes.

'You've upset him, Bridget,' Lacey laughed.

'Shut up, Lacey,' Bridget said.

Lacey shot her a foul look, and went back to scrubbing.

'What do you think, Kallie?' Bridget said.

She looked Bridget in the eyes.

'I'm going to wait,' she said, 'to see where he wants to go first.'

Bridget stayed quiet, looking unsure.

Kallie kept her gaze level. 'So I can go in the opposite direction.'

Bridget shook her head. 'No.'

Kallie shrugged, and got back to work.

'No,' Bridget repeated. 'No, Kallie; we're not splitting up.'

'It's too late, Bridget,' Kallie said. 'I can't travel with him any more. I don't trust him, and can't stand the sight of him.'

'Me neither,' added Lacey. 'I just want him to fuck off.'

'Shut up, Lacey!' Bridget shouted. She turned to Kallie. 'Please, Kallie, I know how you're feeling; I know he's been a complete prick, but we can't split up. We have to stick together.'

Kallie shook her head.

'We're not leaving anyone behind!' Bridget cried.

'Then you stay with him!' Lacey shouted. 'Me and Kallie will be fine on our own, and you can warm his bed. After all, his wee brown lassie's not coming for him.'

Bridget jumped up, her right fist clenched.

'Why are you sticking up for him?' said Kallie.

'I'm not!' Bridget shouted, and fell back into her seat. She started to cry, the first time Killop had ever seen her do so. She held her face in both hands to hide her sobs, while Lacey and Kallie shared a glance.

'We can stay together for a few more days, Bridget,' Kallie said.

Bridget raised her head, and then she stretched out her arms and hugged Kallie. As the women embraced, Killop stood. Ignoring Lacey's stare, he left the cottage and, keeping to the shadows, started to walk.

He felt stupid, and small, and his gaze remained downward, as his feet scuffed the dusty path to the nearby woods. Maybe it would be better if he left the others, for good. He was useless, his mind was so distracted with guilt, and Daphne, and Kallie, then guilt again, that he was making mistakes.

He reached the woods and kept walking, taking a path through the tall, dark pines. A strange bird called out, its cry echoing through the still branches. His boots crunched over the thick bed of dry pine needles, and he tried to think of nothing. It was no good. His mind came back again and again to Daphne, and how he had felt when they had been in his cell. Then his thoughts would race to Kallie, and the moment he had told her, and the look on her face.

And now Kallie wanted to leave. He couldn't blame her for that, and felt a sense of relief at the thought he wouldn't have to see her all the time, but then he remembered Bridget saying they should stick together. Was she crying because she knew she would either have to leave Killop on his own, or say goodbye to the others to remain with him? She shouldn't have to make that decision. He would go back and tell them he was leaving, alone.

He stopped. He looked around at the dense pines, the air dark under their heavy branches. He turned, looking for his tracks to retrace his steps.

Killop swore. His heart raced as it dawned on him that he was lost. He started walking back the way he had come, looking for any kind of landmark, but he had been in such a pre-occupied daze that he hadn't paid any attention to where he had gone. Each way looked the same, endless rows of thick pines, and a uniform carpet of brown pine needles covering the ground.

An hour went by, and he continued to walk. He reached a long stone ridge, which cut through the forest, and he recalled seeing it on the way in. It seemed to stretch endlessly in both directions. He tried to think about where he had been when he had passed it before, and walked straight into a camp of Rahain scouts.

Six soldiers stared at him, frozen in surprise as Killop entered the little clearing. A fire was smouldering in the centre, and the Rahain were gathered around its warmth.

Killop drew his sword as they reached for their crossbows. He slashed out at one just as she was levelling her bow, cutting through her torso. A crossbow bolt flew past his left, and then a second, and as the others pointed their weapons at him, Killop turned, and fled through the trees. He rolled to the ground as a bolt whistled over his head, then sprinted, keeping low, and dashing from side to side. The shouts behind him dimmed, and he kept running until they faded into the distance.

He collapsed to his knees, panting. He looked up, squinting through the treetops, trying to gauge the time. Uncertain, he wiped his sword on the pine needles, re-sheathed it, and got to his feet. He noticed the land rise to his left, and he climbed up the slope. Ahead, he began to see more daylight, and he came out of the forest into the upper terraces of a vineyard, which stretched away in precise rows down the hillside.

From up there, he could see the whole valley, and recognised in the distance the mountain pass they had ascended a couple of days before. From there, he scanned along the route they had taken until he saw the small black speck where the cottage lay. The forest sprawled all the way round the vineyard, along the hill, and down to the valley floor.

Killop started walking down the hill, keeping to the edge of the forest as he descended. Halfway down the slope, he saw movement in the valley ahead, and paused. As he stared, he caught a glint of metal flashing in the sunlight, and saw a group moving through the abandoned fields below. He started running again, as he realised that the group were moving in the direction of the cottage, which was now out of his sight, somewhere behind the treeline ahead.

He reached the trees and kept going, trying to keep in a straight line. His breath was ragged, and his feet ached. In the distance he heard cries and angry shouting, and he slowed as he came to the edge of the forest. Ahead of him was the farmyard, barns and cottage where the four fugitives had stayed the previous night. The shouting was coming from the other side of the buildings, and so Killop ran in a crouch to the nearest wall, at the rear of the old gaien stables. He drew his sword, still sticky from the confrontation in the woods. He tried to control his breathing, but his legs were wobbly, and his lungs burned. He crept up the side of the stables. When he got to the end he ducked down behind a leaky water butt, as four Rahain soldiers scampered past from the left, their crossbows in their hands.

Without thinking, Killop leapt up and attacked, swinging his sword two-handed, and laying into the soldiers from behind. In a second two were down, slashed across the back, and as the other pair turned, Killop swung out again, taking the arm off one. The other loosed his bow, and a bolt drove through Killop's leather armour, deep into his right side under his shoulder. He grunted, and drove his sword through the soldier's chest, killing him. The Rahain he had wounded was trying to crawl away, a trail of blood leading back to his arm. Killop hacked his head off with a downward lunge, then put his left hand up to where the bolt was embedded in his side.

He staggered with the pain, then heard another cry, from a voice he recognised. He crossed the courtyard to the rear of the cottage, leaving the four bodies staining the ground behind him. He edged to the corner, and peered round. Smoke was coming out of the open side window, and several Rahain soldiers lay scattered on the rocky ground, crossbow bolts studding each body. Killop crawled round to the front.

At least a dozen Rahain soldiers were attacking the main door, hacking at it with swords, while holding their shields above their heads to fend off the bolts. Another five lay dead around them. He saw another bolt flash by, and looked up to see Kallie, wreathed in smoke, shooting from the cottage's upper storey. One of the soldiers threw a lit torch through a ground floor window, smashing the glass, and more flames and smoke belched out.

Killop picked up a fallen shield, and charged. He yelled as he ran, a guttural roar of pain and frustration. He barrelled into the soldiers, knocking over three as he pushed his way through them. He lashed out with his sword, using his longer reach to strike a Rahain in the stomach. He felt a blade cut into his shield, and swung again, blocking a blow from another soldier. Soon he was surrounded. He swerved to avoid a lunge at his back, then barged into a Rahain on his left, knocking him down.

Several soldiers disengaged, and started to reload their crossbows, while the others circled him, their swords out. A bolt whistled by, and one fell.

The front door of the cottage burst open, and Bridget ran out, her shield up. Lacey was right behind her, loosing her crossbow. As they crashed into the Rahain, the soldiers broke, and started to run. Bridget cut down two as they tried to get away, and all the while, Kallie's crossbow sang from the roof, each bolt finding its target. Killop staggered, panting, sweat in his eyes. Blood was seeping from his right side. He looked up. Bridget was attacking a soldier, forcing him back across the yard, while Lacey was finishing off a wounded Rahain by the front of the cottage. Smoke was now pouring from every window, and the door. Kallie was still on the upper floor. As he glanced up, he saw her aim her bow at him.

He froze, dropping his sword. His left hand was holding his wounded side, now drenched in blood. Kallie was looking right at him, her bolt pointed straight at his head.

Bridget turned, having put down the soldier she had been fighting.

'Where the fuck have you...?' she started to say, then stopped, as she noticed Kallie.

Kallie pulled the trigger. The bolt flew past Killop's ear, so close he felt the air from it brush his skin, and there was a grunt behind him.

Killop turned, and saw a final Rahain soldier fall to the ground, a bolt protruding from his chest.

Bridget looked up at Kallie, her expression wary. 'Get down!'

Kallie nodded, and climbed out onto the tiled roof, as flames billowed from the windows, and the fire inside the cottage roared. The Kell woman jumped down to the ground, and Lacey joined her.

'There are more soldiers coming,' Killop grunted. 'From the south, by the forest.'

'Out scouting, were you?' Lacey said. 'If so, you fucked that up, too. We never had any warning they were coming, not until they were right on top of us. And now we've lost all our supplies.'

'Shut up, Lacey,' Bridget said. 'He's back now.'

She turned to him, and glanced at his side with a sharp intake of breath.

'Looks nasty,' she said. 'Can you run with it, for a while? We've got to get out of here.'

He nodded, and the four of them turned, and began running up the path to the north, away from the burning cottage. They reached the edge of an old stone wall and followed it down to a stream at the bottom of the valley, where they turned north-east, and began climbing again.

For the entire journey, Killop remained silent, his mind on fire with the constant pain. He stumbled so many times he lost count, his feet like lumps of lead. Bridget urged them onwards through the afternoon, until every step Killop took was torture. He could see her looking back at him occasionally, as if trying to judge how much further he could go.

They reached a turn in the valley where the ground fell away into steep crevices and dark wooded dells. They started to climb down, but Killop lost his footing on a loose stone, and half-slid, half-fell to the bottom of the narrow gorge.

He lay still in the cool, dark air, a few feet from a small stream. Large trees spread their branches overhead, blocking out most of the light. He heard a thump on the soft ground beside him.

Bridget.

She studied his wound, then positioned herself, putting her left foot under his right armpit.

She shook her head. 'What the fuck were you doing?' she whispered, grabbing the crossbow bolt with both hands.

'Sorry,' she said, then yanked with all her strength.

'We can't stay here,' Lacey said.

'We're not leaving him,' Bridget replied.

'But we're only a few hours from the cottage,' Lacey went on. 'This area will be swarming with lizards soon.'

Killop kept his eyes closed as he awoke, lying on the cool ground. His entire right side was a burning sore of agony.

'We have to go,' Lacey said again.

'No,' Bridget said. 'If we leave him here, he'll die. He needs food, and water, and rest. He'll be moving again in a few days.'

'We haven't got a few days!' Lacey cried. 'We'll all be dead by then! Better only one dies, rather than all of us.'

'Shut up, Lacey,' said Kallie.

Despite the pain, Killop strained to hear.

Kallie sighed. 'He's still one of us. Can we carry him, Bridget?'

'Aye,' Bridget said. 'We could rig up a stretcher. If we head up this valley, and stick to the stream, we should be able to manage a few more miles tonight.'

'Lacey,' Kallie said, 'start cutting branches.'

Killop heard an annoyed sigh, and a pair of feet walking away.

'Thank you, Kallie,' Bridget said.

'Just until he's on his feet, Bridget. Then I'm leaving him, and you can make your choice.'

CHAPTER 29
STRIPPED

Rahain Capital, Rahain Republic – 20th Day, Second Third Spring 505

'We're going to need a bigger office,' Laodoc said, gazing at the organised chaos before him. Young party activists sat around, drinking cups of scalding tea, writing letters, and holding rowdy debates.

'Bloody students,' Juarad muttered. 'I blame you, you know. Filling their heads with all this pacifist nonsense.'

'But, my dear fellow,' Laodoc said, smiling at his old Hedger colleague, 'if you're serious about joining the Radicals, then you too would have to oppose the war.'

'That's different,' he said. 'I'm against this stupid war because my businesses are being ruined, not because of any childish dreams about love and harmony.'

'Yes,' Laodoc murmured. 'I remember feeling that way.'

'So,' Juarad said, 'just how many councillors have signed up so far?'

'None,' Laodoc replied, 'but three have given me their personal pledges, and are just waiting for the committee to finalise its membership. If they join the Radicals before that happens, they'll have no chance of being selected. And there are a few more who might join, if they see others do so first.'

Juarad scowled. 'I see.'

'To be honest, old friend,' Laodoc said, 'I think my stance on slavery might be putting people off, rather than my opposition to the Rakanese siege. In fact, I'm a little surprised to see you here. Don't you have thousands of slaves at work, in your mines and on your farms?'

'I do,' Juarad said. Several of the young volunteers turned at these words, frowning at the old Hedger. 'Don't look at me like that,' he growled.

Laodoc waved his activists back to their work.

'Thing is, Laodoc,' Juarad muttered, 'damn slaves are unproductive buggers. They're cheap to run, but you get sod all work from them unless you're prepared to beat, starve and torture them, which just adds to the delays and hassle. I reckon I'd double my overheads if I were paying them instead of owning them, but productivity would triple. At least.'

'Then you don't care about their welfare?' a fresh-faced young woman said, looking up from where she had been stuffing leaflets into envelopes.

'Not a damn bit, girl.'

'Then you shouldn't be in the Radicals.'

'Come now,' Laodoc said, 'the economic case against slavery should be one of our principal arguments.' He paused, as the room quietened. 'If we only oppose slavery because of its undoubted cruelty, and emphasise solely the rights and suffering of the victims, we risk alienating those who might be persuaded if they realised that our policies would also benefit them financially.'

'But we don't want people like that on our side,' someone said.

'We want every vote,' Laodoc said. 'We'll need every tactic we can think of if we're to ever dream about abolishing slavery. That includes targeting those who would assist us only for their own selfish reasons. Think of it as a matter of presentation, if it helps you. By using the economic argument, as just laid out by Councillor Juarad, as well as the moral argument, then we can show that everyone wins from abolishing slavery, not just the slaves.'

Many nodded at these words, although a few looked sceptical.

Laodoc turned to Juarad.

'If you were to join,' he said, 'I would offer you the economics team, to analyse the costs and benefits of a Rahain society free from slavery.'

Juarad snorted, then paused, considering.

'Maybe,' he said, chewing over his words, 'though it'll all come to nothing. Even if the committee weren't throwing its weight around like a deranged gaien, the City Council would never ban slavery in a million years, and even if by some miracle they did, then the High Senate would overturn it, as soon as they had stopped laughing.'

'It's a start,' Laodoc said. 'In truth, I think you're right. We shall not succeed, at least not in our lifetime. However,' he went on, holding Juarad's glance, 'somebody, somewhere, has to make a start.'

Juarad nodded. 'Another pointless exercise, then,' he said. 'Another hopeless cause.' A smile appeared at the corner of his mouth. 'I'll think about it.'

'Excellent,' Laodoc replied, putting his hand on the man's shoulder. 'Now, about that cup of tea I promised you.'

As he was guiding Juarad towards the small kitchen at the rear of the office, there was a loud banging at the front door. Laodoc turned, an anxious hush descending upon the room.

The doors burst open, and soldiers rushed into the office, fanning out by the front wall.

'What is the purpose of this intrusion?' Laodoc shouted, amid confused and angry cries. 'Who is your commanding officer?'

A middle aged woman stepped forward.

'I am Colonel Dhaienet,' she said, holding out a piece of paper. 'I have here a writ from the Requisition and Mobilisation Committee, declaring the immediate dissolution of the Radical Party, as an instrument of sedition and agitation against the state during a time of conflict. All present here are under arrest.'

'All?' Laodoc said.

'But I am only visiting!' Juarad cried. 'I'm not a member of his stupid party! I have nothing to do with any of this!'

The officer glanced at her lieutenant, who shrugged.

'It's true,' Laodoc said, keeping his tone friendly, though his heart was pounding. 'Councillor Juarad is a member of the Merchant Party, and was only here on a social call. He has no connection whatsoever to the Radical Party.'

The colonel sighed, and nodded.

Juarad got several dirty looks as he jostled his way through the activists to the door. He turned before leaving, and gave an almost imperceptible shrug to Laodoc, then disappeared into the crowd of soldiers gathered outside the party headquarters.

Once he had gone, the colonel turned back to Laodoc.

'Now, Councillor,' she said, 'if you would come quietly; we don't need any fuss.'

Before Laodoc could reply, the crowd of young activists gathered to form a barrier between him and the soldiers.

'Leave us alone!' cried one.

'You've got no right coming in here, this is private property!'

'My uncle will sue you for this!'

The colonel turned again to her lieutenant. 'See that they're all arrested,' she said, 'but try not to kill any of them. They're all children of nobles, remember that.'

The colonel walked from the office as more soldiers piled in, each wielding two-foot truncheons and small round shields.

'Please!' Laodoc cried over the growing shouts. 'No violence!'

Ignoring him, both sides eyed each other until, at a word from the lieutenant, the soldiers charged, wading into the packed crowd of students, laying them low with truncheon blows.

As they pushed their way towards him, Laodoc sighed, and shook his head in dismay.

Laodoc and his twenty-four volunteer activists, many of whom were sporting injuries, were held in a cold, dim chamber for several hours, deep within the City Council complex. Medics made the rounds, patching up wounds, cleaning off blood, and splinting the occasional broken bone. Each of the youths had been shackled, with chains connecting their ankles to their wrists.

The mood among them was mixed. Some wore their marks of battle with pride, and were already exaggerating their own part in the fight. Others remained upbeat without the bravado, while a minority seemed to be seriously regretting their decision to help out with the Radical Party.

'The political establishment will never give up their power without a fight,' one of the more cocky youngsters was saying, while a nurse held a cold compress to the side of his head. 'And slavery is all about power. The siege of the Rakanese is all about power. The invasion of the Kellach was all about power. To defeat them, we have to destroy their power!'

Laodoc smiled at the simplicity of youth. After a lifetime of calculated compromise, and subtle realignments of allegiances, he could barely remember feeling as certain about things as many of his young activists did. He had lit a spark. It was small and fragile, but whatever the authorities did today, they could never go back and un-light it.

'Don't you get it?' someone else cried. 'It's over! They banned us! We're all going to jail!'

'Rubbish!' said another. 'My great-aunt is on the High Senate, she would never stand for that. The laws clearly state that one cannot be prosecuted for holding an opinion.'

'But the committee don't care about the law,' another said. 'My uncle's mines were requisitioned at their order, and no one did anything to stop it. One minute he owned them, the next, soldiers and city officials moved in and took over. I heard the senate secretly approves of the committee, even though they would never say so in public. They get things done.'

'Of course they approve!' the first one said. 'They were always complaining that the City Council took an age to decide anything, and often watered down their proposals. Now that the committee has tossed out the constitution, they can command whoever they like to do whatever they want. Look at the number of mages they've rounded up for the siege. No way the council would have had the guts to do that.'

'You sound like you admire them.'

'Pah!' he spat. 'I hate them. But, as an enemy, I admit that I also respect them. They are a worthy opponent.'

Laodoc sat listening, and pondering the future. He was the only one who hadn't been shackled, as a sign of his position. Having experienced a few days in the cells under the High Senate, he had no desire to go back, but he couldn't predict what the committee would decide. They seemed to act as the whim took them.

'When we go in front of the committee,' he said to the crowd of activists, 'hold your heads high, and stand straight, you have nothing to be ashamed of, but at the same time keep any provocative opinions to yourselves. Watch your tongues. Don't give them any reason to act capriciously. Once you are released, you will have plenty of time to plan and plot.'

As the assembled students watched him, the door to the chamber opened, and a council official entered, flanked by soldiers.

'The Requisition and Mobilisation Committee are ready to hear your case,' he said. 'Follow me.'

With the official leading the way, Laodoc left the chamber, followed by the shuffling, clanking ranks of activists. Outside the door, more soldiers were waiting, and they were accompanied through long dim corridors, along ways Laodoc knew well from his two decades as a councillor. They reached a room that Laodoc recognised as one that had been used to hear legal suits, and were marched in.

In front of them, on two rows of tiered semi-circular benches, sat the ten selected members of the new committee. There were three Conservatives, three Patriots, two Merchants and two Liberals, with a further two positions that were yet to be filled. Councillor Ziane sat at the centre of the lower bench, with the others beside and above him.

Most of the committee members smiled as they watched Laodoc and the students fill the other half of the room, although his eldest son

Ruellap's face was grim. Douanna was grinning as if delighted at seeing an old friend. Pleonim nodded at him.

A clerk stepped forward, as soldiers spread out among the activists. Laodoc was shepherded to the front, directly before the committee.

'Case number five hundred and forty-eight,' the clerk called out. 'The accused are charged with being members of the banned organisation known as the Radical Party, carrying out seditious activities, and calling for the overthrow of the established order of the Rahain Republic.'

'Thank you,' Ziane said, leaning forward onto the lectern in front of him. 'So, Councillor Laodoc and his band of misguided helpers.' He smiled. 'Preaching treason at a time of war. Whatever shall we do with you?'

'Reform is not the same as treason,' Laodoc said, his chin up.

'Silence!' Ziane cried. 'The accused will speak only when directly addressed. This is not a routine, peacetime court of law, it is a summons before the Requisition and Mobilisation Committee. As I'm sure you are aware, normal law has been temporarily suspended in the capital, until the Rakanese emergency is over.'

'An emergency of your own making.'

Ziane looked enraged for a moment, then his face relaxed, and he chuckled.

'I'll give you that one, Laodoc, for old time's sake,' he said. 'But be warned. If you, or any of the other accused speaks out of turn again, I will add a year in prison to each of your young volunteers' sentences.'

There was a gasp from the students, several of whom glanced across at Laodoc, their eyes wide.

'I'm glad that we now understand each other,' Ziane went on. 'In light of your crimes, the committee is sorely tempted to seek the harshest possible punishment, and have done with you. The last thing the Republic needs in such a crisis are the miserable stirrings of a group of deluded youth, led by an old man who, let's be frank, should have retired some time ago. We discussed a range of sentences. Committee Member Douanna suggested execution for you all, and persuaded the Patriots to vote with her, but she was beaten six to four.'

Laodoc staggered in shock. His own son had voted to have him executed. Ziane was watching, a grin close to his lips. His tongue flickered.

'The Liberals then suggested that you all be let off with a slap on the wrist,' Ziane continued, 'but their proposal also failed, this time by seven votes to three.'

Pleonim gave Laodoc a small shrug.

'And then it was my turn,' Ziane said. 'I'm happy to say that my compromise prevailed, nine votes to one, with only Committee Member Ruellap dissenting. I therefore declare the following. For petty acts of subversion, all of the activists are hereby sentenced to three years imprisonment, suspended on the guarantee of good behaviour. Your names have all been registered, and if any are found to be engaging in similar activities in the future, then rest assured that you will see the inside of a cell. Furthermore, each activist has been fined a sum of five hundred ahanes, payable by third's end. Let's see how your parents feel about your choice of pastime when they see the bill you bring home tonight.'

The students smiled, and hugged each other.

'And on to you, Councillor Laodoc,' Ziane said, sighing melodramatically. 'Such is the gravity of the nature of your offences that I'm afraid a fine and a suspended sentence just wouldn't do. As you seem to love the lower classes more than those of your own mage-blood, it was thought fitting that you should join them, in body as well as in spirit. You are hereby stripped of your rights and legal privileges as a member of the mage class, and relegated to the peasant class. Naturally, this means that you can no longer serve as a city councillor, effective immediately. Your property will, in its entirety, be treated as if you were deceased, and will pass on in the normal manner to your two sons, and your former wife will receive a widow's pension.'

Laodoc gasped. This was unprecedented. He had never even conceived that such a punishment was possible. Several of the activists looked at him in utter horror, and he heard the soft tinkle of Douanna's laughter.

'Arrangements will have to be made, of course,' Ziane continued. 'Housing, employment, and so on. You will remain a guest in the cells here until everything has been organised. The rest of you are free to go. Each will receive their fine as they are unshackled.'

Many of the young activists flocked round Laodoc, shaking his hand. Some were sobbing, while others looked enraged on his behalf.

'Stay true to your principles,' he whispered to them. 'There may be dark times ahead.'

The soldiers soon separated him from his volunteers and, as Laodoc was escorted from the hall, Ziane smirked. 'Bet you wish you had retired now, eh?'

The prison cells under the City Council were more spacious and comfortable than those Laodoc had stayed in after Killop's arrest and Simiona's death. They looked little used, and the few prisoners he had seen as he was marched through the prison seemed to have arrived recently, since the committee had taken charge.

He was taken to a clean cell, and locked in. Before the soldiers departed, he was handed a set of standard peasant clothing, the familiar brown tunic and trousers worn by the under-classes. Laodoc ignored the garments, and left them sitting in a pile by the bars. He sat on the wooden bench and prepared for a long wait, his mind struggling to come to terms with what had happened.

He was interrupted after only a few hours.

'Father,' Ruellap said, keeping his distance from the bars of the cell.

'Son,' Laodoc replied, rising.

'We will never call each other by those names again,' Ruellap said. 'You are dead. A dead person.'

'You will always be my son.'

'I voted for you to die,' Ruellap said. 'I didn't want this for you.

Ziane didn't say it, but I was also the one who voted with the Liberals to have you released.'

'Thank you.'

'I know that deep down you're still an honourable man,' his son said, shaking his head, 'and I believe that, once you experience life as a peasant, you'll come to wish you had been executed rather than endure the shame such a miserable existence entails. Then maybe you will understand the reasons for the way I voted.'

There was a painful silence. Laodoc felt bereft, and utterly hollow.

'This may be the last time we meet,' Laodoc said, the words bitter on his tongue. 'Know that you have my love, despite all that has passed between us. Also, pass on my love to your brother Likiat.'

Ruellap nodded. Laodoc could see the conflict in the younger man's eyes.

'Farewell, then,' his son said.

'Farewell,' Laodoc replied. 'Son.'

Ruellap grimaced at the word, then turned and walked away.

'Not wearing your new clothes, I see,' Laodoc heard Douanna say, the words awakening him from a half-doze as he lay on the thin mattress.

'I find the colour does little for my complexion,' he replied, swinging his feet off the bed. He reached for the nearby water jug, and filled his wooden mug.

'That's a pity,' she said, her long sapphire robes flowing almost to the floor, 'I don't think there's all that much variety in the peasant range of clothing. Go on, put them on for me. You can trust me to give you an honest opinion.'

'Thank you,' he said, raising his mug, 'but I'll put them on when a squad of soldiers with crossbows forces me to, and not one minute before. Now, did you come here for any purpose other than to mock?'

'I confess it would have been worth the visit for that reason alone,' she said, 'but I do have something I wish to discuss. Do you mind if I smoke?'

'Would you care if I said yes?'

'No.' She pulled a box of Holdings-branded cigarettes from her bag and lit one. She inhaled, and sighed. 'Ahh, the Holdings,' she said. 'A strangely flat land. One can travel for days and not see a hill, did you know that?'

'Is this what you wanted to ask?'

'You're positively no fun whatsoever, Laodoc,' she said. 'You have just ruined my whole lead-in. We were to chat about the Holdings for a while, and then I was to gently steer the conversation towards a certain citizen of that country, whom I happen to be looking for.'

'I assume you mean Daphne?'

'However did you guess? Yes, it is she. As you may be aware, she is wanted for questioning over the escape of your old Kellach slaves. There was a soldier that the foolish girl didn't quite manage to kill properly, and when he awoke from his injuries, he had the most curious tale to tell.'

Laodoc cursed inwardly, not knowing if Douanna was trying to trick him. 'Sounds absurd.'

She sighed again. 'Can we skip this bit,' she said, 'and go straight to the "I know you were involved" part? Because, to be frank, I know you were involved. Did you think that I wouldn't have someone watching her house, noting who came and went?'

Laodoc shrugged. 'I have already been questioned by the authorities regarding this.'

'You misunderstand me,' she replied. 'You see, I am rather anxious to find Daphne before the authorities do.'

'Why?'

'To assist her of course,' Douanna said. 'Poor girl, helpless and alone in a foreign city, pursued by assassins and hunted by soldiers. Now then, Laodoc, where is she? Before you answer, consider this. Imagine your future for a moment. Think about what it will mean to be a member of the peasant class. Living with them, working in a field or a factory, queuing up for bread each day. I can make that life a million times more bearable, give you enough wealth to lift you out of the shit on the slum streets. Or, I could make your life difficult. Peasants are very easily bribed, I find. For a few ahanes, one can get them to do all kinds of unpleasant things. For a modest investment, I could hire a whole team of Laodoc-harassers, dedicated to making your life a misery in a dozen mean and petty ways.'

She smiled beatifically at him. 'So, I ask again. Where is Daphne?'

Laodoc shook his head. 'Your threats are meaningless to me. I have no idea where she is.'

'Then where did you last meet her?'

'At her apartment,' Laodoc replied. 'I visited her there. I thought you already knew that.'

'You were only there once, you old fool. Where did you meet her after that?'

'I didn't.' He folded his arms. 'We communicated, but I never saw her again.'

Douanna narrowed her eyes at him.

'I think you have more important things to worry about right now,' Laodoc said. 'Like, for example, the imminent uprising of the lower classes of this city, due to the shortages and hardship caused by the Rakanese siege.'

Douanna's face relaxed, and she laughed.

'Oh, I wouldn't worry about that,' she said. 'Something is in motion that should bring all that unpleasantness to an end far more quickly than most people expect. Yes, I would imagine that the siege will be lifted soon, and our armies can demobilise, and we can all go back to normal again, with the Rakanese threat firmly, and irrevocably removed.'

Laodoc paused, dread building within him. 'What's going to happen?'

'Don't be ridiculous!' she laughed. 'I'm not going to tell you. Although I'm not too modest to admit I had a hand in the planning of the whole enterprise. Ahh, it will be quite something, believe me.'

Laodoc stared at her.

'Well,' she went on, 'it's been a lovely chat. I just had one more thing to tell you, regarding your runaway Kellach slaves. They were spotted a couple of days ago, fifty miles north of the city, and a squad of slave-hunters has been sent to apprehend them. Or kill them, whichever is easier.'

'I thought Killop was needed alive,' Laodoc said, his heart sinking, 'as a hostage.'

'No,' Douanna replied. 'He is no longer required. The mage has agreed to do our bidding, as she knows nothing of his escape. And once she has carried out what we ask of her, well, she will most likely also become superfluous to our requirements.'

She laughed. 'It was worth it, just to see that look on your face. Now, did you say it would take a whole squad to force you to change into your new clothes?'

She smiled as he stood by the bars, raging and powerless.

'Don't go anywhere,' she said. 'I'll be right back.'

CHAPTER 30
WALL TO WALL

Akhanawarah City, Rahain Republic – 23rd Day, Second Third Spring 505

'We're holding on so far, Commander,' Polli said. 'Our water supplies are back up after last night's rainfall, and the rooftop gardens are starting to become productive.'

'What about the front line defences?' Shella said, sipping from her glass of sour spirits, distilled by Sami in the basement below.

'Everywhere is quiet this morning.'

'Even down in the mud?'

'There's been no hostile activity on the southern front since yesterday, Commander,' Polli said. 'Even their throwing machines have stopped.'

'Odd,' Shella said. She looked over to Kylon. 'Maybe we should check it out.'

'Aye,' he replied. 'It does sound... wait. Did you feel that?'

'Feel what?' Shella said, raising an eyebrow at the big Kell.

Kylon said nothing, but had tensed his body, and was looking around.

Shella smirked. 'You look like you're about to shit yourself.'

Just then, a low rumble began, and the entire building shook.

Shella was thrown from her reclining couch onto the floor, her glass arcing through the air and smashing against a wall. She held her hands to her head as the floor jerked and bumped. The noise was tremendous. Screams rose above the grinding of bricks, and the clatter of roof tiles falling to the ground outside. In a few seconds it was over and Shella, her whole body quivering, opened her eyes.

Everyone around her had also been knocked to the floor, along with tables, and the contents of every shelf. Books and scrolls lay scattered next to broken bottles and gently rolling glasses. Kylon was the first to his feet.

He rushed to her side, and helped her sit.

She grabbed the nearest intact bottle, uncorked it and took a swig.

'Rijon told me that couldn't happen!' she cried. 'A fucking earthquake! It's not supposed to be possible!'

'Come on,' he said. 'Get up. We need to go outside, see what the damage was.'

Her mind turned to the dams and sluice gates, the only things holding in their supply of fresh water.

'Shit!' she cried, allowing Kylon to pull her to her feet.

They ran for the stairs, picking up guards and staff along the way. Shella issued a constant stream of orders, and soon as many were rushing away to carry out their new duties, as there were joining her. Most were sent to rustle up squads of workers to check every water supply and well in the city, while Shella herself was headed straight for the river. It had been sixteen days since the level of the waterway had fallen away to nothing, and eight since the battle for the Northern Heights. There had been no major assaults from the Rahain side following that confrontation. As Shella had predicted, winged gaien patrols had flown by several times during the day after the battle, scanning the heights, and watching as the Rakanese army solidified their defences along the ridge.

'They're preparing to attack,' she yelled to Kylon, as they raced down the stairs and into the courtyard.

Shattered roof tiles lay strewn across the ground, across which a large ragged crack had appeared, splitting the brick cobbles. They ran through the arch and into the street, which was thick with dazed and injured civilians. She pushed her way to Palace Square, noticing plumes of smoke rise above the tall blocks of the city.

'We need to organise fire teams!'

'Let the government deal with that,' Kylon called back as they ran. 'You should be thinking about the army.'

She skidded to a halt in the middle of the square, while all around, her aides tried to stop. A few slipped and fell, while Shella stood, her fingers rubbing her forehead.

'I don't get it,' she said. 'I need to think.'

She started moving again, this time walking.

'First, the earthquake,' she said. 'Rijon said that their stone mages couldn't make one here, because we built the city on clay, not rock.'

'I remember he said that the bedrock was too far away for any one mage to reach,' Polli said.

'Right,' Shella said. 'They must have gathered every mage in lizard-land to pull that off. We have to assume that if they can do it once, they can do it again. But why now?'

They reached the canal which ran along the palace side of the square, and there was a collective groan. The water level in the canal had dropped by at least four feet, and was still falling. A team of city workers was already trying to mend the wooden sluice gate at the far end of the canal where it met the river but, judging by the cracked and torn planks, Shella guessed that most of the water would be lost before the leaks were repaired.

She gazed into the canal as they walked, seeing her hopes drain away. She knew she could expend her powers, and save this one solitary canal, but it was pointless. She didn't have the physical energy to save even a small fraction of the other pools and sealed waterways across the city.

By now they were almost at the river, and the press and bustle of maintenance and repair workers increased. All along both banks, she could see springs leaking from every dam and gate, their fresh water spilling into the cracked mud of the dry riverbed. Her guards and staff fell into silence as they stared at the sight of their water being sucked down into the parched earth.

Shella felt a hand tug her sleeve.

It was her sister Tehna the priestess, the only sibling that Shella had allowed to stay with the queen in the palace, after she had removed Dannu and Pavu from power.

'Mage sister,' she said, her face red from running. 'Please come quickly to the palace. The queen needs your help.'

'Is her well damaged?'

'Yes,' Tehna said, her voice fraught with fear, 'but that doesn't matter. It's the spawn pool, Shella, one side of it has cracked, and the water is draining away. Obli's spawn will die!'

Shella stared at Tehna, overwhelmed by the magnitude of the disaster that was unfolding. She turned to Kylon, but he wasn't paying any attention. Instead, he was gazing up-river, with the same expression on his face that he had been wearing the moment before the earthquake struck.

'Kylon?' she said. 'What are you looking at?'

'Something's coming,' he said, in a tone that caused several of her staff to stare at him. Shella looked up the river bed to the west, straining her eyes, but could see nothing unusual. Then she noticed a spiral of birds, all rising up from the course of the river. Hundreds, thousands of black specks swirling and dancing in the distance, all flying up and away from the river.

Then she heard a rumble.

'Kylon!' she said. 'What's happening?'

'I think,' the big man said, 'we should step back from the riverbank.'

The rumble increased, like the roar of a giant wave. By now, everybody on both banks had stopped what they were doing, and had turned to stare up-river.

Shella stood, transfixed, her mouth open.

Kylon gasped.

'We have to go!' he called out. 'We need to leave, now!'

Shella couldn't move.

She saw it too, a giant wall of mud surging down the river towards them. Already its powerful current had taken it past the edges of the city, and the deluge was flooding both banks in a thunderous wave.

'Run!' Shella screamed, as all around people panicked, their cries drowned out by the roar of the massive surge sweeping towards the centre of the city.

Shella coughed. That smell. Her mage powers sent out feelers into the approaching wall, and her senses sickened as she felt the poisons that saturated the mass of mud. Arsenic, lead and mercury, all in concentrated amounts, enough to kill anything that drank or swam in it. She pulled her flow powers back to her body as her knees gave way.

Kylon caught her arm, and started to drag her away from the river.

'It's poisoned,' she gasped, her voice a whisper amid the sky-breaking roar of the current of mud. The earth began to shake again, just as the wall of mud hit the central docks and bridges, ripping through them in a second. Shella and Kylon toppled to the ground, as the cobbles buckled and rippled, the cacophony of grinding brick competing with the thundering river of mud.

As the vibrations slowed and stopped, Shella felt big arms pick her up, and carry her.

Kylon held her close as he barged his way from the crumbling dockside. The roar of the current of mud grew deafening. Kylon leapt over a fissure, his boots crunching on the broken ground, while Shella gripped onto him with all her strength. They reached the square, which was packed with fleeing Rakanese. Terror consumed everyone, a mass hysterical panic. Anyone who slipped to the ground was trampled by those around them, and Kylon's bulk and strength were the only things keeping the same from happening to Shella. The palace gates were closed, and the two soldiers guarding the gate-house tower levelled their spears as they neared them. Without wasting a second, Kylon tossed them aside like dolls, and charged through the door. He kept moving, finding the stairs to the upper level and sprinting up them. Reaching the battlement at the top of the tower, Kylon came to a halt, and lowered Shella onto the flat rooftop.

She ran to the edge and looked out over the square, just as the mud wall hit the docks where they had been standing only moments before. The thick brown sludge crashed down in a giant wave over the low quayside, sending a tidal surge of dark mud six feet high across the bank of the river, sweeping everything in its path. The screams from those trapped in the square rose to where Kylon and Shella gazed down in horror. The wave of mud reached right up to the palace gates, before splashing down and rolling a few more feet, covering more than half of the square. Hundreds of bodies, covered in brown mud, lay bobbing and floating upon the sludge.

Shella started to cry, and she felt Kylon's arm pull her near.

The noise of the wave faded, as it was borne away eastward.

Shella was shaking. 'Kylon,' she croaked, her mouth dry and bitter.

He squeezed her, saying nothing.

'What have they done?' she cried, hearing her own hysterical voice, and hardly recognising it. 'Polli, Tehna... all of them, all of them. What have they done?'

The mud below them was starting to drain away, leaving behind a thick, dark residue staining the cobbles, its surface glimmering with an oily, metallic sheen, and littered with debris and corpses. A few living Rakanese, covered in sludge, were crawling towards the untouched half of the square, where thousands were gathered, lamenting and weeping. The river level had returned to beneath the height of the ruined docks, and was flowing rapidly. Every bridge in the city had been destroyed, along with the tied-up barges and boats, and every quay and pier. The side-canals, which an hour earlier had been filled with fresh water, were now thick with tarry sludge, their sluice gates wrecked and hanging loose, their dams breached.

Kylon touched her arm, and pointed upwards. She gazed into the sky and saw, amid the pillars of smoke rising from the city, several winged gaien, circling overhead.

'They're watching us,' he muttered.

A hatred filled her, a hatred unlike anything she had experienced before.

'Fucking Rahain bastards.'

'Aye.'

'You tried to warn me.'

'Even if you'd believed me,' he said, 'you couldn't have stopped this.'

'We're finished.'

'Maybe.'

She remembered her sister.

'Obli,' she cried. 'The palace!'

They ran back down the steps, and into the gardens ringing the palace. No one challenged them as they raced through the parched orchards to the main doors. Once inside, a captain of the queen's guard saw them.

'High Mage!' she called out. 'This way, the queen needs you!'

They fell in with the captain and her guards, and hurried towards Obli's private quarters.

'Did you see what happened?' the captain asked, a wild edge to her voice.

'Yeah,' Shella replied. 'Does the queen know?'

'I don't know,' she said. 'The last I saw, she was by the spawning pool, in the basement. I was sent up to await your arrival. Where is Priestess Tehna?'

'She was at the dockside when the wall of mud hit us.'

The captain looked away, her face distraught.

They carried on in silence, the only sound coming from the clanking and jangling of the guards' armour and weapons. The officer led them down a set of stairs, and they followed a corridor through the basement, where Obli and her aides had lived for thirds, to be next to the wells and spawn pool. The entire level had been tiled, in blue and white.

Shella knew something was wrong from the faint chemical smell pervading the air. She quickened her step. She hadn't seen the queen in many thirds, since she had left Silverstream, and she had never once laid eyes on her children-spawn.

There was a scream.

The captain looked at Shella, and they began to run.

They burst through the door into the spawning room. The small pool was in one corner, and there stood Obli, her white gown drenched, a bloody knife in one hand. To her right, crouching on the floor, a young woman was holding her arm and crying, blood dripping from a wound near her wrist.

'I told you to stay away!' Obli shouted at her, rage lighting up her eyes. 'No one goes near my babies until the mage gets here.'

'Obli!' Shella called out across the chamber.

Her sister looked at her, her expression transforming from anger to desperate hope.

'Clear the way!' the queen commanded, and a dozen terrified nurses and servants shuffled aside.

Shella ran all the way to the pool, and nearly vomited in horror. She slipped on the blood, landing painfully on her knees, as her gorge rose. She put her hand to her mouth. She heard Kylon halt beside her, and curse deeply.

On the still, oily surface of the pool, all nine of Obli's spawn-babies were floating, dead. The water level had dropped, and the pool was only half full, but a black, viscous liquid was seeping in through a dozen small cracks, poisoning the water. Shella poured her mage senses into the small bodies, trying to feel for any life, but it was too late, and she was nearly overwhelmed by the presence of so many contaminants.

'Obli!' Shella cried. 'I'm sorry, Obli, they're dead!'

Her sister turned to her in fury. 'You are the high mage!' she screamed. 'Revive them! I order you!'

'I can't,' Shella sobbed. 'It's too late.'

Obli's face twisted in grief, and she lunged at Shella, her knife outstretched.

Kylon pushed Shella to the side, and struck Obli's arm, sending the knife spinning across the tiled floor.

'You will suffer for that!' Obli shouted. 'Arrest them both!'

As the guards looked at each other, Kylon acted. He drew his longsword, and pulled Shella in close to his left side, his arm gripping her.

He began edging his way to the door.

'What are you waiting for?' Obli screamed. 'Kill them!'

The guards drew their bows, and Kylon ran, lifting Shella off her feet as he barrelled his way through the chamber. Crossbow bolts whistled past them, and Shella heard Kylon grunt once, then twice, but his footsteps never faltered, and they crashed through a final pair of guards at the doors.

Kylon fell to his knees as Shella slammed the door shut, jamming its lock with a fallen pike.

'Can you run?' she asked him, trying to ignore the two bolts protruding from his back.

Kylon grimaced. 'I hope you know a quick way out of here,' he muttered, hauling himself to his feet.

Ten days had elapsed since the Rahain had released the river of poisoned mud, and transformed the settlement of Akhanawarah into a city of the dead. Tens of thousands had perished in the initial wave, drowned or swept away, and thousands every day since, poisoned by contact with the toxins that had seeped into nearly every water supply that remained. There were some sealed, unaffected cisterns supplied solely by rainwater, but these were too few to meet the needs of the city's inhabitants.

All the precious spawn-children were dead, or dying, their pools unable to keep out the contaminants. Their attendant lower-level flow mages had been overwhelmed by the rush of toxins, helpless to stop the poisoning of the feeding water. Those few spawn that survived had been moved to a rain cistern, but were sickly and weak, and no one held out much hope for them.

With every bridge destroyed, the city had been split in two, and it was only now that some were venturing across on rebuilt barges, to rejoin their loved ones, or in search of food and water. The river itself was running clearer and cleaner. A few hours after the deluge, the sludge had been replaced with fresher water coming down from the mountains, but it would take years, perhaps decades before the river would fully recover. The metals and other contaminants had spread into the earth all around, using the Rakanese-built waterways to reach the orchards and rice fields, and poisoning the land, killing all of the trees and crops.

Fires burned daily, as relatives tried to cremate their dead, but it was never enough, and the bodies piled high in the streets, by the side of every canal, and thrown into every cracked and poisoned well. Extreme thirst was forcing people to drink even the most polluted water, and many died silent and lonely deaths in their beds, ill and fevered from the toxins in their blood.

Shella had retreated to her tenement, where she had blockaded herself in, along with all of the building's survivors that she could find. Bowda was still alive, and working every hour of the day for her, trying to piece control of the city together. Her fears for Polli, however, had proved correct. She had been drowned by the deluge, along with Braga, and Tehna.

There was an enormous cistern carved out of the clay beneath the tenement, fed by dozens of nearby rain gutters. The water was rank and stagnant, but contained none of the toxins that were laying the city low, and the block's inhabitants queued gratefully each day for their ration.

The only people who seemed unaffected by the poisons, who seemed to be able to drink any water without ill effect, were her Kellach Brigdomin. Kylon, whom she had been convinced was going to die after being shot twice during their escape from the palace, was already back on his feet, looking gaunt but well, and eating everything he could find. She had watched throughout the night as his fevered body had seemed to expel the toxins through the two bolt holes in his back, and she guessed that his people had an almost mage-like power to heal themselves, although to them it just seemed normal, and it was the Rakanese they considered weak.

So healthy were they amid such sickness, that Shella had them running the whole building, defending the gates and cistern, doling out the daily rations, and providing reports from their frequent scouting trips out into the city.

It was from them that Shella had learned that the Rahain army had attacked one night, a few days after the deluge, and re-taken the Northern Heights. The news had been confirmed when a trickle of exhausted and wounded soldiers had staggered down the hill the next morning. General Darra had been killed in the surprise assault, along with nearly half of the division. All that day, Shella had awaited the start of the expected bombardment, but it didn't come, and she realised that the Rahain had only moved to ensure that the Rakanese could not flee the city. The siege continued. All the Rahain had to do was wait, and the city would die.

The stench of death and corruption was everywhere, and Shella had taken to wearing a perfume-soaked handkerchief over her mouth and nose so she could cope, though her spirit was breaking, and she was starting to wish for an end to it all.

'We should do as he says, Shella,' Sami said. He looked withdrawn, and his skin was grey. His stomach and guts were perforated and swollen, and when he coughed there was blood on his lips.

'No,' she said, barely listening.

'We have to get out of the city!' Sami spluttered, clenching his chest in pain. 'Kylon can get us out.'

'How many times do I have to tell you?' Shella exploded. 'I'm not abandoning the people. There are still thousands alive! I'm not going unless we can all go.'

'But most are too ill to move,' Clodi said. She was still in good health, though always thirsty, having never strayed from the tenement since the siege had begun.

Shella shook her head. 'If this is to be the grave of the migration, then I don't want to survive. I would rather die here, with my people.'

Kylon frowned. 'I understand how you feel, Shella. Many in Kell faced the same decision, and many chose to die, rather than flee or be captured. And you are right to think that the people are your responsibility. You have led them, ultimately, to their ruin, though that is the fault of the Rahain, not yours. But how do you best serve your people now? By dying here, or by living, for revenge, or justice?'

Shella laughed. 'What possible revenge could exist to match this? What justice?'

'Someone has to tell the free peoples of this continent,' Kylon said. 'Tell them what happened.'

'You're fucking delusional, Kylon. No one will care. No one cares now.'

'Fine,' Kylon grunted. 'I swore I'd remain by your side until this whole thing was over, and I'll stand by that oath, although it will mean my death, and the deaths of the other clansfolk here. So be it.' He shrugged. 'I still think you're wrong.'

'You won't die here, Kylon,' Shella snapped back at him. 'Of that I'm sure. When the last one of us succumbs to illness or starvation, you lot will still be alive and thriving.'

Kylon said nothing.

'It's not his fault,' Clodi said. 'He can't help that his people recover from sickness and wounds the way they do.'

'I knew you fancied him,' Shella sneered. 'He'd break you like a twig.'

'Shella!' Sami groaned, as Clodi's face went red.

Kylon glared at her, shaking his head. As he opened his mouth to speak, a shout came from the door.

'Commander!' the soldier called. 'You're needed up on the roof!'

'Come on,' she said to Kylon. 'You can deliver your reprimand to me later.'

The big Kell frowned, and followed her up the steps to the flat roof.

The evening sun was shining low to the west as Shella gazed upon the stricken city. So many dreams and lives, dragged hundreds of miles from Arakhanah only to end in poisoned mud. The red and brown bricks of the countless buildings glowed like autumn in the fading light.

'What is it?' Shella asked, looking around at the soldiers on the roof.

'Over there, Commander,' one pointed to the north, by the foot of the hills.

Shella stared out in that direction, seeing a few plumes of smoke amid the towering apartment blocks. She scowled, not understanding what she was supposed to be looking at. Then she saw it. One of the fires seemed to leap across to the others, making it grow in size, then another, so that several individual street fires were combining, and growing.

'What is that?' she said.

Beside her, she heard Kylon groan, a heartfelt noise torn from his lungs.

'No!' he whispered. 'Please, no!'

'What's happening?' she asked again, an edge of alarm in her voice.

Kylon said nothing, but his face paled, and for the first time, she thought he looked afraid.

She turned back to the north. The combined fires were forming into a wall, which was spreading to the east and west in a thin line. Screams were coming from that district, as the flames began tearing their way through buildings, always keeping to a straight line.

'Fire mage!' one of the soldiers gasped, and Shella turned to Kylon.

'Kylon!' she shouted, grabbing his arm. 'A fire mage? One of yours? Tell me what's happening!'

The big man fell to his knees, his head lowered. Shella stared at him, stunned, as he began to sob.

'Your fire mage...' she whispered. One of the soldiers cried out, and she turned to see that the wall of fire, now some four hundred yards in length, and still growing, had started to move forward, devouring everything in its path. It was half the height of the tallest building, but seemed to sweep right through them, causing the floors above and below to explode in flames. Up the streets it crept, while people ran screaming.

'It's coming right for us!' Shella cried. 'Evacuate! Everyone out! Into the cellars, or down to the river!'

As the soldiers around her fled, she pulled Kylon's arm, but the big man wouldn't budge.

Shella started punching him, and kicked his shin, but he remained immobile. 'Great time for your fucking girlfriend to show up!' she screamed at him.

'They have forced her to do this,' Kylon said, his voice hoarse. 'They have her brother hostage. She would do anything to keep him alive.'

'It doesn't matter! We're going to burn if we don't move!'

Kylon looked at the approaching wall of fire, and got to his feet.

'She's up there,' he said, pointing at the ridge which crowned the Northern Heights.

'Can you stop her?' Shella asked, pulling him towards the stairs.

'It's too late.'

They rushed down the steps, and Shella noticed the temperature rising. The courtyard was abandoned when they reached it. They were about to race to the arched tunnel leading to the street, when there was a tremendous roar as the northern wall of the tenement was hit by the rolling line of fire.

'The cistern!' Kylon shouted, pulling her in the opposite direction.

They sprinted across the courtyard. Kylon smashed open the door to the basement, just as the flames consumed the walls behind them. The blast of heat and energy threw them forwards, and they fell through the door, and tumbled down the steps. Kylon dragged her to the trapdoor in the middle of the floor, and broke the lock with the hilt of his sword. He opened it, and gestured for her to climb in, but the heat was too much, and she felt her eyes close, as her skin blistered, and her hair frazzled.

The last thing she remembered was being dragged along the floor, and the sudden shock of a deluge of freezing cold water on her skin.

CHAPTER 31
FROM ON HIGH

Akhanawarah City, Rahain Republic – 3rd Day, Last Third Spring 505

Daphne lay still among the tangled hawthorn bushes that dotted the hillside, her squad of Holdings troopers huddled and hidden around her. She watched as the sun lowered in the reddening sky to the west, the last rays of the day's light shining down on the Rakanese city and making it glow.

She stretched out her left leg, shaking off the cramp that had been attacking her since they had arrived that afternoon. Their gaien-borne transport had glided in with the others, separating at the last moment to deposit the squad onto the side of the hill above the city, where they had scampered into hiding places. The Rahain army were dug in along the top of the ridge above and behind them, giving them the perfect view of the devastation that the flood had caused ten days before.

The city was a mess. Daphne could see the dirty brown stains left behind by the torrent of mud, marking out the streets and buildings near the river. The bridges had all been swept away, and the network of canals, fish-pools and waterways lay brown and dead. Dozens of small pyres were burning the heaps of bodies that lay piled everywhere, easily visible from half way up the hill, where Daphne and her borrowed squad lay.

Father Ghorley had told them about the earthquakes, and the mage-powered release of millions of tonnes of waste from the scores of mines close to the two river-heads, in the mountains on either side of the Tahrana Valley. The Rahain had then demolished the dam, allowing the toxic sludge to surge downstream and flood the city, drowning thousands and contaminating the food and water supplies. Daphne and the troopers had sat in horrified silence throughout Ghorley's speech, unable to comprehend what it meant to destroy a whole city, and all those who lived within.

Even now, as she looked down at the brick tenements, workshops and apartment blocks, and the mourning and purging fires at every crossroads, she had trouble taking it in.

'Get ready,' she whispered. 'As soon as the sun touches the hills, we're going in. Remember the meeting place if we get separated. Good luck, and may the Creator guide us.'

She shuddered as she spoke the name of the Creator. Following her conversations with Ghorley, she had been left in little doubt as to the existence of the being called by that name, and she remembered the deal she had made with the voice she had heard in the Sanang forest. If he helped her escape, she would help him. The thought that it was real unnerved her. She felt even more uncomfortable to imagine that he had been watching her and might, even now, be observing her actions. She pulled her hood up and over her head.

To the west, the bottom curve of the sun kissed the top of the far mountains. Daphne rose into a crouch and started jogging down the hill, using a thread of her powers to help guide her steps in the growing darkness. There were three others in the squad who also possessed battle-vision. The ambassador had been reluctant to let them leave, but Ghorley had over-ridden him, and insisted that Daphne had the best troopers available to her.

As they ran, Daphne noticed the size and intensity of the funeral pyres start to increase. She kept going, getting closer to the northern edge of the city, where a series of half-built tenement blocks sat in a row.

'Miss!' hissed her sergeant. 'Look!'

Daphne glanced over as she ran, and pulled up in surprise.

The fires in this part of the city had joined together, making a long, continuous line, and were growing, both outwards, and in height. People were screaming, and Daphne could hear the flames tear through nearby buildings.

The Holdings squad jogged to the side of a low wall, and watched open-mouthed. The wall of fire was still spreading, forming a line hundreds of yards wide, running east to west. The eastern edge was only a hundred feet ahead of Daphne and the troopers, cutting them off from the centre of the city, and their mission.

'Ghorley said nothing about this!' the sergeant cried. 'How are they doing it?'

'Fire mage,' Daphne said.

'Shit,' the sergeant grimaced. 'The Kellach mage.'

Killop's sister, Daphne realised, unless the Rahain had captured others. She looked out past the edge of the line of fire, trying to see if there was a way around, and the entire wall of flame started to move south, away from them, rolling through the streets and buildings, devouring everything in its path. Within seconds it had travelled several feet, leaving smouldering ruins behind.

Daphne signalled to the squad, and they moved out, jogging down the last slope of the hill and into the abandoned streets that ran between the empty and derelict tenements. They passed pockets of Rakanese squatters who were staring in disbelief at the flames raging through their city. Most of them looked diseased and emaciated, their skin peeling and blistered, or covered in sores, and their hair lank and falling out. Corpses lay piled by the side of the road, bloated bodies, grey, green and dark red, and Daphne's extended senses were assaulted by the sickly sweet smell of decay.

Ahead, the wall of fire continued to crawl south, and Daphne followed it, rushing past any Rakanese on the way, most of whom were too ill or distracted to notice them.

They passed another street, with a small square, and entered the burnt zone. The ground was warm beneath their boots, and covered in ash and debris. Daphne noticed that the wall of fire had not reached everywhere. Seemingly at random, some buildings had been left untouched, and in the corner of the square was a tree with not a single singe mark on it, standing alone in a sea of devastation.

Daphne led them down a burnt-out street, the blocks to either side still burning, while always keeping a healthy distance behind the fire wall as it rolled towards the centre of the city.

They reached a canal, filled with burning corpses, blackened and rotten, and Daphne stumbled from the smell. It was starting to give her a headache. She called the squad to a halt under the arch of a collapsed building. Her troopers were looking as sick as she felt.

'Wrap up your faces,' she shouted over the roar of the fire, 'and don't touch anything.'

She soaked water over a scarf she had tucked into her belt, and pulled it around her face.

'I'm going to take a quick look.'

She glanced around for the highest landmark and saw a tower to the east. She shot her line-vision up to it, and turned to scan the city.

The centre was now cut in two by the wall of fire, with an enormous black swathe of charred and burning remains on one side, and the rest of the city, still standing, on the other. Beyond was the river, and the southern bank of the city. She took a closer look at the palace, still safe for the moment, then trained her sight on the block where she had met the Rakanese high mage. She pushed into range-vision, using the weathervane at the corner of the palace square, and focussed in on the massive tenement. There was a group standing on the roof, pointing and gesturing towards the approaching line of fire. Among them, she picked out the mage, and the Kellach warrior Kylon.

'I see the target,' she said, pulling her vision back to her body, and staggering under the strain. Her senses felt battered, and the fumes from the burning city were making her feel sick.

She looked at her troopers, unsure how many would make it back if she pressed on.

The wall of fire was now well over a hundred yards ahead of them, crashing and incinerating its way closer to the palace square. She needed to move.

'Everyone but the battlers,' she said, 'head back to the meeting place.'

The troopers glanced at each other.

'Now,' Daphne said, and all those without vision skills saluted, and started to jog back the way they had come. Once they had gone, Daphne pulled out a stick of keenweed and a box of Rahain matches from a pocket.

She lit it, while the three battlers watched. She allowed the narcotic to focus her senses, blocking out the stench, and filling her with an artificial feeling of energy.

'Smoke this,' she said, passing it to them. 'Just a couple of draws each.'

They each did as she commanded.

'Ignore the pain,' she said to them. 'Ignore the smell, and forget all your feelings about what you are seeing. We're here to do our duty to the Holdings, that's all that matters. We'll get the mage, and any other royalty or leaders we can find, and then we're getting out. Are you ready?'

'Yes, miss,' the sergeant said, her eyes wide.

Daphne started running towards the fire, and they followed.

She allowed the keenweed and vision to guide her feet. Ahead, she saw the palace struck by the wall of fire, its towers and spires islands in a sea of flame. The pain in her head increased, but she ignored it. She dodged and ducked as an enormous block of red-hot brickwork fell from a nearby building, smashing on the cobbled street below, sending fragments of broken bricks in every direction.

As they approached the northern entrance to the square, she saw it was blocked, by a heaped pile of smoking and charred debris. Bodies, she realised, hundreds, maybe thousands of bodies, as if a stampede had developed at the bottleneck, a surging tide of Rakanese too slow to escape the rushing wall of fire.

They skirted to the right, avoiding the mound of dead, and ran down a blackened and scorched alley. They burst out into the square, and saw the fire-wall raging at the far end of the open space, still rolling towards the river. To their right stood the mage's tower. The massive tenement block was belching smoke and flames, its roof ablaze, and its windows blown out.

'Damn,' Daphne muttered. 'We might be too late.'

'Look!' her sergeant called, pointing.

Daphne followed her lead, and saw movement around the base of the building.

'Kellach,' she cried. 'Come on!'

They sprinted across the square. Two big Kellach Brigdomin were pulling beams and bricks from the collapsed archway at the front of the tenement. One, a blonde woman, Daphne recognised from her trip down the river.

'Leah!' Daphne shouted.

The Lach woman turned and stared as she watched the four Holdings approach.

'Where's the mage?' Daphne cried as they reached the arch.

'I don't know,' Leah yelled above the roar of the fires. 'In there, maybe. With Kylon, maybe.'

Her companion, a big red-haired man, paused from clearing the piled debris. His clothes were ragged and scorched, and ash and grime smeared his face.

'Help us!' he called.

Daphne and the three troopers ran over, and began clearing the arch. Daphne climbed to the top of the pile. She removed the rubble from under the keystone, creating a small gap.

'I think I can squeeze through,' she shouted down to the others. 'You keep clearing, and I'll go look inside.'

'The building's not safe, miss,' the sergeant called up to her. 'It could collapse any moment.'

Daphne shrugged, buttoned down her rising fear, and crawled into the gap. She extended the climbing hooks under her left arm, and used them to wriggle through the tight, dark space. The archway rumbled above her, and the weight of the burning building swayed and rocked as she crawled, dust from grinding bricks falling onto her like a shroud.

She reached the far side, and pulled herself out into the open, clambering down into the courtyard of the tenement. While the upper floors still burned, everything on the ground level was blackened and scorched.

'Mage Shella!' Daphne bellowed at the top of her lungs. 'Kylon!'

There was a crash of falling bricks to her left, as a floor somewhere in the upper building collapsed. She was about to start shouting again, when a small group emerged from an archway to her right. Two Rakanese and a Rahain, all males. One of the Rakanese was injured, and the others were helping him stand.

They eyed Daphne as she approached. They stank, and their clothes were drenched.

'Where's Mage Shella?' Daphne asked them.

'Who are you?' wheezed the struggling Rakanese.

'Rescue party,' she replied, keeping her hand near her sword hilt.

'It's okay, Sami,' the other Rakanese said. 'I recognise her from before; she visited Shella a while back. She's the one who punched Rijon.'

'That treacherous weasel?' sneered the Rahain. 'Well, Holdings woman, you can't be all bad.'

'Is Shella here?' Daphne said. 'Do you know?'

'She was with me,' the hurt Rakanese, Sami, said. 'Upstairs. We were told to evacuate, but I can't move like I used to, and these two helped me hide when I got down the steps.'

'In the sewers, by any chance?'

The three men looked at each other, sniffing and grimacing.

'I was waiting down here for Kylon,' the renegade Rahain said. 'Everyone else ran for it, but I stayed. He didn't show.'

Daphne glanced at the burning upper floors.

'If they're up there, they're dead,' she muttered. 'Are there any other sewers?'

Sami's eyes lit up. 'The cistern!'

Daphne smiled. 'Show me.'

An hour later, not long before midnight, the survivors from the mage's tenement huddled together at the edge of the square, sitting in one of the spared patches of ground where grass was still growing, surrounded by ash and smoking piles of burnt-out rubble and bodies. Seven had made it out, including the two Kellach they had met at the arched entrance to the block.

Shella sat scowling, her hair frazzled and burnt at the tips, and her clothes filthy and ragged. Her skin was an angry red, blistered and burnt. Next to her sat her brother Sami, coughing and shaking, and their guard, who Daphne had learned was named Jayki. They were the sole Rakanese who had come out of the building alive. Kylon was with Leah and Bedig, the red-haired Kellach. Two of their number had been lost to the flames, and the Kellach Brigdomin were locked together in a mournful embrace. Baoryn, the renegade Rahain, was keeping a watchful eye close by.

Daphne and her three battlers stood at the edge of the green patch, watching as the last remnants of the wall of fire scoured the southern bank of the city, having somehow leapt the river while Daphne had been inside the tenement pulling Kylon and Shella from the cistern.

'There it goes,' her sergeant frowned, the enormous line of fire starting to falter as it reached a huge area of mud beyond the last buildings. The flaming wall lowered and fell, and sputtered out, leaving countless smaller fires burning in its wake.

'An entire city, incinerated,' muttered one of her other battlers. He took a draw from the stick of keenweed Daphne had passed around, and held it out to her.

She took it.

'We have two of the Kanawara royal family,' she said, smoking. 'One more to look for, then we're heading back. Kylon!' she shouted.

He walked over, the other Kellach following.

'I'm going to the palace,' she said. 'I need a guide.'

'I'll take you,' he replied, his face twisted with raw emotion. 'But first, please, if you could use your powers. I need to know if this... all this, was Keira.'

She nodded. 'Where?'

'Up on the ridge,' Kylon said, pointing. 'The fires were directed from up there.'

'It's too dark to see much,' she said, 'but I'll try.'

She sat on the grass, while the others watched. She squinted in the direction of the ridge, which she could barely make out through the smoky night air. She looked for something closer, and saw a tall spire at the northern edge of the city. She zipped her line-vision out to it, and looked up the hill side. There were tiny pinpricks of light up at the top, and a patch of cliffside was visible in the reflected light of a lamp. She concentrated, and fired a line of range-vision to this second point, and scanned around.

The summit was crowded with Rahain soldiers, who stood staring at the devastation below. Standing a foot taller than anyone else on the ridge, Daphne noticed the fire mage, and gasped. The family resemblance to Killop was strong. It was his sister, Keira.

She was in chains, standing motionless on the cliff top, her head bowed. Tears were streaming down her cheeks, but her face was a mask of rage. In a half-circle around her, dozens of soldiers stood, their crossbows pointed. Behind them, a long cylindrical carriage was waiting. Daphne noticed that Keira's chains led inside the structure and, at a signal from an officer, soldiers began to pull the chains, heaving Keira towards it. She strained against them but stumbled, and fell to the ground. Soldiers ran to her side, and with a dozen pikes pressed against her, they tied a bag over her head. They leapt back out of her reach, and the other soldiers dragged the fire mage inside the carriage.

Daphne's strength gave out, and her vision shot back to her body. She panted and wheezed, closing her eyes. Someone pushed a mug of vile cistern water into her right hand, and she drank, trying not to be sick. She lit a cigarette, and coughed.

'Give her a moment,' her sergeant said.

Daphne opened her eyes, and saw Kylon's nervous, expectant face, as he knelt next to her.

She nodded. 'It was Keira.'

Kylon rose to his feet, clenching his fists, a low roar coming from his throat. He sobbed, his chest shaking, and he put his hands to his face. Leah stood back a pace.

'How was she?' asked Bedig.

'In chains,' Daphne said. 'They took her away in a flying carriage.'

'How could she do this?' Leah spat.

'They must have forced her,' Bedig said.

'Fuck off,' Leah said. 'Have you ever seen Keira forced to do anything?'

'I can't believe it,' Bedig said, shaking his head.

'The city was already dying,' Shella cried out, and they all turned to look at her. 'She just put it out of its misery.'

No one said anything.

'It was a mercy killing,' Shella snorted.

'Shut up, Shella,' Sami said.

'The Rahain army will be arriving at dawn,' Daphne said, before Shella could open her mouth. 'Our transport out of here leaves just before then, from the base of the hill. Kylon will be coming with me to the palace. My soldiers will escort everyone else to the meeting place.'

'I'm coming too,' said Shella.

Her guard Jayki stared at her. 'It's not safe, miss.'

'Ha!' she sneered. 'We'll have a flow mage, a vision mage, and a grumpy Kell with us. I think we'll be okay.'

Daphne nodded to her sergeant. She frowned, but saluted.

'Let's go!' the sergeant called out, raising her arms.

Daphne lit another cigarette and sat, as the others got up and followed the battlers across the square.

'Why are you here?' Shella snarled once they were alone.

'Don't you want to be rescued?' Daphne said.

'Our dreams are poisoned ash and scorched bone. Why are you here?'

'We had word of what was happening. We had to see for ourselves if it was true.'

'Then why the fuck did Rijon leave?'

'They changed their minds,' Daphne said, smoking. She saw Kylon turn, and crouch down next to them. His face was tear-stained but set firm.

'You ready?' Daphne asked.

He nodded, and they got to their feet.

'Let's go see the queen.'

Kylon and Shella led Daphne across the square, through the blackened wasteland of the royal gardens, and into the palace. The main structure was a burnt-out shell. The towers and spires had toppled through the shattered roof, leaving enormous fragments of ruined brickwork scattered around. They saw no one living, and descended to the basement level. The smooth, tiled walls were smeared in ash. Shella lit a lamp, and they walked down the silent passageway.

'Last time we were here,' Shella whispered, 'she tried to kill us.'

Daphne kept quiet, not knowing if Shella was joking.

They came to a stout door at the end of the corridor. Its latch was broken, as if it had been forced recently. Kylon pushed, and it swung open. The interior was well-lit and Shella extinguished her lamp. They walked into a large chamber, its walls shining in blue and white tiles, untouched by the fire.

Daphne saw a pool in the corner of the room, and next to it a table, at which a woman sat alone.

'Obli!' Shella cried, and ran towards her, Daphne and Kylon following.

They raced across the tiled floor, and Daphne saw that the pool was drained and empty.

'Where is everyone?' Shella shouted, reaching the table.

The woman looked up. Her face was grey and expressionless. She looked exhausted, and sat slumped, her hands under the table.

'I sent them away,' the queen said.

Shella sat at the table across from Obli. She said nothing. A tear crawled down her cheek as she stared at her sister.

'Your Highness,' Daphne said, breaking the silence. 'We're here to help you escape.'

Obli laughed, a harsh cutting noise.

'How is my city?' she asked Shella, her laugh fading. 'How has it fared, since you took it from me, sister?'

Shella's mouth opened in surprise.

'This is your doing,' Obli continued, her stare fierce and keen. 'This day was ordained the moment you murdered their people during the visit of the delegates.'

'No,' Shella whispered.

'We can argue about this later...' Daphne began, but stopped when she felt Kylon touch her arm.

'You were always plotting against me,' Obli went on, her voice rising. 'Right from the beginning, right from the moment we left. You were always jealous of me, a disloyal, treacherous rat, despite the many times I forgave you and kept you close. Well, you won, sister. You beat me, and you took my city from me. My babies all died, Shella, sister dear. Nine little lives. Poisoned, like the whole city, like the whole migration! The holy migration!' she shouted at Shella, who flinched

409

backwards. 'We are destroyed, the migration is destroyed, because of you!'

Obli spat at Shella.

'Enough,' Daphne said. 'We're leaving, your Highness. Are you coming?'

Obli scowled at her, a venomous expression on her face.

'I'm not cowed by you,' Daphne said. 'Are you coming?'

'No,' Obli said, her face dropping again. 'I shall die here.'

'Come with us,' Shella said.

'You're fleeing with these foreigners?'

'Someone has to bear witness.'

'And you think you're suitable, sister?' Obli sneered. 'Oh, I can just imagine the way you will twist things around, how you will leave out the countless who perished at your hand, and instead paint yourself the hero, the righteous one!'

'I will tell the truth.'

'Now I almost wish I was leaving,' Obli said, 'if only to counter the web of lies you will spin. But it's too late, even if I wanted to.'

'What?'

'I have drunk deep, sister,' Obli smiled. 'Deep from the waters of death. I've seen what happens. In a few hours I'll be dead.'

Shella recoiled, her eyes wide.

'There will be torment before the end,' Obli said. 'I have also seen that. If this knowledge disturbs you, sister, I'll allow you to end my life with a wave of your hand if you wish. It matters not to me.'

Shella broke down weeping, her hands clutching her face. Kylon stepped forward, and lifted her from her seat.

'Farewell Obli, Queen of Akhanawarah,' he said. 'I'm sorry for the loss of your children. I'm also sorry that your grief has hidden the truth from you, that nothing would have prevented the Rahain from destroying the migration, just as they destroyed my own land. They are the enemy, not your sister.'

He pulled Shella towards him, and began to lead her from the room.

Daphne gazed at the queen, as her eyes followed her weeping sister. For a moment she looked troubled, as if she regretted her words. Then her face hardened.

'Don't trust her,' she murmured. 'She destroys everything she touches.'

Daphne said nothing, turned, and went out after the others.

CHAPTER 32
EXTINGUISHED

Mountains north of Rahain Capital, Rahain Republic – 4th Day, Last Third Spring 505

'With every step,' Kallie said, 'we get further from Kell.'

'You think I don't know that?' Bridget called back, struggling to keep the frustration from her voice as they trekked up the long stony slope. The sun was setting behind the mountains to the west, shrouding the hillside in shadow.

'There's that gaien again,' Lacey said, as they reached the summit.

They halted, and looked up at the flying lizard, circling a hundred feet over their heads.

'What I would do for a longbow,' muttered Kallie.

Killop was panting, worn out from having been on the move since dawn. After a few slow and tortuous days on the stretcher, he had been back running with the others as soon as he had been able to stand. It had increased their speed, but the constant movement, along with a lack of food, had kept the crossbow injury from completely healing. Most evenings he discovered that it had re-opened, weeping watery pus and blood through his stained tunic. Killop took a swig from his flask, his side throbbing in agony. He refused to let the others see him suffering, not wanting them to think he was slowing them down.

They had given up trying to hide from the flying beasts. Having left the settled, farmed areas far behind, the land they were traversing was barren and dry, a rocky landscape of broken slate crossed by deep, sudden ravines or blocked by sharp cliffs and ridges. Killop knew that Kallie and Lacey would have left by now and gone off on their own, if the dogged Rahain pursuit hadn't kept them running every day. The gaien overhead shadowed them continually, directing a company of slave-hunters led by a stone mage to their position.

'I see the bastards,' Bridget said, pointing into the distance. 'They're catching up.'

'We can't run at night,' Lacey said, waving her arm at the unforgiving land around them. 'Not here.'

'We'll just have to take it slow,' Bridget said. 'Come on.'

She started walking down the other side of the hill. Killop forced himself forward, and they trudged down the track in the fading light.

As they neared the bottom of the long slope, they saw a dark crevice blocking their path. Bridget put her arm up and they stopped, scanning the route ahead.

'I don't think we can get across that,' she said, pointing at the ravine, thirty yards down from them.

'Can we go round?' Kallie asked, squinting into the gloom. 'What if we...?'

'Listen!' Lacey hissed, staring back up the slope.

There was a quiet sound, a tinkle of rocks from above, and they all turned and looked.

'I can't see anything,' Bridget muttered, while the sound grew into a low roar of stones and rocks moving, tumbling, falling.

'Rockslide!' Kallie shouted. 'The lizards must be at the top of the hill!'

'Their fucking mage is up there!' Lacey cried.

The earth began to shake, the stones beneath their feet sliding and vibrating.

'Run!' Bridget shouted.

The hillside bucked as a wave rippled down the slope, and they were flung into the air, each landing onto the rocks, and sliding down-hill, caught up in the turbulent flow of stones and boulders. Killop tried to get to his feet, but the whole hillside was moving like a river, spilling its contents into the deep crevice rushing towards them. Power-less to resist the current, he pulled his arms up to protect his head, and closed his eyes.

He felt the ground disappear, his legs and body hanging in the air as he went over the edge, before he plummeted downwards, surrounded by an avalanche of rubble. Darkness enveloped him as the air rushed past.

Killop crashed into the deep, cold waters of a fast flowing river, the current hauling him down. He hit the rocky bottom, panicking, his arms flailing, as the falling stones churned up the waters. He re-surfaced, his head above the water, and he gasped for breath in the utter blackness, before he was dragged back under.

Just as he thought his lungs would burst, the rushing current lifted him again, and he rose back up, away from the rockslide, the speed of the flowing water carrying him swiftly downstream. He caught a last glimpse of the sides of the crevice where he had fallen, and could see rocks still tumbling over the edge, before the river turned him round again, bearing him north into the night.

Hours later he lay sodden and exhausted on a pebbly bank, deposited by the river, which was flowing just beyond his toes. He had managed to haul himself that far, and had then collapsed. He had vomited up blood and water where he lay, unable to move. Some part of his memory recalled every second of the terrifying trip down the river, but in the darkness he had no idea of how far he had travelled, or where the other three Kellach were. He knew none of them could swim, having no experience of any body of water large enough to need to learn.

His hearing was dulled by the constant torrent of the river, but he thought he heard a soft noise to his right. He lifted his head from the smooth stones. He could see nothing, but his senses were alert, and he could feel the presence of someone close by.

There was a cry of pain, and a clatter of stones.

'Who's there?' Killop said.

'Killop?' came the reply. Kallie.

'Aye,' he groaned. He pushed himself to his knees. 'What are you doing?'

'Trying to walk along the side of the river,' she said, 'but it's too dark to see anything. And now I've just banged my knee.'

'Any sign of the others?'

'No.'

Killop rubbed his arms. He was cold and aching all over.

'Cover your eyes,' he said. 'I'm going to spark.'

He held his hands out from his body, looked away and generated a low, dim burning light between his fingers, using enough power for a few seconds.

As his eyes adjusted, he saw that they were still at the base of the long ravine, though it was shallower here than before, and the sides of the crevice were set more apart from the river, creating a thin strip of flat pebbly ground on either side. Nestled under the sheer cliffs, squat bushes grew. Just before the light faded, he looked to his other side, where he saw Kallie sitting on a boulder, nursing her leg. She was covered in scratches and bruises, her hair and clothes drenched. She was looking at him, and their eyes met for a moment as the spark went out.

'You hurt?'

'Been worse. You?'

'Same.'

They sat in silence for a while.

'Stay there,' he said. 'I'm going to find those bushes over by the cliff, and make a torch.'

She didn't reply, so he started crawling off to his left. In the brief light, the base of the ravine had seemed an easy enough journey to make, but in pitch darkness, it was hard going. After scraping his hands and knees, he reached the thorny bushes, and searched with his fingers for loose, dry branches. He collected several and, narrowing his eyes, shot a spark out at the largest branch, which took up the flames. He held his new torch aloft, and pushed the other branches into his belt.

Kallie got to her feet, nodded, and they set off, following the river downstream.

Killop sat brooding on the smooth stones by the shore of a large, still lake, as the dawn's first rays split the eastern hills to his right. He wondered where Keira was, and if she knew he had escaped. He doubted that the Rahain would tell her, but didn't know what they would do if she insisted on seeing him again. He missed her. He went through imaginary conversations in his head with her, trying to explain about Daphne and Kallie, and hearing her sharp reproaches back at him. Even in his own mind he could never seem to win an argument with her. His excuses sounded feeble and, no matter how he tried to word it, his infatuation with Daphne came out sounding foolish. A few moments of lustful abandon, and he had destroyed his closest relationship with anyone except his sister.

But he loved Daphne. Didn't he? He was sure he did, but nothing seemed real about her any more, as if he had dreamt the whole thing.

Kallie was real. He glanced at her. She was poking at their small fire with a thorny stick, her face tired and drawn, but otherwise emotionless. How could he have hurt this woman?

He heard her sigh.

'I don't know if I have the will to keep going,' she said, so quietly he had to strain to hear her.

'I thought you wanted to go back to Kell.'

'I do,' she whispered, 'but it's so far away, and I don't know how to get there.'

Her face was cast down in despair, but she laughed before he could speak.

'Why am I even telling you this?' she said.

'Look, I'm sorry for...'

'I don't want to hear it.'

'But...'

'No, Killop,' she said. 'I don't want to hear your "I didn't mean to hurt you" speech. I'm not interested. You lost all right to say anything to me the second you took that cow into your arms.'

'It wasn't Daphne's fault.'

'Don't you say her name to me,' Kallie snarled, then stopped, and laughed again. 'Why the fuck do I even care? I'm past being jealous. I'm past giving a rat's arse about what you do, or say. You threw away everything we had.'

'You're right,' he said. 'I did. I made my choice.'

'And now I'm making mine,' she snapped back. 'To be as far away from you as possible.'

'You're going to walk to Kell alone?'

'If I have to.'

'You won't,' called a voice.

They turned, and saw Lacey and Bridget stumbling over the rocks towards them. Both looked exhausted, and sorely bedraggled.

'You won't have to,' Lacey repeated. 'I'll come with you.'

Bridget staggered over, and sat down by the fire, shivering.

'Good to see you both,' Kallie said.

'We only really got moving when it started to get light,' Lacey said, warming her hands by the low flames.

'You okay, Bridget?' Killop asked.

The young Brig woman nodded. 'Need some sleep.'

Killop looked around. 'We must have bought ourselves some time from the slave-hunters. We should get a few hours' rest.'

Kallie looked unconvinced, as if she was anxious to be away, but Lacey and Bridget nodded.

It was a warm, sunny morning, and they lay out some of their damp clothes by the entrance to a shallow cave, high above the southern bank of the lake. Killop slept fitfully, conscious that he kept bumping into Bridget, who lay between him and Kallie. They awoke near noon, and put their dried rags back on in silence, the tension heavy in the air.

Bridget eventually spoke. 'I think we should head round the eastern side of the lake...'

'The road to Kell is north and west of here,' Kallie said.

'Aye,' Bridget said, 'but there's a Rahain town on the west side of the lake. We should avoid that.'

'It's a tiny place. I saw it on the map. It should be easy to get round.'

'But it's the way they'll expect us to take.'

'So?'

Killop watched as the two women glared at each other.

'I'm not going back to Kell,' he said.

'What?' Bridget asked, her mouth open.

'Not yet, at any rate,' he said. 'I need to find my sister first.'

'And how the fuck are you going to do that?'

'Let him go,' Lacey said. 'We don't want him coming with us anyway.'

Bridget looked for a second like she might punch Lacey, who inched back.

'It makes it all simple,' Kallie said. Everyone turned to her. 'He goes east, we go west.'

'We?' Bridget asked.

'You can come with us,' Kallie said. 'I hope you do. Or...' She shrugged.

Bridget sat back and sighed. 'This is so fucked up,' she said. 'No wonder the lizards beat us, when four of us can't stick together.'

Killop pulled on his battered boots, as Bridget shook her head.

'I'll be glad of the company Bridget,' he said, 'but choose what you think is best for you, not me.'

He stood.

'Kallie, Lacey,' he said. Lacey averted her eyes, but Kallie kept his gaze. 'Good luck getting back to Kell, and Lach. I hope you find your families.'

'Goodbye, Killop,' Kallie said.

He turned, keeping his eyes low.

'Bridget?' he said.

She looked up at him, her eyes full of indecision.

He nodded, and turned for the cave entrance.

'Wait!' Bridget called. He looked back, as she grabbed her tattered cloak.

'Goodbye, you two,' she said, pausing to embrace Kallie.

Killop waited as Bridget wiped her eyes, before she turned, and followed him out of the cave. The sunlight was reflecting brightly off the calm waters of the lake below them, and they squinted.

'You all right?' he asked.

'Not really.'

They turned east, and began walking down to the shore.

'Can I ask you something?' Bridget said, as they walked up the side of a low ridge, the lake a mile to their left. 'Are we just searching for Keira, or are we really looking for Daphne as well?'

Killop smiled. For four days he and Bridget had been travelling alone, and he had to admit he had been half-enjoying it. It was a relief to be without Lacey's caustic tongue, and although he felt a weight of guilt over Kallie, it was lifting the further east they went.

'Bit of both,' he said. 'Why?'

'Isn't it obvious?' she said. 'After the way Daphne rescued us, don't you think it would be sensible to get her to help us free Keira? Plus, she probably knows where all the prisons are, she can use her mage powers to find your sister.'

Killop frowned, annoyed that he hadn't thought of this first.

'Imagine how they'd get along,' Bridget chuckled. 'Daphne and Keira... Imagine them getting into a fight...'

'You seem interested in talking about Daphne, all of a sudden.'

'I admit,' she said, 'it's a relief to be able to talk about her at last. Couldn't in front of Kallie, for obvious reasons. But you're forgetting that she was my friend, too, way before you ever shagged her. There was something about her I liked from the start. And when we saw her take on those six lizard guards? Fucking amazing.'

'That surprised me, too.'

Bridget laughed. 'You had no idea that she was a mage?'

'Not until she rescued us, and even then I only thought she could see into people's dreams.'

'I'd forgotten about that,' Bridget said. 'Wait, do you think that's why you kept dreaming about her? Was she coming into your dreams at night?'

'No,' he said, shaking his head. 'She came into my head on the night of the rescue. It was a... unique experience. I'd know if she'd done it before.'

'That's just weird,' Bridget said. 'Imagine, if you two ever actually get together, she'll be able to tell if you're lying, by reading your thoughts. And she'll be able to check if you dream of other women!'

'You'd better hope I never dream of you then.'

She snorted.

They slowed their pace as they neared the top of the stony ridge. The bright morning had turned into a beautiful afternoon, the sun shining to the west amid a clear blue sky. Killop had noticed more vegetation as they had travelled that day, first small shrubs and tufts of long grass, and now there were patches of thin silvery trees. There had been no sign of any Rahain since the rockslide, and the entire length of the lake's southern shore lay empty of farms or settlements.

At the top of the ridge to their left the lake was gently curving round to the north, where a range of low, dark mountains brooded. Several miles away, among the squat and broken foothills that nestled between the lake shore and the mountains, a small tendril of smoke was rising, and Killop and Bridget crouched, in case anyone was watching the skyline.

'What do you think?' said Bridget.

'I don't know,' he said. 'Travellers? Decided to camp early for the night, maybe.'

'Should we take a look?'

'Normally I'd say no,' he said, 'but I'm starving. Might be worth the risk to see what's there.'

She nodded, and they began to descend the other side of the ridge. It was steeper than the gentle slope they had climbed, and it was getting dark by the time they got in sight of the cause of the smoke.

Three wagons were gathered around a large campfire, their gaien beasts tethered and grazing nearby. The two wagons closest to Killop and Bridget were covered in heavy canvas, while a crowd of Rahain sat near the fire, eating and talking. As they edged closer, trying not to look into the light, they saw the third wagon, and gasped.

It was filled with Kellach slaves, crammed inside a high-barred cage sitting upon the wagon's chassis. They were sullenly eyeing the Rahain, filthy in their tattered rags. There were men and women, and a few children also, pressing their dirty faces to the bars, watching as the Rahain ate and drank.

Killop had to bite down on the rage he felt rising within him, and he sensed Bridget tense to his left. He started to crawl back the way they had come, and she followed him.

When they had got out of earshot, he turned to her.

'I don't think I can walk away from that.'

'Me neither,' Bridget said, 'but there's eight of them, and only two of us. They have crossbows, while all you have is a crossbow wound.'

'They were drinking brandy,' Killop said. 'We'll wait till they get drunk, then sneak in and kill them in their sleep.'

Bridget smiled. 'Spoken like a true savage, Killop. I'm in.'

CHAPTER 33
ASYLUM

R ahain Capital, Rahain Republic – 5th Day, Last Third
Spring 505

The raw peal of the brass handbell jolted Laodoc awake, and he rolled out of bed, to stand unsteadily to attention. Up and down the low-ceilinged dormitory, twenty other old men were doing the same. In the passageway running between the rows of beds, the gang-master paced up and down with a cheerful grin, ringing the bell like it was the end of the world.

Laodoc stood by his bed, his heart pounding an irregular beat, his thin and patched-up nightgown fluttering in the breeze from the broken window at the end of the long room. He hoped it would be fixed before winter. As the last man staggered to his feet, the bell stopped ringing, and there was an audible sigh of relief.

The gang-master turned for the door towards the washroom, and they all trooped out after him, keeping quiet and respectful. Laodoc had learned that there was a strict hierarchy among the peasant class, and unproductive old people resided somewhere near the bottom of the heap. Having no legal family, Laodoc had been allotted a bed in a workhouse, with old men occupying one wing, and old women the other. They could mix at mealtimes, but were kept segregated after lights-out each evening.

After washing and dressing, they were led downstairs to the refectory. They queued up at the counter, where a slave handed each a bowl of weak broth and a cup of water, and then they went to their table. There was a collective murmur as they sat, as speaking was permitted for twenty minutes during breakfast every morning.

There had been a bustle of curiosity around Laodoc when he had first arrived, but that had worn off after a few days, and he was mostly ignored, not through contempt, but more because he was unaccustomed to speaking with peasants, and often said things that sounded a little odd to them. He hadn't told anyone the truth about his past, as he was worried they would think he was crazy, and now just tried to listen and not offend anyone.

He supped at his broth as the others at the table castigated the hike in the price of the foul spirits that were sold in the workhouse shop. They were paid in tokens that could only be spent there, and one old man was complaining that it took two days' labour to earn enough for a small flask of what he generously called brandy. Laodoc had tasted it one evening, during their rest hour before bed, and had had to fake a sore stomach to avoid having to drink any more.

After breakfast their gang-master, who had eaten with the other workhouse officials at the top table, led them off to that day's scheduled work. There was a mixed reaction as he informed them that they would again be repairing workers' overalls. Some complained that they wanted to be outside, working in the orchards on the surface on what was looking likely to turn into a beautiful day, while others grumbled about the needle cuts they were sure to get on their callused fingers.

As they were crossing the central atrium of the workhouse, the group's attention was distracted by a news-teller, who was up on a podium. A crowd had gathered to listen, and were cheering. The old men's ears pricked up and they looked pleadingly at the gang-master, who nodded his permission. Laodoc followed his room mates as they jostled their way into the busy crowd, trying to get near.

Laodoc pushed to the front. The news-teller was a young man, dressed in official senate heraldry. He looked like he had already given out his news several times that morning, but was still relishing the reaction it got.

'The siege is over!' he was calling out, to the raucous cheers of the assembled peasants. 'The siege is over! The Rakanese invaders have been eradicated, and their illegal occupation of our land is at an end. The victorious army of the Rahain Republic is coming home! Conscripted peasant battalions will be demobilised, and rationing will be phased out. As a gesture of goodwill to the steadfast peasantry of the Republic, the High Senate has proclaimed today a holiday, and brandy rationing is suspended until tomorrow!'

This last piece of news garnered the loudest cheer, and Laodoc could hear comments all around, praising the wisdom of the High Senate and gloating over the defeat of the Rakanese.

Laodoc approached the news-teller, who was basking in the cheers of the crowd.

'Did you say eradicated?'

The herald looked down from the podium. 'What?'

'You said "eradicated",' Laodoc repeated. 'What did you mean?'

'Annihilated, old man,' the news-teller beamed. 'Smoked out like an infestation of cockroaches.'

Laodoc staggered backwards in shock, as around him there were more cheers at the news-teller's words.

'About time!' someone shouted. 'Slimy frog-eyed bastards!'

There were laughs from the crowd, and the news-teller grinned.

'Indeed!' he called out. 'And thanks to the clever plan of the High Senate, the destruction of the Rakanese camp was carried out at no further cost in lives to our own soldiers!'

'A cheer for the High Senate!' someone called.

The peasants roared their approval as Laodoc slunk his way backwards away from the crowd, despair and horror threatening to capsize him. He felt a hand grab his arm.

'You all right, old man?' the gang-master shouted in his ear as if he was deaf.

'Never better, sir,' Laodoc replied, scrabbling to regain his composure.

The gang-master frowned at his accent. They all thought he affected his upper class tone, another reason why he usually kept quiet.

'I was wondering, sir,' he continued, before his courage failed him, 'as it's a holiday, could I be permitted a pass to go out into the city, please?'

The gang-master let go of Laodoc's arm and rubbed his chin. 'Why?'

'Just for a walk,' Laodoc said. 'I've not been out of the workhouse since I arrived, sir.'

'You'll miss the free brandy.'

'Yes, sir.'

'You know the punishment for breaching curfew?'

'Yes, sir, I do,' Laodoc said. 'I'll be back before the dinner bell, I promise.'

The gang-master frowned, but pulled a wad of papers from his side bag, and a pencil. He filled out a printed pass, and handed it to Laodoc.

'Behave yourself out there, old man,' he growled, and walked away.

Laodoc clutched the slip of paper like it was the most precious thing he had ever held.

He stopped off at his bed in the dormitory to collect a few things, then made his way to the front gates of the workhouse.

The guards eyed him with contempt but let him through. Laodoc practically ran up the street, feeling a rush of freedom. He had only been in the workhouse for fifteen days, but already it seemed like an eternity. Every day was the same, and the lives of the inmates were controlled by a suffocating blanket of rules and regulations. Some of the old men had been inside the workhouse for years, and Laodoc had in no way come to terms with the fact that this was to become his life.

As he walked through the streets the lamps were being brightened, to signify morning. This was the first time he had been out in public wearing his peasant clothing, and he found he had to quickly adjust. Slaves still got out of his way, but the upper classes acted as if he wasn't there, and he had to scurry aside if he saw them coming. The soldiers on the street corners glared at him in the same manner they regarded all peasants and slaves. No one really looked at his face. His uniform was everything, his place in the structure of society as fixed as stone.

By lunchtime Laodoc's feet were getting sore, and his stomach was rumbling. He still had far to go and he realised that, if his plan didn't succeed, he would be late getting back to the workhouse. Three nights in the punishment cells beckoned, and he felt his anxiety rise.

He reached the huge cavern where the government buildings were clustered a couple of hours after noon. He stopped for a moment to gaze up at the beautiful spires of the High Senate, and then the more modest towers of the City Council, where the Requisition and Mobilisation Committee continued to rule.

Soldiers patrolled in heavy numbers, stopping members of the lower classes to check their papers. Laodoc knew the ways of the cavern well, and kept to the narrow back streets, where long shadows masked his presence. He came to a junction, and saw what he had been looking for.

The Holdings embassy.

He had never visited before, but remembered sending Simiona to find out the address for him.

Boldness, he said to himself, striding towards the wide steps leading to the embassy doors.

'Halt!' one of the two Holdings guards yelled as he approached. Laodoc doubted that they spoke to the upper classes in such a tone.

'Good day, gentlemen,' Laodoc said, continuing to walk. 'I have an appointment inside the embassy today, regarding a visa to trade with your homeland.'

The guards looked at each other, then back at him. They kept their spears out, blocking his path.

'Let's see your appointment card,' said one.

'I didn't receive one,' Laodoc replied. 'I was told to report to the main reception.'

'I don't think so,' the guard said. 'Sorry, mate, not today.'

Laodoc stopped, a spear point twitching a few inches from his chest.

'You must let me in,' he said, his resolve starting to break. 'I have important news.'

'Oh yeah? Tell us it, then.'

'I can't,' Laodoc replied, then whispered. 'I must speak to Daphne Holdfast.'

The guards glanced around. They knew the name, Laodoc thought. He noticed a squad of Rahain guards on patrol turn a corner and approach them. His heart raced, and he began to sweat.

The Holdings guards looked up, noticing the reason for his increased anxiety.

'They after you?' the first guard asked.

'Yes,' he said. 'I must speak to Daphne Holdfast!'

The Holdings guards hesitated, trying to gauge the situation.

'All right,' the first one said. 'Come with me.'

Laodoc raced after him, and followed the guard up the embassy steps.

'You'd better not be bullshitting us,' the guard said as they reached the main doors.

'No, sir.'

They entered the building, and when the entrance was closed behind them Laodoc nearly staggered in relief.

'Who's this, then?' said an officer by the doors.

'He claims to know Miss Holdfast, sir.'

'And you thought you'd just invite him in?' the officer said, a frown on his face. 'You know the rules about letting peasants into the building, don't you?'

'Yes, sir,' the guard replied, glaring at Laodoc. 'He also claimed that he was about to be arrested, sir, and that he had vital information for Miss Holdfast. I had to make a split-second decision, sir. Apologies.'

The officer eyed Laodoc up and down.

'Well?'

'May we speak alone, sir?' asked Laodoc.

'You don't sound much like a peasant,' the officer said. He gestured to the guard. 'Go on; back to your post.'

'Yes, sir,' the guard saluted. 'Thank you, sir.'

The officer led Laodoc past the reception desk, nodding to the woman sitting there. They reached a small meeting room, and sat.

The officer raised his eyebrows at him.

'Up until a few days ago,' Laodoc said, beginning the little speech that he had been practising in his head for hours, 'I was a member of the City Council. After being found guilty of sedition against the state, by opposing slavery, and the wars against the Kellach and the Rakanese, I was stripped of my wealth, rights and position, and cast into the peasantry.' He looked the officer in the eye. 'I now wish to claim asylum with the Realm of the Holdings, and beg for sanctuary.'

For several hours, a tired and hungry Laodoc was passed between Holdings embassy officials, who each asked him the same questions about who he claimed to be and what his intentions were. One of the officials had, when pressed, told him the whole tale of what had befallen Akhanawarah City. The horror of it gripped his heart in despair, and he knew he needed to cut himself off from those responsible.

He was taken to a plush office, just as the lamps were being dimmed for evening. Laodoc realised that by now he would have been reported missing by the workhouse.

'Former Councillor Laodoc,' the Holdings man behind the desk said as he entered and sat. 'I am Secretary Joley of Hold Vale, second only to the ambassador himself. We have discussed your situation at length, and I regret to inform you that your appeal for asylum has been turned down.'

Laodoc sagged into the armchair, his hopes in tatters.

'It was felt,' Joley went on, 'that it would set an unwelcome precedent. Things are a little tense between our nations at present, and the embassy does not wish to antagonise your government.'

'May I speak with Miss Daphne?'

'Unfortunately, Miss Daphne is not presently available. If you were to leave her a note, I will see that it falls into her hands.'

The door burst open at that moment, and a dishevelled and red-faced priest barged in.

'My apologies, Joley,' the priest blustered. 'I've just spoken to the ambassador. There's been a change of plan.'

Joley looked irritated at the intrusion. 'What is it now?'

The priest turned to Laodoc.

'I am Father Ghorley,' he said, still out of breath. 'Forgive me, I ran all the way, to make sure I got here before you could leave. Joley,' he said, without turning to look, 'get us some drinks, there's a good chap, and Laodoc here looks a little hungry to me. Order him some food, please.'

Joley tutted, and got to his feet.

'I'll order up some food,' he said as he went through the door. 'The drinks are in the cabinet.'

The priest raised his eyebrows as the door slammed.

'My appearance here has ruffled a few feathers,' Ghorley said, 'but carrying out the work of the Creator has always brought its burdens.'

He walked over to the cabinet, and gathered bottles and glasses.

'Do you know anything about the Holdings religion?' he said.

'Not much, I confess,' Laodoc said, as he was handed a glass of red wine. 'I looked into it a little after I met with Miss Daphne.'

'And what were you meeting her about?' he asked, pouring himself a glass of water.

'I would rather speak only to Miss Daphne regarding that.'

'Were you plotting to free your ex-slaves?' the priest asked, a sly smile on his lips.

'How did you know that?' Laodoc spluttered. 'Did Daphne tell you?'

'No,' Ghorley said. 'The Creator did.'

Laodoc swallowed hard to stop himself from laughing. He had read that the Holdings priesthood could be fanatical in their devotions, but this was the first time he had been face to face with someone who believed that a god spoke to them.

'I can understand your scepticism,' the priest went on, 'however, whether you believe or not is immaterial to me. My orders are clear, and it is purely coincidental that they happen to benefit you.'

'Benefit me?' Laodoc asked. 'How?'

'This world will be united, my friend,' Ghorley said, 'but not under the oppressive heel of the current Rahain government. The Holdings are coming to understand what needs to be done. We already had the example of the Kellach's fate before us, and now with the massacre of the Rakanese migrants, the minds of the king and church are hardening.'

'War?'

'Not if it can possibly be avoided,' Ghorley replied. 'What we need right now is a friendly Rahain, say a liberal ex-councillor, for example, in the heart of the new Holdings capital on the Plateau; someone who would be able to advise on the political situation, and wisely prevail upon His Royal counsels.'

Laodoc hung his head. 'You want me to betray my nation?'

'We want to remove the current regime that is so badly misruling this republic. I thought this was your desire also?'

'It is,' he whispered.

'As I said,' the priest went on, 'this world will be united. The Rakanese homeland is turning to us for assistance, and there are sizable numbers of Kellach refugees prepared to ally themselves also. The Sanang, well, we shall see, but the fact remains that the Rahain government is the main obstacle to peace and unity on this continent, and it is our aim to remove it, before it tries to remove us.'

'And what does your Creator have to do with all of this?'

'He guides us,' Ghorley replied, raising his hand. 'He wishes for peace and unity, and so we labour to fulfil his word. He sees all, and his great heart weeps for the pain your government has caused, and how you have abused the gifts he bestowed upon your people, and not only your people, but how you forced a Kellach fire mage to abuse her power also. A most despicable act. The Creator's plans for this woman are now in ruins, so polluted are her hands with death.' He shook his head, lost for a moment as Laodoc watched him in silence.

'But peace will prevail,' Ghorley said, calming himself, 'for the Creator has foreseen it.' The priest pointed at him. 'You can help us. You can help bring unity to this world, and an end to the wars that have so crippled us.'

Laodoc considered, but began to feel he had no choice. The priest's religious talk had made him uncomfortable, but his heart filled with a base terror when he thought about returning to the workhouse.

'I accept,' he said. 'I will work with you to overthrow the present government, but I will never betray the people of Rahain.'

'Excellent!' the priest beamed. Just then, the door opened, and a servant pushed in a trolley, heaped with plates of food. Laodoc's stomach rumbled at the sight. When the door closed again, Ghorley began unloading the steaming contents onto dishes on the table.

'I have a question,' Laodoc said. 'How exactly will I be getting to Plateau City?'

'It just so happens,' the priest replied, 'that Miss Daphne will soon be travelling that way. I'm sure she won't mind escorting you.'

'Daphne is going to Plateau City?'

'Yes,' Ghorley said, a hint of worry on his face. 'If her present mission is successful, of which I have no doubt, then she will be required to escort certain people there. I'm sure she could cope with an additional passenger.'

'What is Daphne's mission?'

Ghorley smiled. 'We sent her into the Rakanese city to rescue the flow mage, and as many of the royal family as possible.'

'But the city was destroyed!' Laodoc exclaimed. 'What happened? Did she make it out?'

'We have not yet had any contact with her. I don't know her current situation.'

'She might be dead!'

'Not at all,' Ghorley replied. 'As I said, I have no doubt that she will succeed. A few days late she may be, but our Daphne is a very resourceful young lady.'

CHAPTER 34
SURVIVOR

Tahrana Valley, Rahain Republic – 6th Day, Last Third Spring 505

'She's a fucking pain in the ass, Sami,' Shella muttered. 'That's what she is.'

Her brother coughed. 'She's doing her best. It wasn't her fault we crashed.'

Jayki remained silent, trying not to get embroiled in the conversation. The three Rakanese sat in the shade under the thick branches of a tree, as they watched Daphne argue with the Kellach Brigdomin over which direction they should take next. The squad of ten Holdings soldiers stood around, waiting for their orders. Off to the side, the Rahain Baoryn watched, arms folded.

They had been walking for two days, ever since their lizard-borne carriage had come down. It had carried them clear over the Rahain lines and up a long, wide valley, travelling scores of miles in a few hours, before something had gone wrong with the four flying creatures. They had stopped working as a team, and had started pulling in different directions. As none aboard had any expertise in piloting the great lizards, Daphne had been forced into freeing one after the other, which had at least allowed them to descend, until the last beast had lowered the carriage to the ground in an untidy skid, which had sent the passengers tumbling about the inside of the wooden tube.

'Can you not wait a bit longer?' they heard Daphne say. 'We need to get to the meeting point, and we're already late.'

'And once we're there?' Kylon said.

'You'll be able to pick up supplies, while I present that lot to Father Ghorley,' she thumbed at the three Rakanese. 'And we can ask him about searching for Keira. See if he knows anything.'

'I don't want to lose another day.'

'The Holdings might be able to help you search. Don't leave until we get to the meeting place.'

'I still don't understand why you're not coming with us.'

'This is something I need to do, Kylon,' Daphne said. 'I need to go home, and see my family. Also, I can't let Rakanese royalty travel to Plateau City unescorted. When we parted, Killop said he would come for me. When you find him, tell him to look for me there.'

Kylon gazed off to the south, in the direction of the Rahain Capital.

'All right,' he said. 'One more day.'

Shella looked sideways at her brother. 'She doesn't like us.'

'She has her own life,' Sami whispered, 'and her own problems. She saved us, remember?'

'Why do you keep defending her?' Shella snapped. 'You fucking fancy her, don't you?'

Sami blushed.

'You don't stand a chance,' Shella went on. 'I heard Kylon say that she's in love with a Kellach. Do you honestly think you could do anything for her, after she's been with one of those big hairy bastards? No, brother, your whoring days are over. State you're in, you'll have to pay for your girlfriends from now on. Though maybe you could ask Daphne for a sympathy fuck.'

'Miss!' Jayki cried, as Sami lowered his head, his bottom lip trembling.

'Don't you start,' Shella sniped at him. 'Shit. Of all the possible survivors, I had to end up with you two halfwits.'

Jayki looked away, biting his tongue in anger.

Shella frowned. Why did she do this? Why was she pushing them away? Her devoted brother, who had always looked up to her, and Jayki, the most loyal soldier she had ever known? She hated herself. Obli had been right. She was responsible for the annihilation of Akhanawarah City, all those deaths. The destruction of the spawning pools, before a single baby had emerged from the warm waters. All her fault. Why couldn't Sami and Jayki see that? Why weren't they blaming her?

She saw Daphne approach.

'We're leaving,' the Holdings woman said. 'We've got to make ten more miles today.'

'When will Rijon be joining us?' Shella asked, as Jayki helped Sami to his feet.

Daphne scowled, shrugged and walked away.

'Bitch,' Shella muttered under her breath. Daphne paused for a moment, then kept walking.

They made good time, the three Kellach taking turns to carry Sami on their shoulders. They followed the narrow trail along the bottom of a gorge, every now and again catching a glimpse of the great, broad Tahrana Valley to their north. The day before, they had passed the point opposite where the enormous tunnel through the Grey Mountains began. It was nearing completion, Shella had heard, and once finished it was estimated that it would knock a third off the time it took to travel from the Rahain Capital to Rainsby, on the shores of the Inner Sea.

Rahain bastards, thought Shella. They had destroyed the Kellach and the Migration, and now they were casting their greedy lizard eyes on the Plateau.

Just as the sun was setting, the group reached a small farmstead, abandoned and overgrown.

They halted by a gate next to the crumbling walls of an old barn.

'Hello!' Daphne called out into the fading light.

After a moment a torch appeared from round the corner of a building, and a solitary man in uniform approached across the cobbled courtyard. Holdings, Shella guessed, judging by the darkness of his skin.

'Miss Daphne!' the man said, a big grin on his face. 'You're late.'

'Good evening, Dale.'

The man reached the gate, holding his torch aloft.

'This is Flow Mage Shella,' Daphne said, pointing at the Rakanese. 'And her brother, Prince Sami. And Jayki, Shella's servant. We also picked up a few Kellach, and a renegade Rahain.'

Dale smiled, his eyes focussed on Shella. 'Well done, Daphne.' He pulled the gate open. 'Come in,' he said, welcoming the group. 'The old farmhouse at the back has beds made up, and I can warm some food for you all.'

'You got anything to drink?' Shella asked.

'Yes, ma'am.' Dale bowed to her as if she were royalty. 'There's wine, and brandy.'

'I've heard of those, but never had them. Which one will get me drunk quicker?'

Dale frowned.

'Brandy,' said Daphne. The Holdings woman glanced up at Sami, who was riding on Bedig's wide shoulders. 'Does her mood improve when she's drunk?'

'If we're lucky,' Sami rasped. 'Sometimes it makes her worse.'

Shella snarled. 'Shut up, you useless cripple.'

Daphne moved to confront Shella so quickly she stepped backwards in shock.

'Don't call him that,' Daphne growled, inches from her face.

'I'll call him what I fucking like,' Shella blustered. 'He's my brother.'

'Miss Daphne?' she heard Dale say. 'Please?'

Daphne pulled back from Shella, but her face remained grim.

Shella noticed Kylon watching. She wondered who he would have helped if she and Daphne had come to blows.

'Come on,' said Bedig. 'I'm starving.'

The group moved off. Dale led the way to a long, single-storied stone farmhouse, with thick shutters covering the windows. They walked through the main entrance into a large room, with a fireplace, and a huge dining table along one wall. In a chair next to the roaring fire, an old Rahain man was sitting.

'Councillor Laodoc!' Daphne called out. 'What are you doing here?'

'Good evening, Miss Daphne,' the old man smiled. 'Such a relief to see you! I'm here to accompany you on your journey to the Holdings city on the Plateau.'

Daphne glanced at Dale. 'Where's Father Ghorley?'

'He's not here, I'm afraid,' Dale replied. 'He did, however, leave you a message, which should explain everything about former councillor Laodoc.' He walked to an open chest on a table, and withdrew a letter.

Daphne took it from his hands and began reading.

Shella looked around the room, as everyone unloaded their packs onto the floor. Dale and the old Rahain man were the only ones who had been awaiting their arrival, it seemed. Jayki stood by her side and Bedig set Sami down next to her. She watched as Dale sent some guards to the kitchen to ready the evening meal. He then turned to Shella.

'I have prepared a room for you, ma'am,' he said, clutching his hands together. 'Do you have any luggage?'

'Nope,' she said. 'Nothing but what we're wearing.'

'We're well-stocked here,' said Dale. 'There are three wagons in the rear stables, all packed with supplies for your journey. Mostly provisions, but Father Ghorley did insist we brought along a selection of clothing. Hopefully you will find something that fits.'

'Very thoughtful of you,' she said. 'You seem awfully keen that we travel to your capital city, Dale.'

The Holdings officer opened his mouth, but didn't reply.

'Of course,' she went on, 'it's not like we have much of a choice. Where else could we go?'

Dale nodded. 'And now you have another fellow traveller,' he said, flicking his eyes over to the old man sitting by the fire.

'Yeah,' she replied. 'Can't wait to spend more time with a Rahain.'

They gathered the seats and chairs round the long table, and ate a warm meal together. Shella noticed that Daphne kept to the other side of the room, talking to the Kellach. Dale had seated himself to Shella's right, and kept up a constant stream of polite chatter, which she ignored, not even bothering to nod occasionally.

After dinner, the wine and brandy flowed and Shella approved of both, following several thirds of enduring the rancid rice spirits they had distilled in the tenement's basement. As the evening wore on, Shella noticed the old Rahain man glancing at her. She had avoided him throughout the meal, and he looked away when she returned his gaze.

She got up and took a seat by the fire next to him.

'So who are you, exactly?'

'I am Laodoc,' he replied. 'Not, as Miss Daphne said earlier, a councillor. Not any more. I am a fugitive from Rahain, condemned for opposing the war against the Kellach, and the atrocity carried out against your people.' He paused. Shella stared at him, betraying no emotion on her face. 'Please believe me when I say,' he went on, 'that what happened fills me with the most profound regret.'

For a moment Shella felt like giving in to sadness, and allowing her built-up tears to overwhelm her, but guilt and shame filled her again.

'Even after I killed your delegates?'

'That was you?' he said, the colour draining from his face.

Shella held up her right hand, and the room stilled, as everyone turned to her in silence.

'Yeah,' she said, staring at her hand.

'Maybe you should put that down,' said Daphne.

Shella glowered at her. 'Or what? You might be used to everyone else obeying you, but I'm not happy being ordered around.' She turned to Dale. 'Does she have to come with us?'

Dale squirmed. 'Father Ghorley has placed Miss Daphne in command...'

'Well,' Shella said, 'I'm not sure I care to recognise her authority.'

Daphne tensed.

Shella rose from her chair, and walked round the table to where the Holdings woman sat. The rest of the room remained hushed, watching them.

'I'm not frightened of you,' Shella said, a crooked grin on her lips, as she stepped up close to Daphne.

The Holdings woman got to her feet and faced her.

Shella hesitated, then smiled. 'Two killer mages in the same room at the same time,' she said. 'See how they all look at us, Daphne. See the fear in their eyes.'

Kylon muttered something in his own tongue. He took a step forward, and guided Shella back to her chair by the fire, where Laodoc was sitting, his tongue flickering.

As she sat she saw Daphne shake her head in anger. She stormed out of the farmhouse, slamming the door behind her.

Shella groaned. 'I can't believe I'm going to have to put up with her all the way to the Plateau.'

'You and I will be saying our farewells in the morning, Shella,' Kylon said, as he sat down beside her. 'Let's get drunk together one final time.'

'More drunk, you mean.'

'But first,' he said, 'go outside and apologise to Daphne.'

'Why?'

'She saved our lives, Shella,' the Kellach man said, 'and now she's giving up looking for Killop, to make sure you're safely escorted to Plateau City.'

They paused as a Holdings soldier placed a fresh bottle of brandy onto the table in front of them. Laodoc reached out, and poured himself a glass.

'She doesn't like me, Kylon,' said Shella.

'No wonder,' he said, 'the way you speak to people. But you'll be travelling together for thirds. You'd better learn to get along with her.'

'Then she'd better learn to stay out of my way.'

He shook his head. 'I know why you're turning on everyone. You blame yourself for what happened to the Migration. Queen Obli knew nothing of what was going on before the end. She was shut up in her palace, while the whole burden of defending the city fell to you. You may have made some mistakes, but the Rahain were going to destroy the Migration, no matter what you did.'

Hatred filled her. 'How do we make them pay?'

'You travel to Plateau City,' he said, 'and present your case to the king. If anyone's strong enough to resist the Rahain, it's the Realm of the Holdings. Daphne and Laodoc are your allies in this. They are witnesses. Bedig will also be going with you. He told me that he has decided to follow you to the capital.'

'You're letting him go?'

Kylon shrugged. 'He's a free man. He can go where he pleases.'

Shella nodded, then rose to her feet, picking up the bottle of brandy. 'I think I'll see how Daphne is doing.'

Kylon raised an eyebrow.

'I'll behave,' she said. 'I may even be polite.'

She walked to the front door of the farmhouse, opened it, and slipped outside.

The evening air was cool in the gorge. Shella looked up, and noticed the seven stars shining in the eastern sky. Ahead of her, she saw Daphne alone in the darkness, sitting on a low stone wall, a red glow by her mouth.

'Hello,' she said. Daphne ignored her, her face an expressionless mask.

'I'm sorry about before,' Shella said, sitting down on the wall beside her, 'and I realise that I've never actually said thank you for rescuing us, so, thank you.'

Daphne sat smoking for a moment. 'You're welcome.'

'I have some good news,' Shella said. 'Dale mentioned to me earlier that they have brought your horse. I don't know what that means exactly, but he seemed to think it would please you.'

Daphne said nothing.

'So,' Shella went on, 'what's that you're smoking, then?'

'Keenweed. From Sanang.'

'Then how come you've got some?'

'Kellach and Sanang bandits smuggle it through the mountains to Rainsby, and from there...'

'Bandits? Do you think we'll see any?'

'I doubt it.'

'Why?'

Daphne glanced at her. 'We won't be going anywhere near the Sanang Mountains. But if you want to see wildlife, there's plenty of it in Rainsby. The place is run by gangsters, and over-run by Kellach refugees.'

'I want to make the Rahain suffer, Daphne.'

The Holdings woman nodded, then passed her the lit smoke-stick. As Shella took it, she noticed that Daphne's left arm was at an awkward angle.

'What's wrong with your arm?'

Daphne shrugged. 'It got injured a couple of summers ago, when I was fighting in Sanang. A man by the name of B'Dang D'Bang crippled it.'

'Crippled?' Shella repeated, her face going red. 'Oh, Daphne, I'm sorry.' She looked away, thinking of her brother. No wonder everyone hated her.

'It's all right,' Daphne said. 'My other one works well enough.'

Shella laughed. She took a swig of brandy, then passed it to Daphne. She glanced at the smoke-stick. 'Is this stuff addictive?'

'Probably,' Daphne muttered, and took a drink from the bottle.

Shella shrugged, and inhaled. Nothing happened for a few moments, and then she felt her senses expand, her eyesight, her hearing, her sense of smell.

'Wow,' she said, blinking. She looked at the farmhouse, taking in the tiniest details. She gazed back at Daphne, and it was like seeing her for the first time, her nut-brown skin, and long dark hair, tied at her neck. Her green eyes shone in the starlight.

'You're actually quite good-looking.'

Daphne almost smiled, and shook her head.

Shella pulled on her mage powers, feeling out the currents of liquid flowing round Daphne's body. Different from the Rahain, and the Rakanese, she thought. She drew a little more, and her senses were flooded with the complex physiology of the Holdings woman, the narcotic-tainted blood pumping around her body, the alcohol in her stomach, her organs, her heart, her womb…

She pulled back, almost crying out. 'This stuff's amazing!' she yelled, gazing at the keenweed stick in her hand.

Daphne nodded, and took a sip of brandy. 'Maybe you and Kylon are right,' she said. 'Maybe I should stay in Rahain and look for Killop. I also have some unfinished business with the woman who betrayed Laodoc and Simiona.'

'I thought you had family waiting for you in the Holdings, now that you've been pardoned.'

'I do,' Daphne said, 'and I want to see them; but Killop's out there, in the mountains somewhere. It feels like I'm abandoning him.'

'But you'd have to live in the wild, like a bandit.'

'So?' Daphne said. 'I've lived rough before.'

Shella stared at her, her mouth opening in surprise. She doesn't know, she thought.

'What's the matter?' Daphne said, her eyes narrowing.

'Daphne,' Shella said; 'maybe you shouldn't be drinking so much, or smoking, and I don't think you should be living up the mountains.'

'What?' Daphne said. 'You sound like my mother.'

Shella sighed. 'Daphne, you're pregnant.'

AUTHOR'S NOTES
APRIL 2019

Thank you for reading *Book One – The Queen's Executioner* and I hope you enjoyed it. For those who have also read *From the Ashes* and are hoping for more Keira, then I can reveal that she's one of the main point-of-view characters in book two of the series – *The Severed City*, which begins a few days after the ending of book one.

As I write this, there are only six more weeks until the release of *The Queen's Executioner*. It'll be the culmination of a long-held dream, to have a book out that people will enjoy reading. Following that will be the rest of the series, which will be available in the next few months. It's been an incredible year and my thanks go to everyone that made it possible, especially my wife who has inspired and supported me at the same time.

ABOUT THE AUTHOR

Christopher Mitchell is the author of the Magelands epic fantasy series.

For more information:
www.christophermitchellbooks.com
info@christophermitchellbooks.com

Printed in Great Britain
by Amazon

32730250R00263